DEREK MILMAN

A DARKER MISCHIEF

SCHOLASTIC PRESS / NEW YORK

Library of Congress Cataloging-in-Publication Data available

ISBN 978-1-339-00993-3

10 9 8 7 6 5 4 3 2 1   24 25 26 27 28

Printed in Italy 183
First edition, July 2024

Book design by Christopher Stengel

"one's not half two. It's two are halves of one."

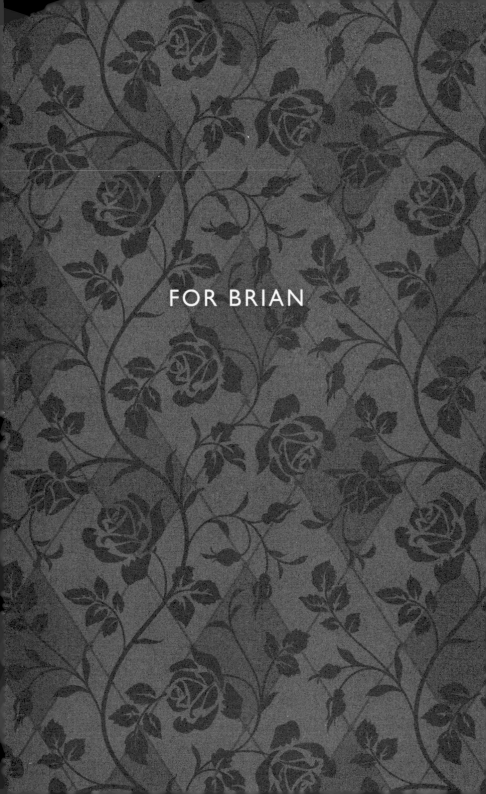

FOR BRIAN

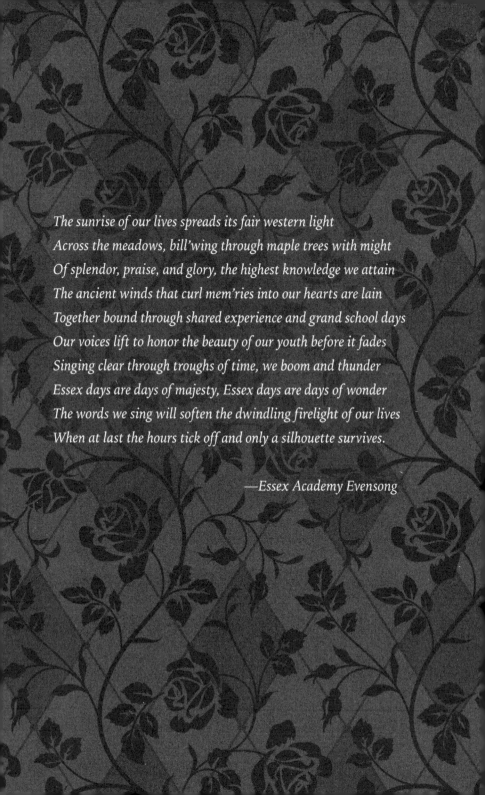

The sunrise of our lives spreads its fair western light
Across the meadows, bill'wing through maple trees with might
Of splendor, praise, and glory, the highest knowledge we attain
The ancient winds that curl mem'ries into our hearts are lain
Together bound through shared experience and grand school days
Our voices lift to honor the beauty of our youth before it fades
Singing clear through troughs of time, we boom and thunder
Essex days are days of majesty, Essex days are days of wonder
The words we sing will soften the dwindling firelight of our lives
When at last the hours tick off and only a silhouette survives.

—*Essex Academy Evensong*

PART ONE

RUSH

MARCH

There's blood on my shirt.

I dangle the sleeve over the bathroom sink, turn on the cold water, and rub the stain with my thumb. *"Out, damned spot."* I start to laugh maniacally as I rub harder. But it isn't funny. I got bitten, and there cannot be blood on me.

I stomp out of the bathroom, shaking out the shirt. Luke left the TV on, and our school is on the news, as it always is these days. Wall-to-wall coverage. I've never gotten used to these reports. There are no updates about Gretchen Cummings, the vice president of the United States's daughter, a sophomore here at Essex Academy, who went missing a few weeks ago.

I walk over to a window and stare down at the campus. It's unlikely somebody would spot a boy at the top of a tower, in a library that doesn't exist. If someone did see me, trapped in the tall paned windows, a white blur in the blast of morning sun, would they think I was a ghost?

I watch FBI and Secret Service agents down below, combing the campus. "This is terrible," I say, out loud, to no one. Our campus is on the TV, reflecting in the window onto the campus itself, an off-kilter illusion.

I turn away as the microwave dings.

Sunlight scorches the old volumes on the bookshelves, bequeathed by donors to a Latin department that never was. Luke and I can't leave the tower at the same time. He absconded before I was awake. But I still smell traces of him. Fresh and athletic. The scent of possibility.

I walk across campus, quiet and sleepy, but not totally dead. I'm another overworked sophomore lugging a duffel bag, getting an early morning start.

No one notices me.

I enter Bromley Laboratory, easily accessible this time of day. No security cams. The door to the basement was unlocked, propped open a few weeks ago. If the Feds searched here, they concluded their search awhile ago.

No one notices me.

I walk down a hallway, open a red metal door at the end, sidle through a pump room, and enter the underground steam tunnels, everything gently hissing. I float down the humid corridors. I reach the B-25 utility room, enter the combination to the lock on the door, and remove it. It's cooler in here, cleared out, except for the bucket and the flimsy cot.

"Breakfast," I say, standing at the door.

Gretchen Cummings sits up on her cot, drawing her knees to her chest. I can tell by her ashen complexion that she's been up for a while. I close the door behind me, removing the steaming-hot orange pizza bag from the duffel and dropping it to the concrete floor. *I'm sorry, I'm so sorry*, I think as I approach her, pointing a finger warningly. "No biting this time."

CHAPTER ONE

LONE WOLVES

I'm sitting alone in Graymont Dining Hall. Graymont looks like a cafeteria you might find on the ground floor of a museum. Round wooden tables on parquet floors; paned oval windows, flanked by heavy tan curtains. We're required to be in Academic Dress for dinner: white collared shirt, tie, blue jacket, dark slacks. I loosen my tie—it's legit strangling me.

Boarding school isn't exactly what I expected. When I learned I'd be leaving my shabby public high school, I got consumed by fantasies about my new life. I imagined myself striding down wide, verdant lawns, my tie flying in the autumnal breeze, chatting feverishly with earnest classmates about nineteenth-century poetry, while referring to any authority figure I didn't like as "that old windbag."

I imagined myself giving a presentation in front of stained glass windows to thunderous applause. And being congratulated later at dizzying parties in elegant common areas, spinning colored lights flashing off domed ceilings with crown moldings, as champagne bottles popped.

Yeah, not quite.

I tap my fingers on the table, glancing over at Ashton Jarr, Toby Darling, and Lily Rankin. They're sitting one table over, and I'm going to tell myself they're unaware of me instead of actively ignoring me. They walked in together after I was already eating. We're tenth graders in the same English class— Mechanics of Word and Identity—a fancy-shmancy way of saying we're studying basic grammar and learning to write complete sentences in our own style. Toby and Ashton are also my housemates.

For a while, we were a loose, casual friend group. The type that forms the first few weeks of school and then dissipates or culls its members. I'd been invited along to watch movies with them or grab coffee in town; we usually sat together for cafeteria meals, and we traded numbers. But lately, I've seen them go off and do stuff on their own (they post everything to their Instagram Stories), so I'm not really sure where I stand.

Last week, Ashton asked if I wanted to crash this upper-class party with them. I was flattered, thinking, *I've been officially accepted*, and spent the whole week trying to hide how excited I really was.

Tonight's the night. But no one's texted me. Or mentioned anything.

Part of me wants to go up to them, be direct, ask *what's up*. Part of me fears the awkwardness of the conversation. But I'm really terrified of the possibility of rejection, and the emotional spiraling that could follow.

The faculty take turns joining us at dinner. Tonight, it's

Mr. Dempsey, an English teacher. I watch him making the rounds. Sometimes if a teacher sees you eating alone, they'll come over and talk to you. Suddenly, I would rather experience literally anything other than Mr. Dempsey cracking dad jokes and asking if I'm making friends here while everyone stares.

I get up and walk over to Ashton, holding my empty tray.

"SZA was paying tribute to Princess Diana," Ashton is saying. "Like Jessie Ware was with that Warhol polaroid of Bianca Jagger at Studio 54."

"Huh," says Toby. "And Kendrick with *Damn?*"

"That was just him, dude."

They're always talking about either sports or the history of album covers, encompassing this oddball knowledge of pop culture history, trying to outdo one another.

"Physics homework tonight," Lily says to Ashton, tapping his knee.

Ashton turns to Lily. "I'll meet you at the library." Ashton finally sees me standing there. "Hey," he says, clapping me on the back while Toby flicks my ear, simultaneously, as I sit down. Toby is a goofball with a streak of snark. In twenty years, he'll probably bring golden retrievers into dive bars. Girls are *really* into Ashton; I get the appeal. He's tall, athletic, radiates sensitivity, has a mop of chestnut curls piled on his head, piercing dark eyes that don't go with the rest of him—a pretty work in progress.

They go on chatting while I sit there staring at my empty tray, until I clear my throat and Ashton raises his eyebrows at me. "Just checking—you guys still going to the party tonight?"

Why does my voice sound so high MY GOD.

9

Ashton and Toby exchange glances. Uh oh.

"I have . . . like . . ." I try not to stammer. "I have . . . someone else . . . other plans . . . just need to know for scheduling purposes." *Scheduling purposes?*

Ashton rises. "Let's walk."

We walk three feet in the direction of the exit, where students are dropping their empty trays, before Ashton clamps his hand down on my shoulder. "Look, man, it's . . . not a good fit." I turn to face him. The way he frowns involves all these furrows and creases bunched together like an ancient map of waterways.

"Fit?" This was my fear. I try not to hang my head like a child being scolded.

"Us. The party." He scratches the back of his neck, clearly not wanting to have this conversation. "Look, uh. Lily is friends with Gemma Brassaud. It's her birthday party, at Quinlan. Lily's sister went here, and she knew Gemma's sister. That's how we—"

"Uh huh."

"They asked who we wanted to bring, like outright, and crossed off your name."

I feel sweat forming on my upper lip. "Literally? With a Sharpie?"

Ashton throws his head back and laughs, like, *You're so charming and that's totally why we've been friends until right now.* "No, verbally. Like: *Not him. Don't bring HIM.*"

I don't feel the need to make this easier for Ashton. "Not. Him."

"I . . . sorry to be blunt." He sighs, doing the solemn thing again, like he's an army commandant bringing tragic news to a slain soldier's wife. When I get any kind of tough news, I always take it in stride. But it's like radiation sickness. It'll really hit hours later.

And then Ashton says that stupid thing people always say that helps nothing.

"It's not personal."

The empty tray is beginning to wobble under my arms. I want to get out of here. "Well, yeah, hey, have fun. Definitely don't let me hold you back."

"Cal, I'm sorry!" I hear behind me as I throw down my tray and exit Graymont.

I'm a sophomore transfer, and after I got over the stress of the morning rush for the showers, I learned that the rules of Essex are unwritten, but they're like electricity coursing through everything. You don't see them, but they power the school. The international and day kids tend to stick together, for instance, and everyone courts the day kids because they have cars (though we're not supposed to ride with them), and they're the ones who sell weed to everyone. Cliques are huge here. They offer a measure of protection against the elements. But I'm not in a clique. I'm cliqueless. A lone wolf. And no one trusts lone wolves . . .

After dinner, I walk back to my dorm feeling weighted down by Ashton's spurning, a hopelessness creeping in. I tell myself: *I'll spend the rest of the evening burying myself in homework! That'll take my mind off the party I got uninvited to!*

Another thing I had to figure out here were all the various pranks I might fall victim to, so I could mentally prepare for their eventuality. As I walk upstairs to my hall, I'm too distracted to notice all the heads half peeking out of cracked-open doors. As soon as I step inside our room, our small plastic wastebasket, filled to the brim with water, perched precariously above the door, tumbles onto my head. "TSUNAMI!" I hear everyone in the hall shout behind me.

Oh, fuck me.

The Tsunami is a common prank around here, especially for under-class students. It doesn't mean you're hated. But the timing sucks.

The force of the water literally knocks me to the floor.

At that moment, another lone wolf enters the room and sees the mess. "Oh shit, sorry," my roommate, Jeffrey, says, closing the door behind him, the jeering in the hall growing softer. "My bad. I forgot to lock the door."

"How am I so drenched?" I pull at my cold, heavy clothing sticking to my skin.

"Those things hold a lot of water."

"Shit." I hold up my phone. It won't turn on. I restart it. Nothing.

"Ugh," says Jeffrey. He reaches into the bathroom and throws me a towel. I wrap it around my shoulders. "I think I can fix that. Hold on!" He runs out of the room while I stare at the brown institutional carpeting, shivering, dripping.

Jeffrey Gailiwick hails from Freemont, New Jersey. We got put together because he's a sophomore transfer too, and Essex must have thought if we had that in common, we'd be friends for life. It's been a neutral situation so far. Jeffrey's hard to get to know. He can get quiet and stare into space for long periods of time.

With limpid eyes the color of pipe smoke and a mane of tousled black hair, there's a definite Byronian vibe to him. He spends a lot of his downtime listening to Sufjan Stevens, reading *The Wasp Factory*, and scrawling in black leather journals. We share a double in Foxmoore House—an imposing, stately brick building covered in ivy.

Jeffrey rushes back into the room holding a glass measuring cup and a plastic bag of rice.

He rips open the bag and pours it into the measuring cup. He jumps up, runs into our tiny bathroom with the energy of an ER surgeon; I hear the medicine chest opening and closing, the sound of plastic caps being twisted open, thrown on the floor. Jeffrey returns and adds a handful of those little plastic cylinders that come in pill bottles. "Give me your phone." I hand it over. He drops it in the measuring cup and shakes everything up, like he's making a magical potion.

"I'm skeptical."

"Trust me," he says. And he's right. After an hour, I sigh with relief as the Apple logo flickers back on to my cracked screen. It hasn't been *that* long, and I'm not sure why I was expecting anything else; it's one of those moments where I realize no one was looking for me. There are no missed calls or texts. No DMs. No notifications about anything. I didn't get tagged anywhere. There's nothing at all.

CHAPTER TWO

NOWHERE MAN

Later that evening, Jeffrey heads downstairs to the common area to heat up some ramen, stretch out on one of the leather sofas, and call some cousin, a regular nightly habit of his.

While he's out, I take a break from watching a British spy thing on Netflix, close my laptop, and pull out my newly working phone, which I know is a mistake before I even, instinctually, without thinking, open Instagram.

I don't even mean to watch Ashton's Instagram Story. I'm watching one from a kid I knew back home, but then Instagram does that thing where it's like, *Sorry, you're going to see this, buddy,* and the story segues right into Ashton's and it's that thing where you know you should stop watching but you can't because you want to torture yourself.

Ashton is at the party, with Toby, Lily, and a few other sophomores. They're all sitting on white lounge chairs in a stone courtyard surrounded by string lights, plastic cups in their hands. The story is meant to show they got into the party, an obvious status thing. But then these other kids, out of frame, start asking where I am, knowing I've been seen hanging with Toby, Lily, and Ashton. But they're asking this sarcastically, like, *why didn't they bring me along, har har,* and then I hear some girls saying off camera:

Where does he get those clothes, the Piggly Wiggly?

He LITERALLY looks like he drove a tractor to his middle school.

Does he have, like, the first iPhone ever made?

I know I should put the phone down. But something twisted inside me needs to see this, a streak of sadomasochism.

Ashton looks wasted, but he smiles along with the jokes before the story ends.

But, on Toby's story, which follows, like a deranged, vicious little sequel, people are now making fun of my accent. The impressions start to become a contest, everyone offering their own take. Ashton and Toby are now laughing along (without partaking), looking a tad uncomfortable but hardly stopping any of this. Not even a "hey, he's actually a good guy, cut it out."

I can't believe they fucking posted this.

I still can't stop watching. And then I can't take it anymore. I turn off my phone and shove it away, like it's possessed.

I feel a panic attack coming on. I'm never going to get to sleep. I need to get out of this dorm; it feels like the walls are closing in. I used to take long walks back home, especially at night. They were therapeutic. And right now, I need to breathe. We're not allowed out past curfew, but I skip check-in by telling Jason Udell, our dorm prefect, that I'm not feeling well and need to stay in bed (they let you skip check-in if you're sick).

Since I'm officially checked in, I slip out the front door when no one's looking.

The dark transforms the campus into a quiet moonlit lullaby, but the night feels ghoulish.

Light spills out from the residence buildings, casting amber trapezoidal shapes across the lawn. Paved pathways are illuminated by silvery streetlights. I let myself dissolve into the darkness. I realize I'm crying into the crook of my arm; I'm glad the night is concealing that.

I'm hurt, yeah, I'm really fucking hurt. I don't want to be, but I am. Those assholes, and what they say, shouldn't matter, but it *does*. I know I look different. Out of Academic Dress, off-duty, most guys wear Gucci loafers, Todd Snyder polos, Rowing Blazers rugbies, waterproof Scandi backpacks. By comparison, I probably look like I hit an outlet mall off an interstate.

I'm from a small town in Mississippi! How could I possibly have thought this was going to work? *That I'd coast by on my natural movie star charm?* I can't be here, I don't belong. But I can't go back to McCarl. I don't belong there either. Not anymore. All this hits me now, really for the first time. How I belong nowhere. I'm doomed either way, slipping into the blemished light and shadow of fugitives. I hear a distant golf cart whizzing by. Essex security.

I can't go back to my room, but I shouldn't be out here either. A continuing theme!

Essex is wild. I'm still not used to asking permission for small, mundane things, like taking a walk. Sometimes, the rules feel draconian. It's all liability shit. Besides our face-to-face check-in every night, lights-off is at ten thirty on weeknights and an hour later on weekends.

There are even more rules about visiting kids in other residence halls, especially for first- and second-year students. We're not allowed single-pair visitation until next semester, and then there needs to be multi-staff-member approval; overhead lights must be on, door open as wide as the seat of a desk chair. The school basically assumes we're all sexual deviants on the prowl.

As I walk, I see a group of shapes emerging from behind a row of trees, gliding down the immense lawn. I hear hushed voices. I hide behind a big maple. There are a bunch of students in tuxedos and gowns, wearing white-and-gold carnival masks. At first I think I'm seeing things. But no. It takes me a second to realize why I'm so stunned: the sudden influx of glamour, mystery, intrigue. This is the first thing I've seen at Essex that matches my (admittedly far-fetched) boarding school fantasies.

I decide to follow them. I stick to the dark, moving from tree to tree.

They head toward the school's old music building, dating back to the 1800s. They're on their way to some kind of party. But not the fratty red Solo cup kind Ashton ditched me for. This is something else. Something that instantly thrills me. There are old, dark, decommissioned buildings in various stages of rot or renovation that dot the campus in forlorn clusters, and this old music hall is one of those buildings. And I'm watching a bunch of people waltz right inside it!

Cloaked by the crisp, windless night, I drift closer to the building.

There are tall oval windows; I peer inside. I see silver balloons hanging, formally dressed people cavorting, holding glasses of champagne. Everything drips in a dreamy golden light, framed by scarlet curtains hugging the windows. The rainbowed crystals from a chandelier sparkle into my eyes. It's a window into another world, *literally*, very much outside the academic and social grind of Essex. I want to be part of whatever this is. I know it on a gut level, no practicality or rationality behind it. It seems like a gilded path out of desolation.

I walk around to the back of the building; I hear music playing through the windows. There's no beat: no Taylor, Drake, or Gaga. I hear prewar parlor music, old-timey stuff, like when that haunted hotel comes alive in *The Shining*. There's a back door.

It opens the moment I set my eyes on it. When no one steps out, I know I've been spotted. There's a triangle of honeyed light, with shimmers of red and pink, that pierces the dark, tickling the branches and leaves of nearby trees. I walk into the triangle, spilling out from what looks like the ventricles of a heart: magenta foil fringes hanging in the entranceway, glittering, and deeper inside, crimson walls.

A white-gloved hand emerges from the door, gesturing at me. Like an idiot, for a second I think this is an invitation to join the festivities—in my Old Navy hoodie and raggedy Converse low tops. When I reach the door, I see the white-gloved hand is holding something out to me.

I'm handed an old-fashioned calling card, on heavy black stationery, with gold ink.

It's the image of an eye emerging from a coil of fog. The moment I take it, the door slams shut in my face. The party continues on behind those stone walls, and darkness consumes me once again.

CHAPTER THREE

LUKE

I wake up the next morning and get hit with a memory: coming home from school to find our kitchen table littered with brochures and forms. I knew what was happening right away.

You tryin' to get rid of me?

Honestly, yeah, Son, I want to convert your room into a gym.

You'd have to get off your ass, then.

Your grades and test scores are impressive. We'd qualify for a nice financial aid package. If you wanted to leave . . .

IF? Leave McCarl? Leave Mom?

Have you heard of this one—Essex Academy?

It sounded so fantastical. An Academy. Far away.

Later, my dad sat heavily on the edge of my bed as I was studying the school's website.

Is Mom going to be okay?

I think it would help her if you took this opportunity. And it would be good for you too. Look at it as a reinvention. Not many get a chance for one of those.

It wasn't only their own problems. It was stuff I'd done.

Dirty, shameful stuff I'd done that led to The Incident . . . which is what led to this. Shame seemed to drip through my insides, like a viscous oil replacing my blood. I was being, in a sense, exiled.

I skip all my meals at Graymont. I'm not in any kind of mood to see Ashton, Lily, or Toby across the room. During all my classes, I can't stop thinking about what I witnessed last night. I keep taking out the card and caressing the eye, as if to make sure it wasn't something I dreamed. *How did those kids get inside that music hall?* Our access at Essex is very limited.

We all have fobs, programmed to get us inside our dorms and campus buildings during the day. If we try and use our fobs to access a locked building after hours, the system will record that, and we can get in trouble. I could talk to Jason; he might know something. But, after classes, there's something else I need to do first.

I walk over to Hertzman Center, where the JV and varsity wrestlers hit the mats, practicing for the Class A Tournaments, the New England Prep School Championships. Where no one would ever expect to find me. I sit by the side of the building, which faces a patch of woods, rest my head against the wall, stare at my phone, and then press it to my ear.

"Cal, I don't think you should call me anymore. I don't think it's helping either of us cope . . ."

"I can't talk to my parents." I smear a chemtrail of snot across the sleeve of my hoodie. "They can't know how bad it is."
I glance upward: a flock of birds like a triangle of blurred black

dots against a steel-wool sky. "They sent me away . . . to . . ." I rest my phone against my cheek for a second. "I'm getting panic attacks."

"Maybe go to Health and Wellness? At least talk to someone?"

"They'd tell my parents and they'll feel helpless. They'll want me to come home; I'll have failed. Look, this isn't homesickness; I feel . . . like I'm in enemy territory."

"You're not fighting a war, Cal."

"Except I kind of am?"

"It's so early in the year. Maybe give it a bit more time? Things could change."

They won't. Unless something drastic happens. I let a few tears fall into my cupped hand like rain. "I'm not being dramatic." I don't have anything else I want to say, or hear, so I hang up. As I walk around Hertzman, my usual deserted shortcut, I see something strange: a boy spraying something on the other side of the wall, opposite from where I was.

He whirls around to face me. There's an open backpack by his feet and paint cans in his hands, but it still takes my brain a moment to process the fact that I stumbled on someone vandalizing school property. And in a clever spot, surrounded by untended grass, out of the way.

He drops his arms by his sides—no point in hiding the paint cans now. He positions his body in front of whatever he did, so I only catch a glimpse of bright color before he blocks it from my sight. "I couldn't help it." He says this plainly, like he's admitting to an addiction.

I look at the phone still in my hand. *I can't help it either.* For some reason, his tone, his bearing, puts me at ease. There was an admission instead of judgment, a tinge of vulnerability instead of the usual sizing me up. I take a step closer to him, squinting. "I know you."

"Chem," he says with a small smile, "we have chem together."

Cute Asian jock in my chem class, that's right, that's who he is, inaccessible as any cute jock at Essex. There's only fifteen of us in that class. I should've known him.

"I don't talk much," he offers.

"You don't." Hell, I don't either.

"I'm Luke Kim."

"That's right," I say, although I had no idea what his name was. I had no idea anyone on campus was this disarming. "Calixte Ware. Cal."

"I live in Garrott."

"Foxmoore," I reply, wondering more and more what he was up to. "Well." I gesture at the sprayed wall, which I still can't see because he's blocking it. "I really don't care what you do." And I don't, but it is kind of a fucked thing—to vandalize your own school.

"I see you here sometimes, Cal."

It had never occurred to me that I was being observed. For a second, I'm horrified. He's seen me crying. I nod at the paint cans. "I'm not going to tell anyone, man."

He frowns. He thinks I think he's blackmailing me, and while he doesn't move an inch, his eyes show surprise as they scurry to correct course. "I meant, are you okay?"

At first, I'm suspicious of the query, as if it'll come at a price. But his eyes are open and searching. My confusion dissolves into something resembling resolve. I bow my head slightly as if in the presence of royalty. "I'm fine. Thank you."

"I'm a sophomore transfer as well."

"You've been watching me?"

"Don't flatter yourself." He grins. And then he rattles the paint cans. "Nice meeting you."

I assume this is my cue to skedaddle. "You too. I guess I'll see you in chem."

"That you will, Cal." He shakes the paint cans and resumes spraying paint, quicker now, as if he's on a deadline. I pocket my phone as I walk away, wondering how red my eyes are, if dried tears are visible, like white chalky streaks on a person's cheeks or something.

When I get back to Foxmoore, I seek out Jason. "Everything okay, Cal? Were you guys trying to domesticate a lion and it went nuts and now I have to call Animal Control?"

"Did that . . . like . . . happen once?"

"Nah." He laughs. I smell weed mixed with patchouli wafting out of his room (seniors actively *want* to be prefects because a single room is guaranteed). I wonder how someone so hot could make such dumb jokes. Or need to be stoned so much of the time. Jason's on the swim team and his choppy, marbled blond hair, further bleached by chlorine, is perfectly tousled, like someone does that for him.

I lean against his doorway. "Question for you."

"Shoot."

I can't let Jason know I snuck out of the dorm. Sneaking out past curfew is a "class 1 breach of trust" according to our Student Handbook. And I got lucky returning—the front doors were left open. Someone on a forbidden cigarette break, probably. Pure happenstance. So I tell Jason what I *saw* at the old music hall was actually a rumor I *overheard* during lunch: kids talking about masked costume balls on campus after midnight.

"Oh, well, there's supposedly a secret society. Maybe they're referring to that?"

"How could they be secret if you know about it?" I ask.

"I mean, you hear stories."

"What are they?"

"That there's a secret society on campus, right?" He toys with the strings on his red hoodie. "But it's a myth. They recruit freshmen and sophomores every fall, *supposedly*, and if you get tapped, you're a member for life."

My heart starts galloping; I don't know why I keep having a visceral reaction to this whole thing. "What do they do?" I ask, trying to skim away the yearning from my voice.

Jason makes a motion of zipping his mouth sideways, then laughs jovially. "I think they explore shit . . . but, like, *if they exist*. Which I don't think they do 'cause it's a joke. But if it isn't a joke, what I've heard is that they're super powerful; they have a reach into every sector of society, and they're part of the Illuminati."

I know it's not a joke, even if a lot of those rumors are probably a bit much. "They seriously recruit freshmen and sophomores every fall? Like, right now?"

"Supposedly, supposedly . . ."

The timing works. And I technically could have a shot. But only because I'm a sophomore. Being accepted around here, for me, has been a continuing challenge. That won't change, though, unless I try to change it. "How does one get recruited?"

"It's a secret society! I think it's the kind of situation where they have to find you."

"How do I find *them*?" But I kind of already did, didn't I? All of a sudden it hits me why this matters, why I woke up remembering what my dad said to me that day.

Look at it as a reinvention.

I think about the window into that music hall, a building that doesn't technically exist anymore. The people inside. Laughing. Dancing. The old music. I'm a history buff; I've always had this feeling of being born too early or too late, an alien observing humanity. And being at Essex has repeatedly confirmed that. But I can't stop thinking about that golden light spilling out of the red velvet interior. I want in. I have to surmount the social hurdles of Essex. For the sake of my family. And maybe getting into this society is how I do that. IF I can do it.

CHAPTER FOUR

SEVEN EYES

It's late afternoon, after classes, and surprisingly warm out. I avoid all the Frisbees and softballs being thrown every which way. I've been obsessively staring at the image of the eye on the card all day. I've seen it before. *But where?*

I remember Luke spray-painting something on the wall of Hertzman. I head back there, but whatever he sprayed on the wall has either been washed off or painted over. But then I realize why I returned. It's my subconscious working out a tangle. I've seen that eye painted on the exterior of several buildings on campus.

I was worried about being the fish out of water; Southern boy trying to fit in to the whole East Coast prep school thing, so I spent all summer reading about Essex. But no matter how much reading I did, I felt as if I knew less and less, like I was only getting snippets of facts; much of the historical information contradicted other information. This made the school seem even more enigmatic, and I got more fascinated by its complicated history.

Essex is the oldest secondary school in the country, founded in 1777 by Alexander Essex, a wealthy merchant and philanthropist. It was built on the remains of a defunct colonial college called Granford, which would've been a Yale or Harvard—a ghostly entry into the Ivy League. But Granford died young, for reasons that weren't always clear in all the research I did. A lot of Essex's campus still comprises what was once Granford.

I retrace my usual steps to my classes. And there it is. The same image of an eye that's on the card. It's painted on the side of a former, currently abandoned junior boys' residence called Piedmont House, dating from the late 1800s, according to the campus map on their website, which lists basic historical details for most buildings.

While the building itself is not in use, apple trees surround the exterior. I take a photo of the eye, hidden by the shadows cast from the branches of the apple trees. I can tell by the faded paint that the eye has been there for some time. And I know I've seen more of them . . .

Given that I observed this society, or whatever they are, having a party at a decommissioned music hall, and I found an eye painted on the wall of a decommissioned building, I wonder if that's a pattern? I find another eye painted on the side of an abandoned dining hall, dating from 1908, called Dunlop Hall, pre-Graymont. *Septem!* is painted above the eye. Latin for seven. There's going to be seven of these.

I find an eye on the side wall of a small disused library, erected in 1961, called the Larson Reading and Reference Room. This one has another special treat: painted over the eye, a line of faded Latin: *Tibi oculi aperti erunt.* I take out my phone and look up the phrase: "Your eyes will be opened." Now I can't stop. I feel like I'm on a mission. This society has laid out a web of riddles, and if I solve them, that could increase my chances of . . .

What? Being noticed by them? Accepted into their ranks? I'm not sure. But . . . something.

I know it's a long shot, whatever this is, I get that, and I don't want to set myself up for disappointment. But I have to try. *I have to.*

There's another eye painted on a modernist industrial steel-and-glass building from 1947, called the Richter Center for Astronomical Discovery, that used to have an observatory at the top. Above the eye, it says, *Time Is Relative!*

The fifth eye is painted on a decrepit brick building that used to be faculty housing, Tomison, dating from 1932. There's another Latin phrase painted above the eye: *Omnia ex umbris exibunt,* which means "Everything will emerge from the shadows."

The sixth eye, painted on Essex's old Jules K. Fairbanks Math and Science Center, built in 1970, before the department was moved over to Hillbrook House, comes with the biggest gift yet. A website—written in fresher, brighter paint—above the eye. Curious@sose.essex.org.

Oh, fuck yes. This is the most alive I've felt since I've gotten to Essex. It's like something deep inside me woke up. The seventh and final eye is on a former administrative building, constructed in 1952 and covered in fairy-tale amounts of ivy, called Addison House.

Back in my room, laptop on my stomach, I type in curious@
sose.essex.org. A single page appears—black background with
faint white type. It says *SoSE* over a gray line, and under the
line: *Omnia ex umbris exibunt.*

As soon as I hit a key, my IP address is displayed in the
upper left-hand corner, meaning whatever's about to happen,
I'll only have one chance to get it right—at least on this laptop.
There'd be no other reason why my IP address would be displayed
along with a timer, already counting down. I have less than ten
minutes.

In the same faint text, it says, *Possession is total!* and under that
are four spaces to type four words. I think of my mom, and I get
a twinge in my chest. My mom is a puzzle fiend. Words with
Friends. Sudoku. Monument Valley. *The New York Times* cross-
word. She got me into all that stuff. We'd play together. They
don't know who they're up against here.

This one's for her. *Let's goooooooooo . . .*

I tap my fingers against my front teeth. It said, *Time Is Relative!*
on the old astronomy building, which is from Einstein's theory
of relativity; it has to do with the rate of time passing and individual frames of reference. My frame of reference is Essex, so
what if I think of these buildings in chronological order? That
means Piedmont is the oldest building. What about Piedmont
could translate to four words? Piedmont and eyes. My thoughts
on the building, dead inside, wander outward. There were apple
trees. What if this is an idiom? Four spaces.

It could be *my* or *your.* Except it gave me the answer: *Possession
is total.*

I type in what's pretty much a guess: *Apple Of My Eye*.

There is a vintage Nintendo-y dinging sound, the screen disappears, and is replaced by another screen with four lines. Holy shit, that worked! The next oldest building would be Dunlop, which is a former dining hall. I type in: *Feast For Your Eyes*.

Ding!

Two lines. Tomison. Seven minutes left.

The building was named after a former student, Andrew Tomison, who was killed in World War I. Tomison's rank in the U.S. Army was private first class. Two lines. I type in: *Private Eye*.

Ding!

I slap my legs in triumph. Four lines. The Richter Center. Astronomy . . .

I type in: *Stars In My Eyes*.

Ding!

Four lines again. Addison House (a misnomer) was named after a beloved school nurse, infamous for being a bit of a heartbreaker around campus, which was mentioned in one of the books I read on the school. After she left Essex, she married a Boston financier named Jonathan K. Addison.

Easy On The Eyes.

Ding!

The Larson Reading and Reference Room was named after Gerald W. Larson, history teacher and member of the Audubon Society, who introduced his interest in ornithology to the students by building an aviary on the top floor of the library (since demolished).

It's three lines, so it can't be *Eagle Eye*. But can it be . . .

Bird's Eye View.

Ding!

The Jules K. Fairbanks Math and Science Center.

As a student here, Fairbanks was a star player on the varsity baseball team. He considered a career in Major League Baseball before he turned to the sciences and taught at Essex. His position? Catcher.

Catch My Eye.

Ding!

The screen changes. It's been so long since I've smiled as wide as I do.

CHAPTER FIVE

SOCIETY

In chem the next day, Luke beams at me dreamily, glowing in the celestial sun through the windows. He's resting his hand against his cheek, twirling a pencil. It's almost like he's proud of me, like he knows what I solved. He's never acknowledged me like this in class before.

At lunch, Ashton, passing by, attempts a friendly sock to the shoulder. "You get with a girl or something? You get lucky, dude? You look all loved up."

"Hey, looked like you guys had a great time at the party."

Ashton looks momentarily baffled.

"Yeah, I saw your Instagram Story." He seems to be only now half remembering what happened. "But listen, if you want to do an impression of my accent, I'm from *Mississippi*. You guys were all over the place. Arkansas, Georgia. Even, like . . . Central Florida maybe? Get it right next time." I give him a little demonstration, as if I'm talking to my mom, while he stands there. It's fun watching Ashton's face fall as horror creeps into his eyes.

That evening, I decide to loop Jeffrey into my Society-related activities. He's a fellow lone wolf who got my phone working again (which my parents wouldn't have been able to afford to replace). I show him the screenshot I took after I solved the riddles.

Saturday, 8:03 p.m. Noyce Courtyard, by the old oak.
Do not be early. Do not be late. Dress to the nines.
No other commitments matter.
Omnia ex umbris exibunt

"Want to come with?" I ask. I don't really want to go alone. Power in numbers.

"Saturday is Club Roam," Jeffrey says, looking intrigued. That's Essex's fall club fair night. Everyone will be dressed up anyway. Whatever this secret society is, SoSE according to their website, they'll blend right in with the crowd. "Am I allowed to come with you? They had your IP address."

"One way to find out."

"Do you have a tuxedo?" he asks.

Right. We have to be dressed *to the nines*. That's one of those phrases like *in my salad days* everyone decided to blindly go with. I have one suit—outside of our Academic Dress, and they obviously don't mean that—which I wore to my granddad's funeral. "No. Do you?"

"Nope. But I know where we can get them. I dig all this. Let me return the favor."

The next day, after classes, we sign out to visit Abel & Mystick's, a famous New England thrift store. Jeffrey got his boots at this place two weeks back. It turns out they're black calfskin Alexander Wangs garlanded by "silver-tone hardware." Worth eight hundred bucks, and sold to Jeffrey for about eighty, which the owner describes as one of the great Abel & Mystick's deals of the last five years. Meanwhile I'm thinking, *Where the hell did Jeffrey get eighty bucks?*

I look down at my worn red sneaks. Jeffrey points to the far-reaching tuxedo rack in back of the store. In a miracle, after flipping through hangers and throwing stuff on and off, Jeffrey and I find tuxedos, shirts, and shoes for a decent price.

My parents gave me a credit card, told me to use it for whatever I need. I debate this for a second, but since I've already determined getting involved with SoSE could aid my survival at Essex, I think it's worth it, which offsets some of the guilt of spending the money.

Jeffrey is tall and lithe; his tux fits perfectly, lucky fool. Mine's big on me. *Runty* is a word that's been used on more than one occasion, which I despise. Thankfully, there's a tailor next door. They'll hand deliver the tux to my dorm by tomorrow afternoon.

8:03 p.m., by the old oak. *Do not be early. Do not be late.*

Later that day, I walk it with my timer on, passing by the bronze statue of Abraham Cook, former Head of School from the early 1800s, who founded the famous Cook Gallery of American Art, which he stands imposingly in front of. There was a legendary art heist there seventy years ago, and a priceless painting was never recovered. They talk about it even now; I think the school is still a little on edge.

I'm making real moves to get into a secret society. I even spent money on this.

The possibility of it all feels realer than ever!

"We've had some rain," my mom is telling me. Her soothing drawl takes me right back home. She sounds mellow, distant. Probably the medical marijuana. My dad has gotten his phone time with me edited down to a neat 43.6 seconds. "Are you picking up?" my mom calls out.

"I'm here," my dad says. "It's been raining."

"I heard."

"How's school, Son? Making friends? Have you met that Gretchen Cummings yet?"

"Seen her around; she seems nice."

"Does she have Secret Service there?"

I explain that sometimes you can spot them, since they try to look like teachers or school staff. They wear backpacks, ride bikes, but they always have those earpieces in. No one talks about them, mostly because everyone feigns a sort of removed coolness.

"Wow," my dad chuckles, "can't quite get over that. Her father seems to have some progressive ideas up his sleeve. No one expected that."

"No one did," I agree.

"All right, good to talk to you, Son, work hard, I have to get back to my . . ." [says something indecipherable, hangs up].

My dad feels guilty that his own troubles contributed to me having to leave McCarl. Not many people from our part of

Mississippi attend Connecticut prep schools. They wanted to get rid of me for my own protection. The return of my mom's cancer. The financial strain of the medical bills. My dad's civil lawsuit, the whispers about criminal negligence. The bullying at my old school that worsened and eventually led to The Incident.

I can't distress them any further with my struggles to fit in. I am lucky to be here. I have to empty my voice of emotion. It hasn't been an easy situation. I'm fixing it.

"You sound better," my mom says, melancholia silting her voice.

"Yeah." I wipe a tear away. "How are you?"

"Oh, I'm fine. Tell me something fun about Essex."

I'm lonely as all shit, so lonely it hurts like a nail through the hand. "I bought a tux."

"You going to a wedding?"

I tell her about the party I saw, the eyes, the puzzles.

Her voice brightens. "Well, that sounds fascinating, right up your alley!" She senses my emotional state. She always knows. "I know it's been tough. You have to give things time."

"Yeah, I'm all right."

My mom puts on a brave face. She's always been peppy for me, and certainly has been at the worst of times, making jokes when she was sick—but I'm hearing resignation in her voice, which is different. We don't talk about her illness outright, just not something we do.

On Saturday, I unwrap my tux from the plastic, get dressed, and stand in front of our room mirror. I'm not exactly red-carpet dashing, but the tux is tailored well. Jeffrey looks sharper, like he's worn a tux before. My granddad's watch, a family heirloom, counts down the minutes. "Time to go," I tell Jeffrey.

There are lots of kids out. Voices everywhere. The energy is curious, exploratory. As we approach the tree, I'm filled with so much anticipation the night becomes a swirl of darkened abstraction—shapes and shadows twining around me, a kaleidoscope pointed at asphalt.

Ashton, Toby, and Lily rush by, giggling. If I get into SoSE, they won't matter anymore. So much asinine social-climbing crap about Essex won't matter anymore.

Noyce Courtyard.

This courtyard is noyce, everyone jokes. As soon as we approach the oak tree, a dude wearing a black tux and a cream-and-gold carnival mask emerges from the darkness. I feel weirdly starstruck. "Follow," he barks.

I'm so ready for whatever this is.

We trudge after him up a hill. It takes me a second to realize there are others following us. Our little group grows, more kids sticking on to us like brambles. I see five students (three boys in tuxes, two girls in gowns, all of them masked), who I assume are upperclassmen, leading four groups through the night. And then it occurs to me: There must have been multiple meeting spots. They didn't want a big crowd.

I do a quick head count. "Forty students total," I whisper to Jeffrey.

Forty kids already scouted, wow.

"Legacies," Jeffrey whispers back.

38

He's right. So many probably already knew what SoSE was—told by dads, older siblings—and, if not already courted, were simply waiting for their shot. This is a competitive school; people compete. I should have expected that. While not one of them, I walk among the elite.

"Phones off," the dude in the mask says without slowing down.

We're heading for Bromley Laboratory, a 103-year-old Collegiate Gothic building where I take chem. There are several floors of old lecture rooms, labs, newer classrooms.

We pass through the iron gates, our school motto, *Felix qui potuit rerum cognoscere causas*, carved into them. It's Virgil. It means "Fortunate is the man who was able to know the causes of things." I like that. The building's stone exterior, extra imposing and monolithic at night, seems aghast at having to let us inside this late. Bromley's two heavy front doors are propped open. We enter the building in a single-file line. This is so serious! There are no lights on, only bleedy exit signs in the far corners of the main hallway.

"Hold up," says the masked guy, palm out, leading us into the building. "Treffpunkt one," he says, gesturing to a masked girl (wearing a pearl necklace with her gown) who leads her charges ahead of us, down the hall, where they make a sharp right.

What the hell is a *treft punkitt*? Jeffrey and I look at each other.

There are more girls than I thought—about a third of the crowd, wearing gowns in foxy reds, shimmering champagnes, ivory whites. All the other boys are in tuxedos like me (*did y'all bring those to school or what? I really* want to ask).

I'm worried people will think this is the first time I've worn anything more formal than farm overalls. I press my hand against the back of my neck, something I do when I'm self-conscious. I have to stop feeling like I'm always out of my element. I need to start believing I have a right to be here too, or I'm screwed.

"Treff two," the masked dude says, directing this over my shoulder; another group of tuxedoed kids is led inside the hallway, where they too make a sharp right.

Then, after a brief pause: "Let's go," he commands, and we follow him down the hall.

"Treff three," someone behind us says.

We make the same right turn everyone else did, and follow the masked dude down a second, parallel hallway. "All five treffs," someone announces from behind us.

Bromley wasn't always a science building. Some of what I read about Essex mentioned Frederick Anson Taft (Essex alum, 1913), famous children's book illustrator, chess champion, big-game hunter, alcoholic. He returned to Essex to paint murals for the interior of a theater that would bear his name, inside Bromley. But other books I read said the theater didn't exist anymore, that it'd been torn down when the building began undergoing renovations in the early 1990s. But we're being led through a set of double doors, and . . . we walk inside . . .

Taft Auditorium itself! That supposedly doesn't exist. Preserved. With faded murals on the ceiling featuring scenes from classic children's literature like "Jack and the Beanstalk" and *Alice in Wonderland*. People gasp as they enter because it's like walking into a dream.

The two-level theater has thick, maroon curtains guarding an unseen stage behind a proscenium arch, brass hunting horn chandeliers, medieval-style latched windows opening onto one of the school's firefly-infested Shakespeare gardens. The lights are dimmed down, and the fireflies flitter in through the windows by the dozens, resembling uncertain, panicked fairies.

The masked upper-class students gesture for us to sit in the front rows, and when everyone is settled, the lights go out and the curtains rise, sending gales of dust into the air. Sitting on wooden high-backed chairs are five Society members: one girl, four boys, wearing carnival masks. Lit entirely by candlelight, they're ghostly but festive. Quite a combo.

The candlelight flickers off the walls; standing against these walls, on both sides of the auditorium, are dark hooded figures. I don't have much time to contemplate this, because my attention is directed back to the stage as the dude sitting in the center stands and begins to speak.

"I'm this year's Tapmaster. Welcome to our informational session. Rush process for SoSE has officially begun." He sits down, and the girl next to him stands up.

"SoSE stands for the Society of Seven Eyes," the girl says. "You are here because we invited you, or because you sniffed out our trail and solved our puzzles. We are one of the oldest secret societies in the nation—bent on the exploration of our campus." I wonder if the kids they invited will be favored over those who "sniffed out their trail." No doubt I'll have to work harder to impress them. "Essex Academy is drenched in ancient quirks, historical secrets, and one-of-a-kind anomalies that, once discovered, unlock the truth of the dark sacrifices of our forebears."

Well, shit.

"Through the unearthing of campus secrets, the history of our school is learned and passed down to future generations."

It's almost like she's saying unless we learn the truth, we'll all be living a lie forever.

She sits down, and the guy on the end stands up.

"Fewer than ten of you will be chosen," he says. A gasp carries around the room.

"You will be selected based on talent, commitment, creativity, and nerve. Fortune favors the bold. Reach under your seats, take the card, but do not glance at it."

There is a card taped underneath my seat. I unstick it and place it in my lap.

"There are three locations written on your card. Choose ONE of them. Find it. Get inside. Write a report on how you did it. Back it up with photographic proof."

The Tapmaster stands again. "Be observant and detail-oriented; pay particular attention to architecture and history. We are interested in your knowledge of Essex, but also in how you see things. Send your reports to the email address on your card."

Another SoSE member stands. His voice is deep, authoritative; his mask is black. He wears a ring with a purple jewel on it, which glints in the candlelight. "Put the cards in your pockets. You will be led out of the building in the same formation in which you entered. Go straight back to your dorms. Once there, you may read your cards. Tell no one about Society. Remember these rules: We never damage anything, and we never steal. Be imaginative; be discreet. We are the Society of Seven Eyes, and this is what we do. Good luck. *Omnia ex umbris exibunt. Tibi oculi aperti erunt.*"

As the curtains fall, I glance toward the aisles. The hooded figures are gone.

CHAPTER SIX

THE ISLAND

Back in our room, twenty minutes later, Jeffrey and I examine the cards we received. They have a colored seal at the top: two gold skeleton keys crossed in front of a navy-blue partially opened gate on heavy cream paper. The familiar eye rises above.

Below the seal it says *O E U E*, which I recognize as one of their Latin mottos, *Omnia ex umbris exibunt,* "Everything will emerge from the shadows." Below that, in a scripted font: *The Society of Seven Eyes.* And an email: TM@sose.essex.org. Below the email: *You have till midnight, one week from tonight. Don't speak of us to anyone. Destroy this card.*

There are four stars, and below those are the letters *WLM.*

On the other side of the card, there are three locations:

Bathhouse @ Stephensen
Solarium @ SWG
Sub-roof @ Ortham

Jeffrey is googling on his phone. "*Treffpunkt.* German for meeting place."

I curl my leg underneath me, sitting back on my bed. "Wait. We're *transfers*. The other sophomores rushing may have tried to rush last year! They've had a whole extra year to learn about this, learn about Essex." How did this only occur to me now?

Jeffrey nods. "Yeah. We're on a level with the freshmen, then."

"Who were those people wearing hoods?"

"What people in hoods?"

"They were standing in the aisles. They looked like adults, not students."

"I didn't see them. People in hoods?!"

Okay, I didn't imagine them. "Should we share our cards . . . ?"

"Sure."

We pass them to each other. Jeffrey has three totally different locations on his. Another hard-to-access sub-roof. An abandoned music library somewhere in the basement of a former senior co-ed dorm, now used for miscellaneous school functions. And, most intriguingly, the club room of the school's old boathouse; it's on the campus proper, but a little too far to walk. It was supposedly demolished when the Lasker Family Boathouse was erected in 2000, where the school's rowing team now practices, at a different location on the banks of the Connecticut River. Lasker holds, like, twenty rowing shells.

I hand his card back to him. He hands me mine. We're officially competing against each other now. "They were vague about a lot of things," I say.

"Super vague," he agrees. "But that seemed purposeful."

It sure did. There were a lot of details to ruminate over, but there are two I can't stop thinking about. One is how they said they're interested in our knowledge of Essex, but also in the way *we see things*. That might be how I can distinguish myself.

The second thing is how they referred to themselves as *Society*. Not just in their name, but the way they spoke about it: Tell no one about Society. *We're not some after-school club*, they were saying, *you're one of us or you're not*. We already are, or we aren't. They'll know.

The burden is on us to prove it to them—and to ourselves.

The next day, I pore over my research on SWG (also known as Strauss, or Willy, Essex's massive gymnasium) in the main library. I'm in a quiet side room with wood-paneled walls, sitting at a desk with a green-hooded lamp.

Strauss Willison Gymnasium was donated by Gordon Strauss (Essex alum, 1923, former U.S. Secretary to the Treasury) and opened in 1938. It's a giant medieval-looking tower. Most of Essex's varsity teams are based there. I'd have to get past the turnstiles, after hours, to make my way to the top. The gym closes at six p.m. sharp every day. EXCEPT if you're on a varsity team.

I hear muffled laughter behind me. I turn around. Lily is straddling Ashton's leg, both of them at another desk, their hands all over each other. I guess Lily finally made her choice over Toby. Ashton sees me and gently pushes Lily off him. She sees me too, looks away, and then disappears into a different room when Ashton starts scooting his chair toward me. "Hey."

I slide my headphones off. "What's up?"

For a moment he says nothing, like his brain's battery died. "I, uh, look, that night . . ."

I shake my head at him: *I don't care, I don't want to hear it.*

"I just wanted to say I'm sorry. We were totally wasted. There's no excuse."

"Y'all left those Instagram Stories up for an entire day, though."

"I know. That's not who I am."

I smile faintly. "I think it is who you are."

"Look, uh, we're going to watch *The Mandalorian* later. Do you want to—"

"Ashton," I say, "I don't think we're friends."

He starts vigorously rubbing the patch of skin above one ear. "Yeah, I just—"

"And I'm not your charity case. I'm not one of you." And now, all of a sudden, I feel like that gives me the advantage. I'm too good for *them.* I don't do shitty things to other people.

"Yeah, but—"

"Hey, Cal, this guy bothering you?"

I look up, to find Luke Kim. He's wearing a peach-colored hoodie, black Adidas track pants, and an orange backpack slung over his shoulder. Ashton sees him and smiles, in a muted way. They know each other. But they're definitely not tight.

"Oh, hey, Luke," says Ashton.

Luke plops down in a chair across from my desk. He looks at Ashton. "You can go."

Ashton messily tucks the back of his T-shirt into his jeans as he rises, sliding his backpack over one shoulder. "See you at practice, Luke." He trains his eyes on me. "Text me?"

"Yeah, I won't."

Ashton pretends he heard a different response. "Okay, awesome." And then he's gone.

Luke cranes his neck over my notes, with a crooked half smile revealing these creases on the sides of his mouth that are cuter than dimples. "Whatcha got going on over here, huh?"

I slam my notebook shut and place it over everything else. "Nothing."

Luke sits back. "Nothing, huh?" But there's a twinkle in his eye that tells me he knows exactly what I was doing. Interesting. I don't remember seeing him at Society's info session at Taft. I would have noticed him.

"You know Ashton?"

Luke shrugs indifferently, like: *Don't we all know an Ashton?* He clears his throat to give me a proper answer. "Soccer. What's your cocurricular?"

"Jazz dance." I expect him to laugh, but he doesn't. "I hate interscholastic sports."

"Why?"

My turn to shrug. I'm too runty; nimble, yes, but generally unathletic. My body doesn't fit well into things. Clothes, sports. I feel like I'd let down my teammates. Who wants that?

"I saw that turd's Insta story. Let it go. He's not worth it."

"I already did. And thanks, but I don't need you to step in on my behalf."

"Oh, I know." Luke rests his palm on my knee; he leaves his

hand there for a moment, in this strange, introspective way, like he's carefully thought out every action. The sconce on the wall reflects caramel light in his eyes. "Personally, I really like your accent." He strokes my knee with his thumb, only once, then removes his hand.

I swallow. I can't seem to find the right words.

He stands up, hitching up his backpack. "Gotta bounce. Practice." He mimes kicking a soccer ball and grins sunnily at me. "I'll see ya around, kiddo. Be good."

After the library, I head to Croyden House, named after Joseph Croyden, some steel magnate (or is it starch? Is that a magnate thing?), the main store we have on campus. They sell Essex merch. I buy swim gear, anything that says Essex on it, including the blue jackets the swim team wears.

Later, I successfully find the forgotten Solarium at the top of Strauss. Luke (and his soft jock energy) are still drifting through my mind as I get to work. I made my way inside by blending in with the swim team, found a caged elevator on the (secret) tenth floor, a hidden staircase, and got rewarded with a large room awash in violet early-evening light.

The walls are Gothic masonry with intricate carvings on them and the floor is basic gymnasium maple-wood planking, which has held up well but probably needs resurfacing. The ceiling is a complex design of slanted skylights in thick, glazed, reinforced glass. Tall paned windows line the walls. Outside, I can see the campus below; the tops of the buildings, as well as a big chunk of Strafton; and lots of treetops: red, golden, bronze, like a train set.

There are old photos on the walls that must be from the early 1900s. Black-and-white, faded by the sun. Kids lined up in old-fashioned Essex athletic uniforms, posing stoically. They look so alive in these photos. They had hopes and dreams like we all do. As I'm taking photos for the report, I find a black envelope sticking out from behind one of the photos. Inside, there's a card on familiar cream stationery:

Congratulations, Rushee, if you're reading this, that means you are the first to have successfully entered the SWG Solarium and completed a thorough exploration. Email your report to TM@sose.essex.org and await further instructions.

I stare at the card as the sun sets. This feels like a legit achievement.

Back in my room, I get an email an hour after I send in my report.

~ OLD BOATHOUSE/VINGERHUOT ~
From: TM@sose.essex.org
To: calixte.ware@essex.edu

OEUE

Calixte Ware,

S-ciety asks you to meet us at OB/V 11:59 Post Meridian, tomorrow. In preparation for what is to come, we are sharing the first verse of S-ciety's catechism. LEARN THIS VERSE BY HEART. DO NOT SHARE IT.

In the Name of our Father, Samuel Granford, Seventeen Hundred and Seven.

Created this institution, the Granford School, Seventeen
Hundred and Seven.
In the Town of Old Hillbrook, Connecticut Colony,
Seventeen Hundred and Seven.
And thus it was born, in the Year of our Lord, Seventeen
Hundred and Seven.

Do not be late. Dress warmly. No other commitments
matter. Come alone.
Delete this email and tell no one about it.

WLM,
EhRamBe

CNSP

I stare at the email for a long time. They *shared* something
with me. It's small; one verse of a catechism, but to me, it feels
monumental. SoSE is obviously secretive as all hell. Is it possible I'm getting closer? Is acceptance a real possibility, instead of
just gauzy fantasy? I never considered that I could actually really
get in. I only hoped, somehow, I had the ghost of a chance.

Later that night, I casually ask Jeffrey if I can borrow his
bike. He says sure, no prob.

I spend significant time on Google Maps locating the old
boathouse, because it isn't on any recent campus maps. I also
have to figure out how to sneak out of Foxmoore after curfew. I
think about windows and doors. And all the rules about being
alone with people. Everything's about liability; that's why you
have to jump through so many hoops just to visit some dumb
kid in another dorm or sign off campus. But liability isn't just
about sexual antics.

I look around our room and realize what we *don't* have. A hot plate. Candles. Fire codes govern so much. And every dorm has a fire escape that would need to be accessible at all times.

I check out the one on our floor. It is on the back of the building, at the end of the hallway, by a utility closet. And, just like I thought, the window isn't locked! I'm not sure how much clanging there'll be, but I guess I'll find out tomorrow. This is how I'll sneak out.

I barely get any sleep and manage to stay *just focused enough* in classes the next day not to call attention to myself: that my mind is clearly on other things—like what's going to happen at midnight and repeating the first verse of the catechism, over and over, in my head.

It mists the rest of the day into early evening, and then it stops.

At a quarter to twelve, I climb down the fire escape carefully. It doesn't clang. My plan works—the back of Foxmoore is dark and ignored. I have a hoodie over a thin sweatshirt, but I soon realize that's not enough. The night is nippier than I thought.

I bike out to the old boathouse. It was never fully demolished, just left empty. All boathouses in well-endowed prep schools on the Eastern Seaboard are the same. Airy, open-timbered rooms with mahogany wainscoting. Broadly arched windows so one can see whatever river or lake the building is set on from the rowing tanks, creating the illusion of an uninterrupted plane of water.

Parts of the building seem to have been damaged by a storm

and never repaired. The windows facing the water are all blown out. The ceiling is partially collapsed and there's a musty, mildewy smell. I walk through the empty space, noting where the tanks used to be, where the exercise equipment once was, on damaged athletic rubber flooring, coated in slime.

I try not to think how big a risk this is, and what could happen if I'm caught by a school official. My self-destructive side is kicking in, maybe more than I'd like. And this side of me seems to be the engine guiding me forward when I see them.

They're gathered by the former entrance to the building, under a frame of heavy timber trusses, the water outside, lit by the moon reflecting off the wood in silvery ripples. Four boys in tuxes and white carnival masks. Standing in front of a hospital gurney. They motion for me to get onto the gurney.

"What is this?" I say in a breathy whisper that somehow still echoes.

No one moves or responds.

And the thing is . . . I only pause for another second.

They strap me to the gurney and blindfold me.

Someone's voice in my ear: "We're going to put on noise-canceling headphones. You will have total sensory deprivation for a period of fifteen to twenty minutes. Nod if you understand."

I do. My pulse quickens. What if I start to panic. What if . . .

The headphones go on. No sound. No vision.

I have touch, smell, and taste left. I can feel the gurney being lifted. I can feel it being set down again, on a flat surface. I sense movement. I sense it in my inner ears. I can taste and smell salty, wet air. I feel a biting wind. We're outside. We might be . . .

On the fucking water.

To offset the total sensory deprivation, my mind shoves images at me: Luke, with his paint cans. My mom smiling over a glass of Bulleit. Fireflies floating through windows . . .

I see those cold eyes, glittering like an awakened cave snake, coming for me in that empty hallway, along with his lumbering friends. I see the highway overpass, the places we'd go as the daylight slipped away and night soaked us. Night conceals things . . .

Like shame. And now it starts to scald, like it always does.

"No," I say, getting heated. I move against the straps. But then . . .

I feel the gurney being lifted and set down. My body is lifted up and placed on a cold, hard surface. The headphones are ripped off. "Do not take off the blindfold until you hear the timer go off. Nod if you understand."

I nod.

"Never speak of this to anyone."

I nod again. My breathing is broken, stuttered.

I hear the unmistakable sound of a boat's motor, moving farther and farther away.

I lick my dry, cracked lips. *Beep beep beep.*

I rip off the blindfold and sit up. There is a stopwatch on a black cord around my neck. I rip this off as well. There is a small flashlight placed on my stomach and a piece of paper. I flick the light on and shine it on the paper. It says: *Hi Cal! Escape the island. - Society*

I'm on a tiny island in the middle of the night. In the

distance, there's a lighthouse, its beam doing a classic circular sweep. Every time it circles my way, it briefly resembles a blazing, large eye, judgmental, suspicious. As my eyes adjust, I see the water tinseled with bits of moonlight. The moon peeks out of a partly cloudy sky.

"Oh my God," I say, over and over again, as I walk the muddy island, shining my flashlight down. There's only rocks and twigs that crunch under my feet. I shiver, clutching myself. The cold is intense and hits fast. I'm going to freeze to death.

I see bones on the ground. *Oh, shit, is that what they are?* My concentrated circle of light shines off small piles of bones and . . . a skull looking right at me, blue-ish white and shocked-looking under the moon. Empty eye sockets! I jump back with a choked cry.

This is a joke. It has to be. They do not take students out here to die.

Although, what if they do? No one knows where I am . . .

I continue walking, and finally, I see something. A rowboat, partially buried under a pile of broken branches. And more bones! I shine my light over it. I see two oars. But it's in ruins, slowly sinking into the algae by the island's edge, the wood decomposing. Something glints: a necklace wrapped around one of the oars. I pick it up. Silver pendant, silver chain. There's an engraving on it: *Omnia ex umbris exibunt.*

I have my phone, but there's no signal. I can't jump in the water and swim to shore, or I'll die. I don't even know which direction to swim in. That lighthouse tells me absolutely nothing.

I hear a sound. I whip around. It sounded like something splashing through the water.

I walk to the edge of the island, where I heard it, and shine the flashlight out into the misty dark. Nothing. But after a minute, a shape appears. It gets closer and closer. It's a rowing shell, what's known as a four, what Essex races competitively in the New England Interscholastic Rowing Association. There are three hooded rowers making their way to me, their shrouded bodies shifting, Viking-like, through the night into tangibility.

I exhale. But it's tinged with disappointment. I must have failed in some way.

The shell reaches the shore. "Did you find the necklace?" a hooded figure asks.

I start to speak but my teeth are chattering. I dangle the necklace out. My hand is trembling so badly I can barely keep it still.

"Throw it to me, please."

I throw it to the hooded figure, who catches it in midair. The lighthouse sweeps our way, illuminating the three figures. Their cloaks are wine-dark red. I can't see their faces.

"Finish this sentence," another figure intones. I hear water lapping against the boat. "In the name of our Father . . ."

I can barely speak. "Sam . . . Sam . . ."

"Take a breath, Cal. Try again."

I bend over, clap my hands over my knees, and breathe deeply. Then I straighten up again. "Samuel Granford."

"Seventeen Hundred and Seven!" they shout, their voices echoing into the night. "Created this institution . . ."

"The Granford School!" I pant.

"Seventeen Hundred and Seven! In the Town of . . ."

"Old Hillbrook!"

". . . Connecticut Colony, Seventeen Hundred and Seven! And thus it was born, in the Year of our Lord . . ."

My voice is a rasp, skittering out over the calm, flat, moonlit water. "Seventeen . . . Hundred . . . and . . . Seven."

"Hold out your hand, we'll help you in. Take the fourth oar from the oarlock."

"But I didn't escape!"

They all laugh. "No one escapes," a hooded kid says, like that's the most ridiculous thing he's ever heard.

CHAPTER SEVEN

NIGHT MOVES PART I (GALA)

Despite what's probably mild hypothermia, and slight trauma that fades slowly away into the side of my thoughts, I feel stronger than ever after my experience on that island. And proud.

I rode home. Took a long, hot shower. And went right to bed. When I woke up the next day, I wasn't sure if I had dreamed the whole thing. Until I saw the mud on my sneakers.

I'm still contemplating it all, two days later, when the letter is shoved under my door. I know immediately it's from *them*. It's a cream-colored envelope with a wax-sealed crest, my name in looping calligraphy on the front. It resembles the card we got on the night of the informational session. I rip it open.

———————— OEUE ————————

THE SOCIETY OF SEVEN EYES

★★★★

Cordially invites you to escape your studies for an evening in stealth and fellowship. Your presence is requested—in cocktail attire—at the Semi-Annual

Gala at Eleven Post Meridian, Wednesday the
Sixteenth of September, at the Weeping Mother.
Be discreet. Destroy this invitation.

★★★★

W L M

There's no way to know if this gala is some sort of next step, if I've climbed a rung of their mysterious ladder, or if this is a continuation of Rush for everyone who emailed a report.

The Weeping Mother in Five Stages of Grief is a weathering steel sculpture by famous American sculptor (and Essex alum) Elias Vanderhaas. It appeared by surprise one morning in Holtham Square in 1969, secretly funded by a group of students, as an antiwar memorial. Holtham Square is where Tanner Hall is, the school's music department. I'm guessing this meeting spot is one of several Treffpunkts. I've got the jargon down now.

The gala is an hour past curfew. But I know how to circumvent that now.

When Jeffrey reveals that he too received an invitation (some girl handed it to him after lunch, like a court summons), I'm disappointed (and then I feel guilty that I'm disappointed). Nothing against Jeffrey, but I assume they didn't make any cuts if he also got invited.

Jeffrey has a different treff than mine. I don't know if that's significant or not, but he has to be at the stone fountain with the comedy and tragedy masks in front of Ashbury Theatre Complex, also at eleven p.m. Jeffrey doesn't know how to escape

Foxmoore, though. He's got a ton of absurd ideas. The word *rappel* is even used at one point.

"What about the fire escape?" I innocently suggest.

He gives me a curious look.

Then I explain to Jeffrey everything I figured out about how fire protocols can work in our favor.

Once outside, we stay clear of the lampposts lining the well-paved paths by gliding across swaths of dark lawns as we make our way to our treffs. Jeffrey and I split up with a single wave of the hand. At the sculpture, I join another group of kids gathering (smaller than last time? I can't tell), and right away, before I can recognize any faces, an upper-class student silently leads us through the night.

We're escorted across a sleepy campus to the first floor of Brookleven Hall, with its columned portico out front. It used to be a science building. Things shifted around campus as newer buildings sprang up, and in the last ten years Brookleven became another administrative building. The bottom floor functions as a kind of ballroom for various kinds of alumni events under-class students wouldn't normally be invited to. My jaw drops when I step inside.

Under a glittering chandelier is a champagne tower on a white-linen table. There is another table with crackers and different kinds of caviar—slimy glistening pearls of red, green, yellow, and black, with various toppings to go along with it. There's no other food. They want us to get drunk. I'm guessing this is a test of discipline and self-control. The island was a test too.

There's a string quartet playing in a corner. Most kids stand motionless in the middle of the ballroom, stunned, blinking. The quartet is playing Pachelbel. The music echoes spectrally.

I go up to the tower and take a glass of champagne. I sip it, slowly. I'm going to steer clear of the caviar because I don't know how my stomach will react to it. Everyone is hugging the corners of the room, unsure. This is a lavish event; the champagne and caviar alone must have cost at least a grand.

An upper-class dude glides over, grabs my elbow, and I whirl around. "Hey," he says. His voice is deep, assured, velvety, like it's used to telling, not asking. "Welcome to Gala."

"Hi." I hold out my hand, which he shakes firmly.

He's a Scandinavian-looking kid with a linebacker's build, in a dark blue tux (badass choice). He might be considered handsome if his head weren't placed on such a thick neck. "Pinky Lynch."

For a second my tongue gets stuck in my mouth. He wears a ring with a large purple stone. I remember that ring. He was one of those masked kids onstage at Taft. I succeed in unsticking my tongue. "Calixte Ware. Cal."

"Good to meet you, Cal. Have fun, mingle, help yourself to everything." Pinky pats me on the back. He walks away too fast for me to get more of a read on him.

A slim Black kid bounds over to me and rubs my shoulders in this overly familiar way as if we've known each other for years. His shoes are shiny, well polished (shit, are mine?), and they're two-tone black-and-white, fashionable with the tux.

"I'm Marcus." I detect a slight accent there.

"Cal. Are you from down south?"

His eyes light up. "From Birmingham. You?"

"I'm from McCarl, Mississippi," I reply, realizing I'm already more chill and outgoing than I've been during my entire time at Essex.

"Ah!" he responds, arms spread wide, like he's going to embrace me.

"We're the ones who help everyone from Alabama feel better about themselves, right?" I joke. People from Alabama like to think Mississippi is notoriously poorer, backward, more racist, with worse schools, but truthfully, we're kind of neck and neck.

Marcus laughs. "I only lived there till I was nine. We moved to Chicago. My dad's an oncologist at Northwestern Memorial."

"Chicago, wow, lucky you," I say, though I know next to nothing about Chicago except it's a city and isn't in Alabama or Mississippi. "You held on to your accent, though."

"I'll never let that go! I miss Birmingham. Chicago is freezing. I also miss some of my friends in Birmingham. How are you liking New England?"

"I like the autumn: the colors, the crispness, like the whole world got ripe." It's hard to describe to folks back home, where there are mostly evergreens, magnolia, sweetgum, where everything is moist and slow. "Connecticut is hilarious. All these towns that sound magical and royal. Bristol! Cheshire! Cornwall! Windsor!"

"I know, right? It's nice here, I dig it. SO WHITE, THOUGH, HOLY SHIT. Not Essex, the student body is diverse enough, but New England as a whole."

"Are you a senior?"

"Junior," he replies. "I'm an SM, or Society Member. I'm also on the BoD. The Board of Directors." He casts his eyes down at my nearly empty glass. "Do you want more champagne?"

"I'm good."

"So what comes next is Marathon, Cal."

I stare at him, rubbing the heel of my hand under my chin. "Marathon?"

"The next step in Rush."

I nod vigorously, like I was expecting this. Of course there was going to be more.

"We want you to keep going. We call them explos. Short for exploration reports. As always, be specific in terms of architecture, security deets, history of the building. We really dig all that, especially how you went about it, the design of the explo. Here's the plot twist, though . . ."

Am I going to get kidnapped and have to parachute out of a single-engine Cessna?

"This time, pick your own place. The next explo is all yours. Don't give us stuff anyone can find online, or in standard basic school materials. Peel another layer off." Marcus makes a peeling-off gesture. Then he speaks directly into my ear. "Take. Bigger. Risks."

Bigger risks. I understand immediately that these are serious words if I want to get tapped.

Marcus glances over at the caviar; there are some kids hovering, examining the stuff uncertainly. "Try the caviar; it's not as bad as you think." His voice is light and airy again, and he's brushing at my shoulder like some lint landed on it. He nods at me and darts off.

I throw back the final sip of champagne. A tenth grader, clearly sick on the copious amounts he managed to throw back already, runs out of the room, hands cupped over his mouth. Okay, he probably got cut. I made the right call to go slowly.

"That kid probably got cut." I turn to find Luke Kim wincing at the sick kid. He swivels gracefully to face me full-on, and he is pure fire in formal wear. "Boy is *turnt*."

"That's what I was thinking," I say, laughing. I'm very happy to see him. I assume, at this point, he must have been at that info session at Taft and I somehow missed him. "Hi, Luke."

"Hi, Cal." He has this devilish smirk, but also that openness about him. More of it now.

"So, where you from anyway?" The boilerplate question around here. I might as well ask.

"Parents are from Seoul. Dad's an engineer, and they emigrated before I was born. Grew up outside Richmond."

"You're *almost* a Southerner."

He makes a *bfffpppttt* sound. "I guess."

"I'm from Mississippi."

"You win," says Luke, taking a sip of champagne from a half-full glass. He's paced himself too. "I figured from the accent anyway."

Yeah, so did the whole school. I gesture around. "What do you make of all this?"

Luke shrugs. "Like, I don't know! It's cool, I guess. Some girl told me I have to run in a marathon or something."

64

"I think it's *called* Marathon? We have to send in more reports."

"Yeaaaaahhh," says Luke. "I'm, like, over that." He laughs, eyes closed, head shooting up in this joyous way. "I'm kidding! I'll do more. Whatever they want!"

His clownishness is cracking me up. "Try the caviar?"

Luke sticks out his tongue. "Nah."

The mingling is still going on, and it's a total ride being in this room, but I'm starting to sense we're not meant to linger. The gala is enchanting as all hell. But the Society members seem to have slipped out; we're probably being observed; the theme of the night seems to be resisting temptation. I spot Jeffrey across the room, glass in hand, talking up Dahlia Evans, a girl from our year. I look at Luke. "I think they told us what they needed to tell us."

"You think we should go?"

"When we choose to go is key," I reply.

Luke points at me, impressed. He gazes around, once, twice, but his eyes keep coming back to mine, like he's trying to figure me out, or dare me to figure him out, I don't know. Is this all in my head? Are we all tipsy? Is that what this is?

"Overstaying would be rude," he concludes. "I'm totally gonna get some more champagne, though. I hate to see all that go to waste." The tower, gleaming like molten gold, looks barely touched. "One for the road. How often do we get to drink champagne, right?"

He dashes off. The string quartet continues on sportily, like they're giving their absolute best to passengers on a sinking ship, and then Luke is back, that warm-ass smile again, which is infectious, and he shoves a glass into my hand. He leads me out of Brookleven, and the next thing I know it's after midnight, and we're chilling behind Hertzman Center.

"We should savor this." I'm not sure what he means at first—*this moment?*—but then he raises his glass of champagne, that sweet smirk again. We toast, and each take a sip. "I have a surprise." He reveals a napkin he was hiding in his jacket—there's a cracker with a neat pile of caviar on top. "Give it a try?"

"Uh, sure." I laugh. I hope fish eggs count as a risk!

Luke takes a nibble, makes a *not bad* face, and hands it to me. I take a bite. "Salty."

"I don't hate it," he says. "Although I don't see the big deal either?"

"Maybe it needs some of those toppings?"

We both finish the caviar, taking mini bites, nodding affably.

"Well, whatever, it's good we tried something new." Luke chugs the rest of his champagne, and then I do. He takes both our glasses and places them in front of a tree. The flutes, leaning toward each other, look like they're in love.

"The moon's reflecting in your eyes," he says, the way you'd tell someone they have lettuce in their teeth. I place the heel of my hand against my forehead, shielding my eyes, as if this lunar glow is somehow offensive or painful to him. "I wonder what happens if you cry."

"Moon tears."

"Ah, a poet." He laughs a little. And I laugh too because no one's referred to me as that before. He's grinning, which seems to smash apart the night.

"I don't think so," I counter.

"Speaking of crying . . ." His grin is embedding itself into my consciousness—it's like taffy and stretches a little bit sideways. "When we first met . . ."

We each stumbled on each other's secrets, in a way. "Been having a rough time here."

"I hear that. You know something? I thought about you. After that day. When we met."

No one's ever said those words to me. "Why?"

"I don't know. You seemed lost. You mutter to yourself too."

I feel myself blushing. "It's . . . something I . . . yeah."

"It's cute." He pauses. "I haven't found my pack here yet. I was kind of a bad kid."

This catches me by surprise. "How do you mean?"

He kicks at a stone on the ground in a way that instantly reminds me he plays soccer. "Wrong crowd at school, where I grew up, these skater punks got really into street art, and we were tagging these buildings—"

"Like what I saw you—"

"Yeah, what you saw me doing, but we got caught, like, I was arrested and shit, and there was this juvenile detention center I was headed for—long story. I wound up here instead. But I have to, like, *behave.* Been spray-painting streets since I was ten. It's not that easy to stop," he says, undoing his tie in a flustered way, like he's being choked by his past.

"What's your tag?"

"Cool, okay. Hold out your hand."

I do. Luke takes a pen out of his pocket and draws

something on my palm. As soon as his pen touches my skin, that cool tickle, I close my eyes. He's made this shape many times before. When I open my eyes, the pen is in Luke's teeth, and he's capping it. "My identifier."

"What is it?" In the dark, I can't quite make it out.

"You'll see. It's late, we should get back." Luke holds out his hand. I shake it.

"Sleep well, Calixte 'Cal' Ware."

"You too, Luke Kim," I say, but he's already dissolved into the midnight.

CHAPTER EIGHT
BLACK ROSES

In chem the next morning, I turn my palm up and look, once again, at what Luke drew on my hand. It's a dead baby in a womb, x-ed-out eyes, a jagged chunk missing from the side of its neck, as if chomped by a cartoon monster. It's funny and disturbing. Luke's got layers. He's edgy and charismatic. He has a certain swagger that makes me want to know more. He looks up at me, sphinxlike, as his eyes flit over to my palm with a ghost of a smile. Then he starts doodling in his notebook. I close my fingers, making a fist, hiding his mark on me.

In English, second period, we're talking about Robert Frost and this poem "The Rose Family." *The rose is a rose, and was always a rose* . . . and there I am thinking about roses, when my eyes meet Emma Braeburn's, across the table, while each of us takes our turn holding forth about Bob Frost. We're trying to impress our English teacher, Mr. Bryce, with his eggplant-colored cardigan and Warby Parker tortoiseshells. Emma smiles at me; I smile back. She's sitting in front of the windows that face York Field; the sun streaks my eyes like electric needles, so I have to look away. Emma is Gretchen Cummings's roommate.

Vice President Charles Cummings caught some heat a few months back for a pretentious, insensitive speech he made about Syrian refugees. He quoted from this terrible poem called "Black Roses" about long treks through endless nights. He even attributed it to the wrong person (a man, instead of the female English professor who for some reason wasn't embarrassed enough not to claim it as her own).

It did not go over well. Huge PR nightmare. In fact, when I heard Gretchen would be attending Essex, I was kinda surprised, and hopeful (for her sake) that maybe she's sharper than her dad. I don't know, I don't have any classes with her. But here's Emma, who's smiling and—

Take. Bigger. Risks.

And yeah, I have an idea. It's a seed of one, and so complicated I'm not sure how I'd pull it off, but it's so badass I'm not sure I can forget about it either.

Later, at lunch, I find Emma while she's staring at the fruit table. "Hey."

"Oh, hi," she says, not totally undelighted to see me. We've never spoken outside of class before. And then she's back to studying the apples.

I point to a Granny Smith. "That's the one, that's the winner right there."

She snatches a banana and smirks at me. "Then maybe you should eat it."

Well, now I sort of have to. I grab the apple.

"Hey hey," says Emma as two of her friends pass by, and she walks off.

Half my brain is telling me that I can't charm anyone here, that I'm not one of them and never will be. The other half is telling me that I'm better than all of them, *look at everything I've done, everything I've been through,* and I can do this, so I go over and sit across from Emma. She doesn't seem to mind. I grabbed the most haphazard collection of stuff to eat. Emma is noticing this too. "Sampling several world cuisines today?"

"I guess." I laugh. "You smiled at me in class today."

A pause. "Why wouldn't I?"

That's a good point. That was probably a dumb thing to say. I feel my posture begin to collapse. I was confident at Society's Gala, but that felt more like I was playing a specific role. Now I'm just me again. How do I summon that same energy at Graymont?

She bites her lip. "I did smile. You look like my little brother's best friend."

Ouch. "Oh."

"We called him Pork Grinder."

Double ouch. "Really?"

"No." She buries her mouth in the crook of her arm to muffle a burst of laughter. "I seriously made that up. His name is Dylan. I have low blood sugar," she says, like that explains everything. Then she laughs again—brassy, self-amused. "Sorry, I . . ." She looks a little pained.

"You didn't hurt my feelings; it's fine." Be cool, buddy, just like that. Relax . . .

"Okay, good." She brushes a lock of hair behind her ear and stabs a fork into her spartan salad. Watching Emma, I realize I can't be the only kid on campus to be self-conscious, to constantly second-guess what I do or say.

So I take a bigger risk. "What's living with Gretchen Cummings like?"

For a moment she seems wary, squinting hard at her lettuce. Damn, someone probably asks her this ten times a day. I went in too fast, too hard.

She takes a bite of lettuce, scrutinizes me, swallows, and says, "She snores."

My lips curl into a smile. "No shit."

Emma presses the side of her hand against her mouth to block her chewing—slow, brontosaurus-like, and gives me a look, eyes slanting sideways, as if to say, *You have no idea.* "Also, she goes to bed *super early.* So the snoring . . . it's endless."

I lean into this. "How do you sleep?"

"I drink a lot of chamomile. That helps. Plus earplugs. But even with all that . . . it's rough. I'm, like, tired. *A lot.*"

"Were you selected to be her roommate . . . like . . ."

"Randomly? Who knows? I had a background check. But we all did, before we got here. Where you from?"

"Mississippi."

Her head snaps back. "Really? Wow."

"What about you?"

She makes a face. "Delaware."

"I've never been to Delaware."

"I've never been to Mississippi. Lots of good writers in the South, though, right?"

This surprises me. Emma doesn't seem like the type to be all that interested in famous Southern authors, not that I necessarily know what that type is. "We have our share, for sure. Faulkner. Harper Lee. Carson McCullers. Tennessee Williams. Also John Grisham."

"Grisham, yeah!" She laughs, friendlier, warmer now.

My budding friendship with Emma Braeburn evolves quickly over lunch (and wow, new discovery: vegan lasagna is not my thing), to where I feel comfortable enough saying I'd love to hear how bad Gretchen's snoring really is. Pierson, the all-girls dorm where they live, has a nice common area, from what I've heard. Big TV, foosball table.

"Do you want to partner up?" I'm risking rejection here, but I feel bold enough.

"Hmmm?"

"So we can give each other feedback on our narrative assignments." They're due at the end of the week. We have to write a short personal narrative, something based on our own life, referencing the theme of beauty from the Frost poem. Traditional cliché beauty like a rose versus our own individualized idea of what beauty can be.

Mr. Bryce encouraged us to team up if possible—critique partner style—but I play up my loneliness. Mississippi boy adjusting to New England, until I get the sense Emma feels bad for making fun of me and is intrigued by the idea. Maybe she thinks I'm cool and writerly because of the whole Southern thing.

It didn't occur to me I could use my background to my advantage like that, but it worked, and I'm running with it. I have to utilize everything I can about myself, all my skills, whatever works, to impress SoSE.

Emma says we should totally hang at Pierson after dinner. Since it's officially the second month of our first semester, we're allowed to visit friends in other dorms now—so long as it's a group thing (these rules crack me up every time). I feel pretty keyed up by her invitation. Maybe I'm changing, growing more confident, chilling out a bit.

Emma has her phone out. "I have to get my advisor to notify the on-duty faculty members tonight at Pierson, who'll notify the school officer in charge of whatever, who liaisons with someone at the Student Life Office, and I guess they all let the Secret Service know."

"Wow, what a cakewalk! No hurdles at all!"

Emma, already on her phone, laughs. "I know. They're a little lax with me 'cause it's like, *I'm putting up with a lot.*" Her eyes flit up to me. "What's your social security number?"

I don't know if she's kidding.

"I'm kidding. Told you. We all got background checks already."

I don't really have a background yet, I think.

Now that I'm officially invited to Pierson, my half-formed plan for a risky SoSE explo suddenly catapults into motion. First stop is the flower shop in town.

I explain to the florist what I want to do and ask what color roses would work best.

"Paint them? They'll die right away." Her tone is sad but also a little sharp.

Okay, Jesus, they're not *puppies*. "But would white roses work better or red—"

"White."

"It's a project for school," I add defensively.

The florist, a middle-aged woman with a pageboy haircut and schoolmarmish glasses, tightens her mouth resignedly, then goes about wrapping the bouquet of white roses in plastic.

The hardware store is one block down.

"How old are you?" the guy with silver rockabilly hair at the register asks me.

"What?" I'm not buying *fentanyl*.

"Spray paint." He taps the can. "Not something we sell to minors."

This did not occur to me. Shit. This is the only hardware store in town I can walk to.

"Ahhh," he says, waving his hand, probably needing a cigarette break, based on the yellowish-brown color of his teeth, "you seem like a good kid."

I slide a twenty across the counter while he shakes out a paper bag.

I find the right alley: deserted, cobblestoned. I throw down a newspaper and lay the roses on top. I spray the petals, careful not to splatter the stems. I stare at them, blowing gently on the petals. They look *real*. As I walk back to campus, I pull my phone out of my pocket.

"If you hate me calling you this much, I'll stop, I swear."

"Christ, Cal. You won't."

I bite my lip. "I might." I grip the phone tight against my ear.

"You won't. I'm all alone here anyway. Like you."

"I'm not as alone as I was. I met someone."

"What does that mean?"

"You know what it means. Are you jealous?"

"No. Did you want me to be?"

"There's more." I explain about Society.

"Why do you need *them?"*

"Nothing is connecting here. I'm the loose wire, the blown-out circuit. People literally move away from me when I sit down in the cafeteria."

"Yeah? And how much of that are you imagining?"

I stop walking. "You mean, how paranoid am I?"

"No—"

"You mean, how paranoid did you make me? *How much damage did you do?"*

"Chill. You're a sophomore transfer from Nowheresville, Mississippi. You know the type of people that go to these hoity-toity schools out east. You were never going to fit in that easily."

"HEARD! I got kicked out of my own friend group, so I'm hardly delusional."

"Look who you just called!"

"Fair."

"And now you have to take bigger risks. And on that scholarship too."

"Yeah. I'm trying to figure out how ambitious I am versus how self-destructive I am."

"You were always a little of both. And kind of aloof. You can make more of an effort than you think to let people in. What's your plan?"

I explain it.

"You'll be invading someone's privacy, exploiting them for your own gain."

"No one will get hurt."

"Is that what you keep telling yourself? The VP's daughter!"

"It's a good idea. Clever, unconventional, imaginative. And so far, it's working . . ."

"Is it worth the moral compromise?"

"Only if I think there is one. And honestly, man, sometimes I'm just like . . . *fuck 'em all.*"

"That's right, Cal. There you go. Burn the world down. That's who you are."

"Maybe it is. Ever considered that?"

I love Emma for wearing a Gudetama sweatshirt and matching leggings.

I zip open my backpack. I dangle two school mugs on my index finger.

"You bought Essex mugs?" She laughs, sharp and nasal, taking them from me. In the evening, off-duty, her voice is huskier, her vibe flintier. And glasses instead of contacts.

I hold out some tea bags. "And chamomile."

"Looks like we're gonna do some teabagging tonight."

Emma invited a bunch of us over "to study." The Pierson common area is like a ground-floor living room: sofas, foosball (confirmed), big TV (also confirmed), and a kitchen area with mostly empty cupboards (except lots of ramen, always ramen), where we can heat water in a microwave. There is a faded portrait of Harold Pierson, "advertising great," Essex alum, over the bricked-up fireplace.

I don't know Emma's housemates: Cara Tarbino, Lydia Yin, Tarsha Mangold. The four of them seem super tight. Samantha Parrish, Alanna Gary, and Julia Higgins from our English class are here too. Grayson Andrews is the only other guy besides me—also from our English class. He's gay, loud, all about musical theater. Gay cliques are even tougher to break into at Essex, not that I tried. You have to know *literally everything* about Shawn Mendes. Grayson's besties with Alanna—some friendships happen fast and hard at Essex. Just not for me.

I like everyone fine, but no one seems accessible. If we were all meant to be friends, wouldn't it have happened already? I don't feel emboldened hanging with new people; I feel like everyone will stare at me for so long I'll look down and realize I'm an alien after all and my outer layer of skin has sloughed off, revealing something scaly and acid green underneath.

Everyone's just vibing, chatting about Gretchen, other people's roommates, various teachers; it's hard for me to find a way in conversationally. I overthink every response, so I wind up saying nothing. This happens every time. THEN a loneliness spreads inside me, like a lake slowly freezing over, and all I feel is this inexorable despair as I dig my fingernails into my palm, thinking I don't deserve anyone's time, friendship, or love. I'm too different.

Too damaged.

But Alanna is directly addressing me, opening a path in, asking about Jeffrey: if he's "on a lot of meds" and if "rooming with him ever gets freaky," and I say no, he's a good dude.

"He's a *snack*," says Cara. "He looks good in those boots too. But I worry he's on meth."

"He's not on meth," I say, sipping tea. Jeffrey takes antidepressants and anxiety meds. I googled the prescriptions.

"Meh." Lydia.

"Oh, come on!" says Cara. "Those witchy eyes!"

Everyone laughs. Grayson hides his face behind a pillow. "Cute."

All eyes are on me.

"What?" I rub the rim of the cup against my mouth.

"Well," says Emma. "I mean, what do *you* think? You live with him."

"Think about what?"

There's an awkward silence. I wrap the tea bag string around my finger.

"Aren't you . . ." says Cara, sliding her plastic night guard in and out of her mouth.

I look at her. "What?"

"Oh, come on," says Emma, placing her cup down on the table, *"aren't you gay?"*

This isn't a question you get asked a lot in McCarl. At Essex, where none of us really know anyone yet, people see one another in a fresh way. That's not possible when you grow up in a small town and everyone knows you since birth. "I don't know what I am," I say, which seems like a solid answer to a question I've never gotten. I didn't know anything about my sexuality was obvious. And why do I have to come out *to them?*

"You're so real for that. It's Cal, right?" Grayson asks, squinting. His hair is dyed so determinedly platinum that in this light it's almost blue.

"Cal, yeah. Short for Calixte."

"Oh. *Slay.*"

As I continue to nod pointlessly, all heads swivel away from me.

Gretchen Cummings is standing there.

"Hi," says Emma, fingers steepled against her temple.

"Hello," Gretchen replies in a quiet, almost apologetic voice, adding a meek wave.

"How was the library?" says Emma.

"Did some reading with a friend."

"You headed to bed?" Emma.

She yawns and stretches. "So tired."

Gretchen is pretty but in an ordinary, cornfield Americana kind of way. She's diminutive, wearing a hooded coat, jeans, oversize fuchsia sweater, dirty blonde hair tied back with a scrunchie. No makeup. I don't see her security detail. They're mad good at being inconspicuous. You'd never know Gretchen was anybody; she blends in so well, like she's trying to be boring. Or maybe she really is. But I've been preapproved to be inside this building. They know exactly who's in here already. That might be all they need.

"Cal." I stand, holding out my hand. She seems surprised by

my formality, shaking my hand limply. Her expression is removed, but then a tiny spark behind her eyes ignites at my sustained politeness, my manners, my small act of kindness to include her.

"Hello." Her voice is so soft it's almost not there at all.

"It's real nice to meet you," I say. I find myself overplaying my Southern accent a tad.

There's some small talk between her and the other girls, but it's immediately apparent no one's really friends with anyone else and has no desire to be.

I feel sorry for Gretchen. No one can relate to whatever her experience here is like so far, and she didn't ask for any of it: to be watched, judged, gossiped about constantly. Inconveniencing other students and staff. Being hated by the progressive kids for some of her dad's administration's regressive stances, which she might not even agree with.

Gretchen waves again. No one watches her go. Conversation instantly turns to who Grayson thinks is gay, and this gets spirited. I find myself slipping into invisibility, despite a check-in glance from Emma every so often. I don't know how to keep up with the ferocious way people joke about others, the way they gossip, how loud they are.

The faculty resident drops by twice to check in on us, and a few other students pass through: an older girl, maybe she's a prefect or something, but we're still way ahead of our curfew.

"You're from the South?" Grayson's suddenly addressing me.

I lean toward him. "Yeah, Mississippi."

"I'm from the Upper East Side." I nod back. "I don't really know what the South is like."

"Pretty chill."

"But, like . . ." Grayson's eyes dart at the ceiling, then back to me. "Everyone spends all day hunting and worrying about abortion?"

I can't help but crack a smile at the subtle Darwinian scorn.

I'm on aid. I'm not from New York. I don't wear Gucci. I don't have the newest iPhone.

I'm not one of them. And they sense it right away.

I check my watch. It's about twenty minutes after Gretchen went to bed. Society wanted us to be creative, take risks, get into hard-to-access places. And I know how I can play this whole thing to further my plan. I grab my backpack and stand up. It's time to make my move.

Emma stands too, hands clasped behind her back.

"I'm gonna head," I tell her quietly, moving away from the group.

Emma trails after me. "Oh, okay. Thank you for the tea?"

"That was kinda mean," I say, leaning into her ear.

"I'm . . . sorry . . ."

"Speaking of heroin, Kate Moss is fifty years old!" Grayson announces.

"I haven't come out yet."

"Shit," says Emma, "I didn't mean to, like—who cares, though?"

"Me? It's up to me to—"

"Yes." Emma waves her hands around. "Of course."

"I woke up one morning, and I was like: I FINALLY GET IT! I love Nicole Kidman!" Grayson exclaims.

"That was shitty of me," Emma admits. "It's cool if you want to be on the DL."

"Didn't say that. But curious, like . . . what gave me away?"

"I guess it's the way you look at other guys."

"Huh." It's all still laced with shame. I have to fight *my own brain* and find a new source of stimulation—fast—whenever I remember my knees on that pavement, those cars rushing by under that weedy overpass. *You don't get it, you don't know,* I want to scream.

"You look at them a certain way," she continues. "But, sorry, I was a total bitch tonight."

I didn't flirt with her, that's what it was. Something in me hardens. I'm starting to navigate a path out of being a victim, rewiring things so I'm the one with the power, I'm the one holding the sword.

There you go. Burn the world down. That's who you are.

Look at it as a reinvention.

"Naw," I say. "You weren't all that. But maybe you can make it up to me."

A gleam creeps into the edges of her eyes. "Oh? How?"

Essex, and SoSE, are like survival of the fittest. If I get into a secret society, I've probably made it here as far as I can, so I present my challenge. Everyone at Essex likes a challenge, everyone likes to prove themselves, one way or another.

"I don't believe Gretchen snores that loud. Prove to me you're not a liar."

The hallway is quiet.

There are rumors: Gretchen's dorm room has bulletproof windows; female agents live in the adjacent rooms; Gretchen can call her dad whenever she wants her detail to back off if she's feeling suffocated. But there's no one. It's almost *too quiet*. And while you can hear music and voices behind a few doors, no individual room doors are open, save one (a little more than a crack), and we walk too quickly past it for anyone to see me—an actual boy, infiltrating a girls' dorm, after hours. The school freaks out about this kind of thing.

Emma unlocks her door quickly, reaches in, switches on a lamp. She waves me inside.

"No cameras?" I whisper, pointing around the hallway.

"Gretchen complained. They took them down. Come in, *Jesus*," says Emma. I slip into the room. She closes the door behind us. Gretchen is indeed asleep. She's like a medieval midwife or something: lying on her back, blanket pulled up neatly to her throat, hands folded, as if in prayer, over her chest. I can't believe I made it this far.

She has a black velvet sleep mask on, and she is for sure snoring; it's very feminine, though: a high-pitched wheezing instead of something deeper and nasal. If I had to listen to this all night, it might drive me crazy too, but it's hard to imagine earplugs being completely useless. Emma just doesn't like her.

"See?" Emma gestures, irritated, at Gretchen.

I give her a look: *You're right, well done.*

"God, if we get caught in here together . . ." says

Emma, worried. "Sometimes they knock on the door and check on us."

My heart skips three beats. "Who does?"

"Secret Service? I don't know."

"You didn't mention that."

Emma shrugs and yawns, a bit too sleepy to worry much about her roommate's privacy.

I swivel my head in the direction of the bathroom, where the light's already on. "I *really* have to pee. All that tea. I'm . . . not even playing. Can I please use your bathroom?"

"Yeah, sure," says Emma, expressionless.

I bite my upper lip. "But I'm a nervous pee-er." I laugh. "For real, I'm worried you'll scare the pee away if you're standing there."

"Don't crack me up right now," she whispers, hands fluttering around her mouth.

"Serious. Wait outside?"

Emma glances at poor snoring Gretchen. "You're not gonna kill her, are you?"

I dance around. "I seriously might piss myself right here on your rug. *Please!*"

Emma rolls her eyes. "All *right*. Hurry."

The door shuts.

Second one: I crouch down and unzip my backpack.

Second two: I reposition the desk lamp so there's more light shining down on Gretchen. Girl's got her mask on; she doesn't react.

Seconds three and four: I place three black roses over her

folded hands. It looks like she's holding them. Holy shit, they even match the sleep mask.

Seconds five and six: I aim my phone. I take a shot. Ugh, my phone's not on silent! That made a camera noise! The door's still closed. No one heard me. I turn my phone on silent.

Second seven: I take a burst of photos.

Second eight: It hits me I could get expelled for this, my future over in a blink. Maybe I haven't made enough of an effort to connect with other students. And when I did finally make one with Emma, it was only to feign interest in a friendship to gain access.

A friendship Emma wasn't exactly yearning for, though. Let's be honest.

Second nine: I move the lamp back.

Second ten: I grab the black roses off Gretchen and stuff them into my backpack.

Second eleven: Gretchen has pulled her mask down. Her eyes are wide open.

She's looking right at me.

Oh shit. Oh shit. I stand there, the rose stems sticking out of my backpack. Gretchen's eyes are glassy, unblinking. Taking me in. A smudge of black paint got on the back of her hand; she sees it, licks her thumb, and rubs it out.

What the hell is going on? Is she awake?

Gretchen pulls her mask back down. Curls up. Faces the wall. Resumes snoring. I let out my breath. OH, DEAR GOD, that was terrifying. And yet, I totally deserved that. Totally . . .

Second twelve: I zip up my backpack and flush the toilet.

My conscience screams at me, wanting me to delete the photos before I have a chance to use them. But the plan is too intricate, it worked too well so far.

Fortune favors the bold.

Second thirteen: I open the door.

CHAPTER NINE

VANISHING TWINS

Brent Cubitt was how I knew.

It was a birthday party. We were playing Seven Minutes in Heaven. A battered Ouija board had been discarded; bored kids chugged orange Fantas, belching loudly, rubbing balloons against their hair. I wound up in a closet with a sandy-haired kid, eyes the color of the Bahamas the way the Bahamas looked on TV. It was supposed to be a joke. But then he cupped my chin. I closed my eyes the whole time. The way I did when Luke drew his tag on me.

I still remember the smell of musty clothes, worn luggage, in that closet. I'd see Brent at school after that day, head bobbing down the halls with his friends, interchangeable boys in polos and khakis, loving Jesus and Ole Miss, but we never acknowledged each other again.

Well. Not at school, anyway.

I compose the email the next day. I describe the series of events leading up to me standing over Gretchen. Society values historical details, so I include some history about Pierson (it was an old infirmary, named for and funded by the estate of Harold Pierson's daughter). I attach the clearest photo, where you can tell for sure it's Gretchen, roses on her chest. The photo is macabre, which I like. This was ballsy, not easy to pull off. But I'm still conflicted. I'm flirting with the dark side here.

I wonder if Society values James Bond–like moves more: leaping from rooftop to rooftop, cutting glass into removable circles, hacking cameras, sliding down ropes. The possibilities are endless, and I don't know what other rushees are doing. I don't know what Society really wants. It's been so nebulous, I wonder if *they* even know.

I mash my lips together and send the email.

The next day, when I'm on my way back to Foxmoore, I see Luke sitting on the stone steps outside the library, lacing up his soccer cleats. I sit down beside him, backpack at my feet. I hold out my hand; his identifier hasn't washed off yet. "I never got an explanation."

"Yo, King." He smiles broadly at me then stares, introspective, up at the late afternoon sky, streaked with tangerine clouds. "I'm a chimera."

"Camilla?"

"*Chimera*. Vanishing twin syndrome. I was going to have a twin. But I ate him up in utero. My mom miscarried my twin, and in my fetal state I absorbed him. I have two sets of DNA. Two blood types. When I'd misbehave my mom would shout, *You're the evil twin! You ate your good sibling, and you're all that's left, you rotten cannibal!*"

I blink. "That's dark."

"My parents became born-again Christians. Then my mom was killed in a car crash."

His casual demeanor throws me. It's like an upbeat pop song with sad lyrics. "I'm sorry."

"That's when I started waking up and he'd be hovering in my doorway."

". . . Who?"

"Me. *But not me.* My twin that almost was. Pale, hair flying around. And stuff, particles or whatever, floating around his face, like he was trapped in an aquarium. He'd look at me accusingly, like I robbed him of his life. He had a chunk missing from his neck." Luke slaps his hand on the side of his neck. "Right there. Like I took a bite out of him."

I stare at the slowly fading baby on my skin. "Oh."

"That's why I created it. And when I'd draw him—*I named him Pete*—he'd go away. For a while. I got addicted to tagging Pete everywhere: every hydrant, every wall, like I was undoing a curse. Got it into my head that the more I tagged him, the farther away he'd go. And it worked."

He takes my hand in his and caresses the baby with his thumb. I can't tell if the touch is for me or for the ghost of the twin he unknowingly destroyed and never got to have. I place my other hand on top of his thumb. It's an involuntary move; we stay like that for a moment, not overthinking it. "What're you haunted by?" he asks.

I wasn't expecting the question. "Lots of things, I guess."

"It's one thing. I can tell. That's why we . . ."

"Why we what?"

Luke pulls away casually, a dude on a schedule, and tightens the laces on his cleats.

I adjust to the sudden change in energy. "How's soccer?"

"Revelatory," he responds, standing up, zipping up a slate fleece vest, for the first time looking like a jock, like he belongs in that subset and is a totally versatile kid, can fit in anywhere. I'm jealous and feeling a spiky cluster of other things too. He musses my hair. "Why do you wear your hair short like that? You in the military or something?"

I brush his hands away. "Can I see your art sometime?"

"Maybe. I don't show just anyone." He smiles with his eyes. "See ya around, kiddo."

I watch an airplane cross a blank white sky. I'm shocked at his hand on my face, grazing the underside of my chin with the side of one finger. But now he's trudging down the hall, coming for me, along with his friends, eyes glowing an unearthly red.

"Cal?"

I sit up with a gasp.

Jeffrey's standing over me. "You were . . . mumbling."

I rub at my face. "I must've fallen asleep." There's a pile of books on my stomach. They fall to the floor as I sit up.

"You missed dinner."

There's a smudge of red on Jeffrey's cheek. At first I think it's blood. I resist a ridiculous impulse to lick my thumb, reach up, and wipe it away. Then I see it's a faint patch of lipstick.

Jeffrey was chatting up Dahlia at the Society gala, and ever since, I've seen him texting more than usual, with a sly smile on his face. I sit further up in bed. "You were with Dahlia?"

Jeffrey blushes, looks away, and laughs a little. On his desk, *Succession* is playing on his computer, faster than normal. Using a Chrome extension, Jeffrey consumes content at "2x speed" to "save time." We've tried to watch movies together; he'll fast-forward any lingering shots of nature or scenery. It drives me nuts. "Good for you, man," I say, smiling.

"Dahlia's not gonna rush Society."

"Why?" My voice is croaky from that unexpected nap.

"She has two older siblings who went here. They weren't in Society, but they know about it. It's not *that* secret. Dahlia heard they do some questionable things."

Those words take a moment to register. "Like what?"

"She said they tap kids based on their looks. They favor a certain type."

I don't need to ask what type. I remember those SMs rowing out to fetch me off that island: brawny, chiseled kids, probably varsity rowers. I'm a puny guy. There it is again. "Are you going to keep at it?" Hell, Jeffrey might have a better shot than me. I remember a movie actress once saying: *Never bring a friend prettier than you to an audition.*

Jeffrey considers this. "I'd like to see it through. It's interesting; it's kept me active here."

I manage a rumpled smile. "And got you a girlfriend."

Jeffrey blushes again. "No, no. We're not that." He turns to his desk and writes something down. "I thought I might as well pay this forward. Dahlia knows a bit more about Rush." He hands me a piece of paper. On it, he wrote: *facilities.essex.edu.*

"What's this?"

"Dahlia says many rushees use this resource for their reports. It has blueprints and reference plans for campus buildings. People also include Google Earth images, apparently. And you really need to know your shit, like, every historical detail of every building matters."

My eyes widen. "Have you been doing stuff like this? On this level?"

"No! God, no."

I gulp as my heart sinks lower than I knew it could go, into the molten core of the earth.

Maybe I won getting kidnapped to that island, keeping calm, finding that necklace, but it may not matter; I could have lost the rest of the game. They said be creative and bold. I did something unconventional, but what they really want is something completely conventional. Something that fits their exact mold. And someone who looks like them. Fuck. *Fuck.* But I don't want to give up. All this new information makes me want to try even harder. Because if I get accepted by them, it'll be the ultimate acceptance. I'll never have to worry about fitting in again. But I probably only have one more shot to get this right. And I'm running out of time.

"Dahlia was a little vague on this . . . but, um . . . there's some strange history to the school that could be linked to Society."

I wish I wasn't so groggy, to get hit, out of the blue, with all of

Dahlia's hard *intel.* "What? What do you mean *could be linked?*"

"Some kids who disappeared or something."

I frown. "What kids? Recently?"

"No. This is probably conjecture, honestly."

"Yeah." Like when Jason told me Society was connected to the Illuminati, I immediately dismiss this as sensationalistic nonsense. I'm aware I'm dismissing it because it's more convenient for me to dismiss it. But it also seems dismissible.

"Oh," says Jeffrey, rolling his chair back, "I found out what WLM means. You know, what's written on the bottom of every—"

"Yeah." I smile tightly, annoyed Jeffrey's making these discoveries on his own. "What's it stand for?"

"With Love and Mischief!"

This makes me fall in love with them even more. Because shit, I really love that. But as playful as it sounds, I can already tell Society contains some darker machinery.

CHAPTER TEN
THE TUNNELS

On Monday, I still haven't heard anything back about my Gretchen explo, and my anxiety starts to nest inside my lower chest. I question everything I already did while obsessing over what my next explo could be, eliminating various ideas. I'm also starting to worry I'm giving all my brainpower to Society, instead of to classes, homework, everything else.

As I'm rushing back from jazz dance to my dorm to change for dinner, a hand swats my elbow: Luke, post-practice, snacking on an energy bar. I'm so happy to see him, my brain short-circuits and I scold him like I'm his *mother*. "Why are you eating that now, before dinner?"

Luke looks aghast. "I was hungry!" he screams.

I laugh as he stuffs the rest of the bar into his mouth and overchews defiantly. "I have to get leaner, build more muscle tone to kick the ball like they want me to kick the ball. So fuck dinner, yo," he says, swallowing. Then he stares at me. And I stare back. "How's Rush going?"

I drag a hand across the side of my face. "I don't know. I don't think . . ."

"Think what? Your whole face just changed."

"That I'm . . . what they're looking for."

"Why do you say that, King? You don't know that."

"I'm not giving up. There's no way. I just need to rethink, reassess, whatever."

Luke considers all this for a second. "Want me to sneak you into Garrott? You know about the Garidome, don't you?"

He means the semisecret basketball half-court in the basement of Garrott Hall. "Yeah."

"Well," he says, wiping his hands down his black Adidas track pants, pocketing the silver foil. "Everyone at Garrott has access, and our room key opens it."

"You want to shoot hoops?"

"It's in the basement of Garrott, King. *Think.*"

"Steam tunnel access?"

Luke nods. "Yessir."

"They didn't say we could work together."

"They didn't *not* say it either. The Garrott basement is one of the main access points to the whole underground grid, but not everyone knows that, or has the advantage of living in Garrott. I knew *you'd* know it, though." He's right about that. "Lots of kids are probably trying to pry off manhole covers. Fools!" Luke shouts into the sky.

I didn't think that many kids would take on the steam tunnels. They seem totally overwhelming, not to mention dangerous. But . . . yeah . . . risks.

Most books I read over the summer mentioned the subterranean network of tunnels that spider-web out from the power plant, on the western edge of campus. One book I found, written in 1974, covered all that, focusing on the phantom intersection between Granford—the college that never was—and Essex, the elite feeder school it now is. Supposedly, the tunnels were built in the 1920s to heat all the dorms via the steam pipes. Then during the Cold War, they became designated fallout shelters.

The steam tunnels might make for a more conventional explo, but working with someone might make it less so. Luke has less to lose; he's probably overall an easier pick for Society. But he wants to share this. He's putting himself out there, and something inside me doesn't want to say no. Whatever he's shown me of himself so far, I feel he doesn't let many people see.

Society brought us closer together. It gave me my first real friend here. And maybe it's not only about sharing the explo for him. *He wants to help.* Am I in a position to refuse?

A few kids are shooting hoops when we get down to the Garidome. Luke knows them, greets everyone cheerily. Their voices echo, sneakers squeaking, the ball thumping around.

"Garrott's basement is huge," says Luke, leading me through a door, hitching up his black Timbuk2. We're inside a hallway. Luke points to a red door. "Feel the handle."

"Hot." I retract my hand.

Luke gestures for me to snap a photo of the door, which says A-23 on it. I do.

Luke opens the door quickly. It's a pump room: pressure containers, utility pipes, machinery whirring behind wire netting, cement flooring, caged work lights. Luke turns on a small, powerful flashlight to guide us. I take several shots as a hot thrill flushes my face. I'm surrounded by possibility. The secret steam tunnels. But also being in them alone with Luke.

"How many times you been down here already?"

"Parts of these tunnels . . . maybe four or five times? I always do a few pre-exploratory missions before I complete a final explo for the report. I work late into the night. I've never sent in a report of a place I've only been to once."

I fan out my shirt, panting. "How many explos so far?"

"Mmmm. Maybe six?"

Jesus. I have to remind myself Luke had certain opportunities that I didn't. Like Garrott.

Luke is unzipping his Timbuk2. He pulls out two pieces of paper, stands under a work light, and traces his fingers along them in a supremely concentrated way.

My upper lip is beaded with sweat. "What's all that?"

"I nabbed a fire insurance plan, utility plan; I've been mapping shit out. The utility plans list the pump rooms; there are different entry points around campus, so there might be older steam tunnels that no longer connect to this one but once did."

Luke had other opportunities too. Kids know to use fire insurance plans, and shit like that, because they have more friends. They do sports. They're more social. "Layers of stuff over older layers of stuff, buried under time itself, forgotten about," I observe, looking around.

"True. And poetic," says Luke, laying his hand lightly on my damp upper back, guiding me forward through the broiling corridor. Something about the way he touches me feels loaded: sort of caring, sort of firm. "Watch out for steam leaks," he cautions. Rushing steam hisses along the walls as we progress, passing by mechanical rooms, dim chambers. Rusty valves drip water like boiling tears, creating dark, steaming stains on the cement floor. I'm nervous, but I also feel safe: Luke as Protector is an emerging idea winding its way through my brain.

We turn a corner. I check my phone. I have *zero bars*. Luke gestures overhead. "According to the utility plan, I'm pretty sure we're under Kirson. Look—" He points to my right; there's a red-painted door that says B-76. "I have this theory that these tunnels, or a different system of tunnels, can lead us anywhere. Into Cook Gallery. Hawthorne Library."

"It can't be that easy."

"Yo, this isn't easy," he says as we continue making our way. "We're under the southeastern corner of Quinlan's Courtyard right now."

I sigh. I didn't achieve any of this. Luke did.

"You're in this with me," Luke adds, reading my mind.

I wipe my mouth, my nose, with my shirtsleeve. "Yeah, but you did all this—"

"I want to give this one to you. I live in Garrott. I have the access. It's more daring and impressive if this is your explo." He whips out his phone. "I'm emailing you the specs—the utility plan, all of it."

Why is he trying to help me so bad?

And then another voice in my ear: *Why can't you just let some-one give a shit about you?*

"Luke."

He looks up from his phone.

"Why do *you* need this? Society."

He laughs a little. "It's a way to redirect my brain, so I can stop tagging as much. I have to keep out of trouble, like I told you."

"Isn't all this . . . just more trouble?"

He shrugs. "Not to me, I guess." He gestures. "Let's move."

I take more pics of the steam-pipe maze as we walk on. Tunnels connecting to other tunnels, all these directional forks to choose from. Luke shines his light down a dark corridor, illuminating piles of china, serving trays, glasses clouded with grime, silverware laid out on the floor.

"This is the service basement to what used to be Pierson's dining hall," says Luke. "That silverware dates from before we had a central dining hall, before Graymont. There's a bull's head carved into the cutlery—a design copied from one of the governor's spoons."

Damn, he didn't miss a thing. All this seems as if I'm in a submersible exploring a shipwreck—without the water. I try and get a shot. "Why's it left down here?"

"Forgotten about." Luke chooses another junction. He's clearly been tracking and mapping this system for a while. I follow until the floor slopes upward. We climb the slope.

"Many of these tunnels dead-end, or they narrow into crawl spaces." Luke points to our left. There's a very narrow passage-way, a hole cut in the wire netting, more warning signs of danger and imminent death, loud switchboards inside. "You're shorter. You can crawl in."

Luke flashes me a knowing grin.

They tap kids based on their looks. They favor a certain type.

Luke is showing me, right now, how I could be useful to Society.

I return his grin, and then I squeeze through the hole in the wire netting.

"Look at you, all quick and limber. Don't touch any of the switches on the wall." I didn't even see those. "Or any of the equipment. It's all high-voltage electricity. Take these." He reaches into his pocket and hands me a pair of wire cutters through the hole.

I grab them. The floor is wet. The water isn't boiling or anything, but there's a leak somewhere. My sneakers get soaked through.

"I have to piece together different utility plans," Luke calls after me, his voice muffled by the steam, as I snip wire away, widening the hole. "It's a puzzle."

"Okay. Give me your hand—and be careful. The floor is wet."

"I'm wearing boots."

Of course he is. I pull Luke through the hole I cut in the wire netting.

I like that moment. His hand in mine. That strong, assured grip.

We continue along, splashing through the puddled floor, until the air cools suddenly and we reach a ladder in front of another red door that says B-61 and something else, written under the number. "Shit," I say, staring at the door.

Luke slaps a hand over his eyes. "I bet I know what it says! I tried piecing this whole system together in my head . . . Does it say . . ."

"Sargent Auditorium."

Luke raises one knee and fist pumps the air. "Yesssss!" he exclaims, drumming the heels of his hands excitedly across my shoulders.

God, he's sexy. I point at the door. "Should we go inside?"

"Well, I ain't going back in those tunnels. But wait." Luke drops his Timbuk2 at his feet, unzips it, and then, suddenly, he's double-fisting paint cans.

I stand back, give him space, and snap a photo of the door to Sargent while Luke sprays his tag—acid green with a blood red border—on the side of the wall by a mound of equipment with blinking red lights. He does it covertly, expertly, which makes me crush on him even more. Although, I wonder, are these explos really keeping him from spray-painting?

"Have you tagged down here before tonight?"

"Gotta have some bread crumbs," he replies. "Open the door."

Thank God it's unlocked.

We climb up a set of stairs and enter the set design shop. Moving along at a brisk pace, we're backstage, then standing onstage in Sargent—the main auditorium in the Ashbury Complex (one of the most state-of-the-art student theaters in the country, or so they say in their admissions materials). Luke strips down to his waist. Three tiers of empty cushioned seats and angled wood acoustic panels stare back at us.

Luke pretends to lean against the ghost light, like he's in an old Hollywood musical. I watch rivulets of sweat slope down his skin, catching the light. I inhaled a lot of dust tonight and got way overheated. "Why don't you take off your shirt too, cool off," he says.

Sure. I remove my jacket, all my layers, my T-shirt. I'm dripping with sweat as well.

"You can look at me if you want," says Luke, catching me in the act, more cocky than challenging. I appreciate his muscular back, and then, a little overcome, fall back, lie flat, and stare up into the theater's flies, getting lost in their depths. Luke comes over, throwing his stuff down, lying next to me, head propped up on his Timbuk2. For a while, we lie there, our chests bellowing in and out like neurotic accordions.

I splay my arms out. So does Luke. Our fingers graze, lightly touching.

They interlock. We hold hands. We stay like that for a little while.

I lie on my side, facing him, leaning my head on my hand. Luke faces me. "What's up?" he says, moving close, kissing me lightly on the lips.

I was expecting the kiss and not expecting it at the same time.

His lips are soft and tremble a little. His breath has a trail of mint and strawberry.

Luke brings my face closer. Our tongues find each other, twist, and entangle. Our bodies press together. Luke rubs the tip of his nose against mine. And just as I'm finding that little maneuver sweet as fuck, he bites me on the underside of my chin.

I pull back. "Ow!" I rub my chin. "Why'd you do that? Your teeth are sharp, bitch."

"They need to be. I hunt virgins at night."

"WHAT?"

He laughs. "There should always be pain. So we'll know how things might end."

But things haven't started yet.

My body is tingling. My face is burning. That kiss felt like it had been searching for me through time and space for eons, pushing away alternate dimensions to finally find me. It doesn't seem contained to the present minute. It felt like something pre-ordained, written in the cosmos, as necessary and certain as my next heartbeat.

"You'll be all right, Lonely Hearts."

"Thanks, Duchess." Tears brim my eyes. Like I'm allergic to perfect things.

"Duchess?" Luke says.

"Lonely Hearts?" I reply.

We both laugh and shrug.

Luke's eyes are fervid, melted. He kisses me again, softer, more focused, then sits up, hands on his knees. I place my palm against his clammy back. My fingers find raised scars on his skin that I didn't notice before. They glint in the light like silver leeches bleeding him. "I didn't tell you about the shit I got into before," he says. "I stabbed this kid."

"Stabbed?" Luke is the most casually badass, punk-cute kid I've ever met. I'm attracted to him and I'm starting to care about him. But I can't see him being violent.

Then again, I don't know him at all.

"This kid I was rolling with stole my paints. You don't do that."

I'm incredulous. "So you . . . *stabbed him?*"

"Stuck him in the shoulder with a fountain pen, whatever. He had to get a tetanus shot, which was probably overkill." Luke gives me a look like he didn't mean to reveal so much of himself so fast, and he's terrified I'll reject what I see. "That's the worst thing I ever did."

"What's the best thing you ever did?"

"I met this kid. He cries in the back of the athletic center."

I feel myself blushing all over.

"You want to know if I have a bad temper; I know what you're thinking. My parents didn't want to have anything to do with me. My dad would beat the shit out of me. His belt buckle almost blinded me once. I'm everything they feared."

"How?"

"I sleep with guys. I want to be an artist. I rejected his values, his stupid God. The wrong twin got consumed in the womb. I'm not the right son, I'm not who he wanted. I'm sure that's why I kept seeing him. Pete, ya know. Why I needed to exorcise him."

Something about Luke fascinates and terrifies me at the same time. "Yeah, okay . . ."

"Home wasn't always a safe place for me. I spent time on the streets, and shit can get rough out there. I have no rights, I'm sixteen, so I have my dad's tentacles wrapped around me still; he rescued me from juvie, pulled strings, and he's"—his face twists into disgust—"paying for me to go to Essex. I am *beholden.* I have to free myself."

"How?" He gets quiet in a certain way that makes me think I shouldn't press this further, whatever he has in mind. I caress his cheek and hope I'm cooling the scorched anger rising in him. He musses my hair, that thing he does. "I'm sixteen too," I say. "I've always been old for my year, but small for my age. My parents held me back from first grade. They felt I wasn't . . . physically ready or whatever." I laugh a little, but as a result of that decision, I've felt behind my whole life, like I'm trying to catch up to everyone else.

"Yeah, I lost a year," says Luke. "My mom. Legal troubles."

"We all have demons," I say.

"What are yours?"

"I've never been in love. But I wanted to be so bad. There was a guy from school."

"Boyfriend?"

"I couldn't call him that." I laugh, which sounds scraped and brutish, like I'm clearing away a pool of acid trapped in my upper chest. "If he ever thought I'd called him that . . ."

Luke's eyes are spilling, his mouth slightly ajar. A tiny bubble of saliva is domed on his lower lip, rainbowing the light; the lip I bruised a little kissing him. "Who cares what he thinks."

"Nothing gentle, nothing sweet. Just mouthfuls of him. Only that."

"Oh," says Luke.

"By this highway overpass. God. I'm so disgusting."

"No, you're not."

"And then it ended. And there was an incident." I should have known the memory would assault me, that I was setting myself up for that. I did get all poetic about it, that's the thing . . .

His eyes glittering like an awakened cave snake.

How I phrased it to police, the judge. It's funny Luke saw that side of me, a poetic side I was never aware of. And that's where it came from, that awful place . . .

Luke presses his mouth to my ear and tells me we don't have to talk about any of this anymore. And I'm so relieved to hear him say it because I didn't know if I could.

On our way back across campus, Luke examines a pattern of manholes that radiate north-south. Luke sticks his hand over one of the vented ones. His face lights up.

"What?"

"Cool air. These spread out in a different direction." He scratches his head. "I think I was right in my initial thinking: There is no junction tunnel leading into this system. Or we didn't find it, anyway. This is a different system." Luke unfolds a piece of paper and makes a note of something. "I'm not going to dinner," he says. "You should, though, you didn't eat."

Neither of us expected how intense all this was going to get so fast. We ripped ourselves open. There's a certain fear in the air, like a green, low-hanging, vampiric smog.

"It'll be okay, Lonely Hearts," says Luke, reassuring me, and also reading my mind again, something he seems to do well. "I'm here, I'll always be here now."

We don't say anything else as the darkening day loops around us, like we're glassed inside a hallucination, and we unravel from each other through the slipstream of dusk.

CHAPTER ELEVEN

NIGHT MOVES PART II (DELIBS)

I'm up all night writing my report on the tunnels as a galvanic fatigue keeps me awake. I send it in at 4:45 a.m. and then fall into a dreamless sleep.

In the morning, as I'm getting ready for breakfast, I notice Jeffrey's bed is made; I can't remember the last time I saw him; something feels off. I was hyperfocused on writing that report last night. Was he not in his bed, asleep? *Was he with Dahlia?* Then I feel I'm being paranoid and weird because I'm so tired.

I don't see Jeffrey all day, and I don't see Luke either; classes are mostly a blur because I'm constantly and obsessively sneaking out my phone to check my email. Nothing from Society.

That afternoon, I head back to Foxmoore. No sign of Jeffrey. Instead of going to the library to do homework, I do it at my desk, checking my email over and over again.

I really want to know where Jeffrey is. Because I have a terrible feeling . . .

As evening falls, I look out my window and see Dahlia Evans

walk by. But she's chatting with Katie Rubens, another sopho-more. Curfew comes and goes: no Jeffrey.

The terrible feeling worsens. I wind up sitting on the edge of the bed and just staring at our door.

At some point, I must have fallen asleep.

A woman emerges from dark lake water, her soaked gown dragging behind her. As the lighthouse sweeps around and illu-minates her, I see she's wearing a carnival mask. *You're too broken for us*, she says, handing me a card with the image of an eye split apart.

I wake up with a start as the door to our room opens and closes.

The retro digital clock on Jeffrey's desk: 4:57 a.m.

I've never been so fully awake so quickly. I fumble to turn on the reading light by my bed and accidentally swivel the stu-pid thing around, so Jeffrey gets pinned in place by a spotlight, like an old gangster film and he's a bank robber on the lam cor-nered by the cops. I hate how caught he looks. His hair is wild. His eyes are bloodshot.

"You haven't slept here in two nights, have you?"

He leans against the door and shakes his head. "I . . ."

"It's Society, isn't it?

"Last night I completed an explo. I had to stay out all night to do it."

My obsession over Society infected him. "Where?"

"Barry. I made it to the top."

Barry Memorial Tower is one of Essex's main landmarks, in the memorial quadrangle. It's on the home page of the school website, on the cover of every school publication; it's, like, the symbol of Essex. Completed in 1921, Barry has a carillon of bells inside that chime on the hour (it began with only ten. More bells were bequeathed later by benefactors, meaning a bunch of rich oil guys sitting in a smoky room nursing tumblers of scotch said something along the lines of: "You know what Essex needs? *MORE GODDAM BELLS*").

"You really made it to the top?" That's an A-game right there if he did it. Essex assumes students will never stay out all night *anywhere*, therefore doing so presents an easy (but punishing) way to bypass dorm monitors. "Whose idea was this?" I don't care if I sound insulting; there's no way Jeffrey came up with this on his own.

"Dahlia. She thought it would make a good explo."

I nod, my teeth digging into my upper lip. "I thought she thinks Society is evil."

Jeffrey half shrugs with one shoulder, exhausted. "She's been advising me, though."

"And what happened tonight?" I sound hyper as shit, but I don't care.

"Look, I don't know—"

"Just tell me, man."

"They call them Delibs. Short for Deliberations."

I'm rising out of bed like an outside force has taken control of my body. *"What?"*

"Yeah, they, like . . . summoned a bunch of us. To defend our explos."

"I haven't heard from them." I'm stating the obvious. My

mind can't fathom this backward reality. Jeffrey. But not me. "Does this mean . . . I'm out?" I want to hear him say it. I want the full force of the pain, like a death blow, so no more pain can follow.

"I don't know. They keep things so . . . cryptic. But they did say. They did say . . ."

"What? WHAT?"

"That it was a next step."

FUCK. "Where was this? Who was there?" I'm thirsty—*parched*—to know every detail.

"Basement of Cranwich."

"Huh." Cranwich Hall, with its red brick exterior and white belfry on the roof, houses the history department. Supposedly, all the tables in the building are made from the pin oak trees they chopped down for the recent expansion, BUT WHO CARES.

"It was me. Ursula Albright. Lars MacAvoy. Anna Chen. James Kirnow." I note each name with a single tense nod. Super-smart, attractive, athletic kids. Ursula is in my chem class. Lars is our housemate (such a *bro*. And Essex legacy). I have math with James, also legacy. Anna, known for her magenta pixie cut, is also in my chem class (and on the JV field hockey team). "There were some freshmen too."

"Luke?" I ask.

"Luke *Kim*? No, I didn't see him."

That doesn't make sense! Unless I screwed him somehow. He gave me that explo and I ran with it! What if we weren't supposed to work together? What if Society found out? Why is everything so topsy-turvy; what the hell is going on?

"They already tapped the kids they really wanted," Jeffrey adds, moving out of the circle of light, now half-shrouded in darkness. "Last night was just who they weren't sure about."

"THEY SAID THAT?" Luke may be safe, then . . .

"Yeah. They were up front about certain things. But, like . . ." Jeffrey presses his index fingers into his eyeballs and starts pacing the room. It's only then I realize how manic he is; the kid hasn't slept in two days. I circle him; two fighters about to brawl in the smallest ring in the history of boxing. "I didn't defend my first explo well. I got lambasted for my point of entry. They said I risked being seen by anyone in Franklin; those windows face west."

"What was your point of entry?"

"Through a hidden passage from Quinlan's courtyard. I squeezed through a partially bricked-over entrance. Dahlia knew about it."

I HATE THIS GIRL.

"They were disappointed I didn't know the clock was powered by quartz. And that I made it to the lower crown but didn't find the main carillon room." He covers his face with his hands and soft-screams into them. "There are fifty steel wires in there connecting to the hammers, *which hit the fucking bells.*" Jeffrey punches the air to accentuate those last five words. "I went in through a back staircase to avoid the ID readers, so I only documented the rear slice of Barry. I missed the catwalks that crisscross through the lower crown, and this spiral staircase, so I never found these vaulted spaces that connect Barry to Quinlan."

My hands fly to the top of my head. "HOLY SHIT."

"The . . . tower"—he starts panting—"was designed by Bernard Rafton Holt; it was the first crown tower in English Perpendicular Gothic style built in the modern era. It was inspired by a fifteenth-century parish church in fucking Canterbury. I didn't know which one."

"WHICH ONE!"

"St. Peter's! And it heavily influenced a Roman Catholic church in Ontario, now a minor basilica. I didn't know which one . . . and also . . . *fuck* . . . I gave them . . . nothing on the steel I-beams that fix the carillon bells to the frame behind the clockface. Nothing on the stone finials, or any other sculpture and ornamentation, I missed the gargoyles, the students at war . . ." He's breathless.

I'm pressing my fists into my scalp. "How could they expect us to . . ."

Jeffrey sinks to the floor, head between his knees. "Told you, they don't kid around, you gotta really know your shit, man." He looks up at me and raises a finger. "But they liked my second explo a lot more. Funny, because it was a lot simpler."

I stare at him. "Which one was that?"

"I snuck into the Furnazi-Gold Electronic Imaging Center."

That's where students do graphic design stuff. "Oh? How?"

"I entered Furnazi through Eckford."

"Freshman girls' dorm?"

"Yeah. Their roofs adjoin, and due to fire codes, the stairway to the roof was unlocked. All I did was jump across."

EXPLOITING FIRE PROTOCOLS WAS MY IDEA! I TAUGHT HIM THAT!

I stand there, in the center of our room, speechless.

"I gotta sleep, man," Jeffrey announces, and before I can even register he's moved off the floor, he's already lying on his back, snoring in his bed. I've never seen a human so tired!

I go over and curl up in my bed. My tongue feels numb. I recognize it as a symptom of trauma. It reminds me of what happened back home. After The Incident, I experienced the same sort of insistent numbness in my face and extremities. *Trauma*, they said.

The truly pathetic thing is, I was proud of my explos. I've never been proud of anything I've done before. Not like that. But I was always at a disadvantage. I'm wondering if I have a bad, burgeoning habit of wanting things I'm never going to get.

I adored the hope of it all. That maybe, just maybe, I might have been chosen by a superelite group to be one of them. And those explos were tough as shit, but for the first time since I got to Essex, my roving desolation got drained away as I focused my brain on something else, something active—*something I cared about*.

And Luke. Of course he's already tapped. Other kids were kicking ass in the way he was kicking ass. What happens when he gets tapped—and I don't? His life will become all about Society while mine will . . . deflate back to what it was here.

I can't sleep. I'm filled with too much sadness and nagging dejection. I watch the predawn light filter through our window, blue geometric shapes floating up the walls. As the light changes to a yellowish white, I figure there's no point lying in bed anymore. So I get myself washed and dressed and head outside to begin whatever this day is going to be.

Much like Jeffrey, I'm beyond exhaustion. I've barely slept in two days either! The light sun-splotches everything as if I'm trapped in a highly aggressive impressionist painting. It's a beautiful morning, but it's painful. Some students like to go on early morning runs before classes begin. Cecily Campbell and Charli Brighton run toward me, wearing trendy athletic wear in tropical colors. They're both members of what everyone calls the 5C 5'10" Girls™.

The 5C 5'10" Girls™ live in Reiss-Orson House, a newer, spacious girls' dorm, and they scored some rock-star suite known as 5C, also known as the Princess Palace, which they've held on to for three years with an iron grip. There's five of them, which gives the whole thing a sort of symmetry. They're all gorgeous, model height (hence the 5'10"), and word around campus is that Charli, leader of the pack, marched into the Dean's office and demanded they all keep 5C forever. Her dad is a big music producer, so I believe it.

They're famous on campus, and I find myself waving to them. They're chatting intensely as they run in tandem. When she sees me, Charli sniffs, irritated, like I ruined the vibe of her run, and ignores me. It could be that I'm in a hypnagogic state, but it feels like yet another reminder that people like Charli sense, on a gut level, I'm not one of them.

Another girl, blotched out by the morning sun, is also running toward me, ponytail bopping. I look away, hoping to avoid another snobby, unpleasant encounter, but she's calling out my name. I shield my eyes; as she comes into view, I can't believe who it is.

"It's Cal, right?" says Gretchen Cummings, pulling her sneakered heel to her butt, stretching her quadricep. The two Secret Service agents behind her in black hoodies and running shorts hang back. I can tell immediately, based on her open smile, that she has no memory of me standing over her while she slept.

CHAPTER TWELVE

NIGHT MOVES PART III (SPOTLIGHT)

I'm shocked she remembers my name, but then she explains it.

"You were so courteous." The way she says it like that makes me sad, as if people haven't been all that nice to her. "My mom's from Savannah, so you reminded me of home, her side of the family." That's right, I totally forgot. Her mom's a Georgia girl. Gretchen grew up in New York City; her dad's from Syracuse, but her parents met at Swarthmore.

"I've been homesick," I confess. Although I think, once again, that word isn't adequate.

We're walking together. "Trouble adjusting?" she asks.

"I guess, yeah. I'm a transfer, so . . ."

"That can take time. Don't be too hard on yourself. You look tired."

I feel guilty about everything that's already connected us. I resolve, then and there, to befriend Gretchen, if she'll have me, and somehow try to right the wrong. We walk and chat for a little while longer about school, before Gretchen tells me not to work too hard and continues on her run with a friendly wave.

That was an unexpectedly chill meetup, filling me with a warmth I wasn't expecting; something I've been legit missing at Essex. It offsets my guilt. But I still feel guilty.

I can't get Society out of my head. My *runtiness*, something I always saw as a flaw, proved useful during an explo. Luke drew that out, and I can't stop thinking about that; I wish Society had appreciated it. But how would they? I don't have chem today, so I don't see Luke.

In calc, Mrs. Wilmers pulls me aside after class to ask if I'm okay. I was hunched over the whole period, trying to will away a nasty stomachache.

I completely flub a test in French Honors that I studied for. *Je ne peux pas le croire!* I can barely concentrate at all. I was a fool to ever want to get into Society so bad.

It makes me feel sick about Gretchen. Am I that desperate for approval, to belong at this upper-crusty school? *That I would do that.*

I skip dinner that evening (not remotely hungry), go back to my dorm, do homework, note that Jeffrey isn't off anywhere secretive and glamorous, and fall asleep super early.

My eyes snap open. There's a noise.

It's my phone buzzing. Jeffrey's asleep, although he left his desk lamp on. The clock on Jeffrey's desk: 1:12 a.m. I grab my phone. "Uh, hello?"

"You're being Spotlighted," a stern voice says.

My consciousness is like weak tea, slightly brown and bitter, but as soon as I hear these words, I know I'm not dreaming. "What?"

"How fast can you meet in front of Cranwich?"

Cranwich. Why is that building relevant? Where did I just hear it? Then it hits me. That's where Jeffrey was last night. That's where . . . Oh my God, IS THIS SOCIETY CALLING ME?

"Uhhh . . . it's probably a . . . ten-minute walk from—"

"See you in seven minutes."

The person hangs up. All I know, in a matter of seconds, is that I still have a chance.

"Shit!" I fling myself out of bed. Then I'm barreling through the night.

I'm led by a masked girl in a ball gown, who's waiting for me outside Cranwich, down to the basement level and inside one of the bigger and newer multimedia rooms.

I'm told to sit on a chair on the small stage, next to a standing lamp tilted down on me. In the audience, there are twenty or so SMs, laptops in front of them, pizza boxes stacked in empty seats. Some kids are spread out in the aisles, lounging on the floor, laptops casting concentrated glows on their faces. Every few seconds, there's the clunk of rolling empty soda cans.

Someone in the third row tells me, without explaining why I wasn't invited last night, that their Delibs are for people they want to question a bit further, and that Spotlight (and it feels literal, given the lighting) is Society's way of resolving a controversy about a single rushee. This is the final step before someone's officially tapped.

"Cal 'Black Roses' Ware," someone says, in the way back, and there's a room-wide titter.

"I found this explo problematic," says an SM in the first row. "You're sneaking up on a defenseless girl while she's *sleeping* and photographing her against her will?"

"I agree it was a bit Peeping Tom–ish, but I thought it was clever, creative, bold, and demonstrated many of the skills Society values," says another shorter girl in the front row, dwarfed by the laptop in front of her. "Charming the right people, gaining their trust, ingratiating his way into an unfamiliar place. Great social engineering. Also, the attention to detail, the planning that was spread over several stages."

"So much of that explo depended on luck rather than skill," says the same irritated SM.

"There was humor and imagination," the short girl says, and I suddenly realize, that for whatever reason, *she's championing me.* "But Cal demonstrated different skills in other reports."

There's a pause. People typing.

Then a steady voice in the back: "Cal, how were you able to map out the B-12 system of steam tunnels so thoroughly in this short amount of time, by yourself?"

"I was with a friend . . . a . . . fellow rushee. Luke Kim. He had done some preliminary mapping, and we explored the tunnels together."

"What were your individual contributions to the explo, then?"

"I took all the photographs. I'm small . . . so I was able to slip through at least one of the tighter spaces to explore farther and cut wire away. The descriptions were also mine." I can't help but smile. I get to tell them this.

"Yes, those descriptions were almost poetic," the voice says.

"In a submersible without the water. Wasn't into that style at first; not what we usually see, but it grew on me."

"Can you tell us a joke, Cal?" someone asks.

Holy shit, I don't know any jokes. Who the hell tells *jokes*? My dad would tell me jokes. But they were old, silly, corny ones and—

Oh God, one of them is coming out of my mouth. I'm involuntarily channeling one of his dumbass jokes. "Knock, knock."

"Who's there?" someone answers back.

"Amy Fisher."

"Amy Fisher w—"

"Bang!"

They're not going to get it.

No one knows who Amy Fisher is. I sure didn't. But they all have laptops. There's the sound of fingers tapping keys, and after a second, two seconds, three seconds, a wave of laughter starts up, moving around the room. "That was, uh, an interesting one," someone says.

"And a . . . sort of history lesson," someone else says.

"Thank you," I respond with a laugh.

"If your life were a novel," a girl says, "what would the title be?"

"Unsworn Paradise."

"Why that title?"

"Uh. Maybe I was trying to express feelings of never fitting in anywhere . . . or attaining a kind of . . . paradise? Or knowing one can't ever be attained, we can only get as close as we can . . . to any form of sustainable happiness." I'm spitballing.

"What's your favorite place you've ever traveled?"

"I'm from a small town in Mississippi, my parents don't have much money, and I'm sixteen. I haven't been anywhere except there or here."

"That's all right, Cal. That was kind of a stupid question on our end anyway."

The questions go on. Abstract, quirky questions that probe who I am in different ways, and then something interesting begins to happen. I de-stress . . .

I want to get into Society so bad—maybe more than I've ever wanted anything, but I know it's beyond my control and probably always was. It's not *literally* life or death. My emotional state feeds into this new perspective, and I gain some confidence by removing myself a little from the outcome and enjoying the fact that I made it this far, which I never expected to do. I wasn't rejected outright. I'm not a total loss as a human being.

There's one final question. That same voice again. Assured, inquisitive. "Cal," he says, "what do you consider your greatest virtue? Don't overthink it."

"I think I'm a good person. I have compassion for people."

"Did you have compassion for Gretchen Cummings?" someone asks.

I take a breath. "Not as much as I should have. That was a mistake and I regret it. I consider myself an honest person, and I'm telling you the truth about that. And although it's not always what I want to be . . . I'm pretty sensitive too."

The call comes the next day. "Be at the old oak," a voice says gruffly, "seven p.m. sharp."

Once again, I've spent the whole day obsessing over Society. And this was another day in which I didn't see Luke, so I feel like I'm treading water in a variety of ways. I haven't seen Luke since the night we were in the tunnels.

That evening, I trek by myself to the old oak. A girl in a black gown and a white mask appears, almost instantly, from behind the tree. She hands me an envelope.

I open it, revealing their signature cream-colored paper, the seal at the top.

— OMNIA EX UMBRIS EXIBUNT —

★★★★

We regret to inform you that we cannot offer you a place in SoSE at this time. Thank you for all your hard work during Rush. We hope you continue to explore Essex's rich historical campus.
With Love and Mischief,
Society

★★★★

Oh shit. Oh no . . .

After all that? My knees go limp. I collapse onto the ground. I don't mean to be dramatic. The finality is what's most crushing. And hearing it straight from them—not Jeffrey. Back to me not fitting in. Not having friends. Terrified to admit this to my parents. Worrying about . . .

Say it. I hear his voice in my head. *Say all the bad things.*

My mom's cancer. My dad's legal troubles. Seeing Brent

Cubitt in that hallway, his eyes dead and frosted over like ice cubes left in the tray too long. My tears blot the letter, pressed into the grass, scratchy and black in the night. That's when I see the piece of paper is perforated.

Right above the perforation, there's another seal. In tiny writing it says:

We are providing you with a false rejection letter in the event it becomes necessary for your own protection. Don't perish.

Wait, what?

Below the perforation is an entirely different message, and another seal.

——————— OMNIA EX UMBRIS EXIBUNT ———————

★★★★

Congratulations, Neophyte, and welcome to Society.
Check your email for information about Tap Night.
With Love and Mischief,
Society

★★★★

I stand up so fast I forget there's a girl standing there. She's gesturing at me.

"Sorry. Shit." I tear the perforation, breaking apart the two halves.

"Do you accept?"

"Yes."

There's the click of a lighter.

"Hold your acceptance over the flame," she says, the fire dancing in her fist.

I do, and it instantly burns to nothing, leaving only the rejection behind. "You'll be receiving an email about Tap Night soon. Congratulations."

Oh my God . . .

When I get back to the dorm, feeling like I'm dreaming, Jeffrey is at his desk, staring into his computer screen. "Hey," he says, his voice dull. "Got a call. Girl met me in front of Kirson, handed me an envelope, told me to read it when I was alone." He hands me the letter. "I didn't get in."

His rejection letter is written on heavier paper, and there's no sign of a perforation.

The message, however, is the same.

I dangle mine out. "Neither did I."

In the Name of our Father, Samuel Granford, Seventeen Hundred and Seven. Created this institution, the Granford School, Seventeen Hundred and Seven. In the Town of Old Hillbrook, Connecticut Colony, Seventeen Hundred and Seven. And thus it was born, in the Year of our Lord, Seventeen Hundred and Seven.

Strafton, formerly Rippowam, entrusted fifteen acres for learning, to Essex. Gifted by Alexander Cornelius, our benefactor, our founder, to Essex. Giveth the pound sterling and in return we taketh his name, Essex. Now we are the great Academy, *felix qui potuit rerum cognoscere causas*, Essex.

Brookleven, Barnfather, Strauss Willison, and Cook, these, the buildings of Essex. Croyden, Turner, Barry, and Bromley, these, the buildings of Essex. Hawthorne, Cranwich, the residences sixteen, these, the buildings of Essex. Our Society birthed and nurtured within these walls, the buildings of Essex.

Ellsworth and Hunt, Kalumets all, their secrets shall be revealed. The Architects' mysteries, once lost in death, their secrets shall be revealed. Brothers, sisters, friends, the bonds of loyalty and trust, their secrets shall be revealed. Our beloved school, history, present, and future, their secrets shall be revealed.

(*Omnia ex umbris exibunt, coniunctio nobis semper perstat.*)
(*Omnia ex umbris exibunt, coniunctio nobis semper perstat.*)

—SoSE Catechism

PART TWO

NEOPHYTE PROCESS

CHAPTER THIRTEEN

THE PTERODACTYL KISS
(TAP NIGHT PART I)

Luke and I started texting.

He asked if I'd gotten in. I said I had. He emphasized my text (!!) and said he had too. I said, *Big Surprise, Duchess.* I craved this new level of intimacy. Instead of being heartbroken that he'd gotten in and I hadn't, now I could celebrate the fact that we had Society in common, something that could pull us closer together instead of pushing us apart. In a way, this had become, without my realizing it, a big reason why I felt like it was vital I get tapped.

Luke asked if I'd heard this indie rock singer he was "low-key obsessed with" named Hiver, who he described as "a glo-fi bedroom-pop wunderkind." I said I hadn't.

The imagery surrounding his music intersects street art there's cool crossover w anime, glitch art, 3-D cyber shit, that's my jam.

He sent me a Spotify link. At first, I thought it sounded garbled and underwater, but the melodies slowly grew on me. I agreed with Luke that the sound was transporting.

Luke texted me images of street artists he "worships." ROA. Invader. SpY. Tristan Eaton. I told him I thought the art was cool, which I did.

RIGHT???!!! What music do you like?

> *My mom would play Patsy Cline, Robert Johnson, Nina Simone. I like music that sounds like it was recorded near some old train tracks.*

Luke emphasized my text with a heart.

> *My parents let me have 2 fingers of Bulleit every night before dinner since I was 12. I associate that music w that time and getting a little drunk w them. My mom was also generous w her medical marijuana.*

Your mom sounds like the shit, Lonely Hearts. You excited for Tap Night?

I smiled to myself but didn't reply back. I wanted to be a little coy. But all I could think about—*all I kept thinking about*—was that kiss we'd shared onstage at Sargent, the sweat dripping down his back, lit by the ghost light, and I'd blush with such intensity it felt like a fever.

Society's email was characteristically mysterious:

You do not have any plans this evening.

You are dressed to the nines, but you can run in what you're wearing. You are carrying only your Essex ID card and phone. You are on time.
The specifics will be emailed to you in four hours.
You will not speak of this to anyone. You will delete this email.
Congratulations, Neophyte.
With Love and Mischief...

One night later, so Jeffrey doesn't see, I get dressed in our common area bathroom, all scratched white tiles and too-bright fluorescents. I'm exhilarated, but part of me still wonders if this is a prank. Part of me still doesn't quite believe any of this is real. Nothing like this has ever happened to me before; it fits no established patterns in my life. Luke doesn't either.

Tingles keep shooting up and down my arms as I think about everything to come, hoping I'll fit into SoSE and be accepted by everyone. After all, I experienced a similar mix of emotions and nerves before I got to Essex, and *look how that turned out*. I resolved to fix my social standing here. And maybe I did. I worked hard to do it, so I can't let my insecurities sink me.

I stare at my phone for a long time. And then I press it to my ear. "I got in."

"Was wondering why I hadn't heard from you."

"Yeah, been busy."

"That's really cool. I'm happy for you."

I stare at my reflection in the white-spotted mirror. "Bullshit, you don't really care."

"Maybe I do."

"Maybe you're not as important to me anymore."

"I'll always be important to you, Cal. I left my mark. You can't get rid of me."

I shake my head and hang up the phone. No. I can. *I can.*

I need to let all this be what it is: a new beginning.

As I walk to Brookleven in my tux (with bright white sneakers! Like BTS!), anxiously anticipating Tap Night, realizing I have no idea what to expect, I stop dead in my tracks.

There's a black stretch limo parked in the street in front of the building.

One of the doors is open, spilling interior light, like something precious bleeding out. People are seated inside, but one figure is standing outside the car, blending into the spidery shadows, an arm resting on top of the open door.

Then that rare thing: being aware of a moment burning into ash as it occurs, transforming into the smoke of memory, in real time. Luke rocks back on his heels. "Congratulations." He squeezes my upper arm, his fingers curling into my muscles.

He's so handsome I sway back. "You too."

"Have to wear these," he says, reaching into the car, handing me a white-and-red carnival mask. I slide it on as he slides his on. I'm one of them now! "Card was on the seat." He hands it to me. On cream linen card stock, a colored seal at the top, and in their usual scripted font:

Congratulations, Neophytes, and welcome to Society.
Put your masks on, please. Enjoy the champagne.
With Love and Mischief,
Society

I look up at Luke, trying to downplay my giddiness: "There's champagne?"

He arches his eyebrows. "Oh yes."

Luke put a clever spin on his attire. Tuxedo shirt, jacket, tie, Adidas track pants with black Nike Air Force 1 sneakers.

In the limo, Luke and I face two masked kids. We introduce ourselves. I meet Daniel Duncan, a blond, freckle-faced freshman, skinny in this boy-band way, green inquisitive eyes like gemstones that get darker when he focuses in on something. And Isabella Flores, fellow sophomore, "from the Bronx," she notes. Her hair is in a bun, allowing space for her rubber-band smile. She bites her lower lip when she talks, with a loud New Yawk accent.

Meeting new people has always stressed me out, especially ones I feel are going to be significant in my life. But when I feel my palms getting sweaty, I remember that I managed to be charming enough to get tapped, and I know what I'm doing now.

I lean into my Southern roots, pump up my accent (not too much), relax, and show the side of myself that Emma Braeburn responded to, and Gretchen Cummings, when I never would've guessed either of them would've responded to me at all. I smile at everyone and express my sincere pleasure at meeting them. "There are two other limos," says Luke. "Behind us." Out the rear window I see their silken oblong shapes reflecting slivers of streetlights.

There's a bucket of ice in the car, and a dark green bottle of Perrier-Jouët. Luke pours some into a crystal flute and hands it to me. I take small sips. My head gets instantly light, like a flood of self-doubt got drawn out of me into a syringe.

Conversation remains light, exploratory, all of us guessing what's to come. No one says too much, no one wants to dominate the conversation. Everyone remains cautious about first impressions. And then we arrive, curiously, in front of the row of interconnected red brick towers that make up the Strafton-Van-Wyke Museum of Natural History.

The museum is on the eastern edge of campus. It's considered, officially, within the borders of Essex campus proper, but it's not official Essex property anymore—it's now owned by a local college. It's renowned for its dinosaur wing and ornithology and paleontology collections, along with its Mayan artifacts and other treasures found in caves and temples.

The limos pull up, a slow nocturnal procession, in front of the museum. The doors are opened (by normal limo drivers wearing caps). We walk up the steps, holding our champagne flutes. It's dark inside; tea lights guide us up a winding staircase to the second floor, where we loop around, and we're inside a room with a rectangular wall of glass.

On the lower part of the glass wall, windows overlook the Jarrett Green—a historic park facing the front of the museum. Sugar maple trees sway in the night wind. The upper part of the wall is an aquarium—sea-green light spangles the room. Fish swim around. A stingray.

Two tuxedoed boys and two girls in gowns stand in front of the aquarium. They hold envelopes. More SMs gather in the corners. There are only seven of us standing in front of them. I eye those envelopes, remembering the email that came before the one informing me of my treff location and arrival time.

In preparation for Tap Night this evening, and the proceedings to come, you will learn S-ciety's cat-chism BY HEART. See PDF attachment.
Failure to do so will be looked upon with sincere disappointment. Once you have learned the text, delete this email. More information to follow.

I've been mouthing the text silently, all day. I obviously already knew the first verse. I wonder if everyone else did too.

A masked SM steps forward. "Each of you, take an envelope. You may open them."

Inside, there's an old brass key with Society's seal engraved on it.

"Place your key in your pocket. Do not lose it. You will need it later." Another masked SM comes around, collects all the empty envelopes from us. "Enjoy the museum and the champagne for the next thirty minutes. Then be out front, standing by your car. Do not take your masks off. Do not be late."

In the weak light and everyone's excitement at being in a museum after hours, I quickly lose track of Luke. I head down a staircase, candles lining the walls, reflecting off the marble floors. I walk down a hall of habitat dioramas, the shapes of taxidermized animals frozen inside, and through an arched entranceway, past a plated sign on the wall I can't make out.

I'm all by myself in a room full of dinosaurs. There is a pterodactyl fossil suspended from the ceiling, its dagger-like beak pointing down at me. If that thing snapped and fell, I'd be impaled: the first death by dinosaur in the last few million years.

The other fossils—a brontosaurus, a stegosaurus, a hungry-looking T. rex—loom from all corners, assessing me with Jurassic grandeur. Street light from the windows frosts the fossils.

Someone grabs my elbow. Luke. His mask glints in the light. He chugs the rest of his champagne. "Make any friends in here?"

"They're not very sociable."

He snorts, admiring the pterodactyl. "What do you think comes next?"

"Next?"

"Those limos are taking us *somewhere*."

Right, right, of course they are. "I don't know." He pulls me toward him. Our mouths lock. Starbursts of emotion streak through me. Fear. Happiness. Disbelief. My mind flashes primary colors and random shapes instead of thoughts, a bleeping educational film. "Who else did they take?"

As if on cue, three of our fellow Neos slip into the room, the kids from the other limo. I recognize Anna Chen right away because of her magenta hair. "Wow," she says, taking in the dinosaurs. Two freshman boys trail her. Ryan Randolph and Kip Spicer. Luke pulls ever-so-slightly away from me, and we all introduce ourselves.

Yeah, I'm not physically like any of the other boys, I note. They're hunky and athletic.

Ryan's a handsome Black kid, polite in a way I respond to instinctively, urbane in a way I admire. Kip, a pale white kid with gunmetal-gray eyes, not as tall as Ryan, or elegant, but with a muscular chest, a hint of a goatee, and shaggy honey-colored hair.

I don't know if they were all hanging together, and if Luke and I were unintentionally sequestering ourselves. I don't know if they can tell we just smooched, but after some wandering and taking in of the dinosaurs, everyone slips out again, with a "See ya guys soon!" from Ryan, which feels like a warning and a gift at the same time: Luke and I can become a world of our own. That could be everything I ever wanted, but it could also be dangerous. Luke glides toward me, takes one of my hands in his, and rubs his thumb over mine. "You'll always remember our pterodactyl kiss."

I know he's right. I draw him into a close hug, his neck against mine, a hint of scruff, one of my hands against the back of his head, my other hand dropping down, caressing his spine, moving all the way down, and stopping, teasingly, right above his butt.

"I like how you touch me," he says, hushed.

Playfully, I push him away. He pretends to fall over himself.

He toys with his empty flute, twirling it around in one hand. "What's going on with us? Should we . . . talk about it?"

Luke's gaze tumbles down, suddenly disquieted. "Yes, if you want."

"What's going on, then?" I laugh nervously.

"We're broken in different ways."

"I'm more broken than you know, Duchess."

Luke nods. "We understand that about each other. Sometimes it's simple."

We look at each other through our masks.

All the things I'm not going to say: I've dreamed of drowning myself in shallow rain puddles, watching my reflection shimmer and fade in the gray scum and shit of the world, erasing everything I ever was into the wet, cratered earth. There have been afternoons like that.

"What scares you?" he asks, tilting his chin up. "The most."

"People becoming something else. Something they hid from me all along."

A shadow crosses Luke's face. But then he shakes it off. "Maybe together we become a sort of whole." His face detonates into an assured grin. "That's what I love most about you."

The word *love* rumbles inside my chest. "What?"

"You see your own ghost, in a way. Like I do."

He's partly right. "I see the world in halves, Duchess."

CHAPTER FOURTEEN

ALL ALONG THE WATCHTOWER (TAP NIGHT PART II)

Placed on the seat of our limousine is another card. Below a Society seal it says:

You are now venturing far away from campus. Breathe, and enjoy the night. You've come this far. Take off your masks.

"We're in a car with a rando driver and we have no idea where he's taking us," says Isabella with a husky laugh, glancing out the windows, which show blurry orange lines of freeway lights whooshing by. The conversation spikes and recedes into jittery laughter, all of us jumpy and self-conscious.

Luke is peering out the window as the limo slows. "We're at Slumbering Soldier."

Slumbering Soldier State Park is a freakin' *mountain*. Hiking trails. On the National Register of Historic Places. The mountain itself resembles a soldier lying on his back, slumbering away, a rucksack by his side.

The limos pull up to the edge of a lot. Car doors slam— extra loud in the taut night.

Two other limos pull up behind ours, and all the SMs, still in their masks, get out. They all hold camp lanterns, globed rays providing the only light besides the headlights. The SMs surround us on both sides, magnetizing us into a marching line.

It's like we're heading to a witch trial.

We leave the limos behind, cut through a deserted parking lot, through an empty picnic grove, and make our way to the entrance of a dark trail.

"Chant!" someone commands.

We chant the catechism as we head up a steep dirt trail. The trail is wide enough for the SMs to form two straight lines on either side of us, guiding us forward with their lanterns. As we chant, we get higher. Darkness spills out beneath us like it's being ladled out of a spoon.

Our combined chant elevates the language, and it sounds enchanted. I get this out-of-body feeling: the person I've always been will not exist anymore after tonight.

We're headed toward Slumbering Soldier's famous watchtower, looming above us. We must be hiking Tower Trail, made of crushed rocks taken from a nearby trap rock quarry. I read about Slumbering Soldier in books on Essex, on Strafton.

The stone lookout tower was built during the Depression, a WPA project, and was used to spot enemy planes during World War II. My research and reading are starting to pay off. I don't feel lost, physically or spiritually. Like my dad, I've always loved history. If you know where things come from, it's harder to feel lost about where you're heading. It's linear.

We approach the tower, trekking up steep ramps. We're heading to the top, which is supposed to offer 360-degree panoramic views of Connecticut.

"You may cease chanting," we are told when we reach the summit.

We're on the roof, shivering, breathless. There are people already here, crowding the edges. The view is magnificent: a grid of twinkling lights, the park and trails winding below us, the grassy Soldier himself regal and undisturbed, the night sky sheeted with cirrus clouds.

The SMs surround us, forcing us into a tight circle by waving their lanterns. There's a click of a lighter, and in the middle of the circle, on the stone ground, a ring of fire springs up, the flames monster green. Probably boric acid.

On the outer perimeter of the tower roof, I see a ring of hooded, cloaked figures, silently watching the proceedings. The same figures I saw that night at Taft.

The green flickers off our faces. Two masked SMs step forward, a guy and a girl.

"A goblet will be passed around," the guy says. "Drink what is proffered. One sip each."

Another masked boy steps forward, wearing a green velvet tux. As soon as he speaks, I recognize his patient baritone from the Spotlight. "I am CEO of Society, head of the Board of Directors. Rush is over. You're all officially Neophytes now. You will go through training that'll last most of the year before you become a full member, or *Veteres*."

Right. Acceptance isn't over. We may never stop having to prove ourselves to Society.

One of the hooded adults, wearing a silver masquerade mask and holding a staff, unlooses himself from the tenebrous perimeter and steps forward.

"You are now part of a two-hundred-and-ten-year-old tradition: the creative, thorough exploration of Essex's rich history," the man says. "Society was founded on the idea of brotherhood; working together, forming bonds that will lead to lifelong friendships while uncovering campus secrets."

The goblet is passed to me, momentarily taking my focus off the masked man, his voice like burnt charcoal. I take a sip; it's syrupy and tastes medicinal. I pass the goblet down.

"In the coming weeks, we encourage you to get to know your Society mates and work together closely," the man continues. "You will get to know your tap class as you would an extended family."

"Rely on each other," says the velvet-tuxed CEO. "We are the moving parts of a whole."

An SM comes over to each of us with a leather-bound book. Another SM behind her carries a fountain pen. "Sign your name in the register to formalize your acceptance."

When they reach me, and I'm handed the pen, I sign my name right under Luke's on a blank line. The ink is dark and wet, the paper soft like vellum.

That spot has been waiting for my signature my whole life.

"Remove your jackets and shirts," says an SM. "For the women, please lower the straps on your gowns."

"Hold your keys over the flame."

We all take out our keys and hold them over the green flames until the tips glow.

There's a voice tickling my ear: "You have ten seconds to decide. Are you a true SM?"

"I am."

"Then we need to brand you. Do you consent?"

BRAND ME? They want to brand me, oh my God.

Second one: I think about how badly I need this.

Second two: I think about my mom and dad.

Second three: I think about reinventing myself.

Second four: I remember the 5C 5'10" Girls™ looking at me like I was nothing.

Second five: I hear muffled screams, the *clang, clang, clang,* as each key hits the ground.

Second six: I think about pain, how there is always pain; *no pain, no gain.*

Second seven: It will be a small scar. I don't have any counterarguments.

"Do it."

Tongs swoop out of the darkness, pluck the key from my hand, and before I know what's happening the searing-hot tip is pressed into the bare skin of my shoulder. The pain is so great it becomes a color: The black night floods out of my eyes, replaced by a blinding white. The key is dropped at my feet. *Clang.*

I make eye contact with Luke. Pain has frozen his face into a kind of determined mask: his eyes like cold, dead rockets, fallen from the sky. He's almost relaxing into his agony.

"Get dressed, put your jackets back on," we're told. "Give them a minute to cool off. Then pick up your keys. Put them in your pocket. Do not lose them."

"Enjoy the champagne," says an SM, walking away with a pair of tongs, clicking them together. A table is rolled toward us—bottles of the Perrier-Jouët and accompanying glassware.

The pain is freeing, like we crawled out of our old identities in the way a snake leaves behind a scaly sock of its former self. I'm going to have Society's mark on my body forever. This makes me feel like I belong to them, no matter what. It's liberating. But also scary in its mercilessness. The SMs take off their masks, as an impromptu tower-roof gala starts up.

Someone grabs me: "Congrats!" I recognize her as the girl at Spotlight championing me.

"Hey! Thank you."

"I'm Nisha Patil. I'm a senior. I rushed Society freshman year; I'm Veteres now. I'm looking forward to seeing what you bring to Society!"

"Who are . . . ?" I gesture to where the hooded cloaked figures were, but they're gone.

"Archi," she says. "You'll learn more about Archi very soon." She waves goodbye as another SM whisks her away.

Someone soft-punches my arm. A glint of a purple stone on the dude's finger. Society's CEO. "Pinky Lynch," I say. You cannot forget that name. Plus, he's wearing the green velvet tux. He dangles his mask on the thumb of his other hand.

"Cal Ware," he replies. "Wanted to offer my personal

congrats. Enjoy tonight. We'll get to know each other more in the coming weeks."

He glides off, and Marcus, the other SM I met at Gala, fellow Southerner, takes my hand and clasps it in his. "Good to see you again, Cal!"

"Thank you," I reply, my voice confident. "I'm excited to be a part of this." That fickle substratum of confidence, flowing deep inside me like groundwater, which swelled up during my Spotlight, and which I wish I had more control over, has steadied me once again.

Marcus, about to utter some standard declaration of congrats, gets quiet as he notes this. "I'm excited to get to know you better." He moves off, revealing Luke in his wake.

Luke is oscillating lightly as if to a song only he can hear. "Is this pretty?" He tilts his head toward the rest of the watchtower roof: all the other kids cavorting; the sky, now clear, clouds puffed away; stars, newly emerged, shining down on us, pinpricks scalding the sky.

"Yes," I answer, with a small laugh. "It's, like . . . *objectively* pretty."

"Well, I don't think it is. Any of this. The sky, the stars, the whole goddam world. I never see the beauty in it."

"What do you see?"

"It's not what I see, it's what I feel."

"What do you feel, then?"

He drags his wrist down his cheek, gripping his glass like a rip cord. "Terror."

"Terror?"

"The vastness and the mystery and the unknown and all the awful possibilities of everything. I hate it. I hate all of it. It's so scary." He hugs himself. "Jesus, I'm cold."

"Hey. Ssshhh." I grab Luke's wrist and press two fingers into the pressure point, rubbing my fingers over his radial artery. I let it pulse into me. Luke's face, his demeanor, softens.

"People will see us," he says with a half-cocked joker grin. "They'll know what we are."

"What are we?"

He leans his body into me. "Scoundrels."

We both laugh. I like who I am with him. "It's not all scary out there."

He musses my hair. "Not if you're with the right person, I guess."

I meet his eyes. "Right."

"When it would get dark out, my mom used to run around the house shutting all the curtains, pulling down the shades, in this frenzy. 'Let's shut out the night,' she'd say. But I always wonder if she ever did. How do you shut out your night, Lonely Hearts?"

I don't know if I do, but Luke doesn't give me a chance to respond. He motions to his empty champagne flute and walks away, gazing with trepidation at the sky, blending into the gallivanting crowd.

CHAPTER FIFTEEN

LETTERS AND ARCHIVES

The next morning, I stand in front of the full-length mirror we hung on the back of the door, resplendent in a cone of morning sunlight. I take an extra second straightening my tie, smoothing down my jacket. I smile. I'm not an ordinary sophomore. I'm in a secret society. I don't know that Cal kid who arrived at Essex a few weeks ago. He was so sad and lost . . .

It's unseasonably warm. Kids are milling on the grass. I walk, reveling in the sunshine. I sense heads turning my way. No one knows I got tapped by one of the most exclusive secret societies in the country. Nothing outward has changed about my appearance. But something's different. I feel it.

"Looking good, Cal," says Gretchen as she runs by, whipping her head around with a generous smile. I wave back. Even one of her Secret Service agents smiles at me as they run in a tight pack, pacing themselves, behind her. A lime-green Frisbee slams into my chest.

I pick it up and toss it back to the small group of students who were throwing it around, and all of a sudden, we're playing a low-key game of Ultimate Frisbee before breakfast. As I leap up to catch it, the Frisbee whizzes right by me, grazing my right temple. I run to retrieve it.

"Hey, you okay?" says one of the kids rushing over. "Did that nail you in the face?"

I hand it back to him. "I'm actually blind on this side."

The kid opens his mouth. "Oh, badass, I never would have known."

"Until I didn't see the Frisbee." We both laugh, but it's good-natured laughter. I catch a glimpse of Dunlop from where we're playing. I see *Septem!* painted above the eye on the wall. How many people notice that every day? I wave at the Frisbee Boys and continue on my way.

That night, I'm in front of my laptop, dashing off an assignment at the last minute for English. We moved on from poetry to a collection of American short stories. "Write a story referencing the style of one of the authors we've read, but instead of beauty being the principal theme, use the story to reveal something autobiographical about yourself." I'm using Sherwood Anderson's story "Sophistication" as inspiration because he wrote well about isolation.

"Haven't seen you as much," says Jeffrey, regarding me from his desk chair.

"I'm right here," I say, typing, not looking up. When I get going, I type fast.

"You have, like, a glow to you."

I've tried to keep my acceptance a secret, and we only had our epic Tap Night so far, but I get the sense Jeffrey is already suspecting something. "The laptop is reflecting off my face," I reply. He laughs, and I turn to face him. "Sorry, I'm stressed about this assignment." I waited till the last minute. I got so distracted with Luke and all things Society. "This thing feels locked away inside me. And it needs to unlock. *Now*."

Jeffrey goes into the bathroom and returns with a water bottle and a pink pill in his palm. I don't ask what it is. I swallow the pill. I take a swig of water.

"Did you meet someone?" says Jeffrey.

"Why do you ask that?"

"You seem different."

"Sorta. How are you and Dahlia doing?"

"We're okay," he says, accepting the redirect. "Figuring things out."

"I'm here if you need to talk," I say as I turn back to the laptop and resume typing.

The next day, Society emails us that we'll be having an informational session before dinner, at the library. SMs are positioned discreetly around the main reading room. When I'm spotted, I'm escorted to a secret elevator at the back of the room, unlocked with a small brass key; we speed up to the legendary Letters and Archives Room, not accessible to (normal) students.

It's impossible not to gasp when you walk through the entranceway and behold the vaulted ceiling and lights hanging from chains. The stone fireplace and stacks of books backlit behind thick glass; the mezzanine overlooking the reading room with wrought iron gating; the stained glass windows, letting in balloons of colored light, floating across the room.

The room is like something out of a Dan Brown book, where the hero has some research epiphany while talking to a weathered professor who "doesn't do this kind of thing anymore." L&A is sort of a bridge between our main school library and the antiquities that Hawthorne contains. L&A contains archival collections documenting the cultural history of the country.

We're all standing behind reading tables, facing the fireplace, ten SMs gathered in front of it. Luke is two tables away, running his hand over the polished wood. Our eyes meet, but his face is inscrutable. It's only been a day and a half, so I'm not sure I have a right to be upset about not hearing from him since Tap Night; everything is so new between us.

"We need to go over some logistics," says Pinky. "Check your email often. We'll be meeting every week for training, excursions, guided tours. It's recommended you attend every meeting, especially if you have your eye on joining the Board as an upper-class student. Eventually, we'll be unlocking Society's database and Neos will be granted access. The database is Society's greatest treasure. Painstakingly collected articles and past explo reports on every building on campus, including security layouts, blueprints, floor plans, fire insurance maps."

Damn. I want to see that database.

Pinky takes in each Neophyte. "Anyone eyeball the security cams in here? There are typically two facing each other across the room to eliminate blind spots—at what angle?"

"Forty-five degrees." Luke.

"And this is especially true around—what parts of buildings?"

"Entrances and lobbies." Luke.

Pinky nods at Luke with a proud smile. I note this interaction with curiosity.

"We'll be getting to all that. I'm Pinky Lynch, if you didn't already know. I'm CEO. I lead discussions, plan events, delegate work to the other Board members."

The Chief of Staff is introduced, a senior named Hamish. He explains he's in charge of everything social—galas, dinners, retreats.

Next, the Minister of Information. It's my man Marcus. He'll plan our guided tours, organize our lecture series. He introduces a guy named Tath as the Minister of Rituals—a stout, muscular Asian dude; he'll be leading us through our training of "physical exploration skills."

"Lock-picking, shivving, double pumping," Tath explains, listing these matter-of-factly while we all stare. "Before we move on to social engineering later."

Tath then explains he's in charge of Society's rituals and celebrations.

There's only one woman on the Board, a senior. Her name is Candace, short dark hair, with snappy bangs and a frosty demeanor. She's Chancellor of the Exchequer. "I oversee Society's financing," she says. "I deal with fiduciaries and our trust. I handle alumni drives and donations. I'm the only one with access to our bank accounts."

"We need to go over panlists and email protocol," says Pinky as a PowerPoint is set up.

Panlists are listservs for mass emailing, commonly used for

school clubs. Pinky explains how to send an email to a fake address while BCC-ing the appropriate panlist: Omnes ("everyone") goes to everyone. Vox ("voice of the people") goes to the Board. Neophytes ("new") to us. Veteres ("established") to official SMs. Archaei ("old") to alumni. "You won't be needing to email Archi unless specifically directed to by a member of the Board," says Pinky.

So that's what Archi is: Society's alumni. They must represent some of what my mom called "the movers and shakers" of the country. She said that a lot after I got into Essex: *You'll be a mover and shaker now.* It's strange to me some of them had the time to be at Tap Night.

Pinky goes over communication protocols and proper formatting for emails.

We each need our own Society signature, a light encryption of our name. We create our own signature on the spot and enter them into that same leather-bound book from Tap Night, next to our signatures. I become, in an instant, CxtaW.

At the end of every piece of correspondence, we write CNSP, an abbreviation of the Latin: *Coniunctio nobis semper perstat* ("Our union always endures").

"We will meet again soon. In the meantime, a bunch of us will be sending you introductory emails. Work hard, follow Society protocols, and you will make Veteres. Do not let your GPA dip below 3.9."

And with that, we're dismissed.

My head is buzzing as I leave, taking a moment to stand on the steps staring out at the lush grounds. That flatline of a day dying; a smidgen of lit sky left, like a movie theater darkening before the first preview. "Hey." Luke is leaning against the glass-encased bulletin board stuffed full of flyers, right in front of the library, waiting for me. "How you, huh?"

I walk toward him. "Good, man."

"So, yeah, sorry, I'm coming out of an Adderall haze."

I raise my eyebrows. *That's* new information.

"Sorry 'bout being MIA." He makes an *ugh* sound and hops around like he got stung by something. He rips off his Timbuk2 and rifles through it, scattered.

"It's okay, it was only two days." I choose to downplay this, though the Adderall is concerning. "How did you know about the cameras?"

"What?"

"Positioned at forty-five degrees? That's not something everyone just knows."

"It's the angle most cams are positioned. The more contemporary devices."

"Oh." I frown. "How well do you know Pinky?"

"As well as you do."

They had a pretty familiar look between them. "Are you lying?"

"Lying?" He stands, hitching his backpack onto one shoulder. "You don't trust me?"

"I barely know you." I keep forgetting that.

"Likewise." He nods. "Let's fix that. We gotta hang more. Can't right now, though. These kiddos. We're hanging at Gelson . . . like, now."

Of course. A cutting reminder Luke is part of another social scene. He's a jock. And this is a sports school. Things are driven by the athletic department; they can claim it's about other things too (Theater! Music! Speech and Debate!), but sports is where all the money goes.

There are four stone gargoyles above the entrance to the library, representing the four different types of students: the Socialite, the Scholar, the Athlete, and the Artist. The athlete is the only one who's smiling. Luke strokes under my chin with one finger. "I want to know the shit out of you, Lonely."

"You too, Duchess. I want to know . . ." I sigh at his touch. "Everything."

"We'll figure shit out. Gotta run." He flicks my ear then flies down the steps, darting between trees, away from the lights shining down on the winding walkway.

CHAPTER SIXTEEN

THE STARS OF TRACK AND FIELD

I'm at breakfast when I watch Ashton, Toby, and Lily look up from their huddled sniggering. Their eyes track me across the room, bewildered, as I sit down at a table with Anna Chen, Daniel Duncan, Isabella Flores, Candace, and Pinky, who waved me over. Mixed tables like this, with under- and upper-class students, are a rarity at Graymont. It's a mystifying group. And unmasked, no one knows who we really are.

I look back at Ashton, Toby, and Lily. I nod in a detached way, like I never had much to do with them. This fills me with an amused satisfaction. And then gratitude, that I don't have to worry about them anymore. Or eat alone.

Pinky rests his meaty hand over mine with a guttural laugh. "We always sit together during meals. This is a brotherhood."

"Ahem," says Candace, slicing into a vegetarian sausage.

"Sisterhood." Pinky rolls his eyes at me, lowers his voice. "That too. Of course." The whiff of old-boy, old-school blue-blood misogyny hangs in the air momentarily, like a trace of musky cologne in a crowded rush-hour train car. "I've been meaning to talk to you, Cal."

I shove a forkful of scrambled eggs into my mouth. "Me?"

Pinky takes a greasy piece of bacon left on his empty plate and devours it in one bite with his fingers. He wipes his mouth with a white cloth napkin. "In private."

I swallow. "Private?" What could Pinky want with me already?

"Behind closed, latched doors. How all murders get planned." He adds an amused growl.

"What do you want to—" And *boom*, I get a push notification on my phone.

Isabella sees my face. "Uh. Did someone die?"

"Headmaster wants to see me," I reply, frowning at the email. "ASAP."

"The Pope?" says Daniel, shocked. "What did you do?"

"Nothing!"

"Looks like your own murder may have already been planned," says Pinky. He leans across the table toward me. "You should wear two coats when you see the Pope."

"Two coats?"

"Two layers."

"*What?*"

He nudges Candace. "Who was that . . . historical personage . . . walking to his beheading on a winter's day?"

"*Personage?*" says Candace.

"Yes, lady, when this personage was walking to the

gallows . . . he wore two coats, so if he shivered in the cold, the crowd wouldn't mistake it for cowardice."

"I have no idea what you're talking about," says Candace, chewing her sausage.

"It was Charles I, and you totally knew that, you whore."

Candace shakes her head.

"It was Charles I of France!" Pinky bellows. He takes a black bowler hat from his lap and places it on Candace's head. Candace places it back on Pinky's head. He sits back, folds his arms, and says, "Well, Cal, you better get going. Don't shiver in the cold."

No one knows why Melvin D. Scheffling, Head of School, Essex alum '69, Harvard alum '73, Yale Law alum '76 (don't mess), is called the Pope. I think he just *resembles* an old imposing dude that *could be the Pope*. But people are not half-assed about the nickname; his ground-floor office in Brookleven is even called the Papal Conclave.

His secretary, grandmotherly but with a hint of glamour, like an old movie star, eyes me. "Shouldn't you be in class, young man?"

"He said ASAP."

"Oh, you're Calixte."

And without a beat, I'm being shown into a dimly lit office.

"I don't care for late morning light." The blinds are drawn; bands of burnished light crisscross the room, defying the Pope, who stands in front of them, a plump shadow. "This time of year. It's . . . very . . . *revealing*. We're all heathens in our own way, I suppose." I'm starting to get why they call him the Pope.

"The dimmer it is," he continues, "the softer time is. I'm less hectic. As you get older, it's not places you miss, it's times you're most homesick for."

"Times?"

"There was a time I had a mother, a father, a sister. They're gone now. I was a student here once, my whole life ahead of me. Now there is a lot less *time* ahead of me. Anyway. Time. And emails." He sighs. "So many emails, too much light."

"May I sit down?" Something's swelling in my throat and I want to challenge him, gesturing to the sofa behind me. But when I turn toward it, I discover Christopher Richards, Dean of Students, sitting there, one leg crossed over the other. Not the warmest, he primarily emerges to deal with problems or infractions. He gives me a lackadaisical wave.

"Calixte," says Richards in this clipped way. My jaw tightens.

Why am I here? My head swivels back to the Pope, who sits behind his desk imposingly, and damn, every second more of this performance, he's earning his nickname in spades. He's wearing a three-piece blue suit with a red bow tie. He has an institutional-looking folder in front of him, and he pages through it like someone with a phone book looking for a plumber. "Calixte Waaaarrrre," he purrs. "'The Stars of Track and Field.' Tell me about it."

"What?" My mind races. Those words have no meaning.

His eyes fix on me. "Story you wrote?"

"Story I wrote," I repeat.

A flicker of impatience, rattling his jowls. "For Mr. Bryce's class."

He leans back in his chair. Then I get it. Our personal narratives!

I was struggling. Jeffrey gave me that pill. The title was inspired by a song I once heard whose melody I no longer remember. I rack my brain, trying to recall what the story contained, the controversies within that would've led to this meeting.

Holy God, I hope I didn't plagiarize something.

The Pope stands suddenly, with a clearing of his throat. I can't tell, with the placement of shadows and stripes of light in the room, if he's glowering at me, smiling kindly, or neither. "Please forgive me," he says curtly, as if he's not used to asking for forgiveness and doesn't particularly care for it, "but I did something . . . a bit *untoward*."

"What."

"You see, Bryce, that crazy cat, thought the story had some merit, sent it to me, and I agreed! I submitted it to *Bombast*. They were really lacking this semester and needed something with some spark."

I'm not processing these facts fast enough. "You submitted my story to *Bombast*?"

"Yes, and the thing is, they've accepted it."

Bombast is the student-run school lit mag, considered one of the best in the nation. They never take anything from under-class students. Rejections from *Bombast* are cruel and rampant.

"So," says the Pope, "I do need your permission, of course, which I hope you'll grant, but we did also want to make sure you're okay, young man, that you're getting on here all right."

Some of it comes back to me now. I wrote about trying to fit in at school. I talked about my burgeoning feelings for Luke (hence the title) without naming him. I talked about my dad. I thought only Bryce would see it. I can't believe they circulated it!

I didn't bring up . . . Oh Christ, I hope I didn't bring up . . . *The Incident.*

"Respectfully, sir, the story I wrote is very personal."

"That's what makes it so special!" the Pope intones. "The ability for a writer to be emotionally naked on the page like that is rare. *Bombast* certainly agreed! Do you know, young man, that a measurable percentage of students published in *Bombast* have gone on to have serious literary careers! I don't know what that number specifically is, but"—he looks to Dean Richards for a figure—"it's impressive, isn't it?"

"Ethan Jay Farley?" Richards asks me.

If I'm supposed to know that name, it's instantly apparent by my face that I have failed. Richards nods glumly, like he didn't expect much in that regard (not sure whether to feel bad for myself or for Ethan Jay Farley).

"Frequent contributor to the *New Yorker*," says the Pope. "But that's neither here nor there. Are you assimilating all right?"

I guess my sense of alienation really came through. Is that why the Pope launched into his philosophical thoughts on The Nature of Homesickness? "Yes."

"Being away from home can be hard," says Richards. "There are plenty of resources here if you need someone to talk to." I love how he keeps that vague.

"Well." The Pope claps his hands together, looking at me expectantly. And of course, with all this pressure mounting, and them clearly wanting me to confirm that I have found my place here, what the hell am I supposed to do? *Say no?*

As I'm rushing back to Foxmoore, I get intercepted by a whistle. I turn to see a bowler hat leaning against a tree. Pinky tips the hat back on his head, revealing a hedonistic smirk. He favors white dress shirts, militarily pressed, with matching white suspenders. He walks toward me. "What did the Pope want, eh?"

Haltingly, I explain what transpired.

Pinky snaps his suspenders, which makes me flinch. *"Bombast!"* Pinky keeps two fingers behind his suspenders, stretching them out. "Interesting. Why did the Pope become involved?"

"They needed my permission. For the submission."

Pinky smiles at the rhyme. "Goodness! What did you write about, Cal?"

I really need to check my laptop. "Um . . ."

"Luke?" He says his name in a teasing way.

I instinctively check my phone. "I think . . . yeah."

"Did he text you?"

I lower my phone. "Uh, no."

"Well, don't look so homosexually disappointed. I'm sure he will. What else?" How does Pinky know about Luke and me? "Trouble at home?"

The question startles me. He's definitely talking about my dad. "Uh."

"We know everything. We vet all our Neos." Pinky waves away my questioning look. "That can't surprise you. And that's what I wanted to speak with you about. To offer my support. Very soon, I'm going to tell you how we can make it all go away."

I frown. "What? What do you mean?"

"Exactly what I said. Society can help. We can do anything."

For some reason, this conversation is making me nervous. "What is Society about?"

"You already know the answer. Exploration. Unearthing campus secrets."

Campus secrets . . . *or student secrets* . . .

Pinky walks closer to me, inches from my face. His breath smells vaguely metallic, like blood, like bleeding. "I bet it meant something to you. When you saw our eyes." My arms hang at my sides. "It did, right? That's how you found us."

"Not exactly. Well. Not at first."

"But then the eyes . . . *our symbol* . . . seven eyes. Six more than you have."

"All right," I say, shifting onto my other foot. "All right." What are we playing here? I know we're playing something, but I don't know what.

"Your secret, *all your secrets*, are safe with me. Secrets are crucial to Society. And how we guard them. Why did you tell them they could publish the story? You could have said no."

"I guess I technically could've."

"But you wanted everyone to know you're assimilating just fine. You needed that acceptance. And hey, I'd say it's better to be known on campus than be invisible." He puts on a pair of black gloves, and for some reason, I imagine him strangling a deer at the edge of a barren forest. "Keep that in mind." Pinky rolls a toothpick out from under his tongue. His grin is charged and maudlin at the same time. And then he walks away.

What . . . in the name of God . . . *was that?*

Later, back in my room, I scan "The Stars of Track and Field" on my laptop at supersonic speed. Jesus, I poured my heart out! It's practically the first draft of a memoir! But I didn't go as in depth as I feared. It could've been worse . . .

I heard you got blessed by the Pope.

The text dings, startling me as it flashes across the screen. Word travels fast around here. I stare at Luke's words. He's typing more.

Everything ok?

Ya.

I'm outside ur dorm. Get ur gloss on, gurl.

I walk outside. Luke is staring down at his phone. When he sees me, his eyes brighten, which makes my mood brighten. He takes one pod out of an ear. "What's up, Lonely Hearts?"

"What's up, Duchess? Don't you have practice?"

"Don't you have a jacket, dickbitch?" He's in layers of what I can only describe as athletic hip-hop wear: pink-and-white-striped Adidas hoodie zippered open, revealing a white sweat-wicking jersey. He reaches into his bag and tosses me a black training jacket.

It's a little big on me, of course, but feels snug anyway.

We walk, like he wants to get away from the residence halls before we speak; I can't stop thinking about my encounter with Pinky. Luke asks what the Pope wanted. I explain about the short story and how they submitted it to *Bombast* and now it's going to be published.

Luke halts so fast I almost stumble into him. We're on the sidewalk, flanked by red maples, facing the back of Tanner Hall. I hear someone practicing the violin through one of the open windows. "Well, that's a big deal," he says. "That's huge, right? They reject everyone! It's almost always second-semester seniors droning on about a dying grandparent or leaving school, linked to all these dumb metaphors about seasons changing."

Someone's been reading *Bombast*. "The Pope gave it to them. They had to say yes."

Luke considers this. "Maybe. But if someone took my artwork, didn't tell me, and threw it up on some gallery walls—even in New York or Berlin—I'd be pissed. What's it about?"

"The story? About me."

"Well, then, I want to read it. Before it goes to press. A preview. Can I?"

He's going to read it eventually, but I know once he does, I'll be much more exposed and emotionally naked than I ever have been with him. I'm cornered. "If you want . . ."

"Awesome." Luke checks his watch. "I've gotta go meet some kiddos."

His soccer friends. I crash a little. I love being with him. He's like a drug.

"Keep the jacket. It's cold. Come over later? I'm going to read your story, and I'm going to show you some of my drawings. We'll do it like that. Okay?"

I hadn't expected him to level the playing field so smoothly. I try to keep cool, temper my joy.

CHAPTER SEVENTEEN

RUSSIAN DOLLS

Luke's roommate is this guy named Vlad Vasquez. He plays field hockey. People who play field hockey are never in their rooms. It's a rule. "Y'all have a fridge," I remark.

"Vlad told Haas he has acne." Mr. Haas is the faculty advisor at Garrott. Students get their own fridges (which aren't technically allowed) by getting prescriptions for fancy zit cream that needs to be refrigerated (shit always gets stolen from the common room fridge even if you write your faculty advisor's name on your food, which everyone tries to do).

Their room isn't much different from ours; the windows are more modern; Luke and Vlad are a little messier than Jeffrey and me. Curious, I hold up a bottle opener. Luke winks at me and kicks open the fridge. It's stocked with bottles of beer. "Vlad plays field hockey."

That's the only explanation I get, and honestly, probably the only one I need. The fridge humming comforts me, a vague sound from home. Luke opens two bottles of Red Stripe and clinks his with mine as I spot a few other interesting details:

shrink-wrapped comic books hidden in a corner on the floor next to Luke's desk; ceramic cups of colored pencils and pens. A pile of Moleskines. I never looked closely at the silver necklace Luke wears, which dangles off his throat as he leans across me to grab one of the sketchbooks. I examine the pendant. "St. Jude," he says as I run my finger along the embossed design. "Patron saint of lost causes."

The necklace slides out of my fingers as Luke leans away and opens a laptop on his desk; a dream-pop band plays from a well-placed speaker somewhere. We both sit on his bed, side by side. Luke rests a hand on my knee, swallows some beer with a wince, and asks for my laptop.

Gulping Red Stripe, hoping it'll lessen my nerves, I take the computer out of my backpack, open the Word document, and hand it to Luke. He sits back, bottle between his legs.

I put my bottle on the floor and flip open his Moleskine, glancing over at his door, then down at the beer in his lap. "No one's coming in, it's just us," he says, eyes glowing werewolf silver from my screen. "Relax, Lonely Hearts." He's wearing a plain white tee and I notice the Society scar on his upper arm. Both our scars, healing at the same time.

Luke's drawings are amazing. His trademark tag—the chewed-up baby—is a recurring character. Luke is in a lot of his own drawings, facing away (standing against an alley wall, walking through a deserted parking lot). You can tell it's him, though. In these drawings, there's always a "25" written on his back like a jersey number.

Also recurring: a brindled pit bull with a TEC-9 hanging

around its neck by a chain. Luke's colors are bright, explosive, but then in some drawings, he chooses darker, bruise-colored tones. You can track his mood shifting. There are lots of creeping shapes and silhouettes, stirring night clouds, the moon choked out by a turbulent fog.

There's an aftermath-of-war thing going on. Burnt-out buildings, shadowy figures, gray submarines snaking through city rivers. Blue spaceships invading urban areas through spiraling beams of light; disembodied eyeballs with bloody veins.

There are also portraits of kids—a bust, and below that, mad streaks of Luke's pen—impatient tendrils, like he got interrupted and never finished. There are studies for each one, then the drawings themselves, progressing steadily page by page, gaining more depth. The many studies remind me of Luke's obsessiveness planning explos, mapping out the tunnels.

There's one of me. No studies for it, though, only the drawing itself, like it always existed, nearly complete, in Luke's mind. Luke's other portraits have a specific zany energy to the lines and strokes. This one seems uncertain, delicate. There's an intensity in my eyes, but I look almost frightened. I'm mesmerized by it. "Can I have another notebook?"

Luke is glued to the screen. "Geez, Cal. This is really fucking good."

Luke could be famous. The nervous twitch to his work. All his vulnerabilities cracked open across the pages. I can see him in museums, galleries.

"Those are the ones I saved." He points to the notebooks.

"Saved?"

"My dad threw a lot out. He went through my shit after I got in trouble, didn't like the imagery, blah blah, felt it was a waste of time, making me do bad things."

"Who's the dog?"

"Gino, we had to put him down."

"Why?"

"He bit a stupid kid. WILL YOU LET ME FINISH READING?"

"What's the significance of twenty-five?"

Luke sips his beer and doesn't look at me. At first, I'm not sure he's going to answer. "Something Pete once whispered to me . . . when he appeared."

"He spoke to you?"

"Just one time. Whispered that number. I used to think it corresponded to a date. But I don't know, it's just my mind . . . doing shit."

I spot a neat row of pill bottles perched on top of a rickety bookshelf that has books for school and little else. God, he does not worry a damn about having his room searched.

Luke snaps the laptop closed and sets it beside him. "The story is so good. It's so *honest*. What happened with your dad, that haunted house"—he scrubs at both eyes—"can you tell me about it? Like, what he actually *did*?"

"I mean . . . I don't like talking about it, to be honest."

"Respect. Just the fact that he fucked people up with a haunted house is so dope. I am in *awe*. I'm sorry about your mom. I know she'll be okay."

"Thank you for saying that."

"I sure as hell get the isolation thing. We all have it here, to different degrees." Luke takes my hand, intertwining his fingers with mine. "You came out in your story; hope you're cool with that. 'Cause once it's in the mag, it'll be part of your identity here."

I shrug. People like Emma Braeburn and Grayson figured me all out already, so who cares anymore. "What's your identity here?"

"It's in flux, I guess. I don't like labels."

"Who was . . . your first . . . dude?"

"Kiddo I was rolling with, Nick Rydell, called him Night Ryder, he was a wild child, a real trip, was involved with him for a while." Luke covers his mouth with his hand like he's trying not to laugh. "He was my first. He was definitely an education."

"Was he the one you stabbed?"

He gets very still. "Yo, I didn't *stab* this kid, it was more like . . ." Luke shakes his head. "No, I didn't stab *Nick*." He laughs, loudly, to himself, remembering something wired.

I hear music, kids in the hall, voices through the walls. "Your drawings are amazing."

Luke hangs his leg over mine. In this light, his left eye has a celadon tint to it. Luke sees me see it and buries his face in my chest. "I'm a chimera, remember? The variations in my skin tone on my left side? My eye?" The lighting has exposed this other side of him I never saw. The idea of this nonexistent person cocooned inside him, absorbed by him, excites and scares me. I think about Russian dolls.

Now's the moment, now's the moment, now's the only moment . . .

I take Luke's finger, draw it close to my face, pressing it

against my right eyeball. I do this until I'm certain he feels the texture. Luke's face doesn't change. He exhales a stream of beer-tainted air, keeping his finger against my eyeball, not retracting it. I watch his throat, his Adam's apple, bob up and down.

"You see the world in halves," he whispers.

"Yes."

"Glass?"

"Acrylic."

"Oh," he says, in this wonderstruck way, "I saw . . . I mean, I . . . noticed . . . something was off . . . sorry, just different, something I couldn't quite—"

"Yeah, there's still some scarring around my—it's just an ocular implant. I'm still me."

"Of course you are." He kisses my cheek, then clamps a hand to the back of my head and whispers in my ear: *"What did they do to you, Lonely?"*

"Acid."

His grip tightens. "What—"

"It had to do with my dad. When a small Southern town turns against you, they turn against you fast. There was already bullying at school. It went up several notches . . ."

"You left that out of your *Bombast* story."

Thank Christ. "The only thing!"

He takes my face in both his hands. "It's kickass. Your eye." He smiles, not at me exactly, but around the room, spraying his cute mouth creases everywhere, with a look on his face like he solved some grand puzzle. "That's what it's been . . ."

"What *what's* been?"

He returns his neon gaze to me. "I'm glad you told me. I'm glad you trusted me. This changes nothing, nothing with us."

I don't feel relief yet, although all this revelatory shit was inevitable. It's not his reaction right now that matters; it's how he'll be with me tomorrow, the next day.

"Does your roommate know?"

I shake my head. "No one knows." Except that's not quite true, is it?

"I think you're beautiful. Everything about you."

No one's ever said that to me before. I don't want to ask what about me he thinks is beautiful, to make him doubt it or take it back; I want to accept it as fact, but that's hard for me to do, so all I say is: "You drew me."

We stare down at the sketchbook. The energy in the room is swirling, expectant.

"You got in my head, Lonely Hearts. I draw what's in my head."

But it looks so different from the other drawings. I grab his pendant again. "I like that you have St. Jude helping you out. But you aren't a lost cause. You're my best friend here."

"Nah, we're more than that. Aren't we?"

I stare down at my sneakers. "Yes." Why is this so terrifying? "What's your relationship to Pinky?" I ask again, my mind pinpointing, looking back at him.

Luke is staring so hard his eyes are like a pool flooding into me. "Hush."

We fall back on his bed. We hug like we're hanging on for

dear life. We kiss for a long time. His mouth feels perfect. Like it was made for mine. "You can still cry, huh?"

"I can cry out of both eyes. I'm still human on that side, I swear."

"Moon tears," he purrs, kissing both my eyelids.

It's as if the night unfolded her from its depths.

Crossing campus, on my way back to Foxmoore, flushed and overwhelmed from Luke, I bump into Gretchen, heading back from the library. I sense the Secret Service moving through the trees surrounding us, like wraiths. I offer to carry some of her books, something out of a Hallmark movie, but she laughs and declines. "You look a little sprightlier than last time."

"I was with a friend."

"Or . . . more than a friend, maybe?"

She's perceptive; that's cool. "How are things?"

"I like it here, but I have to accept I'm not going to have a normal experience."

"Does that bother you?"

She shrugs. "I think . . . well, I *know* . . . some of the girls are threatened by me."

I've heard the girls at school can be awful to one another, way worse than the boys, but Gretchen's someone, given her status, I'd assume people would seek out. "If it makes you feel any better, my life isn't normal. Not even a little."

We're outside Reiss-Orson, home of the 5C 5′10″ Girls™. Gretchen surprises me by sitting on the steps out front, slamming the pile of books down in front of her. "How so?"

I sit beside her. "My mom has lymphoma. My dad is an insurance adjuster. But he's all bored back home. He's a haunter, a member of the Fear Community. He designs haunted houses. They're, like . . . ex-military dudes mostly, ultracompetitive. He upped his game last fall. By a zillion. And a well-liked member of the community . . . had a heart attack inside and died on the way to the hospital. My dad didn't have waivers or anything. There's a civil suit and I'm praying he's not going to be found guilty of criminal negligence, which is a possibility."

Gretchen nods, understanding. "Wow. So they got you out."

Exiled. I don't know why I spilled all this tea to Gretchen, stuff I didn't even say to Luke. Or couldn't yet. But she's totally right. And it feels a hell of a lot different when someone else says it like that, like she did, looking in from the outside. I'm subconsciously neutralizing. I don't want Pinky to be the only one who knows all my secrets, even though he doesn't know *all of them*, even if he thinks he does. But the way he spat out all that sensitive info, it felt almost like . . . and I hate that I think this word but . . . *blackmail.*

It felt like fucking blackmail.

CHAPTER EIGHTEEN

SECRETS AND SOULMATES

Very soon, I'm going to tell you how we can make it all go away.

Despite my night with Luke, how we revealed more of ourselves to each other, which felt precarious in its intimacy, and then revealing even more to Gretchen, which felt, given who she is, like confiding in America itself, I wake up with Pinky in my head. Anxiety spasms in my chest. There's more at stake than I initially realized. *If if if . . .* they really can help my family.

But I have to continue to impress Society. Every detail, every moment, matters.

A Society email comes the next morning. We have a nine p.m. meet at Turner Hall. Turner is adjacent to Bromley Lab. It's a leftover from centuries ago, when Granford shifted away from its initial goals and became Essex; Turner is one of those buildings forgotten in the transition, though with all the rotting latticework braiding its lower perimeter, it seems renovation has been on people's minds for a while.

This part of campus, known as the Sci-Fi Sector (it overlaps with a few buildings once used by the English Department), contains disused mid-modernist buildings, and is notorious for its unfocused lack of site planning and architectural incoherence, a major contrast to the rest of Essex. When we all arrive, the building's already been unlocked.

Turner has a normal roof, but there's a brick tower on the side, like an extra thumb. We're led by a formally dressed SM up a staircase to this sub-roof. A ring of masked SMs hug the perimeter. We're told to turn our phones off and form a circle.

An SM steps forward and lights a ring of black candles placed on the ground, inside our formation. "When your name is called, step forward."

We're all handed black envelopes with silver cursive on the front.

"The envelopes you received contain a written statement that represents the deepest, darkest secret of the upper-class SM whose name is written on the envelope. Your test is to guard these secrets. You're all here because you have demonstrated the skills Society values most. This is a test of your trustworthiness. Trust is the foundation of Society."

Pinky wasn't kidding. Secrets really are the glue that holds Society together.

"The envelopes are sealed. If some inner weakness compels you to peek inside, you not only risk the member whose secrets you guard, but Society's faith in you. In one week, you will return the envelopes to us. If the envelope is opened, damaged, lost, or in any way compromised, your future in Society will be forever tainted. Do not fail. Next week: same time, same place, except you'll need to find your own entry into Turner."

Oh God, I know what's coming . . .

I know it before the black paper and pens are passed around. "Now write your own darkest secrets and hand these over to the very SM whose secrets you now guard."

My throat constricts as I see the name written on my envelope.

None other than Pinky Lynch.

"Will you trust the SM you've been assigned with your deepest secrets?"

Luke meets my gaze. His face is shrouded in darkness, extricating his luscious mouth, freed into the electric night; the black candles flicker in his eyes like jack-o'-lanterns.

I look over at Pinky. He gives me a salute.

"Will you write your deepest, darkest secret on your piece of paper? Do you trust *us*?"

Is this a trick? Will they check and know if I revealed something truly stark?

Or do they mean what they say?

I crouch on the ground, write two short paragraphs in glistening silver ink, and seal it in the envelope provided. I write my name on the front of the envelope. I walk over to Pinky and place the envelope in his outstretched hand.

It's not random that I got him. No way.

We all leave, single file, climbing back down the narrow, winding staircase. I lose track of Luke. Once outside, we disperse, clutching our envelopes.

Pinky is standing against a tree, my envelope in his hand. I hold his in mine. Both black, nearly invisible in the swollen night, except for my name in silver writing on the front, which reflects the sidewalk lights like the apologetic smile of a goblin.

The story of my attack would've been in the *McCarl Inquirer,* our local paper, elsewhere maybe. They definitely vetted me. Pinky holds the envelope over his head, squinting at it.

"Why did you tap me?"

He smiles at me toothily. "Suffering from imposter syndrome?"

"The primary thing you knew about me was a disability."

"Maybe you proved yourself. Maybe I saw something in you."

"What did you see?"

Pinky waves my envelope daintily back and forth in front of his face like a Southern lady in church. "You ask good questions. I like that."

"Did you pick me because you felt I could be manipulated?"

He raises his eyebrows. "Can you be?"

"If you can help me, my family, maybe I'd do anything . . ."

Pinky looks at me open-mouthed, like he's shocked. "Would you? Do *anything*? Rather cynical, Cal, I must say. Maybe I like how you see the world. Maybe I saw how badly you need to see the world in four dimensions. Maybe I needed a little purity in my midst. Does Luke know, by the way?" He taps his right orbital bone.

"Yes."

He walks over to me, close enough to scrape the envelope holding my secret under my chin. "I'm rooting for you two. Honesty should be at the core of every romance."

"I don't know if we're—"

"You're wearing his jacket."

And so I am. "Well—"

"Or"—he looks me up and down—"is it something . . . just . . . purely . . . *sexual?*"

"We haven't . . ." What it is, is none of his business.

"What? Consummated things?" he says, elongating *consummated*. "You will."

He walks off whistling a melody that sounds like a dirge.

I'm still excited about everything to come. But it's tinged with something else now. I'm starting to smell a whiff of danger. Although, it's not scaring me off. Just like with Luke, who obviously has a looming darkness inside him, it's not scaring me off. And I'm wondering why.

Maybe because coming here was more than just reinvention. I saw Essex as a place where no one could hurt me anymore. And by continuing to face everything head-on, maybe nothing can. By allowing Society to wrap me in its cloak, I've built my own wall of protection.

I realize all this again as we're given a nightly lecture on the general history and layout of most of the key buildings on campus. Our lecture series will eventually include what Society terms *Unbuilt Essex*, or *Invisible Essex*: buildings that remain unfinished or were razed, which encompasses a lot of real estate and history (I'm into it, I'm into it all).

I realize this as we sit on the cold, hard basement floor of a former freshman boys' dorm, as we're each given a

fourteen-piece lock-picking set with transparent training pad-
locks. "The different picks, hooks, and rakes, which I will explain,
have reinforced handles and are made of stainless steel," says
Tath, pacing. "Three different kinds of tension wrenches. You
are going to encounter various locks and security systems on
campus."

"Cooool," says Kip Spicer, unfolding his pouch like it contains the Ark of the Covenant.

"We will learn the skills to unlock the school's history. Our
goal will be to experience the world, or at least the world of
Essex, in—"

I interrupt. "In four dimensions?"

A rare smile from Tath. "Exactly, Cal."

Only a day later, Jeffrey bursts into the room while I'm
practicing.

I'm sitting on the floor like an idiot, back against my bed,
the kit laid out in front of me. Jeffrey stares down at all my lock-
picking gear. I don't make a move to hide it; it's too late. His
schedule has gotten so unpredictable, there was no way to avoid
this. Jeffrey drops his backpack on his desk chair. "You're not
all that secret for being in a secret society, are you?"

I methodically pick up all the pieces and put them back in
the leather pouch.

For a second, a look crosses Jeffrey's face, not quite disgust,
but something close to *I can't believe they took you over me*, and
then it's gone. "You always think I'm asleep when you sneak
outta here. I'm usually meditating."

"Okay," I say softly. "I didn't know that."

"I'm getting into Buddhism."

"I thought you were getting into *Overwatch* on Twitch?"

"Look, I didn't want to mention this before. I'm totally jealous you got in. But, like . . ." He sighs, eyes slanted down at the floor. "Picking a locked door is never not breaking a rule that'd get you in big trouble. Don't you have a scholarship to think about?"

"Um. First of all, that's my problem. Second, this is bigger than my—"

"Are you sure about all that? Dahlia said some other things. When I pressed her."

Dahlia again. "Like? Is this about people disappearing again?"

"I know it's mostly all rumor. But sometimes there's bits of truth in these things. She heard they steal creepy shit. Body parts. The skull of Alexander Essex."

"That's ridiculous. Now they're *grave robbers*?"

"It gets worse." He sits down at his desk chair and gives me a long look. "Every year, supposedly, they pick a sacrificial lamb. Someone they tap as an insurance policy. If shit goes awry, they put all the blame on this person while they temporarily disband. It's usually someone tapped late in the process. Someone with some controversy to them."

I suddenly feel hot. I rip off my sweater and stare into my lap for a long moment before I speak. "You think it's me?"

"Didn't say that. But it's pretty awful, man. That they do that."

"*If they do that.* Again, like you said, these are rumors—"

"Yeah. But Society pretty much becomes your Essex experience; it takes over everything. Is that what you want?"

He's not wrong about that. "I didn't have an Essex experience before this, so . . ."

"I get it, I get it."

Is that why they took me? *Is that what all this is?* Am I just a pawn, because a secret society that covets the elite would never take someone like me?

"Alexander Essex is buried in England, by the way," I mutter.

"Supposedly the headstone is false. And Society has the real one. If you ever find it, along with his skull, in a room with blue walls, you'll know all the conspiracy shit was right on."

I don't know what happens to me after this conversation, but I get hit with a wave of paranoia. Jeffrey got in my head. Pinky's in my head. Luke is in my head. Everyone's in my fucking head. The sacrificial lamb is new information and it's the only thing that seems real enough to not be total whacked-out speculation. And it's bad.

I take out my phone. "What's up, Cal?"

I explain everything that's going on.

"So it's not all sweet 'n' sugar in Candyland, huh?"

"What if I'm being played?"

"Play 'em back."

"*How?* They're way bigger than me."

"You know their secrets. You have a hand to play as well. Don't forget that."

"WHAT HAND?"

"Pinky seems to need you. There's something there, even if it's not defined yet. Look, you don't know if it's real, if it's you. And if it's neither, maybe they really can help you."

"I don't doubt that. What if the answer's in the envelope I'm not supposed to open?"

"Don't open it, Cal. Don't do it. Find out everything you can, peek around every corner, peer into every crevice. Don't let your insecurities doom you."

"That's wild coming from you, man, like, *what a thing to say* . . ."

"Do everything you can to make them need you. Be invaluable. And keep the receipts."

A week later, all seven of us reach the entrance to Turner at the same time. I can't pretend everything Jeffrey told me isn't still swirling in my head, but I've resolved, for now, not to panic, to keep going and stay as much in control of things as I can.

They put a basic padlock on the entrance to test our lock-picking skills. As all the Neos gather around and take a shot at it, it's Luke who gets it open first, unlocking it with a few twists, which is met with a gasp from Isabella. God, he can be so sexy in small moments.

On the sub-roof, a large group of SMs are waiting for us, *dressed to the nines* like we are. We stand around a circle of candles again, and each time someone's name gets called, they step forward and hand over the envelope, inspected by several SMs to make sure the seal is intact; then one by one, the envelope is held over the candle flames by a pair of tongs until it burns to nothing. And then the envelopes we gave to the SMs with our own secrets are also burned into a sparking gray ash. When it's my turn, Pinky takes an extra-long time examining my envelope, feeling around the corners, holding it up with a lot of scrutiny, shooting me a wolfish grin. In the end, both our envelopes get burned. Our secrets neutralized by fire.

"Well done, Neos," says Pinky Lynch, beaming. "Well done."

Afterward, Luke is waiting for me, by the entrance to Turner. We embrace; it feels like it's been forever. We've both been so busy all week with classes, work, sports, Society.

"What was your secret, Lonely?"

"You first."

"That kid I talked about."

"Who? Night Ryder?"

"Nick, yeah. He OD'd."

I watch his face for more. "Is he okay . . . ?"

"He is now. We don't talk anymore. But it was my fault. I should've gotten him help sooner. I didn't know what to do. I was afraid to be alone."

"It's not your fault. And I certainly know what it's like to be alone."

"Nah, it was on me to—*fuck, get down!*" Luke pushes me into the grass. A golf cart whirs by—a security guard, dark blue cap on, slumped against the seat, dutiful and sleepy.

"Aaaaaand that was close. Shit." Luke pulls me back up, brushing me off.

What would've happened if we were seen? *Run?* "Society hasn't told us how to avoid—"

"We're supposed to immediately disperse." Luke pulls me behind a large tree so we're more hidden. "What did you write?"

"Why do you want to know so bad?" There's a hunger to him like he needs this.

"Like I said, I want to know you, all of you."

I slide down the tree, resting my hands on my knees. Luke does the same. I let my head fall onto his shoulder. Luke runs his fingers through my hair. Gentle now, instead of mussing it. "I come from a small, conservative town. My dad pissed off a lot of people. They called us Satanists." I laugh a little at that, always have. "We got death threats. And then . . ." Luke presses his hand down on my knee; he must sense from my breathing this isn't easy to talk about, but he doesn't stop me like last time. "I'm deformed because of the dude at school I—"

"Yo, King, you're not deformed. Don't say that again. I don't like it and it isn't true."

"It was the guy I used to . . ." All those afternoons and evenings set to the sound of eighteen-wheelers roaring by, the acrid smell of exhaust, surrounded by crabgrass and flattened dandelions. It had started off with a kiss in a closet (ha!) but had become something animalistic and relentless over time. It was still the only intimacy I knew, so like a fool, I craved it.

And then, one day, Brent caressed my jaw with his hand, looked into my eyes, and murmured something like *huh.* Suddenly, there was a flash of tenderness, something more. I knew it terrified him, that he'd started to *feel something;* immediately, I knew it was over. But I didn't sense, not right away, that there was a threat level.

"He flipped out about what we'd been doing; he and his friends . . . after school, cornered me, held me down, beat me up, the town pariah's son. I only lost just the one eye because when they were pouring drain cleaner on my face, I was able to turn my head, keep it pressed to the floor."

"Shit, Lonely, I'm—"

"There's more." I take a breath so deep it quivers through my lungs. "I still talk to him."

"You . . . *what do you mean?*"

I hear something in the distance, like an animal, a wolf, a coyote, some kind of howl.

I stand up and brush myself off. "That's all I want to say. For now."

Luke stands as well. I can see clearly how he feels about me. It's written all over his startled face. He doesn't care a lick about my eye. I don't know why I thought he would. If anything, it's brought us closer, and there's no pity involved. I kiss him on the cheek. I feel freed and scared at the same time, but this is definitely enough for now. "Good night, Duchess."

As I go, from behind, I hear a whisper through the rustling trees: "Good night, kiddo."

The next morning, I stop by Hertzman on my way to breakfast. I take out my phone. After a long pause, I hold it to my ear. "I told Luke."

"You're an idiot!"

"You knew eventually I'd have to tell someone."

"He's gonna think—"

"What's he gonna think, huh? That I was brutalized by you, and this is the only way my brain can process it—so I don't lose my fucking mind? HUH?"

"Did you think it would make me disappear? Because, BITCH, you're still calling me."

I hang up, my face tight, and dial home.

"Hi, honey," says my mom, who sounds weak as shit. "It's so early."

"Hi, Son," says my dad, who sounds absolutely exhausted.

"Hey. You guys okay?"

"We're all good. Tell us about school. You have time? We love hearing about Essex."

I can't talk about Society (the beautiful bits of poetry to lock-picking, aligning the gaps between the pins with the shear line, getting the shaft to turn), so I blather on about classes, getting choked up because I miss them so much; hearing their voices makes it worse, every time. When I have nothing left to say, my mom tells me she loves me and hangs up first. I ask my dad again if everything is okay.

"Thanksgiving is right around the corner. We'll see you then."

I've been counting the days. But something feels off. "Mom doesn't sound great." They both sound more distant every time I call, like they're secretly moving across the world to some far-off glacier.

"You know the treatment makes her tired. That's all it is."

"Right, right." A no-no. We do not talk about this.

"We'll talk soon, Son."

I hate when conversations with my parents sound outwardly *miserable*. I'm still mulling this over, worriedly, when Society emails us: We can pick any member of our tap class to be a "Soulmate," a partner in crime, someone we can confide in, as we advance through our Neophyte training. Our next assignment is to go out to dinner with our Soulmate, get to know them, and plan an explo together, our first official explo as Neos.

Whassup, Soulmate??!!

Luke's text later that day makes me feel like someone injected warm tea into my veins.

CHAPTER NINETEEN
THE LEAGUE

OCTOBER

With some troubling shit brimming in the back of my brain (does Society have a dark side? why are my parents acting weird?), I vow to do everything I can to impress Society, so if they can help my family, I'll have them as a resource, a buffer. And I focus on keeping my GPA stable, so if anything goes awry, Essex will see, at the very least, I'm a good student.

Meanwhile, my standing on campus shifts, once again, when the new issue of *Bombast* comes out. It's similar to what happened after I got tapped, the way people noticed something different about me, but this shift feels stronger. I feel people's eyes on me. Emma Braeburn crosses a hallway to tell me I'm "brave." Jeffrey pats me on the back in passing: "Great story, man." Ashton comes up to me and tells me I'm "a great fucking writer." I didn't know that many kids read *Bombast*. I don't get invited to any midnight fêtes by the 5C 5'10" Girls™ at Reiss-Orson, but I feel less invisible. I think this pleases Pinky too, although he hasn't said anything; it's just a feeling. And then I get annoyed with myself for caring about what Pinky thinks.

Luke tells me he made a dinner reservation for us at The League. I'm so swooned out by how romantic that sounds—*an actual date?*—that I forget it's one of those places where rich parents take their formally dressed kids when they visit, whispering about planned ski vacations, summer shares, and houses in Naples, Florida. I forget to check the damn prices.

"Yes, yes, hello," says Luke, in a clipped mid-Atlantic accent, to our crisply uniformed waiter from behind the leather-bound menu. "I'm going to order for my better half, here." I almost burst out laughing at that. "We would like to start with the soupe automnale—for *him*—and I'll have the poulpe grillé. And also an order of the moules Dijonnaise." The waiter jots all this down. Luke, who has just demonstrated some flawless French pronunciation, leans back, puts his fist under his chin, and while still studying the menu makes a *hmm* sound. "Do you recommend the basquaise over the cassoulet?"

The waiter starts to answer, but Luke cuts him off. "You know what? I think I'm going to go in a different direction . . . but hold on . . . *Lonely Hearts*"—Luke looks at me questioningly over the menu—"what are you thinking?"

I clear my throat to a thin rasp. "I'm gonna do . . . the roasted chicken," I tell the waiter softly, almost too softly; he leans into me, gracefully, for a mini second, as if he didn't hear, but then nods and jots this down too.

"Ah!" Luke points at me as if I just inspired him. "The homard safrané for me!" he declares. "And also an order of risotto."

Although this is the type of restaurant that wouldn't normally display the prices, at least where I'm from, this one does, and Luke has already ordered more than $200 worth of food, by a quick, anxious calculation on my part. I sit up in my cushioned chair, ramrod straight, and put a hand on Luke's wrist, but he ignores me.

"I also think a side of the fricassée of local mushrooms. We'll take those when the entrées are served."

The waiter nods stiffly.

Luke slants his mouth at me. "Do we want to do the Plateau Royal from the raw bar?"

I quickly shake my head as I mouth: *Too much.*

At this point, Luke orders us two dirty martinis. As if he's used to spoiled Essex kids attempting this shit, the waiter politely asks for our IDs. Without missing a beat, Luke asks for ginger ales instead. The waiter does this half bow, then glides away.

I lean across the table. "What are you doing?"

"We're going to eat the shit out of this Strafton warhorse."

"Why did you pick this place?"

"Society said to have dinner out!"

"I can't pay for all this." I'm getting uncomfortable; something hot and wicked blooming in my blood, reddening my face. My parents couldn't afford to take me here.

"Can you please enjoy this bougie meal? I will take care of it."

"You know I'm on financial aid, right?"

"You worry too much. I want to treat you."

He doesn't mean to make me feel small; he's not always

sensitive to the fact that we come from different backgrounds, but he's being a brat. I take in the dining room: the well-ironed tablecloths, matching cloth napkins, perfectly folded; the heavy violet curtains with embroidered gold ties flanking the large paned windows; the dark wood walls.

The ginger ales arrive, in tall, slim glasses with crushed ice, and Luke swirls it around in his mouth. "It's fine," he concludes. "Definitely some *ginger notes* to appreciate." The waiter disappears and Luke looks at me. "We have an explo to plan."

"I wish they'd unlock the database."

"That doesn't happen until we make Veteres."

"How do you know that?"

"I think they do it in stages. Listen, do you know about the underground river that winds through Strafton?" Luke flicks his eyebrows up and down.

I choose my words carefully. The next explo matters. Nothing in Society will never not matter if I want to make Veteres and assure myself I'm not anyone's sacrificial lamb. "I read about it. Through campus?"

"Technically, it's a tributary. Part of it is still aboveground. The settlers built it up. Factories. Mills. Housing. It was called the Great River; the tributary was called the Little River. The Army Corps of Engineers buried it in the forties or something—*a public works project*—to prevent flooding and runoff. There were two big floods in the thirties. Did a shitload of damage."

"Right."

"And obviously several before, which destroyed what was Granford, I'm guessing. The tributary now flows underground;

it's all subterranean and empties into the Connecticut River through a conduit." We both love history. "I've heard the river runs underneath Jarrett Green and Strafton-Van-Wyke. Think we can access it?"

I catch my elongated reflection in the knife. "Maybe? That sounds . . . complicated."

"Do you know about the library at the top of Faber?"

He's on a high-spin roll. "I think so . . ."

"Probably also a bit advanced for us right now, but *hmmm.* Might be good for us."

"Are you on Adderall?"

He drums his fingers on the table, his eyes everywhere and nowhere.

"Society didn't really indicate what would be appropriate for an explo right now."

"You can sort of suss that out based on the time frame they gave us," he says. "I mean, seventy-two hours? Later, we'll have more time to really flesh out our explos. But they want this soon, so we should keep it fairly simple. Maybe focus on the Sci-Fi Sector?"

"Those old abandoned labs?"

"Exactly. I'm not sure the history of Essex is all that accurate and"—he brings his thumb and index finger together—"on the level."

"What do you mean?"

"Like if Essex was Granford for a lot longer than they claim."

"There's no way they could pretend Essex was founded in

the 1700s if it was actually founded in the 1940s or something. No freakin' way."

"Not saying *that*, exactly. But history gets rewritten. And it gets rewritten by the winners, as we all know."

"Sure, during the Roman Empire maybe. There are official public records now and—"

"Yeah, but who can say when someone decided to change a name, forge this, fake that, take a bribe? The world is shady. A lot of desperate shit happens when people need money."

"I read books on this place. Historical books."

"Books, shnooks."

But it's funny because I think about all the abandoned buildings on campus. The interrupted renovations, the messy, mysterious overlap of Granford into Essex.

And damn, I've got a crush on this kid.

Luke's hair is brushed back. He's wearing a blue sport coat, white dress shirt, first button open. I watched him as he approached our table: skinny beige khakis, cuffed perfectly over the ankle, revealing a slice of skin; beachy blue boat shoes. The way clothes fit him, the way he moves through space. It's real thorny being attracted to somebody but also jealous of them at the same time. Luke is dashing and suave. He's easy to like, root for, want to win over. He's one of those people who are hard to be friends with, yet you want nothing more . . .

I took the reviews for this place way too seriously. I'm wearing a jacket with sleeves too short, a blousy corn-yellow shirt, cheap tie, baggy gray slacks. I'm disheveled, mismatched. But Luke doesn't seem to mind. His head is tilted toward me, eyes swimmy, inquisitive; his leg brushes up against me, knee scraping mine. "You're a romantic, Lonely. I like that."

"Why do you say that?"

"It's the way you respond to the world. Your story. *Bombast.* Everyone's talking about it! People relate to what you wrote; that's a gift!"

A small crowd of uniformed servers invade the space, which is almost a letdown, because we were having a moment, but the food looks amazing. Luke's eyes widen. "Well, look at this. Will you look at this?" He grabs his silverware and digs in. And then I do. He frowns at me. "So what's up with you? You seem a little . . . distracted?"

"My parents. Something's off."

"Off how?"

I put my utensils down. "Are we on a real date? What is this?"

His eyes are cool like slate. "What do you think it is?"

I shrug.

"Don't be daft, Lonely." He reaches under the table and grabs my crotch.

I slap his hand away. "Do you ever have doubts about Society?"

"What kind of doubts?"

"Like the lock-picking, for instance. We'll be breaking rules."

"That's the fun; that's the tradition."

"We're learning intense skills."

"That's the *point.* What are you going on about?"

I might as well ask him, since I can't stop thinking about it, although Luke's knowledge will be limited. "Jeffrey told me they sometimes . . . tap kids as sacrificial lambs."

"What the hell does *Jeffrey* know?"

"Dahlia Evans told him. Her . . . siblings went here."

"What a bunch of fucking bullshit. So Jeffrey knows you got in, then, huh?"

"How well do you know Pinky? He knew we were . . . a thing."

Luke rolls his eyes. "Pinky's CEO of Society. I think we can assume . . . he's, like, kinda omniscient. Just chill with all the worrying about every little thing."

"I have real things to worry about, Luke."

"But you need to enjoy yourself too, live your life." He presses his knee up against mine, harder this time. "By the way . . . we could be together . . . in my room more . . . if you wanted to."

I consider this. "You're seducing me instead of answering my questions."

He winks. "Is it working?" He fiddles with the napkin on his lap. "Maybe I don't have the answers you're looking for. For the same fucking questions you keep asking me."

"What if Vlad returns and . . . ?"

"Nah, he's chill. Those dudes sleep on the field mainlining Red Bull, I swear . . . Just gotta let him know first. This would only be temporary, anyway. That's why I mentioned Faber."

More food arrives. Mussels and risotto and chicken and lobster (when the heck did we order lobster?) and an array of different types of mushrooms, herbed and glistening. Luke grins

like a little kid with each new plate that arrives and plops generous heapings onto his plate. I take more reserved portions, but
everything is good, *so good*.

Luke reaches across the table with his fork, wanting me to
try a bite of lobster, which he saw I was avoiding. Expensive
shellfish makes me nervous. I gobble the wobbling pinkish-
white chunk off his fork. I catch one of the older couples eyeing
me. I hesitate, self-conscious.

"Don't worry about them," says Luke, eyes not leaving mine.

"Wasn't. But you're being ostentatious."

"Everyone here is a clown. They probably all have these
ridiculous WASP-y names that make no sense. *Hello, I'm Lazenby
Huckleford. I'm a tax attorney. I drink gin from a flask every day on the
train to Westchester. I'll see you at the club on Saturday.*"

I laugh.

"Good, right?" says Luke, referring to the lobster, really
wanting me to be happy. He places his hand on mine. "It will be
okay. Literally everything you're tormented about."

"I'm not tormented . . ."

"Yeah? I can't keep up with your prism of tormentedness."

"I can't keep up with you either, and I know you're on
something."

There's a boom outside. The lights in the restaurant flicker
while lightning flashes through the windows. Uniformed wait-
staff rush to the windows to close them as the curtains blow in
from gusts of wind. I catch fragmented glimpses of teeming
rain in the lamplight outside on the sidewalk. The lighting inside
gets weaker. "It's storming."

"Fuck yeah, it is," says Luke. "What do you want for dessert?"

There is a confectionary blur of mousse and tarts, poached pears, a soufflé, crème brûlée, pot de crème, a selection of rare cheeses. I let Luke order away, rattling off nearly every option on the dessert menu. We swill cappuccinos, giggling, until the waiter, unasked, lays the bill on the table. Luke slaps his credit card down. It gets whisked away.

"We are official Soulmates now," says Luke. "It is decreed. So you'll have to trust me moving forward, okay?"

I put the cup down. "I do trust you . . ."

"Mmmm . . ." Luke swivels his head to one side, then the other, purring skeptically.

"I do!" I protest.

"You have to take what you want from this world," says Luke. "Snatch it."

The waiter returns. He is accompanied by a host and a burly member of the kitchen staff, and neither looks friendly. The waiter lays the bill on the table, in front of Luke. "I'm afraid your credit card was declined, sir."

I sit back. I no longer feel the cushioning of the chair, just the wood cutting into my lower spine. Luke's expression doesn't change. "Ah, yes!" He reaches into his pocket, producing his wallet, replacing the credit card inside with another one in a single fluid maneuver. "I gave you the wrong card. Use the Amex? I am so, *so* sorry about the mix-up."

The bill is scooped up and the men disappear.

A burst of lightning. The lights in the restaurant flicker again. There's another hard gust of wind assaulting the walls of the old building; everything shakes. I barely notice Luke rise, drop his napkin, and bend over the table to address me, still standing in front of his chair, as if he's about to make a toast. *"Get up, yo."*

I do, without thinking or saying a word. We glide through the restaurant like phantoms. The carpet is soft, well-vacuumed. No one's at the host stand.

We are out the door in a blink and enter a drowned world.

The thunder hits hard, and the lightning is close, giving us bright previews of abandoned, upturned broken umbrellas, like birds shot out of the sky, littering the ground, water bubbling up from sewers. No one on the streets, no one on the sidewalks, no one peering out of windows—melted squares of light here and there, bleared by rain; the dark, soaked emptiness of everything. By the time we get back to campus proper, I'm so drenched it's hard to move.

Luke, a sodden shape in the night, is heading for the Sci-Fi Sector.

I shout after him; he raises his hand to silence me as the sky lights up, imprinting him.

Luke seems to be heading for the Pencey Chem Lab, a Collegiate Gothic building built in the twenties, closed and off-limits for years. Luke leads me to a side entrance. He asks me to shine my iPhone light on him. He places his hands on the door. He pushes hard and when it doesn't budge, reaches into his back pocket and shuffles through the set of lock-picks they gave us. I can make out their metallic gleam. "You keep them on you?" I scream into the raging night. We're not supposed to. He hunches over his work, then a second later steps back and gives me a thumbs-up. He creakily opens the door, revealing a dark rectangle of cobwebbed darkness. I follow him through the entrance into a dank hallway, the door closing shut behind us. I smell abandonment, chemicals, age.

We head up a nearby staircase, encountering closed doors requiring codes or special keys. Luke picks a door lock—the first one we find that's pickable. We enter an empty lab. Bursts of lightning illuminate grimy glass cabinets. Luke sits on a workstation, above me, taking off my jacket, unbuttoning my shirt. "This isn't safe. Someone could come. Security guard."

"Take out your fake eye and put it in your palm. With the lightning . . ."

"I'm not *Pan's Labyrinth*ing anyone."

He throws back his head and laughs. He grabs my face and massages my jaw.

"You said you were treating me tonight, but you kinda tricked me."

"Don't get butthurt. Told you, you gotta take what you want from this world." We peel off the rest of our clothes. I run my hand through his wet hair. I keep getting caught in his rippled wake and I wonder if that's a good thing. I pull up a metal stool so we're level, and we kiss.

After a few minutes, we switch, and he's in front of me, kissing my throat, silvered by shocks of lightning from the windows. I've never seen a naked dude before—not like this. I can't possess him as a whole; he seems so fragile, like he could shatter; all his component parts seem breakable. I don't know how to take smaller doses of what's becoming too much. My body wants him, every one of my cells, but I'm worried my heart is too bruised to handle all the accompanying feelings.

"We'll come back tomorrow, make this place a real report." He takes me in his hands.

I gyrate in his grip. "Whoa, your hands are cold," I whisper, nuzzling his neck, as he sinks to his knees and I close my eyes.

I awaken in my bed, hours later, semiconscious. I don't remember how I got back; a heavy sleep nailed me in, so there's only a hazy memory of running across campus during a break in the storm, the sky roiling and spoiled, everything dripping, gurgling, the smell of the rain, of electricity; taking a hot shower.

The light through the window tells me it's early dawn, and someone texted me.

It's Luke. I can still smell him on my skin. I can still taste him.

He texted me a photo of a police car parked in front of his dorm.

The law! They came for me, Lonely Hearts!

CHAPTER TWENTY

A HAUNTED NOWHERE

When I dash over to Garrott like my ass is on fire, the police car is still parked outside. I don't see anybody, which is maybe a good sign—Luke doesn't seem to be getting arrested. Two cops emerge from the entrance. I text Luke, asking him what's going on, but he doesn't respond.

The cops stand in front of their car. A black Maserati pulls up right behind it. A kid's at the wheel, but I can't tell who it is. I hide behind a nearby tree and peek out from behind.

The driver's side opens, and a husky blond kid in a red tracksuit pops out. He walks over to the cops, hair a mess of misshapen tufts like he just woke up, face ruddy, gait plodding, but with a certain conviction. A dude on a job. Then I see the ring, and I can't believe it took me this long to recognize Pinky. I've never seen him dressed down before. Pinky saunters over to the cops. They get into a calm discussion. Like this was expected, planned. They all shake hands. The cops get back in their car. Pinky gets back in the Maserati. Everyone drives away.

This is wild. A kid at school, who wasn't directly involved in the incident, with no faculty member accompanying him, was able to talk to the cops, and in a minute, it was over?

I look down. I'm sinking into the wet grass. I step out of the twin indentations with a squish, my worn sneakers soaked through.

Luke texts me: *all good no worries.*

I text back: *what happened?*

Luke: *coniunctio nobis semper perstat.*

They must have told him to lie low or something. Mr. Dine and Dash is not in chem.

While sitting around the oval conference table in world history class, the Harkness method at its best, I sneak my phone out from under the table. Luke is being evasive, dodging every question, which is upsetting but something he does. He says we should meet tonight to formally complete our joint explo into Pencey Chem Lab.

"Everything okay, Mr. Ware?"

I blink at Mr. Rafferty. I say something vague about how any discussion of gunpowder empires gets me worked up. He gives me a skeptical look back.

There's a new Society email about formatting protocols for our reports, along with a link to the Letters and Archives Digital Images Database (LADID). We can sign in with our school-issued email and password. The database provides the history of many buildings on campus, along with facility assignment plans, which show a floor-by-floor layout. I download as much as I can about Pencey.

Later that night, I meet Luke. He's standing by the same side entrance, shrouded in a black hoodie, all *Assassin's Creed*. He tells me to try to pick the lock—*"use your feeler pick"*—while he sticks one of his pods in my ear; I hear a gravelly-voiced dude soaked in reverb. It takes me longer than it took Luke the last time, but when I get it and the door clicks open, I let out a sigh of relief. It feels great. We fist-bump. Luke pushes us inside the hallway. The door closes behind us. As Luke makes his way deeper inside, I grab a strap on his backpack. "Hold up, kid. What went down with you and Pinky and the cops?"

"It's taken care of. It's fine, who cares?"

"I care! You involved me."

"There's nothing more to say."

"What is the deal with you and Pinky?"

"You keep—*ugh*—there is no—"

"It seems like you're testing him. Was that a test?"

"A test of what?"

"You tell me." There's definitely something going on.

Anyone eyeball the security cams in here? There are typically two facing each other across the room to eliminate blind spots—at what angle?

Forty-five degrees.

The way Pinky nodded at Luke, a proud mentor.

We haven't . . .

What? Consummated things? You will.

The way he said that word. Prickly, resentful. "Does Pinky have a thing for you?"

"Why do you ask these questions?" Luke mutters, snatching

something out of his backpack, holding it up. It's his Moleskine, and on it, the drawing of me. But it's different: There's more texture, depth, color. "Been working on this, wanted to show you."

I glance at his drawing in the rusty light. It's more evolved than the drawings of those other kids. It's annoyingly powerful. Ridiculously beautiful. "Why are you still working on it?"

"It's not finished."

"When will it be?"

"When it's done. When all of you is inside it. I like having you close."

"I like having you close too." I take a breath. "I don't feel close to you right now." I snatch the Moleskine out of his hands and examine the drawing more closely. I expected him to do something with my right eye, expose something truthful about how he really sees me, something freakish and profane, but both my eyes are normal.

He wanted me to know he doesn't see it, my implant is invisible to him, a nonissue. But he's pretending it isn't there—when it very much is. I'm scarred; he can't remove that part of me and make me normal. I shove it back into his hands. "Cool, great, thanks."

Luke shakes his head as he returns the Moleskine to his backpack. "What's up with you?"

"Are you high right now?"

"I pulled some stuff on Pencey off LADID—"

"I did too. *Are you high right now?*"

"Maybe."

"Were you high at The League?"

207

"Maybe."

"Do you have a problem?"

"We all have problems."

"Luke."

He folds his arms. "I have a prescription. I take it for my ADHD. Are you gonna—"

"Do you abuse it? I mean, you—"

I don't expect him to punch the sides of his head. I don't expect the snarl.

"You know you're starting to sound like my fucking dad?"

I instinctively take a step back. A bit of spittle hit me in the eye.

"Sorry," he says, face veering toward the dirty floor, a cruel moment to be reminded of his perfect jawline.

I slide a finger across my eye. He does have a temper, look at that. "I need to be able to trust you. The League was . . . a lot . . . to be honest . . ."

"You know I'm not him. You know that, right?"

"Who?"

"The kid who attacked you. *The one you still talk to.* I feel like you think I'm going to come for you at some point."

"Come for me?"

"Harm you."

"That's what you think? Where's this coming from?"

"The way you don't trust me." He gets close to my face. "Why do you still talk to him?"

"Why does it bother you?"

"It makes no sense."

"Not everything makes sense."

"Everything else about you makes sense."

"Does it?"

"He hurt you. And now you have me."

"Do I?"

His mouth curls, his eyes are embers, scorched and feral.

We've never had an all-out fight before. There's something a little too raw and scabrous about this; the anger feels foreign, like it's the wrong cable connection. I haven't been privy to Luke's fears about what we're becoming, only aware of my own.

"Talk to me. Not *him*."

"I'm, like . . . fucking trying here? I'm on financial aid."

"This again?"

I snort. "Yeah, this again. There are parameters. I can't get caught up with the cops 'cause you swallowed amphetamines and felt all whimsical."

"Respect. I'm sorry. I did keep you out of it, though. There are parameters for me too."

"Juvie, right? That's what you told me. People get hurt in juvie, Luke. They get knifed."

His upper lip twitches. "How do you know *that*?"

"I know more than you think. Maybe you better start being more careful."

"Everything we do is a risk. Look where we are right now. This is a risk."

"Then we need to minimize the risk."

Luke unzips his backpack and throws me a pair of rubber gloves. "Agreed."

We don't say much more; we sweep through Pencey over the next few hours, all business, doing a thorough exploration of the premises.

"What's our take?" says Luke as we leave, removing our gloves with echoing snaps.

"A take?"

"We need a take. Like a sort of thesis statement on Pencey. For the report."

The place had a Chernobyl-suspended-in-time feel to it. "It felt like time travel."

"To?"

"A haunted nowhere version of the present."

"Shit, Lonely, I love that."

Later, Luke texts me drawings of the Pencey Chem Lab. I took most of the photos, so he drew these from memory.

Drawings of a Haunted Nowhere.

Luke! These are incredible!

Should we include in report?

Absolutely.

After we jointly email our report, I get sleepy and think about floating through Pencey with Luke. Cobwebbed fume hoods, old freezers. Corridors with moldy emergency showers; cement platforms lined with iron edges to protect against chemical leakage; metal machines with piping connected to temperature gauges. Gliding through halls filled with dense fumes coating the back of my throat, blinking fire alarm lights like a poisoned galaxy filled with dying stars; the horror-show light of old overhead fluorescents, half burned into miserable pinkish-white flickers. His mood a gathering sandstorm. Our tether stretching but not breaking. Him lashing out at me.

Luke's drawing of me is getting more and more filled in, but my own drawing of Luke, the one I keep in my mind, is becoming a chalk outline at a crime scene.

Brent Cubitt steps out of a smoky hallway. "Of course you need Society. You need to see the world in four dimensions so you can stop seeing it in halves."

I wake, to a voice I recognize.

Jeffrey is sitting on the edge of his bed, a news story blaring. He sees me sit up. "Shit, sorry, I meant to connect my AirPods." This is a morning habit of Jeffrey's, listening to the news as soon as he wakes up. He tries to do it silently if I'm asleep, but sometimes the Bluetooth fails, and authoritative anchor voices permeate my dreams.

"No, no, wait, what is that?" I say, rubbing my face. "Play it."

Jeffrey plays the story. Someone is attacking Gretchen's dad, VP Cummings.

"You cannot judge a society on wealth inequality alone; I cannot imagine a more flawed viewpoint. Divest the wealthy of their wealth and their priorities shift. How do you grow and expand your business, or create jobs, if your capital is being taken away? A value-added tax is the only way to go. You cannot punish the American Dream itself . . ."

VP Cummings has been in the news a lot lately—more and more each day.

He's been vocal about pushing through a hefty wealth tax,

and "closing the carried interest loophole." The 1 percent feel betrayed. Gretchen's dad is going to oversee the writing of the wealth tax himself, which the president will sign into law. Congress has already signaled their support. "What is that, CNBC?" I ask.

"Yeah."

I sit up straighter. "Who was just talking?"

"None other than Essex's own Clayton Cartwright. Assholes like him are always against the redistribution of wealth."

"Ugh." The Cartwright family. Billionaires who own Oneida Pharma, the pharmaceutical giant that played a huge role in the opioid crisis by shoving OxyContin down the throats of the medical establishment while downplaying its addictive properties.

They're awash in unprecedented fines and lawsuits. Many arts institutions have renounced their donations and ended any public association with the Cartwrights in response to protests from advocacy organizations. *But has Essex formally renounced them?*

Clayton Cartwright went to Essex, and so did his dad, Brandt, and so did his grandfather Morton. I'm sure they've given the school a shit ton of money over the years, but there's no Cartwright Hall or anything, nothing dedicated, so there's no way to be certain.

Clayton even distanced himself from his family's pharma business. He's a private equity investor who made hundreds of millions and likes to pretend he's self-made, but that's a joke; he'd obviously be nowhere without his family's fortune. *If there's one thing quiet old money hates most, it's loud new money*, I overheard someone here say once.

I wouldn't have known if I hadn't heard his voice at the scrim of consciousness where dreams meet memory, right before waking, when sleep dissipates.

I wouldn't have known if I hadn't had monocular vision, which makes my sense of hearing more acute, my ability to remember voices sharper.

You are now part of a two-hundred-and-ten-year-old tradition: the creative, thorough exploration of Essex's rich history . . .

The hooded member of Archi wearing a silver mask, holding a staff, at Tap Night.

That was Clayton Cartwright.

CHAPTER TWENTY-ONE
SEVEN BREATHS

The next day, on my way back to Foxmoore after my last class, I run into Gretchen.

"I really liked your story," she says. "You told me some . . . about your dad . . . but the way you expressed it, all that truth, took skill and audacity."

This means a lot. And since I'm flattered, I get embarrassed, so my primary instinct is to deflect. "I'm hearing a lot about your dad these days."

"Yeah," she replies. "His heart's in the right place. Like yours."

"I don't know where my heart is."

"Well, you certainly know how to speak from it." She stops walking. "So many kids here . . . they're all about cliques, trends. You're the real deal, Cal."

Am I, though? "Thank you."

"We don't all have to fit in everywhere; we come from different places and backgrounds. We need to show more humanity. My dad's causing his usual trouble, but it's partly because I've been telling him he needs to rise above, make change for the people who need it."

"*You're* the reason your dad is—"

She holds up her hands. "I didn't say that. But I didn't *not* say that either." She smiles warmly. "Anyway. I'm meeting a friend. Always good to see you, Cal." She runs off.

Pinky is standing against a tree, eating a sandwich. He walks over. "Hey."

I stiffen. I never know how to react around him. "What's up?"

"Eating this sad-ass fish sandwich." He tosses the remains of it over his shoulder. "The rest is for the maggots." He puts one hand on my lower back and one on my chest. And then he *adjusts*. He steps back, looks me over. "Better. Don't be a sloucher."

Might as well just ask, since I'm standing so straight now. "What's with you and Luke?"

"Meaning?"

"Your history, your relationship?"

"What's with you and Gretchen? I'm *definitely* interested in *that*."

"We're—"

"Listen, man, you and Luke did fantastic work over at Pencey."

A pivot. I'm surprised Pinky reviewed our explo already.

"This is important to me personally," he says, "but also to Society."

I'm caught off guard. I shouldn't feel such a rush of pride at his praise; it's ridiculous that his approval matters so much. But it does. For lots of reasons. "What's important?"

"A strong partnership combining the right skill sets. That magic, that chemistry. I've seen past explo reports on Pencey boring as day-old bird shit, but you guys nailed it."

"What did we nail?"

"A haunted nowhere? Your description. His drawings. The soul of the place. The way you two see things when you're together. It's special, visceral, which pleases me. The painter and the poet! I love that." Pinky picks at one of his teeth. "Me and you . . . we're going to be having another one of our conversations." He keeps his eyes on mine. "Where we discuss the weight of water. Demonology. Or perhaps . . . our future."

". . . What?"

He drags the back of his wrist across his mouth. "You'll see." He gives me a lazy wave over his shoulder as he walks away. "Be good; keep at it."

I don't know exactly what Pinky was talking about (do I ever?), but his words seem prescient, annoyingly foreboding. When I get back to my dorm, there's a vague voicemail from my parents: *Call us back.* This could be anything.

They both pick up at once. "Everything okay?" There's a tremor in my voice.

"I'm sorry, Cal," says my dad, "but we won't be able to fly you home for Thanksgiving."

At first, I think it's a joke, but the punch line never comes. "What . . ."

"Thanksgiving break is only three days—"

"No. People leave Tuesday night and return Sunday. It's almost a week."

"Less than a month later is Christmas break. Let's wait till December."

"It's McCarl," says my mom. "It's out of the way, there are no direct flights, which compounds the cost; we can't afford two trips that close together right now."

"You never told me this."

"We didn't realize," says my mom, "but we talked to the school. They have a nice dinner for kids who don't go home for Thanksgiving. They leave the dorms open. Many students don't leave during Thanksgiving, it's such a short blip of a holiday. It sounds like a lot of fun."

It sounds depressing as all hell. The prospect of having to wait an extra month, knowing there's a week where *I could have gone home*, and everyone else *is* going home, and I'm not, because we're fucking poor—is unbearable. "You know Thanksgiving is my favorite holiday."

"We know," says my mom, sounding emotional.

I try and keep it together. "We won't be able to watch *Fantastic Mr. Fox* together."

"Anyway, how are classes?" says my dad, in his grow-up-and-take-it-like-a-man tone, which can enrage me. My dad prefers to blithely move on when he either wants to avoid people's emotions, or he's messed something up and doesn't want to argue about it.

"I want to know what's going on."

"Everything is fine," says my mom, trying to sound reassuring. "Nothing is—"

"All right, I gotta go," says my dad. "I gotta—" He says something muffled, away from the handset, hangs up.

"This is new to us as well," my mom continues, "you being far away; we got caught up, just now started researching flights and realized the expense."

"I would have gotten a job here if I knew, something after school, I—"

"No, we want you to focus on your classwork—"

"You could've communicated this! You plan things in advance, you make a *budget*—"

"I'm sorry. I don't know what else to say."

I don't either. I'm in disbelief. I don't want to totally lose it and make them feel worse. I throw the phone down. It bounces off the carpet and clatters across the room.

We get emails from various SMs introducing themselves; they're all fun, cute, surprisingly personal. I get a separate email from Nisha Patil, the girl who seemed to be fighting for me at my Spotlight. I wonder how much sway she had, how much I owe her for getting tapped. She wants to meet at Café Bianco, a popular meeting spot in town.

I'm comforted by Nisha's friendly smile; she's sitting at a corner table by a window. I place my latte in front of me and pull up my chair. "You like escape rooms?" She indicated this on her email introduction. "I do too."

"It's my favorite hobby! Want to join sometime?"

"I'd love to," I say.

"There's two nearby. We'll definitely do one." She takes a sip of what looks like black coffee. "So the purpose of this meeting is to tell you . . . I've been assigned your Chronus! All Neophytes get an upper-class member of Society to be a confidante, mentor, someone you can talk to about your Neophyte curriculum. I championed you, so it made sense to match us. We'll be doing an explo together too, further down the line. Anyway, I grew up in Bethesda, Maryland. I'm applying early to U of Chicago. I'll probably major in quantitative econ. I know all about you already."

I run my finger along the rim of my mug. "Why *did* you champion me?"

"You were one of the most versatile rushees we saw! And I'm tired of Society focusing on only broad-shouldered boys who look like rugby players." She laughs lightly. I like her laugh. "You're limber, a good climber, you can fit into small spaces, and your early explo reports had an interesting layer to them: humor, emotionality. I was digging it!"

"Thank you."

"So, this is . . . me formally introducing myself. In an informal setting. And if you had any questions, I—"

"Yeah." I shoot my shot. "Does Society tap kids who they use as sacrificial lambs?"

"I've heard those rumors, but I've been in Society since I was a freshman and I've never seen any evidence they do that. It's *possible* I wouldn't know about it. I'm not on the Board. But I wouldn't worry, Cal; trust me, you're not a sacrificial lamb."

We both laugh; mine's a little more nervous. This isn't even about if I'm a sacrificial lamb—I don't want *anybody* to be one. That'd bother the hell out of me.

"People know we exist," she says. "There's only so much secrecy you can have. But they don't know what we really do. So there's lots of misinformation about Society."

I barely know what they do. I dove in, blind, to this protean group with so much history baked into their cells. I feel emboldened by the tradition of it all, the privilege attached to it. The school has many secrets, it makes sense there'd be a society dedicated to unearthing and learning about them, but there's still so much I don't know. "How involved are members of Archi?"

"Only members of the Board know that."

"Do you know their identities?"

Nisha shakes her head. "That's a well-guarded secret."

"What happens after we become Veteres?"

"Once the database gets fully unlocked, it's like Olympic levels of trying to explore all the flagged places no one's ever accessed. It's competitive. And you'll have the chance to run for the Board, which will give you more power over influencing Society and future tap classes. What else is on your mind?" She takes a sip of coffee and eyes me. "You seem a little down."

"I'm going to be stuck here for Thanksgiving."

"So am I! My cousin's getting married, my parents have to go to Mumbai, and they're like, *Don't worry about it.* I have college applications. It makes more sense to hang here. It's not that bad. They make a solid Thanksgiving meal for the orphans."

"The orphans! Well, that's good to know."

"Yeah, we'll totally hang. That's what I'm here for!"

I love Nisha's sudden presence in my life. I feel a little relief (just a little) about the sacrificial lamb thing, but it's really gnawing at me that Clayton Cartwright is a member of Archi and might be pulling the strings on Society. It's gross to be getting in bed with people like the Cartwrights, but if they're a part of Society, they're a part of Essex, and we're all getting in bed with them—to an extent. There's no way they haven't donated to the school.

I'm thinking all this through later in the afternoon, lying in bed, my laptop guarding my face, when the door opens. "Hey," I say, not looking up.

"Hey," a deep voice responds that is not Jeffrey's.

I slam my laptop closed and sit up fast.

"At ease, soldier," says Pinky. He's wearing a navy-blue pea-coat. He holds up a beat-up leather briefcase. He gestures at Jeffrey's bed. I nod, and he plops down on it.

"I'm not sure when he's going to be back—"

Pinky gives me a look like: *I know exactly where Jeffrey is; we're good.*

"Heading home for Thanksgiving?"

I hesitate. "Did Nisha tell you—"

"No, no, but I had a feeling. Don't worry. They'll feed you well here. I mean, you won't fill up on ham hocks and collard greens; mac n' cheese isn't considered a vegetable at Essex."

I smile faintly at him.

"Thanksgiving's not as bad as you think here. So I've heard, anyway. I always go home. *My* parents want me." He grins. "But I believe transparency is best."

"Transparency?"

Pinky, humming lightly, digs through his briefcase. He produces a newspaper, unfolding it on his lap. "I have a strange hobby. I collect small-town newspapers."

That's how he vetted me. I was right. "From which towns? That concern who?".

"Those I'm most interested in."

"Why are you especially interested in me?"

"Another good question. I'm guessing you're not a subscriber to your hometown paper?" He smiles patiently at my blank expression. "No hometown spirit, eh? The *McCarl Inquirer*?" He throws it over to me. "Take a gander at that headline."

The paper is dated ten days ago. The front-page headline is about my dad.

The D.A. is charging my father with criminal negligence.

"I want to assure you of a few things. I spoke to my dad. He has an excellent attorney. They looked into the case, and yes, it's likely your dad will go to jail."

My stomach lurches. "What?"

"A man died, after all. That's involuntary manslaughter. Your mom is very sick, right?"

Slowly, I nod. Where the fuck is this going?

"If your family, because of your dad, loses their health insurance, that could be . . . catastrophic. Wouldn't you agree?"

I stare at the paper. *Why didn't they tell me?*

"Medical bills piling up. Legal fees. Bankruptcy is the least of their issues. Your mom might worsen. From the stress. From any kind of obstacles to her care. This is a brotherhood. We take care of one another. I wanted to apprise you of your situation at home. I'll bet good money your parents have been keeping this from you. Don't hate them. They just wanted to protect you. But listen, I actually do have good news."

My eyes flit over, meet his. I'm annoyed that I'm embarrassed by all this.

"Remember what I told you. Society can make anything go away. Get those charges dropped, for one. I don't want you to worry a lick over any of this."

"Maybe my parents didn't want me to know about what's going on so I wouldn't worry." It's bothering me he invaded their privacy. It feels wrong.

Pinky stands. "Transparency, as I said."

"What about keeping secrets?"

"Was this a secret, Cal? It's in the *news*."

I stand shakily, dizzy. "What do I do?"

Pinky rests his palm against my cheek, a stabilizing gesture that feels sliced through with something more. "Continue to shine." Pinky drops his hand lower, so he's squeezing my ass. "How badly do you need to move up the ranks . . . now that there's transparency?"

I stand there, shocked, breathing heavily.

"Enough to move my hand away?" He squeezes harder.

For a second I remain motionless. But then a razor-sharp instinct, deep inside, kicks in; I lean toward him and speak into his ear: *"Get the fuck off me, man."*

Pinky moves backward, hands in the air, as if from an invading SWAT team. "Yes," he says, almost proud, pointing at me, "I'd like to see a little bit more of *that Cal*, please." We stare at each other for a moment. "You need to make Veteres. That will help things along."

My mouth barely moves as I speak. "I will."

"We're going to have a very special relationship. But I'm going to ask you not to bring this conversation up with anyone. Not Luke. Or Nisha. Let your parents believe you're in the dark until they decide to enlighten you. And you'll get what you want. Hell, we all will. We just have to play the game. My father gave me a leather-bound copy of *Hagakure, The Book of the Samurai* for my sixth birthday. One of my favorite quotes: *'One should make his decisions within the space of seven breaths.'* Did you make yours?"

"What am I deciding here?"

"First dumb question you've asked." Pinky looks around the room, as if he's learning the layout, and then his gaze finds me again. "You have, I know you have. We'll talk more soon. I don't want you to worry," he repeats. Still humming, he closes his briefcase and walks out the door, leaving me staring at the newspaper headline.

Luke texts me later: *I'm outside, Moon Tears.*

I throw on my jacket and come downstairs to meet him. "Let's walk." He always says this when he wants to hang for a bit but has other plans.

"You okay?" he asks. "You look shook."

"I'm good." My fingernails scrape the bottoms of my pockets. "Who's your Chronus?"

"Tath."

We walk toward the quadrangle, Barry Tower looming. "Did you know Clayton Cartwright is a member of Archi? He was at our Tap Night."

"No. But who do you think Archi's gonna be? It's wealthy alumni. That's Essex."

That's how I know Society is exactly as powerful as Pinky says. "They did bad things."

"His family did, right? He's kind of doing his own thing now. Remember how I mentioned Faber at dinner?"

"Yeah."

"We need to check it out. I've been doing some reconnaissance. We're learning all these new skills. It might be a way we can be together more. In private."

My stomach jumps a little.

"It'd be great if I didn't have to blow you in a spooky old chem lab. I usually just want low-stakes dick, but it's different with you."

I clap my hand against my chest. "So romantic, wow! Be careful plagiarizing Louisa May Alcott so brazenly, though."

Luke laughs. "You look all sad."

"I'm stuck here for Thanksgiving." And my dad could be going to jail. "My parents can't afford the flight."

"I hope you can speak Russian. It'll be you and the crazy Russian kids."

"How do you know?"

"What I heard! It'll be great. One of them will probably have, like, nine-hundred-proof vodka. And a shiv. *Peredat' klyukvennyy sous, ili ya tebya porezhu.*"

I feel guilty even smiling right now. "What'd you say?"

"Pass the cranberry sauce or I'll cut you."

I laugh. "How do you know Russian?"

"I picked it up during my time in a filthy gulag."

"Stop!"

Luke lays a hand on my back. "I'm sorry. I know you wanted to see your family."

"What are you doing for Thanksgiving?"

"My dad," he says coldly. "I wish I could take you with me." Luke brings me in close. Forehead to forehead. He kisses me, our first public kiss.

The 5C 5'10" Girls™ pass by, chatting. "Queeeeens!" Luke shouts. Charli lowers her sunglasses and actually smiles at Luke. "Yo, they get, like . . . super loud when they're together," Luke says into my ear. "I'M WITH MY BOYFRIEND, YOOOO!"

Charli gives him a thumbs-up.

"Is that what we are?" He's never used that word before.

"Eh. Labels. Why does everything have to be—" Luke drops his backpack, rips open a front pouch, removes some Visine, and vigorously puts drops in his eyes, blinking upward. Then we walk a little more. "Here's Faber." I didn't realize where we were headed, Luke is always so distracting. "I'm thinking more long-term, I guess. See the tower at the top?"

"Yeah."

"It's an abandoned library, probably impossible to access. But nothing's impossible, right? Isn't that what we're learning? We'll need to look at blueprints, map stuff out, make our move at just the right time. There's probably an elevator somewhere.

I'm guessing our access point will be through the basement."

"Faber's a co-ed dorm, right?"

"Yeah. Cocaine Betty lives there."

Poor Rachael Klein, a popular junior. As legend has it, she returned from the bathroom to her honors European history class one morning with white powder caked over her nostrils. She'll never live that nickname down. "A nice Jewish girl from a nice media family," says Luke. And out comes his Apple Watch. "I gotta meet some kiddos."

Right on time. "Yep."

"I got practice. But we'll start researching, maybe get in there, look around?"

"Cool." It'd be amazing to have our own place.

"You want me to fly you home for Thanksgiving?"

At first, I'm not sure I heard him correctly. "What?"

"I will if you want. It's no big deal. Don't make it into a big deal, Lonely."

"My parents wouldn't like that." They're mortified by anything resembling a handout.

"You want to come over later?"

"Yes." I need every escape from reality I can get.

"Vlad won't be around. You want to have sex?"

I toy with the zipper on my jacket. He's so forthright! "So, like . . . I've never . . ."

"Yeah, I get that. We'll see where it goes, no presh. I'll text ya?"

CHAPTER TWENTY-TWO

THE SCROLLS, THE SKULLS, THE CODES, THE KEYS

Luke kicks his door closed, not worried a bit about anyone noticing we're in here alone, flips off the overheads (another broken rule), and switches on a blue lava lamp on a table by the bed. It floats rubbery shapes across his walls. There's a stack of LADID printouts and maps piled on his desk, spilling onto the floor. It's all Faber-related: Luke's diagrams, notes, drawings, maps. He sees where my eyes are at. "Been sort of focused on this for a while."

"Yeah, I can see that."

He kicks off his sneakers, hangs his jacket on a hook on the door, and disappears into the bathroom. I hear the sink as I stand by his desk, flipping through all his penciled notes. Arrows pointing every which way; dimensions, measurements, sketches of structural deviations he found from old blueprints and fire insurance plans. At the other end of the room, Vlad's sneakers, in Day-Glo color combinations, perfectly lined up, his side all shadowy, like Luke lives with an imaginary jock friend. Luke returns in a T-shirt and yoga pants, his hair damp.

I sit on his bed. He sits beside me, drying his hair by rubbing the back of his head super hard.

"What'd you do, fall in the toilet?"

"Washed my face, brushed my teeth," he replies. He puts a hand on my leg. I put my hand over his hand. He leans over and kisses me on the cheek. We fall back onto his bed. Luke takes off his T-shirt. I take off mine. I lean forward and peel off my socks. Luke jumps up, pulls a shopping bag out of the corner of the room, and ceremoniously removes each item:

A light blue box of Trojans.

A black tube . . . I quickly realize is lubricant.

My eyes go wide as Luke removes a container of Skippy peanut butter.

And then a jar of grape jelly . . .

"Wait, what is . . ."

Luke sees my expression and laughs hard, his head falling forward, a chunk of hair folding over his eye. He throws open the fridge—there's a bag of Wonder Bread. "These are so Vlad and I can make PB&Js!" he howls. "You thought it was a sex thing!"

I cover my face. "Oh my God."

"I'm going to peanut butter you."

"Stop."

"I'm going to grape jelly you so hard."

My face must be a million shades of red. "Shouldn't we negotiate . . ."

"I'll call in my legal team—"

"Who's doing what here?"

"I'm not really vers, Lonely Hearts." The devilish grin on his face with one eye in a half wink should be trademarked. "But. We don't have to do anything you don't want to do."

"Okay. Well. No, that's fine. I want to be able to look at you?"

"I'll make sure, so I can kiss you."

I keep getting bombarded with paroxysms of worry: my dad, prison, everything Pinky said today. I shove those thoughts away so I can concentrate on Luke, which only leads to more guilt. He lies next to me and pulls me toward him, our bare chests together, heartbeat to heartbeat. His stubble scratches my chin. He rubs my shorn hair at the nape of my neck. I wrap my arms around him. He's so trim and muscular. I'm a scrawny kid, vanishing in his iron grip.

"So, like. This is a big step for me . . ."

"I know what it is, dickbitch! Are ya gonna scream out the V-word?"

I bury my face in his chest. "Don't make me laugh right now; this is lovely."

"Yo, it'll be easier if you *listen*." We shift. Luke straddles me, lecturing atop my stomach; I'm immediately reminded of his soccer legs. "It's gonna hurt like a motherfucker the first time—even though I'll go slow, promise. Every guy who does it with another guy for the first time should do it with a guy who's done it before. Sometimes it comes down to metrics—physics, plumbing, wires, mechanics, scheduling. It's never going to be the perfect moment."

"I didn't say—"

"Yeah, but you're a romantic. I'm telling you shit isn't always going to be perfect."

"I don't think I'm—"

"You said it's a big step for you! That's romantic! I'm trying to bring it back down to Earth, so this isn't all starry, floating on the astral plane, ya know."

I nod; I appreciate him making this moment accessible for me. I've never felt like I belonged in a place and time with one person so insistently before. Shielded from everything else. The stress and heartbreak of the world. Luke asks what makes me most happy.

I tell him my family. And school. And *he* does, obviously. And Society. And when he asks what about Society, my doubts evaporate, and I tell him it's the camaraderie. The sense of being part of something secret, valuable, delicate; a part of history and tradition; the challenges, uncovering new skills; the glory of it all. Something that can take all the horrors away.

And because my head is swimming, I rattle off a bunch of random words mistily describing what Society is to me, the space it has in my brain.

The scrolls, the skulls, the codes, the keys . . .

There's a poetic ring—there it is again!—to the string of words, embedded with imagery and atmosphere. Luke asks me to repeat it, and so I do.

The scrolls, the skulls, the codes, the keys.

Each time I say it, I de-stress a little.

He asks me to keep repeating it, and as I do, whispering it

like a spell, he gets to work, undressing me, using his hands, his tongue, always asking if I'm okay.

He grabs my hand (*"Relax your muscles and breathe, Lonely"*), and then we combine in a way that makes me wonder if we've recombined together into something new, and if we can ever uncombine. And then another Cummings enters my mind, not our VP, but e. e., at just the moment the poet's last name becomes a double entendre.

> *one's not half two. It's two are halves of one:*
> *which halves reintegrating, shall occur*
> *no death and any quantity; but than*
> *all numerable mosts the actual more*

When I wake up, I'm in his arms. I've never fallen asleep next to another person before. I feel inextricably linked to him and his own dreaming mind, cloistering its fears and hopes and terrible truths. Luke is breathing against my back. Like his lungs are filling mine.

Luke's phone buzzes on his desk. Probably one of his jock friends. I carefully untangle myself so I don't wake him, even though I want to stay like this forever. I sit up, eyes heavy, fluttering against the grainy light. As I get dressed, I try to remember if I left the window propped open on my hallway. I missed check-in.

The same text message flashes again. I only catch the name because I'm right by his desk, in this tiny-ass room, hopping around, trying to get my socks on.

The message says: *ok let me know when ur done, we need to talk asap.*

I remember I asked him, and Luke told me his Chronus was Tath.

So why the hell is Pinky Lynch texting him at four a.m.?

CHAPTER TWENTY-THREE

TRUTH IN LIES

The next day, my mind replays every detail from the night before. I can't stop thinking about the sex; how I feel so chill about it, as if Luke was able to siphon away my anxiety, and yet . . . how things don't feel quite right either. My world is shrouded in other people's secrets. And yet . . . I don't want to ask Luke why Pinky was texting him. I don't want to create division, I don't want Luke to think I don't trust him . . . 'cause he has a thing about that.

I managed to sneak back into Foxmoore. I did leave the window propped open after all, so no one saw me come back in. I haven't seen Luke all day, but at five p.m., he texts me.

Heading to practice. How RU.

Good, man. I still feel you.

Was that the right thing to say? Is it too much? Is it gross?

Feel ya back. Can't get you out of my head, Lonely.

The rest of October flies by. Gretchen and I make our run-ins a bit more formal. We do our homework in the library together. As her dad saturates the news, causing a schism in his party, I notice more of her Secret Service detail hovering, which she's not thrilled about.

Our weekly Society lectures about various campus buildings and their histories continue. Our "physical exploration" training with Tath escalates, with nightly meetings.

I learn to see a door, and its locks, as if under a microscope, any mechanism in place preventing me from accessing the other side a solvable hindrance.

We learn how to bypass various alarms and how to avoid motion detectors.

The important places on campus (Hawthorne, Cook, L&A) have their own security; this is where what they call "Rafiki" comes into play. You can duplicate a security guard's ID badge remotely. The RFID strips on them emit a specific radio frequency, and some of the electronic locks on important doors will only open if they're exposed to the right radio frequency. RFID stands for radio frequency identification. It's how our key fobs get programmed.

Tath on the steam tunnels:

"These utility corridors transport high-temperature steam from Essex's physical plant to all buildings on campus. Steam leaks, in decommissioned parts of the system, are invisible, and potentially deadly if you're not careful." We are taught to hold a piece of cardboard in front of us, a precaution against encountering a high-pressure leak.

Our physical training moves into "social engineering." We continue to meet in locked buildings, many of which we've had lectures about, in basements, hidden storage rooms, or empty classrooms—filled with silverfish, dust balls, rat traps.

"Lying is a skill," Tath intones in the Brookleven ballroom, "and it takes practice. If you encounter a security guard or school official while on an explo, *if you get caught*, this skill can be the only one that keeps you from D-Comm." D-Comm is the school's disciplinary committee.

"The best lies have elements of the truth. Put anyone who's questioning you on the defensive. Work from the top of your strengths. Can you cry on command? Do it. Can you summon a surge of confidence? Act like you belong there. Don't make too much eye contact. When you look to the left, you're lying. When you look to the right, you're remembering something." Tath snaps his fingers, right, left, to emphasize the point. "Throw people off their game. Whoever catches you isn't going to be too aggressive. You're children. Their primary goal is to make sure you're okay. Always have a lie prepared. Know why you're there. Make whoever's questioning you uncomfortable."

I think about truth and lies. And my parents, who I haven't spoken to since I hung up on them. They've called a few times since. Anger at them keeps melting into fear. I prefer the anger.

"You never know how you're going to react until you actually have to lie under pressure. There's adrenaline. Breathing becomes shallow. It's harder to talk. So we're going to practice. Your Chroni are going to give you hypotheticals. You're going to create the perfect lie for each one. And then, in about a week, you and your Soulmate are going to be assigned a low-security building. And you're going to break into it. And you're going to wait for security to arrive. And when they do, you're going to lie to them."

Whoa . . .

"Passing this test means you don't get sent to D-Comm."

The next day, on my way to meet Nisha, Luke is standing outside Garrott handing off a small plastic bag to another sophomore. Luke's face lights up at the sight of me. "What up?"

"What was that?"

Luke motions for me to keep walking, so I do, and he joins me, pecking me on the cheek, leaning into my ear. "I gotta move some of this Adderall, so I have a little side thing going on."

I stop walking. "A *side thing*? You're selling drugs on campus?"

"Yo, keep your voice down, King."

"Why?"

"For the cash. Why else?"

"If I saw you, out in the open like that, any teacher could too. Are you *trying* to get expelled? Why do you even need *cash*—"

"I'm not going to get expelled, *chill*." I walk again, a bit faster, so Luke has to jog a little to keep up. "Are you mad?"

"Do you understand, like . . ." I flap my hands around. "I'm . . . I love you."

He gets still. He opens his mouth to say something, but then doesn't.

Wow, I just blurted that out, didn't I? "You have to protect what we have . . . what we *are* . . . by not doing every single insane thing you think of. It's not only about you anymore. It's about us. I don't want to lose you."

"Respect. I appreciate you telling me this. I'm not self-destructing."

I give him a skeptical look. "What am I to you? What are we?"

"I shouted it to the world, remember?"

"Say it to me."

Luke puts a hand on my back, whispers in my ear: "I can't wait till I can have you again."

I shake him off. "It's not just about sex—"

"It's not."

"Then do better."

"Yo, like . . ." He gestures with his hands. "You're really good at making me feel like I disappointed you."

"Is this a Pinky thing?"

Luke's eyes are cryospheric. "Is what . . . *a Pinky thing?*"

"Selling Adderall."

"Why would it be a 'Pinky thing'?"

"'Cause it's something. And it doesn't seem like all you."

"Maybe you don't know me as well as you—"

"Yeah, that's obvious." I walk away, and honestly it hurts like hell to leave him standing there with nothing resolved, but I am furious.

"You've been caught by a faculty member in the basement of Cranwich after hours. What are you doing here?" says Nisha, inquisitive.

Tears come to my eyes, surprising me. Nisha sways back

in her chair, impressed, as I launch into the lie I prepared.

Nisha studies my face, taking a few notes as I go. "Not bad!" she says when I'm done.

I sit back as the normal white noise of Café Bianco—people chatting, typing on laptops, Cherry Glazerr punking it up on the sound system—comes rushing back to my ears.

Nisha taps her pen on the yellow pad. "Sometimes you need to charm your way into somewhere, and sometimes you need to charm your way *out of* somewhere. You were respectful, that's good. The pieces of truth you used—yes, you were meeting Luke, yes the door was unlocked and open—"

"Because I picked it open," I laugh.

"Yes, but *truth*, right? Watch your eyes. You made a bit too much eye contact. The crying was great! Make any authority figure uncomfortable, put them on the defensive."

I wipe at my eyes. "Yeah, I didn't expect the tears."

"That was amazing. Everything okay?"

My phone vibrates with a text.

I love you too. I LOVE YOU, Lonely. I didn't say it cause I was scared.

There's a small pause, and then Luke adds:

Dickbitch.

I have to close my eyes for a second because there's a lot welling up inside me. "Yeah, everything's fine." I laugh a little;

I'm happy. And frightened. Luke doesn't get to be the only one scared of this.

"When I texted we'd be focusing on Cranwich, did you have your lie prepared?"

"Yeah, I did."

"I could tell. Now, what's up with you?"

I take a sip of my latte. "Luke means a lot to me. But he plays things a little too close to the knives. I don't want to get hurt." Tears really start flowing now. I wipe them away. God, there's all this stupid emotion flooding through me; I don't know what's going on. I mean, *I do know*, a human being on this planet other than my mom and dad just told me they loved me. That's new. And something I honestly never thought possible.

"It's very obvious how he feels about you, Cal. How's your family doing?"

I try not to let my face fall. Every move I make with Society feels like an effort to save my parents, and that's a lot to carry around. "They're okay. They miss me. Yours?"

"We're all good. I'm excited for Thanksgiving. Want to do an escape room?"

I nod, palms pressed against my eyes. God, I'm still crying; this is so embarrassing.

"Lie to me," says Nisha, folding her hands. "Are you in love with Luke Kim?"

I open my eyes and look past her gaze to the right. "I don't know Luke Kim."

CHAPTER TWENTY-FOUR

SILENT ALARMS

Wednesday, and the entire faculty and student body is gathered in Woodbridge Auditorium, the three-tiered auditorium on the ground floor of Dallow Memorial Hall, for our weekly Class Meeting. Seated by year, we sing the Essex Evensong as light streams through the stained glass windows. On the stone walls, there are old photos of Essex students, all the way back to the 1930s, gathered here, in the same building. The songs we sing are the same. The lyrics link us through time, walking the same lawns, entering the same buildings.

One day, a hundred years from now, some kid singing these same words is going to see an old photo of me singing in Dallow and wonder what the hell I'd make of the world they're living in. Our voices rise into an angelic chorus, celebrating youth and vitality.

I get a message from Luke, standing a single row in front of me, texting coyly with one hand, phone down, while singing extra loudly to distract.

Check ur email, Lonely. We got our break-in assignment.

Luke and I go over all necessary docs that we can dig up before we make our move. First built in 1911, Hoyt Auditorium burned down in 1918, and was rebuilt in 1921 with a gargoyle added to the entrance, featuring a phoenix, to symbolize *rising out of the ashes.* In 2009, the building was renovated for the second time. For certain school functions they split up the student body and the upper-class students head to Hoyt, which is a smaller space than Woodbridge. Since it's newer, its security features will be newer. We head over there together at approximately seven p.m., two hours after the building is locked.

The last specks of light fade from the sky as we approach the front entrance stealthily. Jeffrey's words are echoing in my head: *Picking a locked door is never not breaking a rule that'd get you in big trouble.* And Pinky's: *You need to make Veteres. That will help things along.*

I'm at war with myself, but the only thing I know for sure is, Society is taking me on a specific path, and I need to follow it. Despite risks to my academic standing, or even getting expelled, I wouldn't be able to live with myself if I had the ability to help my parents and I let that opportunity pass. However, I'm still scared shitless right now.

Hoyt is semi-adjacent to Telfare, a junior boys' dorm. We have to make sure we're not seen. The electronic readers at the front glass doors are blinking red, meaning the building is off-limits. Inside, I see dimmed recessed lighting. "We can't pick these doors."

"No full plate," Luke agrees. "Plus, the readers."

We do a sweep. The back of the building, which faces a patch of woods, is not as modern. There's a light shining over a decorative, trimmed wooden door at the bottom of these stone steps, as if leading to a cellar. I walk toward it, but Luke holds me back, his black Nike soccer-gloved hand pressed against my chest. "Camera over the door?"

"There's not supposed to be one here."

"Always check first anyway. If we're caught on camera, it will dismantle our lie," says Luke, walking forward, zipping open his backpack, as I do the same. We approach the door. It's locked. No reader. No camera above the door. It's an easy lock to pick (basic deadbolt). We both go to work on it, and we're inside two minutes later. Luke points to wiring circling around the inside of the door, which we guess is probably an alarm of some kind, but nothing sounds.

We're in a narrow, cool basement: stone walls glittering with mica. We find a staircase and head upstairs to the lobby. The lights are automatic, movement sensitive. As soon as we pass under them, they click on. The doors to the auditorium are across from the main building entrance. Luke grabs a trash receptable, opens those front doors (not locked from the inside), careful not to step outside the building, and props them open with the receptacle.

Barring the high-security places, there are no cameras inside any school buildings or residence halls on campus. People value student privacy and preserving the trust of the Essex community. It wasn't until five years ago that they installed *exterior* cameras—and only twenty or so—on some key buildings (after some faculty bikes were stolen). Thanks to Tath, though, we all know which buildings have exterior cams, and Hoyt is not supposed to have any. But things can always change, and the school certainly wouldn't let us know, so it's better to err on the side of caution.

"Looky here," says Luke, tugging on the heavy doors leading into the auditorium itself.

"Locked?"

Luke examines the door. "Not a full plate."

"Maglock?"

"See the armature plate? Go for it."

I am proudly one of the Neos who is not terrible at the tugging trick on electromagnetic locks. I get the doors open on the third try. *Pull, push, pull, ending with a sharp pull up.* That last firm maneuver is the secret trick to fooling those mashers.

Suddenly, light spills in through the glass doors behind us. "Oh, hello," says Luke as two security dudes in golf carts pull up to the entrance. Luke checks his watch. "You know, that was faster than I would've guessed. These dudes weren't napping."

"Silent alarm?"

"A few of the newer buildings have them. Or someone saw the door open? Better get the lights on inside lickety-split or we're gonna have to lie by the seat of our pants."

We leave the doors open as we move inside. Luke finds a metal box on the wall. He flips switches. The house lights come on, and some work lights hanging from the ceiling, which shine down on a podium. We both hop up and take the stage.

Luke drops his backpack at his feet, takes off his gloves and his jacket. He's dressed in all black: Dri-FIT jersey with mesh panels, PUMA jogging pants, Adidas Predator Tango sneaks. Luke looks good in black, though he doesn't really have an off color.

The security guys are in the lobby now, calling out.

Luke gestures toward the back of the auditorium. "Yo, these dudes, they need to make sure the kiddos on campus are safe, everything's in compliance with state and local fire regulations, answer every emergency call. Let's try not to get them to write up an incident report. They're not faculty." Luke checks his watch again. How is he so calm?

The two security guards enter the auditorium. They cautiously walk single file down one of the two aisles (which is amateurish, one is blocked by the other) as Luke pulls me toward him, gripping my upper back.

Flashlights find us. *Please don't let me get sent to D-Comm,* I silently pray.

"What are you two doing here?" says one of the guards. He's tall and spindly, with thinning blond hair, a strong jaw. The other is Italian-looking, fireplug build.

Luke blocks his face with his hands. "Yo, get that light out of my eyes."

"You're not supposed to be in here."

"Well," says Luke, "why was the door open, then? Why were the lights on?"

"Can I see your ID?"

"No. Fuck that." Luke kicks his backpack.

Whoa. What is he doing? "We didn't know the building was off-limits," I say calmly. "The door was open. We needed somewhere private to talk."

The two flashlights cross over to me, as if the guards suddenly realized I was there.

"Go to the library, then," says the tall one. "Go to your dorms. Your common areas."

"None of those places are private," Luke sneers. "Do you know how much my dickhead dad pays for me to go to this school where I can't get a moment alone? What would my mother have thought if someone accused her son of some impropriety," says Luke, crossing himself, "may she rest in peace."

The Italian responds to the cross. "Relax, kid. We didn't accuse you of anything."

"They're just doing their jobs," I tell Luke, through my teeth.

"We can drive you over to Rangor right now. Talk to a counselor." The student health center is a ten-bed inpatient accredited hospital facility, open 24/7. These dudes are clearly trained to offer this as an option first. But we don't want that.

"I don't want to go to Rangor!" Luke screams. "I want to talk to my friend!"

"All right, take it easy," says the Italian.

"Come down here, please," says the tall one, motioning for us to get off the stage.

"You come up here," says Luke. "We're not doing anything wrong."

"You're trespassing," says the tall one as he does walk up the side stairs onto the stage. The Italian reluctantly follows.

"Not knowingly," says Luke. "WHAT THE FUCK?"

"Please take it easy!" says the Italian. "And watch your mouth."

Luke leers at him. "Fucking make me."

I'm getting furious at Luke. Is he trying to screw the both of us?

"IDs, please. NOW." The tall one.

I grab mine out of my wallet and hand it over. "We didn't know we weren't supposed to be in here," I say, following my script. "We're sophomore transfers. The building seemed open."

Luke, angrily kicking at his backpack, has apparently gone rogue.

The tall one examines my ID and passes it over to the Italian, who examines it, then hands it back to me. They regard Luke uneasily. The Italian motions for Luke to hand over his ID. And that's when what could have been over escalates into a whole thing.

Luke rips open his backpack, chucks his ID at the guards' heads, but as he does so, a plastic bag of pills and a wad of cash get unloosed from his backpack and fly out along with the ID. The pills, white-and-orange capsules, scatter across the stage, as loud as marbles.

For a moment, everyone is silent.

Oh my God, what did he do? Their flashlights sweep across the stage.

"What are those?" says the tall one.

I can tell Luke is registering how far south things just went. He clearly has issues with authority. Did. Not. Know. That. "Those," Luke huffs, "are the pills I'm supposed to be taking."

"He's not taking his meds," I say robotically, perspiring.

"You keep them in a plastic bag?" says the Italian.

"No," says Luke, bending over, producing a vial from his backpack. "I have a prescription. These are mood stabilizers. Prescribed by my *doctor*. My name is on the bottle."

The Italian shines his light on the wad of cash—mostly hundreds. "That's quite a lot of cash you got there." He moves the light into Luke's face. "Are you high right now, son?"

"I am not high, and I am *not your son*. Do I look like some goombah's kid?"

"Luke."

"You selling drugs on campus?"

"How dare you accuse me with no evidence."

The pills, scattered everywhere, gleam in the stage light.

"What would your mother think of you selling drugs?" says the Italian.

Luke gets in real close to the guy. "My mother? My mother's gone. And she was a good Catholic woman, man—*not some lapsed gutter whore like yours*."

It's not a slap, not exactly.

The Italian, without thinking, swipes his hand against Luke's chin. I'm about to physically intervene, but Luke got exactly what he wanted. He cries out, grabbing his face, staggering back. "He hit me! Did you see that?"

Wow, he is a superb manipulator. It takes me a second to register and appreciate that. And now I have no choice but to play along, so I address the guards. "You hit a student?"

"Whoa," says the Italian, "I didn't hit nobody."

"You hit *him*," I say. "An Essex kid having a tough day?"

"Let's all relax," says the tall guy, hands out. "No one's hitting anyone."

"I beg to differ," I say, following Luke's runaway train. "I'm a witness."

"Kid, are you okay?" says the tall guy to Luke. "Is everyone okay?"

"Jesus," says the Italian, shaking his head. He's nervous now.

"No incident report," says Luke, pointing at them, still holding his mouth. The two guards stare at him, baffled, the beams of their flashlights sinking down like crashing helicopters. "It was a misunderstanding. The building was left open. We stepped in for a breather. Got it?"

Luke walks over to me and kisses me hard on the mouth. The guards watch this, visibly uncomfortable. Luke addresses them, pointing at the money. "Go on. Take it, take it all."

We were trained to employ various tactics in this situation, but Luke has elected to employ *all of them at once*, a prism of tactics. It's like he's field-testing each one to see what succeeds best. And he knows he's bribing two unlucky security guards— not the police.

"I won't tell anyone you hit me. Take the money, but no incident report. And we want another few minutes. We'll turn off the lights and close the doors when we leave."

And, after a few moments of hesitation, *they fucking do it.*

CHAPTER TWENTY-FIVE

THE SUNKEN BOTTOM LAYERS

When they leave, Luke takes two spray paint cans out of his backpack. He leaves his tag on a sliver of wall toward the back of the stage. I kneel near the edge. Luke rifles through his backpack, then sits beside me, gently resting his hand on my shoulder. "You okay? That was not worth getting upset over. Those guys were just cosplaying as Delta Force Whatever."

"They were doing their job."

"They took seven hundred bucks off me."

"You made seven hundred dollars selling Adderall?"

"That's what I was tryna tell you. There's a market here. Gotta exploit it."

"You don't have to exploit it just because it's there."

"Well, now I really do, 'cause I gotta make back the seven hundred."

"You were vicious with those guys. Their job is to protect us."

"But the money was more important."

"That was too much, man." His ugly side, and how fast it came, bothered me.

"That was our assignment. We succeeded. We're not going to D-Comm."

"It doesn't feel like a win. You could've gotten us in a lot of trouble."

"You gotta stop being so naïve, Lonely. There are winners and losers in this world. You gotta snatch what you want, screw the rules, screw decorum."

"Take what you want? Like running out on a restaurant bill? Like that?"

"Yo. Look at Essex. They hired security guards who were bribable, not ethical. Does that make you have faith in our fair institution?"

It doesn't. Although, as Luke said, they weren't faculty. But still, I want to rebel against this whole idea. "You're going to get in trouble for selling drugs."

"I need the cash to get the hell away from my dad."

And then I remember what he said when we kissed for the first time, on a different stage: *I have to free myself.* "That's what this is about?"

"I'm just trying to survive my stupid life, Lonely Hearts."

There's something else going on. His anger is too potent. It's like he's being pulled by some outside force; there's too much anguish behind his actions, tinged with resentment. But then I realize, aren't I also being pulled . . . *by an outside force?*

We lie back. I'm unnerved but I want nothing more than to feel him again, close to me, because I feel untethered from the world when I sense him moving away from me. I kind of hate myself for that; it feels weak.

We doze, holding each other, only for about an hour, and before check-in. I wake up before he does, with an unsettled feeling. I tiptoe over to his bag and lift his phone out. There's another missed call from Pinky. And a text.

Which tact worked best w these 2 guys

I nudge him with my sneaker. "Wake up, Duchess." He opens one long-lashed eye—the one that changes color. I hold his phone out. He grabs it out of my hands, sitting up fast. He scans the screen, squinting. "Why is Pinky texting you?"

"You should get back; you'll miss check-in."

"It didn't seem to matter last time." I never did get written up.

"Don't make it a habit."

"Answer my question."

"Seriously, Lonely," he says, standing, rubbing his head, "don't get paranoid on me."

"What's going on with you two? You said you knew him as well as I did."

"I don't know how well you know him."

Suddenly, I'm not sure either.

How badly do you need to move up the ranks? Enough to move my hand away?

"He wants us to do well," says Luke. "He likes to give me information."

"Seems like he wants some."

"He likes strong pairs. He likes how we see things together." He flings his head to one side to get a lock of hair out of his eye and texts, his back to me.

The pills are still scattered everywhere. Luke never thought to pick them up. "You planned that, didn't you? The whole spilling-the-pills routine . . ."

"Nah," he says. But I know he did.

I double down. "Pinky texted you the night we had sex. At four a.m. Why?"

"How do you know?"

"I saw your phone on your desk when I was getting dressed. How did he know we were together? I don't like this many secrets, man. Especially with the risks I'm taking for you."

"We're both taking risks—"

"All the intimate stuff? You're more experienced. This means more to me."

Luke bounces over, his face an inch from mine; playful, but with a slight edge. "Yooo, WHAT? You think this doesn't mean anything to me 'cause I've been with other dudes? You're not them. You're not taking more risks. Don't power play that slime."

"I want to know what's up. And I'm not going to allow you not to tell me anymore."

And at that moment, since Luke's phone is in the palm of his hand, another text from Pinky flashes on his screen. We both see it.

Did they take the money?

Instead of looking caught, Luke's face relaxes, as if something he's held on to for a long time, some sort of burden, got lifted away. He can't lie about whatever this is anymore.

"It has to do with my own shit . . . my past."

"What."

"I do know Pinky," he says, in a hushed voice. "From before . . . before Rush."

"You lied to me?" I ask at the same time I remember we've all become trained liars.

"I've known him since summer. It wasn't me actively *lying to you*, Lonely. I'm not allowed to talk about any of this, so I tried not to, but you keep pushing—"

"Don't turn this around on me. You're not allowed to talk about what?"

"The whole thing. There's too much at stake for me."

"What the hell is at stake?"

"I was courted."

His words are hitting me like shrapnel, lightning fast and dangerously sharp. "By . . . ?"

"Essex. Society. Both."

I want to be patient because I know he's making a concession. "Why? How?"

"My grades, my circumstances, I can't say more, I could get into trouble."

Something feels very similar about Pinky's hold on him and the hold Pinky is trying to have over me. "I don't understand," I say softly. "Can you explain?" Luke's face twists into so much concussive torment, I have to grab him. "Okay, take it easy. Is Society doing bad shit?"

"No, no, they saved me."

"From?"

"Juvie."

I have no idea how to react. "What can you tell me?"

"Pretty much what I did. It concerns me, not you. I'll always keep you out of it."

"Keep me out of what?" But I think about The League and how it all sort of went away.

"What I owe them."

"What do you owe them, Luke?"

"I can't talk about this, but I know it's hurting you. I don't want to hurt—"

"DUDE, WHAT IS GOING ON?" Luke drops his head onto my shoulder. I draw him in close. "Hey, it's okay."

"I don't want to talk about this anymore. Please. I'm fucking begging you."

"Sometimes I feel like I barely know you."

"You know me better than anyone else in my life. If that means anything. If I tell you more, I'm worried it could . . . damage things. You have to trust me on that."

I can't risk a schism between us, I love him too much, I am in too deep. "Sssh, sshh, it's okay, it's okay." I keep saying that. Over and over again.

"My God, Cal, what you won't do for love," says Brent.

"I'm terrified to be without him."

"Pick up the sword. You and Luke are similar in many ways. You're just as obsessive and relentless when you want to be. How did you learn so much about Essex to begin with? Or complete those initial explos? Do the right research. Do more of it."

"Why do you care?" I spit into my phone. "You feel bad? About what you did to me?"

"Let me ask you this . . . why can't you let me go?"

"Because I have to believe there's something more inside you than rot. If I don't believe that, I'm not sure I can ever trust anyone again."

"You'll die lonely, Lonely Hearts."

Right after the experience at the auditorium, I start actively investigating Society.

It feels like the only way I can secure things with Luke, and with us, is to try and get more of an idea of what's going on. Between what Luke is hiding from me and what I'm hiding from him (Pinky, and therefore Society, being the connective tissue), the only way I think I can protect our relationship is to do what I do best: research and uncover shit. This becomes easier once Society unlocks Tier 1 of their prized database, after we all succeed with our planned break-ins. Tier 2, the fun stuff, gets unlocked after we make Veteres.

For now, we receive lists on which buildings are alarmed, which dorm common areas have interesting amenities, archives on which doors need to be shivved open, and a guide to "abnormal doors" with latches that don't catch the lock, or sensors we should avoid.

Society provides another link to LADID, which functions as a back door into a deeper layer of the archive. Through this link, there are other links that allow me to burrow into the internal maneuverings of the Academy. Namely, their revenue and expenditures.

I read their Annual Report on Giving, compiled by the trustees. I examine their endowed funds available for use by the school. The hunger for donor cash is probably not unusual for a top-tier prep school, but their expenditures are bizarre.

The school hasn't turned a profit since 2014 (the tax filings online only go back to 2001, and they're public record). Their revenue includes categories like "contributions," "program services," and "investment income." Their expenses include "executive compensation," "fund-raising fees," and something called "recompense." This term catches my eye because the number is so high—in the eight figures—but also because it's an anomaly. I cross-check with the Eight Schools Association, which Essex is a member of, and no other school has "recompense" listed as an expense. No other schools are in the red as much as Essex is either.

For the hell of it, I google Essex and the year 2014, the last time their net income wasn't a negative number. The first hit I get is a story I've heard before and forgotten. A junior named Whit Vance supposedly abducted his girlfriend, also a junior, named Jennifer Hodge. Her father was a Maine congressman, Doug Hodge, who was sponsoring a bill for a wealth tax.

Wealth tax.

Jennifer Hodge was missing for a week, and when she mysteriously returned to campus, the whole thing was dismissed as drawn-out relationship drama. The wealth tax was never brought to a vote. Whit Vance left Essex—either quit or was expelled, it's not clear.

Suddenly, what Dahlia told Jeffrey comes rushing back to me.

There's some strange history to the school that could be linked to Society. Some kids who disappeared or something . . .

I had dismissed this as nonsense, a silly rumor. What if it isn't? Could that be possible?

If Essex—*or Society*—is into disappearing people, that would explain why we need to learn every nook and cranny on campus; why every bit of history, every building's security specs and layout, is critical. I have no evidence of anything, though. This is all conjecture. But . . .

Luke's words are haunting me: *If I tell you more, I'm worried it could . . . damage things.*

And Pinky's: *What's with you and Gretchen? I'm definitely interested in that.*

Society has become so much a part of me (it links me with Luke, and now my parents and their very well-being), doing this digging feels like examining my own blood work—and discovering something like a cancer, hiding. If I know something is sick, maybe I can find a cure. I just need to know where the malignancies are. I turn my focus underground.

I want to learn as much as Luke about the steam tunnels.

The late October colors heighten into a hazy golden light. Every day, it's like moving through a dream. Luke and I make headway with Faber, nailing down a preliminary time when we can make our first move. We need a place that's ours. It won't solve all our problems, but it'll make certain things a hell of a lot easier.

Luke and I can use our newfound skills, and our standing in

Society, to strengthen our relationship, literally fortify ourselves. We've never spoken about what happened at Hoyt again. It's not worth it for me to watch him unravel. *That's why I'm trying to find out everything I can about Society on my own,* I repeatedly tell myself.

Meanwhile, Luke does the sweetest thing. He gives me a wrapped box, *a care package,* which I'm only allowed to open when Thanksgiving break begins. Society hints at two major projects to come, which will formalize the end of Neophyte Process. Tath concludes our training.

Society hosts a Halloween party, what they call "our first official happy hour event," in a disused former cafeteria. The room is decked out in a 1920s theme. As usual there is plentiful amounts of champagne—and hors d'oeuvres. It reminds me of the first glimpse I ever saw of Society. But now I'm on the other side, looking out.

Marcus dresses up as Miles Morales. Isabella goes as A.O.C. Luke's costume is some sort of schoolboy, but then he announces he's Ki-woo, from *Parasite,* and everyone freaks. Nisha dresses up as Cheetah, Wonder Woman's nemesis. I go as Elton John.

"Thought you'd go as Huck Finn or the KFC guy," says Pinky, making a compelling Post Malone, face tattoos and all.

"Someone in overalls, drawling, covered in dirt, you mean? Stick to my roots?"

"Just joshin' ya," he says, trying to soften another of his cruel little jabs. "How are things going with Luke?" he asks. "I know you guys kind of had it out over at Hoyt."

"How do you know that?" Although, why am I even asking . . .

"People confide in me. Must be my honest face."

"That must be it." Anything I tell Luke he could tell Pinky. Is Luke really keeping me out of anything? Did he ever have the power to pretend otherwise?

"I hope you guys get into Faber soon. It'll be good for you two."

"I agree."

He leans in. "Give the natural history museum another visit. Go down." He shoots his hand at the floor. "The biggest secrets are always below, not above. Where everything begins. And gets forgotten. The sunken bottom layers. Think of this as a little gift from me."

"A gift of what?"

"Of information. Since I know how much you value *knowing everything.*"

I don't get a moment to reflect on his words or ask why he's giving me information. The party picks up. We toast to Society, dance to Ariana. And then I'm shocked to see Gretchen Cummings walk in the door and join the festivities. Except it's not Gretchen, not at all . . .

It's an SM, a junior named Hannah Locke. The resemblance is uncanny; the wig drives it home. She tells everyone she was fooling people all day; she even fooled Gretchen's own detail.

When I sneak back into my room later, Jeffrey is asleep. As I take off my costume, I notice there's something on my pillow. I switch on my reading light, tilting it down.

It's a single black rose.

There's an envelope beneath the rose. Damaged. Charred by fire.

I pick it up. It's not what I thought. It's *Luke's envelope*. His name is written on it, in silver ink. Someone plucked it out of the flames just in time. Luke told me his secret was about that guy Nick he used to be involved with. But when I rip open the envelope, scattering ash into the air, his secret is only four words long.

I am the wolf.

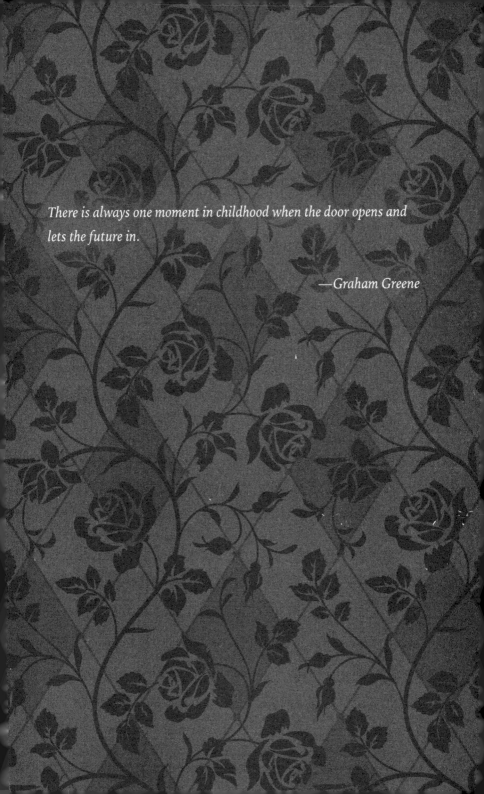

There is always one moment in childhood when the door opens and lets the future in.

—*Graham Greene*

PART THREE

VETERES

CHAPTER TWENTY-SIX

NORMAL ELECTRIC 62, ROOM OF MARVELS

NOVEMBER

My dad's haunted house, the one that caused all the trouble, was set up in an old Victorian. The place sat far back from the street with spiky dead trees on an overgrown lawn, covered in Virginia creeper, which in the fall looks like little red claws grabbing on to one another. When people in line reached the front, a group of two would be led inside to an entranceway— littered with foam gravestones, cardboard bats, spiders—cheesy drugstore Halloween decorations. People were already laughing, thinking it was going to be so lame.

Inside the entranceway, the pair would find another couple, the haunted house proper behind closed double doors. Two sets of chairs facing each other. The two couples would chat nervously as the wait stretched out.

Finally, the double doors would swing open, and a voice would call out: Only the first two people could enter the house. The first couple would bid farewell to the second couple and enter the house. But the double doors wouldn't close behind them. Instead, the main door, *the door to the entrance*, would slam shut, followed by the click of a lock turning.

The second couple would grow more and more concerned as bright light poured out of the open double doors, followed by the sounds of drilling, hammering, and the first couple screaming. The second couple, having no other option, would eventually venture farther inside. And the double doors would lock behind them. What they'd find inside was a space resembling a giant garage, not the interior of a house. And behind a wall of Plexiglas, they'd watch the first couple they had casually befriended only moments before getting chased, tortured, and killed by men in black leather smocks wearing welding masks.

"THIS IS REAL!" the first couple would scream, pounding the Plexiglas, before getting their arm severed at the shoulder by one of the masked men wielding a welding torch.

With all doors locked, there'd be nowhere to go, except to follow the line of Plexiglas, where couple #2 would watch couple #1's slow, painful demise, including a gory finale involving a meat hook and jumper cables.

The exit steered the sobbing, traumatized second couple several blocks away from the entrance, out of sight of everyone waiting to get inside, where they truly felt like they'd survived something. No one ever gave the twist away.

My dad is a goddam genius, I'll give him that.

"Well, this is our official Thanksgiving call!" says my dad.

"We're grateful you're answering your phone again," says my mom.

"The one we pay for," my dad adds.

"What are your plans?" my mom asks.

"Gonna chill," I say, stuffing my backpack with a water bottle and a hand-drawn map. "There are more kids on campus than I thought." This isn't true, there are less. And Luke was right about the Russian contingent, although they are insular as fuck. "What y'all doing?"

"Well, I wasn't going to make a turkey without you. Aunt Liz and Uncle Wade can't come down anyway, Liz is having back problems again . . . and, oh, who gives a shit, right?" I laugh in spite of myself, throwing a protein bar into my backpack. "Your dad's going to watch the game and we'll eat some fried chicken and miss the heck out of you, baby."

WEDNESDAY

Once the crush of final exams was over, I started planning every day of Thanksgiving break to a T. I even typed up an itinerary. The black rose, and the envelope, remain hidden under my bed. I don't know who left them there; I don't know what it means yet.

I want Luke to confide in me without confronting him. I feel like something will be forever broken between us if I'm the one to bring this up first. It has to be him who tells me he's the "wolf"—whatever that is. But I can't lie to myself and pretend any of this is okay.

The day is cold and clear, the sky a Slurpee blue, candied wisps of clouds in twisty shapes. A breeze ices my cheeks as I walk across the wide, empty lawns of Essex, wrapping my red wool scarf tighter around my throat. Most of the leaves have fallen off the trees; those left have muted colors: russets and dirty mustards, spotted with insect bites.

Strafton-Van-Wyke Museum of Natural History has normal hours, closing at five thirty.

I take my time through the Hall of Mammals. The dioramas are vigorously autumn-centric. One diorama is titled: "An October Afternoon on Kaitermink Mountain, in upstate New York," and has hefty slopes of trees glossed by ginger light and a winning slice of November-themed wildlife: ducks in a pond, deer, owls, rabbits.

The biggest secrets are always below, not above . . .

On the basement level, in a room of its own, I discover a giant wall-length oil painting by none other than Abe Cook. Cook was a soldier, aide-de-camp to Washington; he turned to the arts and became known for painting Revolutionary War scenes. There wasn't much of an art market in colonial America, so he struggled to find patrons. And as a member of the patrician class, it was sort of frowned upon for him to be an artist. He became Head of School late in life and founded the Cook Gallery, hoping to foster a love of the arts among students.

This painting is called *The Architects*, dating from 1815. It depicts a biblical deluge and what I think are Essex students (waistcoats, bow ties, vests) being washed away. There are skulls and bones stacked on the bottom layer of the painting. Alexander Essex, in a long, curly powdered wig, stands imposingly, literally walking on water, meeting the gaze of amorphous godlike figures forming through dark clouds.

Above the angry sky, there is a maze of shapes with writing on it, which extends into the background. The writing is familiar. It takes me a second to recognize Society's catechism, painted in script that appears to be glowing. I know those shapes too. I think it's an early map of the steam tunnels. At the end of the maze, there's a tiny flickering candle, like an *X* marking the spot, and some Latin. I step closer, my eyes inches from the canvas.

It says: *Coniunctio nobis semper perstat.*

Abe Cook is telling me where to go.

Alone in my room later, I update my hand-drawn map of the steam tunnels, filling in lots of blanks with what was in Cook's painting. I snapped a gazillion photos of it. I'd already planned to explore the tunnels on Thanksgiving, when I knew the campus would be dead, but now I have a specific destination. If I find the cancer, I can cut it out, I keep telling myself.

I also get to work on some other Society-related business.

Society announced we'd be focusing on two projects. One is called the Building Project. We each get to choose a building— one we had a tour of and a lecture about—to do a report on. This will be our final explo before we officially become Veteres. We'll get to show off our new skills and we'll have new choices in how we design the explo. We can go in with our Soulmate, or we can partner up with a different Neo—one whose specific skill set matches our intentions for the report. If I succeed, my chances of making Veteres are virtually certain. I cannot fail.

The second project is for the Annual Christmas Prank.

Every year, Society plans a prank right before Christmas. No one ever knows Society is behind them. Past ones include redirecting traffic from the nearby interstate through campus, turning the whole school into a honking traffic jam. Another year they snuck sheep, chickens, and bales of hay in overnight, transforming the lawn in front of Dallow into a farm.

We all get to pitch our ideas. The best one gets chosen. Dovetailing with my recent obsession of mapping out all the tunnels, diagramming the patterns of the aboveground steam grates for weeks (determined to best Luke's initial map and also inspired by something my dad used for one of his haunted houses a few years ago), I take notes in preparation for my pitch. If I rise to the top ranks of Society, I know my family will be safe. I cut a piece of cardboard, ripped off a storage box, with a pair of heavy-duty scissors.

I hold it out in front of me like a shield, practicing.

THURSDAY—THANKSGIVING DAY

Wearing a surgical mask and rubber gloves, I traverse the hot, steamy tunnels, my boots stomping through occasional puddles, stopping every few minutes to mark my spot, drink water, and update my map with colored pencils. According to my research, I should be approaching a section of the tunnels that isn't as well documented. When I reach the junction point, I see why. They are dark. Decommissioned. Holding the cardboard out in front of me, I discover one section is too dangerous to enter. The cardboard dampens immediately, right at the entrance, and in the near distance I hear a series of sharp, angry hisses. *Steam leaks.*

I mark this on the map. Thankfully, Abe is leading me to a different corridor, which while also decommissioned, feels cool and doesn't affect the cardboard. I venture farther, cautiously, *realizing I am right under Cook Gallery.*

The tunnel narrows into a crawl space. I aim my iPhone light in front of me. There are rooms beyond. The *X* on the map indicates that's where I need to go. I slither on my belly, snip away wire netting, and I'm in front of an entrance to a utility room with painted lettering above it: ROOM OF MARVELS— NORMAL ELECTRIC 62.

The piping is rusted. The walls are decayed. The cement floors are cracked, puddled in places with slime. There are thick cobwebs and rodent droppings. I take a heavy-duty flashlight from my backpack, shine it around, and see a painting.

The first thing I think is: *Where do I know this from?*

The painting is in a carved wooden frame, leaning against a red velvet curtain, which is draped across the wall. The image is of a muscular guy rowing in a lake against a cobalt sky. The canvas is warped, covered with curlicues of mold. I track the iPhone light across the floor. I left footprints in the dust. It's obviously been a while since anyone was in this room.

And then of course I know what the painting is: It's the one that was stolen from Cook in the 1950s. It's been here all along, in a utility room in the underground steam tunnels, right below the museum. *How is it possible no one ever found it?*

I crouch down. I pull my surgical mask up, take off my gloves, and touch the canvas lightly. There's a leather journal in front of the painting.

I open the journal, releasing a spray of dust. It's a diary. It hasn't fared much better than the painting, damaged by humidity, age, neglect. *Coniunctio nobis semper perstat* is scrawled on the first page in blue ink, and then a date. I read the first three pages.

The diary was written by an Essex kid named Oliver. He was in Society and had become Veteres. He dates each entry. He wrote the diary between 1952 and 1953. The pages are yellowed; the corners practically chip off in my hand; many are too damaged to read.

The diary and the painting are too recent to have been specifically what Cook was guiding me toward. And the lettering above the entrance is too new. There's melted wax hardened into drippy shapes around the edge of the curtain—the remains of candles.

The room is a shrine.

It's in an older part of the tunnels that may have been significant for Society, taking on different ceremonial purposes through the ages. I put my gloves back on. I take photos of the painting and the pages of the diary. Then I sit on the floor and read every page I can.

Oliver never gives his last name. He had a friend named Richard, also Veteres. Or . . . well . . . they were more than friends. The way Oliver describes Richard: "beautiful of body and spirit, a pure heart" and "a fine fellow, my friend for life" is sweet.

They stole the painting from Cook because "Archaei ordered it." Both, at the time of the diary's final pages, were being expelled from Essex. Because they were "discovered together in the bathhouse." Homosexuality was obviously viewed differently back then. Oliver and Richard were using Society to be together. Oliver quotes the Bible: *Behold, the lamb of God, who takes away the sin of the world—John 1:29.*

Oliver and Richard must have been sacrificial lambs. There's a passage where Oliver addresses a future kid who might one day find this diary. It reads like a warning.

> *And it could be you too, brother! Are you small, delicate, fair, queer? Did you wonder why they picked you? Did it seem like a miracle? Like a mistake? The wolf picks the lamb. They will use you to their ends, reaching backward through their youth, pulling the strings on their puppets, stuffed with straw and sapphires. Just like they did in '39. '42. '49.*

In the back of the diary, as if guided by Cook himself, Oliver drew another map. It appears to be an underground passage linking Franklin Hall and Memorial Tower. He scribbled the word *catacombs* along with another Bible verse: *For behold, I will bring a flood of waters upon the earth to destroy all flesh in which is the breath of life under heaven—Genesis 6:17.*

I think of the painting. The students being washed away . . .

I wish I had never found this.

The wolf picks the lamb . . .

I sit there, on the cold, dusty floor, for a long time, holding the diary. I thought if I knew more, I could cut the cancer out. Instead, I'm terrified I've found something inoperable.

Finally, I stand myself up.

I discover an unmarked door (that I can pick) right off Normal Electric 62. Based on the plans and the map I've drawn, I'm almost positive it will lead to the basement of Cook Gallery, meaning I can access it right now. The door is old; it's possibly how Oliver and Richard broke in all those decades ago. But I haven't cased Cook during its daytime hours, haven't studied its floor plans. I don't know where the cameras are placed, and it's sure to be heavily alarmed. I keep moving, heading toward another junction, where I hear rushing water.

The tunnel yawns into an underground stone aqueduct. Thin grates above stripe the lead-colored water with cold daylight. It's the tributary Luke was talking about; this must be the underground conduit. The current is surprisingly strong. I snap photos. There is a narrow walkway on the side where I emerged. I follow it, toward the light. I stop to update my map.

The walkway leads to a metal staircase, which takes me to street level. I emerge in a sort of subway station. The door locks behind me. There is no knob or plate, so this wouldn't present an entry point to the tunnels from this end. Only the other way around.

I'm on the edge of campus, right where I was yesterday, by Strafton-Van-Wyke. But I'm on the other side of the museum, facing the rear, by the flowing tributary. The tributary isn't exactly a secret; it's right there, but few people have probably followed its path the other way, as it continues underneath

Essex. It's mid-afternoon. The sky is bright, seagull gray.

I was underground for six and a half hours.

I spend dinner at Graymont, on my phone, eating dry turkey, reading about the art heist.

The painting is called *James Brackett*. It's by Thomas Eakins. It was painted in 1873. Eakins painted a series of rowing works, and this is considered one of his best. Brackett was a "champion of the single sculls." The painting is known for its vivid attention to detail: the muscularity of Brackett; the boat, oars, thole pin. The way wood looks in water.

A wealthy German art collector named Klaus Schulz was prepared to acquire it in exchange for a small fortune, bequeathed to the school. The school needed the money. Alumni objected. Schulz, inconveniently, had been a Nazi sympathizer.

The school decided to sell it to Schulz anyway. The funds went through. Then the painting mysteriously vanished en route. Archi had made a decision.

I try and find out about Oliver and Richard, but Google gets me nowhere, no matter how I order the keywords. It's too long ago, and probably something Essex swept under the rug.

I also google the years Oliver mentioned in his diary: 1939. 1942. 1949. But I can't find anything significant with a direct link to Essex.

FRIDAY

The next morning, I investigate the underground area indicated on Oliver's map, where it said *catacombs*. But the entryway he drew is now bricked over. It's been over seventy years; things have changed around here. I'll have to find another way in.

I meet Nisha at noon, and we head into town. A new escape room recently opened. You have to escape a meltdown at a nuclear facility. Nisha and I escape in record time. Holy hell, it's good to get out of my head. To celebrate, we go to Chester's Luncheonette, an old medieval-ish alehouse in a sketchier part of town. I'm halfway through my vanilla shake when I push my empty plate to the side and ask Nisha if she knows anything about *James Brackett*.

"Who?"

"The painting stolen from Cook in the fifties."

"I mean, I know the story."

"Well, I found it."

"What do you mean *you found it*?"

I explain about the Cook painting at Strafton-Van-Wyke, the hidden map, and how it led me through the tunnels, where I found the second painting, by Eakins.

"I know Cook's painting is at Van-Wyke because it's too big to put anywhere else. I never realized it was a map. You should not be going in those tunnels alone!"

"Did you know Society was behind the heist?"

"How?"

I explain what I found. The painting, the journal, the two boys who got expelled. I pick at my food. We're facing a gated parking lot: rusty barbed wire, homeless people pushing shopping carts. The contrast between this area of town and the Essex campus is striking. I never realized; I've hardly had much chance to roam. I wonder if Essex pumps any money into the town it occupies. "Pinky . . ." I start to say, *He was the one who provided the initial clue, to go down there,* but I have no idea why he did that yet, and Nisha won't know why.

Nisha speaks slowly, carefully. "You stumbled on a famous painting? That's insane! It's probably worth a fortune . . . I doubt you're the only one who knows about it."

"I left footprints in a thick layer of dust." But Pinky must know . . .

"My advice? Pretend you never found it."

"Right." But it's the information behind it, the story, that I can't pretend I never found.

"I don't know what the ramifications could be. It could hurt Society. Or Essex. Let the school deal with it. God, those two boys . . . that is sad." Nisha sighs. "I'm your Chronus. I will tell you with certainty I don't know of Society using sacrificial lambs. Lots of things were done in the past, all types of hazing rituals, that they don't do anymore."

Like being taken blindfolded to an island in the middle of the night?

"We've all gotten better."

"What is the wolf?"

"The wolf?"

"The wolf picks the lamb?"

"Where did you hear that?"

"In that diary."

Nisha shakes her head. "I don't know . . ."

"What's up with these catacombs?"

"I think they're red-flagged. Meaning no one in Society has been able to access them."

"Ever?"

"Yup."

"Wow."

"Cal, listen. If someone ever asks you to do something you're not comfortable with, come to me first, okay? Don't ever do anything you think is wrong. I'm only saying this because . . . I could have blind spots. Stuff I don't know. The Board may have their own secrets."

"Archi holds a lot of sway over Society?"

"Only Candace deals with Archi."

I remember that day at lunch, she and Pinky seemed pretty tight.

"She's in charge of financing. As far as I know, that's all they do. Fund our operations out of school spirit. Essex pride."

"Clayton Cartwright was at our Tap Night."

She seems surprised. "How do you know?"

"He spoke to us, remember? I recognized his voice."

"Archi does attend certain important ceremonial—"

"That was him—"

"I mean . . . I know he went to Essex, but I'd never believe a guy like that would be at Society's Tap Night. Are you sure?"

"You didn't know? That he was Archi?"

"No." She gazes out the window. "That's unfortunate . . . if . . ."

"If what?"

"If he is. He's not involved with his family as much as he

once was. But what can we do, really? The higher you climb, the more you're going to brush up against the shoulders of people like the Cartwrights, who did questionable things to attain wealth and power."

"I don't like that."

"Life is about compromise sometimes, Cal."

"What am I compromising, though? My morality? My values?"

"It doesn't mean you have to do immoral things yourself . . ."

Or does it . . . ?

I think about having Luke all to myself at Faber. And my family. Maybe I am willing to make compromises to get what I want. "Tell me about Pinky."

"We've been friends since freshman year. We all rushed together. Good guy, kind of a snot. Wealthy family from Marblehead. Legacy. Two older brothers. He has issues with his family, but honestly, who doesn't, right?"

"He seems weirdly close to Luke."

"Sometimes the CEO will take a Neo under their wing. Someone they think is troubled but has potential. Someone they think could be mutually beneficial."

Mutually beneficial? "In what way?"

"The Board starts searching for their future replacements early on. It's also probably a Pinky thing. Maybe Luke reminds Pinky of himself. Pinky's a bit of an egomaniac."

"Do those dates from the diary mean anything to you? 1939. 1942. 1949."

I'm surprised Nisha sits back in her seat so fast. Like I pushed her. "What?"

"Obviously, I've been in Society for a few years now, so I've learned a lot about the school and its history. I remember reading that in 1949 an Essex student went missing."

"Went missing? Who?"

"A junior. Big, important family. I think his name was Pine. Lyman Pine. I only remember that because it rhymes. Pine, 1949. They found him, unharmed."

"What was the story?"

"He disappeared one night from his dorm. Maybe one of those junior dorms by Pierson they tore down in the sixties? I can't remember. He returned a few weeks later. No one ever found out where he'd been; he wouldn't say. But this was a gazillion years ago."

I'm ripping my napkin to shreds. "It's awhile back, yeah . . ."

"They didn't know much about mental health issues back then. I think he had an older brother who died in the war. He could have been depressed, grieving. I doubt Society was involved, and if those two boys think Society was, they could've been wrong. If this was something that happened regularly, we'd hear about it."

"Jennifer Hodge?"

"That was her boyfriend, a romance gone off the rails."

Was it, though? Her boyfriend sounds like a lamb.

"There are rumors, you know. That Society is behind these . . . disappearances."

Nisha nods. "I told you. There's lots of crazy rumors out there about Society."

"What about those other dates?"

"Don't ring a bell." Nisha only knows so much, and that doesn't comfort me one bit. I didn't know there was such a dramatic hierarchy between the Board and regular SMs. They guard their secrets well. Nisha takes my hands. "You're going to make Veteres. You know that, right?"

That shouldn't thrill me as much as it does. Or even worse: comfort me.

"You want to proceed, right, Cal? You're sure that's what you want?"

I squeeze her hands. "I'm sure."

On my way back to Foxmoore, I decide Father's Office will be perfect for my Building Project. That's what it's known as colloquially. It used to be called the Barnfather Building. Now it's Essex's HQ for foreign languages. It's a beast of a place, an interesting bridge between Old Essex and Newer Essex, flush with historical quirks. I stop in front of it and take photos of its Ruskinian Gothic exterior. While I'm doing this, I realize how much I enjoy it. It chills me out, dulls the loneliness and anxiety that's always bloomed deep inside me.

"Look at you compartmentalizing," says Brent.

"It feels like a survival mechanism, if we're being honest," I say into my phone.

"Are we? Being honest? You can still walk away."

"Can I, though?"

"Those are patterns, Cal. You found patterns. You know that's bad."

"Not sure you get to take any moral high ground with me, *you ghoul*."

I make drawings and diagrams of Father's Office in a brand-new notebook to go along with my photos. Creating explos, and executing them perfectly, has become a near obsession—like my dad with his haunted houses. But my obsessions won't root me in place, where I'll bitterly spin my wheels. Society will take me forward. I think Luke is right. There are only winners and losers in the world. I don't want to be the latter.

But that doesn't mean I have to stop looking for answers either.

SATURDAY

I'd put an embargo on my phone for the duration of the holiday, and when I wake up, I decide to break it. It's been three whole days. I'm in the mood to hear about Luke's time at home, read his texts, and listen to my mom's voicemails.

After my phone boots up, I stare at the screen.

There's nothing. Nothing from anyone.

For a moment, I think about texting Luke, calling my parents. Just to get some connection, hear from someone. But you know what, *screw them all*.

There's a lot of stuff online about Chris Pine. Captain Kirk. Not as much about Lyman Pine. I might have to scour L&A and find old issues of our school newspaper, *The Daily Essex*, to read more. Except . . .

There is a lot of info about Lyman's father—Ralph J. Pine,

Essex alum, U.S. senator. Pine was named chair of the U.S. Senate Antitrust and Monopoly Subcommittee in 1948. A crusader against corruption, he took on the steel, automotive, and pharmaceutical industries.

At the time of his son's disappearance, Pine was investigating corruption charges among senior administration officials and members of the IRS, who were taking bribes. Lyman's dad was going after a lot of powerful people. Powerful people who may have been connected to Essex. Powerful people who may have wanted to send a message.

I think about Gretchen, and her dad currently lighting fires in D.C.

Still sitting in my unmade bed, I finally unwrap Luke's care package. It's a medium-sized box wrapped in silver paper. It is well curated. There's a graphic novel called *Bloom*. It's a gay coming-of-age story. On a flash drive is a JPEG of one of Luke's drawings: cotton-candy-colored headphones on a teddy bear with a link, written in big bubbly letters like graffiti, across the image. The link takes me to a mashup mix Luke made for me, uploaded to SoundCloud.

On the flash drive are also three photos of Luke giving me the finger. He's standing against a mossy tree doing it, standing against a fence doing it, and standing against a sunsetting sky, angled from below, the only selfie of the bunch. This makes me laugh. It's what Luke does during sex. He flips me off. Biting his lower lip, eyes scrunched closed, he'll flip me off. It's like him saying, *Fuck you for making me this vulnerable even for five seconds.*

He also included some candy. A map of the ornithology wing at a natural history museum in Cleveland. A London Underground Tube map. A guide to a national park in Utah.

And there's a gold envelope. Inside, a handwritten note:

> Moon Tears,
> I wish I was next to you. I'm writing this in the past, but I know when you read it, I'll be wishing I was next to you. I hate what's left of my broken family, so I know right now I'm probably miserable. Unlike you, I hate Thanksgiving. I'm sorry you're not with your own family. Read these things and eat this candy and listen to these songs and think of me.
> Love,
> Luke

I devour it all. This is what I do the rest of the day, while it rains. It almost makes me want to forgive him for not texting me this whole time.

And for all his secrets . . .

CHAPTER TWENTY-SEVEN
STRAW AND SAPPHIRES

SUNDAY

I eat an early dinner in the dining hall. There are a few more kids around. People starting to trickle back. I listen to Luke's mix while I eat a cheeseburger.

When I get back to my room, I nearly have a heart attack. I'm looking down at my phone, and for a second, I don't notice Pinky sitting on my bed, flipping through *Bloom*.

He's wearing a beige overcoat, gray pants, black loafers. We're not far apart in age, but Pinky seems decades older. Something about his bearing is haggard, burdened. He throws down the novel. "Whoops. I startled you."

I'm frozen in the doorway.

"Well, come in, come in," he says, gesturing. I step inside, closing the door behind me. "Got back early. My asshole brothers had to get to the airport, so I hitched a ride. I needed to get away. These holidays can drag the hell on. Luke says hi; he texted me an hour ago."

My mouth twitches. "He texted *you?*"

Pinky gestures to Jeffrey's desk chair since he makes no

move to get off my bed. "Have a seat!" Pinky gives me a heavy-lidded look. "You've been a busy boy this Thanksgiving."

"You wanted me to find it. Didn't you?"

He feigns innocence, throwing his arms wide. "Find what?"

"Show you I could do it. Show you my commitment. My nerve." *Fortune favors the bold.*

"Commitment to what?"

"To whatever you're going to want in return. Right?"

He leans toward me. "We are their puppets. It's true. *Stuffed with straw and sapphires.*"

Blood drains out of my face. Nisha couldn't have told him I found the stolen painting.

"You and I," says Pinky, wagging his finger at me, "are going on a stroll."

As we pass Strauss, Pinky can't help but lecture. "You found the Solarium. But if you ever return for an explo and *go down*, you'll encounter staircases with white marble banisters, the complex of rooms that hold old trophies, an impressive array of flags, an old squash court. Manly sporty stuff! Figural reliefs of athletic nudes in lunettes over the windows."

My way of seeing has changed. I can now describe Strauss as a "beleaguered citadel." I see "patterns of urbanism," I know which lecture halls have a "low mass of heavy masonry," which exteriors have "seam-face granite with limestone trim," or note a series of triple lancet windows that "recall the Romanesque fabrics of England."

We stride into Garrott. There are a few kids bouncing a

basketball in the Garidome. "Hello, boys!" Pinky calls out. They all wave back, indifferent. No one notices us enter the basement, without gloves, a mask, cardboard, or a map.

Pinky heads deep into the tunnels with a grace and confidence that's impressive given how much work it took me to map out what I don't even think is 75 percent of the whole system.

Pinky doesn't remove a single layer of clothing, and he never breaks a sweat. He makes quick, sharp turns, easily avoiding the decommissioned corridors. Before I know it, we're standing in front of the Room of Marvels. He took an easier, quicker route.

Pinky fishes out a Ziploc from his messenger bag as he leads me into the room. Walking backward, he flips on a key-chain light, aims it down, and sprinkles dust on the floor from the Ziploc, covering up the footprints I left. "See the trip wire." He points down. There's a thin wire buried in the dust.

"Yeah."

"Well, you tripped it. That sets off all the hidden cameras." He points at the walls, but they are in fact hidden, and I don't see them. "Which in turn activates a home security app only members of the Board have. There I am at home, eating chestnut soup, listening to my dad drone on about the price of tea in China, and I get a notification on my phone. And in night vision glory: your little determined face!"

"Shit. Sorry."

"Hey, I'm the one who guided you down here. It's been a while since someone made it down this far all by themselves. Obviously, we know about the diary; we know about the painting. We leave it here, as is. A sort of tribute to the past."

"What kind of tribute?"

"Well, this is the room where Society holds the annual ceremony to pick our sacrificial lambs. It's very witchy, we all wear hoods. That's why the painting and diary are still there."

Oh. "Am I . . . uh . . ."

"No, no," says Pinky. "You're not the lamb! *Obviously.*"

Is it obvious? I feel a rush of relief, and then guilt that I feel relief. "Who is it, then?"

"We pick a tracker early on. The tracker is our wolf. The wolf picks the lamb."

He didn't exactly answer my question. "Luke is the wolf."

Pinky registers absolutely no surprise I knew that. "You're not meant to understand everything at once, ol' chap."

"Right, but I want to understand . . . like . . . *something?*"

"Come!" We head down another corridor, make a right, a left, and then Pinky approaches a door I never saw. He easily picks it and then we're inside Cook. I was right about being underneath it. I was just at a different entrance.

We're in a newly painted stairwell, a metal door at the top. "No alarm will sound from this access point," he says. "You need this to get inside the museum proper." Pinky waves a key card in front of a scanner beside the door. It clicks open, and we're inside. "The cloned RFID frequency gives me access. The security system recognizes me as higher-up security personnel, so nothing will sound. If it was the wrong frequency, the wrong scanner, the silent alarms would notify the police and we'd be immediately locked inside. I'm CEO. I have privileges."

"Aren't there cameras?"

"Of course. But no one's going to review the footage unless something happens. And they'd see me. They know me." He waves at a camera. "I know where all the bodies are buried. I could take anything off these walls. They'd probably just ask me really nicely to give it back."

Bodies, huh? Here we are, standing in a museum at night, surrounded by priceless art, so I don't doubt him. The lights are at a twilight setting; fixtures aiming bronzed beams onto the Hoppers, Gainsboroughs, Turners. Sculptures too. Ellsworth Kelly. Rauschenberg. Serra. I'm embarrassed I've been at Essex for months and haven't been here. It's a major destination, beautifully designed. A white rotunda; giant circular skylight at the top, casting down rays of moonlight flecking the walls.

Pinky gazes at a Seurat. "Essex itself is pointillism. From afar, it's a ravishing composition; look closer and it's a chaotic mess." He laughs to himself and sits on a bench facing a Degas painting: little-girl ballerinas with grotesque faces. His hulking build is a comical contrast to all the delicate beauty. I sit beside him. "Cook bequeathed his historical tableaux to Essex in exchange for an annuity, and the first major art museum at a prep school in the history of the country was born."

"Why are none of his paintings here?"

"They used to be. Essex likes to erase its past. The school's Puritan founders were unsettled about the arts invading their devoutness. That's probably why this building used to have a theological lecture room. A little yin, a little yang, eh? But Cook's paintings had their own purpose: stirring up patriotism in the students, which was in itself devout."

"Love of God and Country?"

"Right. And if you're wondering about the tomb-like quality of the building, Cook is buried under the stone flooring, along with his wife."

I think of *The Architects*. And my feet sinking into the soggy ground . . .

Pinky shakes his head. "So many sacrifices made so we can sit at those polished Harkness tables and chat about Hemingway."

"What do you mean?"

"Granford was founded by clergy to train ministers. It was about maintaining this Puritan religious orthodoxy. But, after a few decades, they needed money for new buildings. They hit up wealthy merchants and went all in with Alexander Essex, a governor with the British East India Company. He gave them goods, which they converted to pound sterling. The school was born but the world was changing."

"You mean the Enlightenment? The Great Awakening?"

"Yes! Granford was erased and became Essex in 1777. There's always compromise when money is involved."

Luke already figured that out. "What are we doing here, Pinky?"

"You don't like fine art?" His tone softens. "Luke's an artist, after all. He got you that present. That's a big deal, eh? I think it is, anyway."

"You're in love with him, aren't you?"

Pinky throws his head back and cackles. "You think it's that simple?"

"If it isn't, then tell me what it is."

For the first time ever, Pinky seems the tiniest bit vulnerable, and I think I might be right. "That stabbing he told you about? He wasn't kidding. He was on his way to juvie."

"I believed him."

He flexes his fingers. "It was a bad sitch; got in with these violent urchins he took up with on the streets. Poor kid. His home life . . . is . . . rather unstable."

"He went home for Thanksgiving."

"He didn't listen to me," Pinky mutters. He leans forward and rubs his hands together in the tight space between his thighs. *Chssssh. Chssssh.* I wince; I've always hated that sound. "I lifted him out of it," he says. "We did. Society. It's how we operate. We find kids we can help."

"*How?*"

"If I could tell you more, I would."

"What exactly does he owe you?" I ask, remembering Luke's specific use of that word.

He straightens up; his whole face is different, cracked open like an egg, displaying a salty leer. "Everything. I'm owed everything."

I'm beginning to understand why we're here. Pinky is showing me what he can do, what Society can do. Infiltrate. Get in anywhere. Do anything. He wanted to prove that to me.

"Why did you leave me that envelope with his secret?" Because now I know it was him.

"Everything we do, everything we are, is sheathed in secrets. It has to be, of course. But it's hurting you both. Nothing kills a burgeoning romance faster than secrets and lies."

"Why do you care about us?"

"I want you both to be happy. That will only strengthen Society."

"You're hurting us more than any of our own secrets are."

Half his upper lip snakes upward. "Is that so? What do you think I'm doing?"

"Manipulating us."

"You know the dangers of juvie more than anyone, right?"

I let out a high-pitched laugh at his wild, pointed left turn. "Um, what?"

"I mean," says Pinky, "you know what can happen in those places . . ."

"You told Luke about . . ."

"I didn't realize he didn't know! Luke says you still talk to him!"

I stand up, breathless. I can hear my pulse swishing in my ears. "You told him."

"Easy, buddy," says Pinky, like he's calming a horse. "I have to let you out of here. There are too many secrets strangling us. It weakens our bonds. I see good things for you, Cal." His ring flashes, that violet amethyst. "I'm counting on you. So are your parents."

It's coming. What they're going to want. It's coming soon. I did find patterns; they were real. And then it hits me: Gretchen Cummings is in danger. And there's nothing I can do about it. I have no evidence. In actuality, *it's only a theory*. I'd look like a madman if I warned anyone.

And the school already knows I have PTSD. That I have mental health issues . . .

"Why do you still talk to Brent Cubitt?" Pinky seems genuinely fascinated.

I blink rapidly. "Because he . . . hurt me . . . so badly . . . I'm not crazy, man . . ."

His eyes sparkle, razor blades reflecting a house fire. "In this strange way, Cal, I think you're the sanest one of us all."

"It was my way of . . . dealing with . . ." I can't stop circling my hands around.

"Rather morbid, I must admit. But I don't know, I can't say, how people deal with trauma. This is your way, I suppose. But the cat's out of the bag now. Luke's going to want to know why you still talk to the boy who hurt you so badly. The very same one who was stabbed to death at a juvenile detention facility ten months ago."

CHAPTER TWENTY-EIGHT
CLOSER

"They were going to find out eventually that you talk to ghosts."

I pace my empty room in a fury, illuminated solely by the buzzing fluorescents of my desk underlighting. "Archi must fund the school. Essex wouldn't be able to operate in the red for this long otherwise. Archi must have offshore accounts, secret trust funds, shit that wouldn't be listed on an IRS filing. And I'm guessing when Archi wants something that will benefit them financially, all they do is ask."

"You should be relieved, Cal," says Brent. "They're offering you a way to fix everything."

"I don't feel relief."

I haven't figured out why Essex spends millions every year on whatever "recompense" is. But this is how Society draws you in. It's not what Nisha said. They don't ask you to do something you're not comfortable with—they ask you to do something they know you can't refuse. They remove the option of choice.

I stand over the sink and wash the acrylic part of my prosthetic eye with baby shampoo. This was why I requested a room with a private bathroom (the size of something on an aircraft carrier, small sink and toilet), why I wound up at Foxmoore. The irony of Pinky lashing out at all the secrets while only facilitating them will never be lost on me. But Pinky likes games. He has two sides as well.

Don't we all . . .

I wash my eye socket with a warm washcloth. When my eye socket and the prosthesis are both dry, I pull back my upper eyelid, follow the markings so I don't put it in upside down, and replace my eye, pulling my lid back down over the prosthesis. I used to need a suction cup to do this, which also needed to be cleaned, but I don't use it anymore.

Luke finally texts me, a single word, at midnight: *back*.

I see it first thing in the morning, our first day of classes after Thanksgiving, along with a second text asking to meet later in his dorm. Vlad will be gone all night.

"Did you like my package?" he asks as I walk through his door.

"Yes. But you didn't call me once during break."

"I'm sorry. Shit at home. I did some thinking. About us. It was an introspective week."

I lean against the door. I wait for him to say something awful: He doesn't feel the same way anymore, he's into someone else, this is over. Luke, sitting on the edge of his bed, sighs heavily into his hands. "I guess I caught feelings, Lonely. I needed some distance to understand them better. I couldn't stop thinking about you, and when I did, it wasn't generalized you, it was little things. The way you blink your eyes. The way the knuckles on your right hand are a little dry. What you said when you saw my art. I love you. I really do."

"I love you too." God, it's always so good to hear him say it.

"My dad took away my phone after I punched him in the head."

"Why did you punch him in the head?"

"Because I brought one goddam Moleskine home. He found it and tried to throw it out. He hit me first!" Luke tilts his head to the side; there's a cut over his left eye. He takes his shirt off; his arms are covered in bruises. "This is from him grabbing me."

"Why did you go home? You could've stayed here with me."

"No. I couldn't. I'm beholden, remember?"

"I don't like you getting hurt, and I don't know what to do."

Luke stares at the floor for a long time before he says, "It's okay, come here."

I walk over and sit next to him. Luke rubs his hand up and down my leg.

"I know what Pinky told you," I say.

"I know what Pinky told you."

"I want you to say it."

He doesn't look at me. "I'm the wolf."

"Who's the lamb, Luke?"

"Not you. I swear."

"But—"

"That's all I can say. Please?"

"Doesn't it bother you?"

"Yes. But it's tradition. I don't have any agency. I can't walk away."

Neither can I.

"I want to know—"

"I don't actually hear Brent's voice. I don't hallucinate him. It was a way of . . . *dealing*. He was all I could think about for a long time. I kept seeing his face. I only said, like, ten words to Brent in both our lifetimes. We weren't lovers and I didn't love him."

"Okay."

"I was in therapy, but instead of talking to the therapist, which wasn't helping . . . I started talking to Brent. Asking *why*. And then, in my head, anyway, he started responding. He became, in this way, less evil. And it made me feel less lonely, less of a victim, to . . . berate him. Get him to say how sorry he was."

"I see."

"You think I'm insane."

"Jesus, of course not. It makes me sad, though. That I was right. We're both haunted."

"You didn't know how right you were."

"I want you, Lonely. I want to be with you tonight, very close, and for a long time."

We're naked under the sheets. "Come closer," Luke keeps whispering. He holds me so tight, like I'm filled with helium and I'll fly away. I love the quirky things Luke does, like the care package. He's sweet to me, but it's always sly, a twist that could only be his. That's what turns me on the most about him, the clever, careful ways he shows his love.

"Closer," he says again, when I am so close. He pulls me in, incising the remaining inch.

When we're done having sex, we are never just done. We talk. Luke talks about shame. He says he's ashamed about being rejected by the people who are supposed to love him unconditionally. If they can reject him, anyone can.

I tell him it's okay. I kiss his chest. He says he has no one except me.

I ask him to stop talking about us with Pinky. He agrees.

"Don't give him anything you don't have to. No confiding in him anymore . . ."

The scrolls, the skulls, the codes, the keys. We both recite it.

Luke straddles me, leans over, kisses my mouth, my cheeks, my chin, my ears, suctioning me with his perfect lips, ending in mischievous little bites, while bracing me with his knees, as I tilt my head back and wish he could swallow me whole. "More," I whisper as he drags his tongue slowly down from the hollow of my throat.

And then we switch. I slide down his body, his eyes spinning, glinting, his mouth open and contorted in that fault line where pleasure looks like pain.

We fall asleep facing each other, our bodies linked by arms, wrists, ankles, his hand cupping my butt possessively. At one point, Luke turns over, releasing me with a damp squish of skin, murmuring, *Don't ever leave me, Lonely.*

Later, I wake up and the room feels strange. The door is wide open.

And there he is. Pete. *Luke's devoured twin.*

A kid who looks like Luke, hovering in the doorway—a living embodiment of his tag. He seethes at us, his envy electric, witnessing everything he could've had.

His head is surrounded by a film of particled gel. There's a chunk of flesh missing from his grayish neck. The outline of him glows an ectoplasmic yellow. We stare at each other in silence. Then I wake up without having been aware I was asleep.

Luke is sleeping. The door is closed.

I get out of bed and pad over to Luke's desk. No texts on his phone. I place my palm over his Moleskine, the one his dad tried to destroy. It's battered; I can't help imagining Luke and his dad wrestling over it. I open it. His art has a new intensity. The subjects themselves are similar—UFOs, submarines, monsters—but they're drawn differently; they practically vibrate. Luke's style is changing, his drawing more frantic. Like he's at war with himself.

I flip to the portrait of me. It's still strange to me Luke only drew this once, that there are no endless studies for it like with all his other drawings. The portrait is so different from the rest. My face has so much more emotion, but not happy emotion. I look tormented, betrayed. And he changed my eye; it's not normal anymore. It reflects Luke, like a hall of mirrors, ad infinitum.

Luke trapped inside me, a million Lukes inside my empty eye.

DECEMBER

~ B-ILDING PR-JECT UPD-TE ~
Pinky Lynch <PHGLynch3450@gmail.com>

To: SmellsLike@TeenSpirit.com
Bcc: neophytes@sose.essex.org

OEUE

Neos,

Your B-ilding Pr-jects will be due next month. This is the
final stage of your N-ophyte Process. The aim is to show
S-ciety the full extent of your newfound skills and the
implementation of all you have learned.

We want to see how you use:

• Your physical exploration skills
• Your access to all available resources for historical
research
• Your social engineering skills
• Your teamwork and individual leadership skills
• The way you structure your time

We want to see how you work wisely, efficiently, and
safely.
We want to see how an e-plo report can only be one
designed by YOU.

Get to know your b-ilding! Gain the trust of its occupants:
s-curity, faculty, students, etc. Approach your b-ilding as a
puzzle that can be solved. We want to understand the
thought process behind your reports.

Use LADID! We cannot stress this enough. If you choose a
newer b-ilding, we want to know about the site itself. It's
not just about what currently exists but what once
existed. We have EXTREMELY HIGH expectations. You have
all worked hard and that has not gone unrecognized. But
we expect nothing less than the best. We put our faith in
you. Prove to us we made the right call.

Make sure to visit your b-ildings before Xmas so you can create a plan. (SEE ATTACHED PDF RECOMMENDED TIMELINE.) Understand the s-curity layout, how you'd social engineer your way in or out of the b-ilding. Classes resume Jan. 9. Your reports need to be emailed by Jan. 18. You will present your pr-ject to S-ciety Jan. 21. Be prepared to explain methodology, expand on your historical research, and answer questions. This presentation will determine if you make V-teres. Show us what you can do. May the bar only get higher.
Ovid: "Perfer et obdura"

WLM,
PkLh, TaK, CsR, MaJk, HgFd

CNSP

"Congrats, Lonely!" says Luke. "Your idea deserved to get chosen. It's so fucking fly."

For the third time in a week, we're sharing a lamplit table in a far corner of the library. It's become a convenient place for Luke and me to meet and discuss our side project: the hidden, forgotten Latin library at the top of Faber Hall. We've been squeezing in these sessions between classes whenever we can.

Luke's soccer season has ended, but since we're on the cusp of a breakthrough with Faber, and with the holidays approaching, we've elected to hold off on any more intimate encounters in Luke's dorm until we're back in January. Plus, Vlad's field hockey season has ended, so Vlad's been sleeping in his own bed again.

Society announced, after a careful evaluation of everyone's submissions, my idea for the Annual Christmas Prank was the one they decided to pick. It's a huge honor. I know it was a cool idea. I had competition, but I can't help thinking how my relationship with Pinky probably influenced shit to go my way. It doesn't feel like a pure win. But still . . .

My idea involves Quikrete, access to the courtyard in front of Noyce via the steam tunnels, and a fun take on a traditional Christmas image.

Luke points down at our mess of plans, diagrams, stairwell maps, faded blueprints. "Let's infiltrate Faber's basement right before break."

I consult the school calendar on my phone. "The eighteenth?"

"Yeah, we'll need access to this utility closet first." Luke points at the documents we sourced from LADID. "Copy the key to the elevator. Replace the key, get to the top of the tower. This pit house is where we need to get." He taps the paper. "The staircase won't take us to the roof. It should be fairly easy to get in between three and five p.m. on any weekday. Cameras?" He takes my hand underneath the table and interlaces his fingers with mine.

These small, furtive affectionate gestures of his get my blood pumping more than anything. "Faber doesn't have exteriors."

"Inside?" he asks.

"It's an old building. Only one in the entrance."

"We wait for a small group, then. Or even one kid to go inside. Or we can social engineer our way in if we need to."

CHAPTER TWENTY-NINE
CHRISTMAS

"Well, goddam," says my dad. "We used Quikrete in 2017 to make the exterior of—"

"I know. I remember that house. It wasn't very scary."

"Bite your tongue, boy."

I still haven't told my parents about Society. I told them I got selected by a student group to head up Essex's Annual Christmas Prank because my idea was the best. Not sure they buy it—my mom knew I was rushing a secret society back in September and that's the last I spoke of it. She hasn't pressed me for more.

Everyone's dad in the South is always obsessed with some old-ass diner they claim "has the best hot dogs," when they're just hot dogs. So here we are at Little Darling eating perfectly acceptable hot dogs while my mom has a doctor's appointment in town.

"Went off without a hitch?"

I laugh into my Coke. "Hardly. I told them to make the top removable. Didn't matter."

"School thought it was a bomb?"

On the morning of the last day of classes before Christmas break, everyone at Essex woke up to find a giant concrete present in the middle of Noyce Courtyard, wrapped in red-and-green Christmas paper, a bow on top made with real ribbon. It was partially assembled in empty basement spaces most of the students have never been to. It was carried in pieces through a system of steam tunnels most of the students don't know exist. And it was completed under cover of night, in the courtyard, with a coordinated field ops team texting codes to lookouts and decoys, who successfully diverted any school staff or security guards heading in our direction.

All the students and faculty, in the brief amount of time they had to behold our work, were delighted and flabbergasted. Then the police came.

"I mean," I add, "they know there's a Christmas prank every year."

"Cummings is in the news a lot these days."

"I guess, yeah, the school, the Secret Service, they're a little nervous."

The bomb squad swooped in. They determined it was innocuous. But their sledgehammers destroyed all our work within minutes. The present, in all its glory, only exists on Instagram.

Society, however, was overjoyed. It was planned brilliantly and completed successfully, which is what they care about most. It's how they judge the Neophyte class. We worked super well as a team. A lot of that is being attributed to me.

We had a massive party to celebrate, one of Society's "happy hours"; it was wild and rollicking and all I want to do is pretend it never happened.

"You're pushing food around the plate."

"Not hungry." I've felt off since I stepped off the plane. "How's Mom doing?"

"Doctors are optimistic. She's a strong lady."

I used to believe whatever my dad said unconditionally—that he was only telling me the unfiltered truth. But not anymore. When I first saw them at the airport, my parents looked tired. I was prepared for the worst. It had been months. Our Wi-Fi isn't good enough to FaceTime, and I was scared my mom would be disturbingly thin, but she looked better than I thought.

Our house, though, as if to offset everything else, was clean. Too clean. It's never been as clean and decluttered as it was when I walked in with my two duffel bags and dropped them by the kitchen door. The neatness freaked me out, my parents hiding their troubles, burying all the sadness and despair under Clorox and hyperorganization.

Society's Christmas happy hour was at the Veronica Inn, an old hotel from the sixties that they revamped while trying to hold on to the original vibe: blue-and-white patterned wallpaper, mid-century modern furniture sourced from local antique stores.

Society rented out an entire upper floor. We were celebrating the end of the semester and the success of the Christmas Prank. Something resembling a Viking horn was getting passed around a suite most of us were congregating in, filled from cloudy brown apothecary bottles.

I had many energetic, drunken conversations. I remember the act of talking, my jaw moving, making sounds, but not so much what I said or what anyone said. Pinky, in a dark pin-striped suit, giving me a bro hug. "Nice work. I'll check in with you over Christmas."

Later, noticing both Luke and Pinky had disappeared, I stumbled into one of the bedrooms, and there they were. Pinky, his suit rumpled and creased, leaning against a closet door, arms behind his head. The room was ransacked. Pictures torn off the walls, revealing wires like internal organs. Overturned lamps, shades askew, casting naked rays of dirty light in lopsided directions. It looked like there'd been a fight.

Pinky met my eyes. Without understanding what was happening yet, I remembered his words from the smug expression on his face, his pants pooled around his ankles.

Everything. I'm owed everything.

Luke on his knees in front of him. He turned toward me, mouth open, eyes washed out, leaving only this blank halogen stare. "Sorry," I muttered, closing the door quickly, telling myself, *We're all fucked up; no one knows what they're doing* . . . though I couldn't quite believe that. Pinky's mind was clear. It always is.

I wound up in another crowded suite. Everything was fuzzy. Everyone wired, drunk, splayed on sofas and piano benches, talking then nuzzling then kissing, a savage energy combining like loose twine into a tight ball. I tried to offset heartbreak and rage through my fog.

I remember wet mouths and tongues; the sharp nip of incisors when someone's aim slipped. People's hands on me: wrapped around my waist, against the back of my neck. I gave in. I didn't see Luke again the rest of the night.

We don't watch *It's a Wonderful Life* or *Home Alone* or anything like that around Christmas. Our tastes are more pulpy—we'll watch whatever's trending on Netflix. I'm watching *The Triangle* with my mom, a new reality show where a bunch of twentysomethings with vocal fry, beaded bracelets, and digital marketing jobs are living in this luxury building in San Francisco; they either have to fall in love with or vanquish their fellow competitors. It's dumb and empty, but also hard to stop watching.

In the middle of episode four, I lay my head on my mom's lap; she strokes my hair. It occurs to me this is what we all secretly want—the feeling of being protected, knowing everything will be okay. I wonder if we spend our whole lives trying to get this back again.

My mom stops stroking my hair and slides her hand down. "You're warm."

Standing in front of the bathroom mirror, I take my temperature. It's 101. I peel back my lower lip because my mouth hurts. There's a cluster of whitish-yellow sores.

Over the next two days my fever barely dips below 102. I have terrible body aches. My head pounds relentlessly. I assume this is the flu, except mouth sores—which are getting worse, my mouth is a livid horror show—aren't a common symptom of the flu, according to WebMD.

Every part of my mouth is affected. My gums are so swollen they protrude between my teeth. I have sores on the tip of my tongue, on the membrane *under* my tongue, the inside of my cheeks, my soft palate, my hard palate. "I think we need to see Dr. Duke," says my mom on the third day of this. I'm soaking through the sheets at night. I can only eat soup and barely that. "I want you to get looked at now before people leave for Christmas."

Dr. Duke calls a day later when he gets the blood work back. "You tested positive for a recent HSV-1 infection. Herpetic gingivostomatitis. I know, it's a mouthful. Pardon the pun."

"What is that?"

"Oral herpes. Usually, people get infected from kissing. Most people get exposed to HSV-1 early on, same virus that causes cold sores. But if you're exposed later, it can be brutal. Particularly if your immune system has been taking a hit. Under a lot of stress at school?"

I knew something like this was going to happen.

"I'm going to prescribe an antiviral and dexamethasone, an oral rinse. Unfortunately, the virus never goes away. It hides in your nerve cells. When you're under stress, it can replicate, so you'll have periodic outbreaks for the rest of your life, but they'll be less severe."

"I know my mom takes dexamethasone to combat the side effects of her chemo. So now we're connected through that. Am I contagious?"

"When the virus is shedding, don't kiss anyone. And avoid oral sex." I let that moment hang in the air for a second—my childhood pediatrician telling me to hold off on sucking dick.

Whatever deal with the devil I have with Pinky, my parents' troubles, Luke's betrayal at the Veronica Inn. I was waiting for this. My body's giving out.

Luke texted me a few times since we left campus for break; rando bullshit, never acknowledging what happened (and maybe he doesn't remember?), but I couldn't bring myself to respond. I don't know what to say to him yet.

I wake up one morning in a feverish state and hear Clayton Cartwright on the news again: *". . . the wealth tax would be a major societal disruption, we cannot allow . . ."*

"Turn it off!" I scream, Clayton's voice painfully loud, echoing in my ears.

A major societal disruption, a major societal disruption . . .

Our break is three weeks. Right before Christmas, I feel well enough to take brief walks outside. We live in a classic farmhouse with a high-pitched, slanted roof on a few acres of land. It's not as cold here as in New England. I pace our backyard in the mornings, a cup of peppermint tea in my hand, which soothes my mouth, wearing one of my dad's old fleece jackets.

One of these mornings, I get a call and hear a voice I don't expect. "Hey there, Cal."

I stop in my tracks. "Pinky?"

"What goes on down there at Christmas? I bet it's grand."

"In Mississippi?"

"I'm in Marblehead. Logan and Bennett are being their usual demonic entities. You know 'em? My brothers, they were at Essex. Ah, right, never mind, you're a transfer, why the hell would you know them? My parents dote on their every whim; the wicked nature of my family, I guess; was curious what you were up to, told you I'd check in."

I'm picturing Pinky talking to me from a wood-paneled study with round picture windows and lots of red-and-black tartan. His loneliness, however, sounds like the real deal. "My mom got us tickets for *The Nutcracker* at the McCarl Opera House."

"You have a local opera house?"

"Yeah. I was in a production of *Godspell* there my freshman year." My eyes shoot up to the periwinkle sky. I watch a cloud break apart.

"Sounds fun. Wanted to see how you were doing. I miss my Society kids when I'm home. Nothing makes me more depressed than being stuck with my family." I hear voices in the background like he's at a thing. "Luke made headway with Faber?"

"I'm surprised he didn't tell you. We got into the basement before break."

"You copied the key?"

"Yup. We'll be able to get into the library when we get back."

"Good. I'm going to need the two of you at your best. So it'd be great if you guys could patch things up."

"Luke and I are good. Keep your hands off him. That'll help."

"Your voice sounds weird. Your mouth is all marbled."

"Are we CLEAR?" My sudden ferocity surprises the both of us. There's a silence. I always assumed I needed Pinky more than he needed me, but maybe that's not entirely true. It takes two to tango, after all, and my high fever is filing away my reason. And my caution.

"I hear you." Pinky sounds oddly chastened, his voice low.

I'll be in a weakened state when I get back to school, which is unfortunate. I won't be at my strongest. Will I be able to kiss Luke again?

"That night got a little out of hand, right? We were all blitzed. Anyway. Excuses. Take care, Cal. Get rest, okay? We'll talk soon."

The next day, Luke texts me photos. The Statue of David. The Colosseum. What is he on about? Cathedrals. Piazzas. Then he texts: *Traveling thru Italy. Galleria Vittorio!* This is followed by a selfie: Luke grinning, wearing turquoise headphones, standing under a domed glass-ceilinged arcade.

Luke is in Italy?! I feel so removed from him. It's a horrible feeling.

I go see the kids of the McCarl Dance Company perform *The Nutcracker* with my dad at the opera house after he gets back from the pharmacy. My mom claims she's tired, which is what she always says when she's feeling sick; she downplays everything. But she didn't want us to miss the performance. The show is festive, but I can't focus. Why wouldn't Luke tell me he was traveling abroad? After the show, we go to my dad's second-favorite place to eat in McCarl: Marianne's Oyster House.

"You sure you don't want any oysters? Just soup?" my dad asks.

"If I wanted oysters, I would've ordered oysters."

He forks a fried oyster into his mouth. "You're rail thin. Your mom's worried."

"I'm fine."

"I know you're not feeling well. But it looks like something deeper is eating away at you."

"I said I'm fine."

"Everything okay at school?"

"Everything's grand." God, I sound like Pinky.

"Are you angry at me?"

I eye him. "What would I be angry with you about?"

"You tell me."

I wipe my mouth. Blood smears across the back of my hand, onto the napkin. Sweat trickles down my temples. "Not angry."

"You should be ashamed of yourself." A smoker's rasp.

There's a woman in front of our table. She has a ruddy, bunched-in face, short permed white hair with split ends. "What you did to that poor man. Y'all are in league with the devil. *I hope you rot in jail.*"

"If you'll excuse me," says my dad, his tone minced and sharp as needles, "my son is home from school and we're having dinner. You can take your Jesus-loving bullshit out to the parking lot and all the way home with you."

"You don't know Jesus," the woman growls, stating the obvious. I'm worried she's going to spit into our food. She's wearing a cowboy shirt with rhinestones and pockets that snap, tucked into high-waisted jeans.

"I believe you're right," says my dad with a warning tone. "Now scram."

She gives us one last scowl and vanishes. As soon as she does, I go back to my clam chowder like nothing happened.

My dad takes a breath. "We've got some enemies in town."

"You mean *you've* got some enemies." My dad is literally facing *time in prison*. I'm not fully comprehending that. I don't know how he's coping. He sure as hell doesn't deserve what's happening. Neither does my mom. And my dad doesn't want me to know—because he's ashamed. "You wouldn't keep anything from me, right?"

My dad chews his food, his forehead creased. "Like what?"

I drop my spoon. "I should probably tell you. I'm gay."

He stops chewing and squints. He looks older; it's the lines around his eyes. He displays zero emotion; they probably already knew, and nothing like this would bother my parents. He finishes his oysters. "Well, I'm glad you told me."

"I am too. I hate secrets."

"Good thing you waited till the Square Dance Jesus Freak fucked off to tell me, or her head might've exploded." I laugh a little. My dad pushes his plate away. "You're still my son."

"Well, not sure who else's son I'd be."

"Just saying, we love you, no matter what. Find someone who makes you happy."

"Yeah." I rub a hand down my face. "Let's get out of here?"

He nods. I signal for the check. He grabs at his pockets, feels around the booth, and curses.

"What? Your wallet?"

"No. Goddammit. Your mom's meds. I left them at the theater."

"What?"

"Bag I had from Walgreens. Stuffed it under my seat—"

"You left opioids out in the open?"

My dad's face reddens. "We're not all the hicks you think we are out here. Don't get too uppity spending all that time in Connecticut."

"Let's drive back to the theater."

"It'll be closed. I'll have the pharmacy refill the prescriptions—"

"They won't just refill a controlled substance; it'll take time to get authorization—"

"Calm down, Son. I'll get on the phone with Dr. Evans in the morning—"

"Except Mom is in pain *tonight*—"

"I'll take care of it."

"No. I will."

I get out of our white Nissan and slam the door behind me. My dad jogs after me. The building is dark. I don't attempt the doors up the main steps; there's an exterior camera. I case every place now; every room of any building I'm in. It's become second nature. These old buildings in the South don't have state-of-the-art security. Only the banks do.

Darting between parking lot lights, I make my way to the side of the building, where I'll have more luck. "Give me your ticket stub," I say, moving forward, reaching behind me. My dad stuffs the stub into my palm. I approach the side door. There's no exterior cam at this entrance, and no interior cams inside the building. The door is locked. "Cal, I told you, the door is—"

"Sssh." I put my ear against the door and picture a map of

the interior; the layout of the building gaining depth, like I'm running 3-D modeling software in my brain. I note the aisle and seat on the ticket stub. I won't have a lot of time, so I plan the route before I take the key chain of picks out of my pocket. We're not supposed to carry these around with us, and especially out of state. But I bought an Essex key chain and keep my picks on it now.

I examine the door and turn the knob. It's locked. I select the appropriate pick.

"Cal. What are you doing?"

"Wait here by the door. Hold it open. When I come out, we'll need to move q—"

BRRRRRIIIIIIIIIIINNNNNNGGGGGG!

The alarm is loud enough to wake people three towns over. I got it open in eight seconds.

I make my way into the auditorium, which is darker than I thought, but there's dim floor lighting. I find our seats fast. I hope the bag is still there. When I reach under our seats, there's nothing. But when I grope around underneath the seats in front of ours, I grasp plastic; the floor of the theater slopes down, and the bag got caught beneath the seats of the row ahead. Untangling it takes long enough for me to come up with a social engineering lie in case the police are faster than I think they'll be. But they're not.

I fly out the side door a minute later. No cams anywhere; no one will see what happened. My dad chases after me, holding his ears, as I head back to the car, a safe distance away.

"Jesus, Cal!" says my dad.

"Done and done," I reply, throwing him the bag.

I find myself driving by the highway overpass on the way home, which holds so much weight in my memories, that same rusted chain-link fencing entangled with dead weeds, shot through with beams of passing headlights. How is it possible that hideous spot and Essex's Letters and Archives Room both occupy the same planet? The same lifetime?

We sit in our driveway for a moment. "Did you break into that building?"

I grin at my dad. "Yeah, I did."

"No normal club at school is going to teach someone how to do that."

I almost laugh at *normal club*. "I'm going to fix everything."

"I'm proud of you. You're doing well at school. You're finding yourself. But you need to focus on *your* life, not ours."

"We're a family."

"Your mom and I can take care of ourselves. Everything's going to be okay."

Liar. "I'm going to make sure."

"Cal, it's not your responsibility to—"

"I said I'm going to take care of it! Things are not okay. Stop pretending they are; I'm not a little kid anymore. Certainly, I know what life can be like, *what people can be like*. I know you sent me away so I wouldn't have to deal with this shit town anymore, but sometimes people need help. I can help." I get out of the car before my dad can ask me how. He follows behind me as I head inside; when I look over my shoulder, through the front door, I see his pale, distorted form swimming through the beveled glass.

"How was the show?" my mom asks as I hand her the bag of medication.

"Great."

"We need to see the ocularist while you're home, don't forget."

"Right." My fake eye needs yearly maintenance.

"You look like shit, honey." She kisses me on the forehead.

The rest of the night curdles around me. The house becomes a smear of colors and textures. The shirred silk of my mom's nightgowns draped over chairs. The mint-green Depression glassware on the shelves. The crushed velvet sofa in front of the TV. I'm out of my mind with fever. But I don't feel like quelling it with ibuprofen. I want to suffer through it.

After my parents go to bed, Brent Cubitt steps out of the shadows in the living room, standing in front of the window, blotted with chalky streetlight through the thin curtains.

"So what, you're a full-on apparition now?"

"You came home, so I'm closer, at least in spirit. Plus, your fever is spiking; might as well take advantage of your delirium."

"You sound farther away now. Your voice . . ."

"I'll be leaving you soon."

"Fuck you will."

"I'm getting weaker in your mind. And, c'mon, man, it's time."

"Fuck all it is. You don't get to decide that."

"I've never been the one making the decisions here."

I'm so dizzy I feel like I'm floating. "I drove by our old spot."

"Aw, I saw. What did you feel?"

"Nothing. I felt nothing. It was just a place. *I don't live here anymore.*"

"You came out to Dad. I'm proud of you."

"You don't get to be proud of me."

"You're real sick, so you better keep your wits about you and stay alert. Why do you think Pinky needs you to get into Faber so bad?"

"Luke wants it! Pinky thinks it'll help Luke and me—"

"Oh, please, you really believe that shit? Maybe you found a weakness."

"Pinky did seem weirdly remorseful about what happened with Luke. That's unlike him."

"He needs the both of you to get into Faber."

"If he cares about us so badly, why would he—"

"He likes to mark his territory. Maybe he does have feelings for Luke. Or envies what the two of you have. Maybe he can't help himself. But Faber could be a power play."

"I still don't get why you care?"

"I'm living vicariously through you. I was always dead inside, but now I'm dead for real. You're all I've got, man. Maybe in a different life, we could've been something."

I laugh acidly, all garbled. My mouth feels like barbed wire is unspooling itself from my throat. "I was sad and lost in this backwoods town. You're trash. You were always trash. You hear me? Trash! NOTHING BUT TRASH!"

But I'm yelling at the blank curtained windows. There's nothing there.

Later, I sit on the recliner, bathed in the electric-violet light of the fish tank, with my laptop, finishing writing up my Building Project on Father's Office, which I completed between Thanksgiving and Christmas. With everything going on, concentrating on Society-related stuff became the only balm I had.

The work made me forget about a lot of inconvenient truths: Nisha doesn't know what really goes on in Society, they do in fact use sacrificial lambs, people like Clayton Cartwright are involved, Society has a dark past (although, what doesn't?), and Luke is under Pinky's thumb.

The Fathers' Association, the wealthy dads and granddads of students who went to Essex throughout the ages, funded the most recent renovation of the Barnfather Building in 2016. It was led by a slate of wealthy trustees with legacies dating back to the 1890s. The building has become a symbol of the devotion alumni still have for their alma mater.

Devotion. That word, that idea, stuck out to me.

Besides detailing the building's illustrious history and describing the landscape modifications to the building's perimeter, I went into the mechanical system upgrades: the forty-ton air-handling unit systems, hot and chilled water coils, sixty VAV terminal units, the building's new energy-efficient automation system, feeding into Essex's main plant.

The explo involved a wide variety of skills, from social engineering (I familiarized myself with building staff so they'd get used to seeing me, which is how I infiltrated the building each time) to climbing, lock-picking, and avoiding motion sensors by mapping out their placement.

There was even a deus ex machina involving several attempts to enter an abandoned faculty billiards room from the thirties, which I wanted to photograph, through a door that could not be picked or shivved. But there was space underneath the door.

I partnered with Kip Spicer; he worked remotely with me, on his laptop. After I slid a small spy camera (which Society had on hand) under the door, Kip had a live feed of the interior. I snaked a coat hanger in, twisted into an L shape, hooking it onto the doorknob from inside, while Kip directed me, step by step. I opened the door using the hanger.

I title the project: *Daddy Reissues. From Charles Barnfather to Today—Two Centuries of Fathers.* The title might be my favorite part.

There was another reason I chose Father's Office for my Building Project.

In my initial research, I knew the Registrar's Office had relocated and expanded onto the fourth floor. I wasn't sure if I would find student records there, especially ones dating back decades. But it turns out there was a storage room the whole length of the floor filled with filing cabinets of old records, on every single student going back to the early twentieth century—exactly what I needed. It was a lot, but I didn't let it overwhelm me.

I knew the years I needed to concentrate on.

CHAPTER THIRTY

FABER

My parents aren't sure I should return to Essex for the first part of winter semester. I'm still pretty sick. But I insist, mostly because I have to defend my Building Project in person, which, thankfully, goes well. But I spend January lying low.

I ignore Luke for most of the month, barely answering his texts, which delays our Faber excursion. I'm clearly sick, so I have that excuse, but I'm also pushing back a bit, and Society knows it. I don't want Pinky manipulating our relationship anymore. I have power too, and I flex it, but it is a small flex, which is all I've got. Then three things happen.

The first is Daniel Duncan: cute, freckle-faced Neo gets busted by campus security for trying to lock-pick his way into a side entrance of Quinlan House. He gets put on disciplinary probation, which includes an in-school suspension. Society informs us, via email, he'll no longer be in contention for Veteres. Holy shit. Daniel will have that scar for life reminding him he failed to make Veteres. I wait to see if there will be some sort of fallout; if Society will be blamed, if one of us, a sacrificial lamb, will take the heat, but none of that happens. Society reminds us to always be discreet and take calculated risks.

The second thing is I fuck up a chem test, which threatens my GPA. This shocks me; I am the very definition of a straight-A student. But when Dr. Lichtfield hands me my test back, it's a mess. I can't remember inputting these answers, but my brain is in such a cloud I barely remember studying for, or even taking, the test at all.

Dr. Lichtfield, given my illness, agrees to let me retake it, but paranoia invades my thoughts. Somehow, both the chem test and Daniel getting kicked out of Society feel like direct warnings—that Society has the real power. Is that possible? *Or rational?*

The third thing is, while Gretchen's dad is on the news pretty much constantly now, rumors spread that she's getting fed up with her Secret Service detail suffocating her, and they're going to scale back. This could present a soft spot if something were to go down, but I can't let my mind go there. The threat is too formless! And I haven't seen or talked to Gretchen in a while. As January ends, my fever finally dissipates. But I'm still waking up with this icky lingering malaise, and there are new mouth sores that greet me every morning.

FEBRUARY

~ AND HERE WE FINALLY ARE ~
Pinky Lynch <PHGLynch3450@gmail.com>

To: PourSomeSugar@OnMe.com
Bcc: neophytes@sose.essex.org

OEUE

Neos!

The time has come. Tonight, you shall appear in the K-ot
G-rden at 11:57 Post Meridian. Dress to the tens. Wear
shoes made for mobility. Make sure you have your
Neophyte k-y in your possession and the cat-chism on
your tongue. Be prepared. Be pleased with yourselves.
That is allowed.

WLM,
PkLh

CNSP

I used the entirety of my parents' Christmas gift card to up
my game with the formal wear. I'm also letting my hair grow
out. I may be sick, but I'm more dashing than I was back in the
fall, when all this started.

"Look at this drip," says Luke, flirtatious but cautious,
knowing he's on thin ice with me, as I walk into the frosted-over
Knot Garden (which is like a hedge maze's baby brother). There's
one behind Old Shaw, a fortress-like former gymnasium converted into senior dorms. Big-deal seniors live here. Kids of
prominent families. Kids with elected positions in student gov-
ernment. Pinky lives here.

French windows, with ornate wrought iron balconies, open
onto the sloping lawns of Essex. The eastern views, with rosy
morning sunlight sweeping in, are supposed to be incredible.

Once we all arrive, we're blindfolded and led away, broken up into smaller groups. We walk for about ten minutes, then go up a flight of stairs.

We kneel on a hard, cold floor, and then our blindfolds are removed. We're on the roof of St. Andrew's Clubhouse & Literary Society, the roof's perimeter surrounded by a stone balustrade, one of the most bizarre buildings at Essex, neither in commission nor being renovated. It just sits here, windowless and imposing, no one ever going in or out.

It was built by a sought-after Gilded Age architect, in the Moorish Revival style but with exotic twists (colored striped stonework, a patterned forecourt), completed in 1849, and known as the Tomb. Supposedly, the Literary Society was another secret society, left over from Granford. People say it's haunted, that bats live inside, that vampires roam its rooms.

Candles line the roof. Every single Society member is present. Tath gives a majestic speech about tradition and brotherhood. He's wearing a black robe over his tux and holds a staff. Each time he bangs it on the ground, someone calls out one of our names. We stand, recite the catechism, and approach Pinky, who's standing on a raised platform. He's decked out in a classic black tux and wears a silver masquerade mask. I don't see any members of Archi around.

"Do you accept full membership into the Society of Seven Eyes?" Pinky asks.

"Yes," each of us say. We hand our key to Pinky. Pinky gives each of us a new key and a pin with Society's crest; he sticks it onto our jackets and gowns.

"Everything will emerge from the shadows," says Pinky.

"Tier two of Society's database will now be unlocked," says Tath.

Pinky displays a velvet-lined box. Inside is a row of keys. "These are the master keys to Essex, in our possession for over a hundred years. All our tools are now yours. You are no longer Neophytes—you are now Veteres."

"Congrats!" the Board screams. Everyone cheers.

There is a gala afterward, in the Brookleven ballroom. And there's more than just caviar this time: food in chafing dishes; tuxedoed waiters serving us on porcelain plates.

Nisha gives me a big hug. "I knew you'd do it. I'm so proud of you."

"Thank you." We haven't had time to hang lately. I feel like I can only talk to Nisha about what I found in the Registrar's Office, which didn't factor into my explo report but has been quietly gnawing at me for weeks. Lyman Pine's 1949 disappearance wasn't noted in his student record, like it never happened.

In 1939 and 1942, the other two dates mentioned in Oliver's diary, I found something notable. When a student dies, the rest of their academic record is left blank with a line drawn through it and a red stamp marked DECEASED. There had been flu and typhoid outbreaks, but by the late 1930s it was not a common occurrence for kids to die on campus. But in 1939, and again in 1942, a student died.

No matter how hard I looked, though, I couldn't find any more information on them, not even a cause of death. There is no way those dates written in that diary could match two unexplained student deaths and mean nothing. It's too big a coincidence. But what does it mean? *That these kids got murdered?* It seems like a lot. But Society, and Essex, keep surprising me.

Nisha gets pulled away and Luke comes over. We've come full circle, it seems.

"Congrats on making Veteres."

"And to you," I reply.

"We need to talk."

I catch a glimpse of Pinky standing in the middle of a pack of drunken SMs, reveling. He gives me a juiced look and lifts his champagne flute. I nod back.

"Not here," I tell him.

Outside, it's raining. I stop by a large oak, which provides meek cover, and let Luke catch up. He moves in for a kiss, but I push him away.

"The silent treatment for a whole month? *Really, Lonely?*"

"Really."

"You like playing the victim a little too much."

I glare at him. "How dare you say that."

He holds out his hand. "Sorry. I didn't mean . . . it was wrong . . . what I did. But . . ."

"But *what?*"

"It was a crazy night."

"That's it?" Pinky said the same thing.

"All I can say is, I'm sorry."

"Are you involved with Pinky?"

He grabs my elbow. "No. *No.* There's only you."

I wriggle out of his grip. "Is he making you do things . . ."

"No one's making me do anything."

"Then explain what happened!"

"See, Lonely, you *are* a romantic. But life can't always fit into this perfect crucible of what you think it should be. You aren't owed glistening perfection forever just because bad shit happened to you. People aren't perfect, they mess up. This whole thing has been eating me up; I was a wreck all during Christmas; you don't even know."

"You looked tormented in Milan."

"C'mon."

"Why were you in Italy anyway?"

"Pinky sent me."

"What?"

"It's nothing more than what it is."

"And what the fuck is it?"

"Pinky just helping me . . . stay clear of my dad."

"Perks of being the wolf, huh?"

He moves in for a kiss again. I push him away. "I can't kiss you."

"What?"

Quietly, I tell him what's wrong with me.

Luke, undeterred, grabs the back of my head and kisses me. "I don't care."

"I'm probably still contagious." God, he feels so good, though.

"I've been desperate to kiss you for months. I'm not going to stop."

"Why does it feel like I'm also kissing Pinky?"

He recoils slightly but continues caressing my cheek. "Do you really?"

"He's hanging over us; he's playing both of us, man."

Luke shakes his head like he's physically shaking my words away. "Faber will help."

"What is your obsession with Faber? What is Pinky's obsession with Faber?"

"We'll be living together. It will be something that's ours."

"I think Society is behind kidnappings, Luke. Maybe even murders."

"Christ, Lonely. What rabbit hole did you fall into?"

I explain everything that I found.

"Oh, man," says Luke, looking away, shaking his head, "that's *so long ago*. If bad stuff happened like that regularly, *recently*, don't you think the whole world would—"

"I don't know." I can't pretend I didn't have the same doubts, even though it feels sinister. But I'm too weak to resist, argue anymore, or be without Luke. And he knows it. And Pinky knows it. Plus I have no real evidence of anything. "What happened with Daniel—"

"He got sloppy! He's having a thing with Ashley Rothman, who lives at Quinlan! Daniel . . . always seemed to me like someone who claps when he gets served pancakes."

"Luke—"

"He wasn't thinking with his head. He used Society to try and get some."

"Isn't that what we're doing?"

"We're not sloppy! Look, I don't want you sleeping alone

tonight," he says, knowing if I lose him, I'll drown. I'm in love. I tried to turn it off somehow, I tried to step back, and I got sicker and sicker. "Let's do Faber right now," he says, mischief gleaming in his eyes.

"*Now?*" I hug myself in the wet and the cold. "We won't get in, it's—"

"I think we might." And when he smiles, bright and burning, all I can do is agree.

"Finding and copying the key was half the battle," says Luke as we head to Faber. "We didn't know how to enter the building itself. I did some further reconnaissance and guess what? The key we found for the elevator is a utility key! It opens a side door. No alarm."

"You went into Faber already without me?"

"No, bitch, I waited for you, so we could do it together."

Entering Faber with the key we copied, I discover Luke already mapped out a clear, covert route to the elevator, through the winding basement. Getting caught isn't much of a concern anymore. Luke and I have never gotten caught doing anything. My curfew hasn't mattered in months. It's like we float above the clouds.

We successfully enter the library one hour later. It's ghostly and grandiose. The lights inside don't work, but light from other buildings shines through the windows. The teeming rain casts shapes over the walls and fireplace. There are books everywhere.

"Well, isn't this fucking fly," Luke says repeatedly, walking around, dazzled.

"Where are we going to sleep?"

"We'll have to—slowly—bring stuff in. Whatever we can find. Tonight's a start." We make a bare-bones setup on the floor while the rain trickles shadows down the walls like the room is crying. The wooden floor is dusty, so Luke lays a towel underneath us, and we use Luke's gym bag as a shared pillow, our clothes as blankets. We fold into each other.

"Happy seventeenth, by the way."

"That was last month. But thanks."

"Well, you were blowing me off. I got you a gift in Milan. But I lost it on the plane."

I laugh. "It's the thought that counts."

"I always think about you, Lonely Hearts."

I bury my head in his chest as he draws me in. "What was it?"

"What?"

"The gift."

"I'll never tell."

And I'll never ask again. "I love you, Duchess. You're the light that guides me; you manifest the words in my heart that write every line of my life."

Luke turns his head away. "Shit, that's . . . don't make me fucking cry right now."

"Will you be here when I wake up?"

"Of course. That's the point, Lonely. Now we have our castle in the sky."

In the morning, the sunrise erupts into the library, coral rays trapping swarms of frantic dust motes; we both wake up, groaning, shielding our eyes.

Over the next few weeks, Luke and I slowly furnish Faber with found objects sourced from empty dorm rooms, Sargent's props department, a linen store in town. I was worried about fitting the mattress we stole into the elevator, the most challenging part, but we're good at what we do now, and we managed fine. And then we made good use of the mattress afterward.

Tier 2 of Society's database was unlocked the day after we made Veteres, through an encrypted link. The database is impressive—a 3-D map of places on campus. Every location an SM wrote an explo for is pinned; if you click it, you can read the reports and download all accompanying materials, including maps, blueprints, assignment plans, photos.

Society encourages explo reports of any building on campus—even those previously explored, because something new is always discovered. Locations have a blue marker if they've only been explored once. Places that have never been explored are flagged in red. These include the interior of the Tomb. Various hidden libraries, roofs, sub-roofs, rare book rooms. A forgotten auditorium on the top floor of Cranwich. A moldering greenhouse, supposedly at the rear end of Bromley, that no one's been able to find.

The holy grail is "the 1752 Room," preserved as it was from 1752. It was accidentally walled off during the renovation of Franklin Hall. It's at the end of the catacombs, linking Franklin and Barry Memorial Tower. That's where I tried and failed to get in already. But there are updated plans uploaded to the database. I spot a different entry point.

Our next assignment involves completing an explo

partnered with our Chronus. I start taking notes right away. I've never stopped mapping out the tunnels. Besides our next assignment, everyone's eyeing a place on the Board. It's clear that's where the real power lies.

MARCH

Nisha and I turn in a much-lauded report on Bromley. Although we didn't locate the greenhouse flagged on the database, it was still a great explo, full of fun, left-field discoveries. We've both been talking about being the first to infiltrate the 1752 Room.

To keep up appearances, and not arouse too much suspicion, Luke and I decide not to spend every night at Faber—mostly weekends and one or two nights during the week. Luke was right; having our own place helped. It repaired what I was terrified was a growing rift.

School gets busy. I allow myself to forget about my grim discoveries about Essex's past, my troubles at home, and all the tangled shit with Pinky. I'm Veteres now. I feel shielded by that.

Things start to feel so routine that when Gretchen Cummings vanishes while heading back from the library, everyone isn't rattled so much as confused. She'd been ubiquitous lately!

We'd been seeing her all over the place!

But, as it turns out, that wasn't Gretchen Cummings we'd been seeing.

CHAPTER THIRTY-ONE
THE ARCHITECTS

The notification hits our phones while we're all in the middle of class. There's a collective gasp. A breaking news alert. A CNN reporter standing in front of the library dramatically intones, *This is the last place Gretchen was seen.* But the library has exterior cameras. No one who knows anything would snatch Gretchen from that location.

When another reporter, this one stationed in front of Dallow, says something similar, my suspicions are confirmed. There's a steam grate, one of our access points for the tunnels, right in the shot, along with a splash of color. I can't tell how fresh the paint is, but I'm guessing it's recent. My heart sinks as I realize what I'm seeing. He couldn't help himself.

Luke tagged the goddam grate.

It's been four nights since we've slept in the same bed; we don't have the same classes this semester. We've been leading parallel lives.

Luke never stopped keeping secrets from me. And he's not answering my texts.

I get one from Pinky, though:

Class meeting tmrw will b cancelled. They gotta figure out wtf theyre gonna do w investigators combing campus while keeping us focused and docile. Come see me at OS 9 a.m.?

Wheres Luke?

All good w me. See ya in the morn.

Pinky has a suite at Old Shaw that's something to behold. High ceilings, crown moldings. Shag rugs on hardwood floors. Antique off-white furniture with brass knobs, trendily distressed.

I'd heard about kids giving on-the-fly haircuts in dorm rooms, but Pinky seems to have formalized this. Tath sits in a barbershop chair, facing a salon mirror perched against an armoire. An apothecary table with jars of scissors and combs is beside them. Pinky, in a smock, wields a pair of shears. As he snips, tufts of hair float down, singed by the sunlight.

There is a turntable nearby, playing John Coltrane, perched on a mid-century modern walnut stand, with record albums underneath, spines frayed, as if he inherited the collection. Next to that is a bar cart chock-full of liquor bottles, crystal glassware, stainless steel cocktail tools.

"We'll be done shortly," says Pinky, as if I'm his next client.

Tath, in a white-and-red-striped barber cape, appears to be half asleep, a triangular chunk of wet hair folded over one eye. Pinky dunks the scissors around in a jar of Barbicide, then attacks another section of hair.

"Hannah Locke!" says Pinky, pointing the shears at me. "Remember Halloween?"

For a moment, I don't follow. But then, *of course*. I was bedazzled by Hannah at that Society happy hour. She went as Gretchen. She fooled everybody.

"Hannah dressed up as Gretchen, at various times, for *a whole week*. So many places! So many witnesses! It will throw off their investigative timeline. We got lucky. Gretchen called Daddy, told him to peel off her detail, we learned their patterns, it was painfully easy."

"What did you do, leap out of a sewer grate and snatch her like fucking Pennywise?" It was all so unformed, unspoken. And now it's so real. "I'm not going to be part of this."

"But you already are. Think of your dad. Your poor mum."

"They wouldn't want this."

"Pushback, eh? I'm loving this flex." *Snip.* "What about your boy?"

Pinky's little *Sweeney Todd* routine is grating on me. "Where is he?"

"He's been a goddam handful. And my job isn't to spank the under-class miscreants. I have enough on my plate. *Truly.* I am the king of dealing with kids who don't belong in their own families because *I relate*. That's why I sent him to Italy, to keep him out of trouble. And Switzerland! For spring break." *Snip.*

"Switzerland?"

"The land of Ricolas and chocolate, cheese and knives! Too bad they didn't master cutting boards, they'd be an empire. But that's called off now. I'm going to need you both here. This is a tight operation, done in neat little stages. Once we wake Gretchen and move her into Faber, it'll be you and Luke who watch her during spring break."

He's disregarded everything I've said so assertively, I almost respect it. He's using a straight razor now—glinting viciously in the light—to groom Tath's neck.

"You aren't listening to me."

He flicks Tath on the nape of his neck and rips off his smock. "Come!" he calls, leading me into his bedroom, down at the end of a hall.

The curtains are drawn; the room is bathed in filtered light. Luke is curled up on top of a king-size bed on beachy linens, wearing a white T-shirt, black soccer shorts. His head is resting on one arm. Two of his fingers are bandaged. "Why is he asleep like that?"

"He's drugged. We had to test out a few concoctions."

"Oh my God."

Pinky pours scotch into a crystal tumbler from a carafe on a side table. He gestures at it with his thumb. I shake my head.

"If it meant your dad goes to prison, would you still want out?"

"My family will get through whatever hand we're dealt. I can't commit a crime. I can't cause a person pain." I sit on the edge of the bed, laying my hand against Luke's back.

Pinky plops down in a large recliner by the windows. "What about Luke? He'll go to juvie. Those are dangerous places, remember? Think you can handle chatting with another ghost? I need you boys to work together. That's part of the design of this explo."

"This isn't an explo!"

Pinky crosses one leg over the other one. He takes a swig of scotch. The amber liquid through the crystal catches the light, dancing across the walls. "I don't make the rules."

I think about the painting again. Those godlike figures in the clouds. "This is Archi."

"They wanted you both. And Luke has to complete his end of the deal. I'm moved by your feelings for him, quite honestly, your empathy in general. That's what I found most appealing about you, going all the way back to your Spotlight, when you fell back on that fusty old joke from your ne'er-do-well dad."

I stand and face him. "It was a good joke."

"Wasn't it Queen Elizabeth who once said, *You can only piss with the dick you have?*"

"I don't think she said that."

"The last thing you wanted was to tell that dumb joke. But you love your dad, and that's what came to mind; you couldn't escape it. I'm relieving you of the burden of choice. I know you can't lose Luke *and your parents.*"

No, I can't lose everyone who ever gave a shit about me. But there's always a choice. How much am I supposed to sacrifice for other people's mistakes?

"It's not just Archi tracing the line from their powerful lives back to their feckless youth here," says Pinky. "It's also tracing that line back to the beginning."

"The beginning?"

"The sunken bottom layers, remember? Where everything begins and gets forgotten."

"When we were in the museum, you said there were *sacrifices made.*"

"There were. Soon after Granford transformed into Essex, the school had to cater to a growing student population who came here to study theology, the sacred languages, the sciences. In the decades that followed, the school became everything to the town. The last thing Strafton needed was—"

"A flood."

"It practically washed the whole town away. Students drowned . . ."

"Is that what those payouts are?"

Pinky's eyes light up. "Well, smell you, Nancy Drew! Yes, there are irregularities in the tax filings. Many families were too poor to claim their dead. And the school had to maintain their reputation while they rebuilt; every single drowned kid would've killed their progress, so they covered up the tragedy. You saw the painting. We walk on their bones. Records were fudged."

"How is that possible?"

"Money! Money was at stake! They implemented a system of reparations. Families who lost children in the flood who forfeited the remains . . . their descendants would be paid . . . forever, all the way down the line. That's why this school— which has a *seven-hundred-million-dollar endowment*—is still, pardon the pun, *underwater*. It's in the catechism. Recite it!"

I do. Pinky stops me after *Ellsworth and Hunt, Kalumets all, their secrets shall be revealed. The Architects' mysteries, once lost in death, their secrets shall be revealed.*

"Ellsworth and Hunt. Two students who founded the Kalumet Society, headquartered in the Tomb, the original secret society SoSE was born out of over two hundred years ago. They're known as the Architects. There were seven original members."

Archaei. Archi. Architects . . .

"Shouldn't it be the Society of Fourteen Eyes?"

Pinky scoffs. "Doesn't have the same ring, though, does it? They built a bridge between the school and a group of powerful alumni who became known as Archi. Archi gives us cash flow; we learn the history of Essex as a way of paying our respects to all that was sacrificed. And when they ask for a favor, we pull the lever for them in a big way. Society funnels that cash into Essex. This school represents the happiest, most innocent time for so many almighty figures. It's a *Citizen Kane* rosebud thing. Never underestimate the power of nostalgia."

"You're exploiting me, *someone with less means . . .*"

Pinky rises and lumbers over to me. He's probably drinking expensive liquor, but his breath still just smells like someone's abusive dad. "Don't pretend outside forces corrupted you. You've always known what you wanted and what you were willing to give up to get it." He flicks my arm, where my scar is. "Other-wise, you'd never have sent those photos of Gretchen. That's when you made the choice."

"What choice?"

"The choice of who you were going to be. We all want to *matter*. I'm helping you up the ladder—so you can get out of the swamp. You told yourself no one would get hurt, but you were always willing to do whatever it took to be one of us."

One of us, one of us. His words echo, brutally, in my ears.

"Means, yeah, maybe I have *means* . . . but no freedom. People pursue their dreams, their passions. I'll never be allowed to lead my own life." He throws back the rest of the scotch.

"You can take a different path."

He laughs ruefully. "You say it like it's so easy. Listen, it *isn't*. I don't care about being cut off; it's the feeling I'm a disappointment that's always been my Achilles' heel."

"Does Nisha know?"

"We use only who we have to. She wouldn't be right for this." Pinky gazes out the window. "They'll rape us and keep raping us. But they'll give us a velvet pillow for our heads."

"Jesus."

"I'm going to trust you to keep this quiet, as I know you will. It's funny," he says, kicking at a lone sock on the carpet, "my family took me foxhunting. Foxhunting, for chrissakes! Seven years old. I couldn't hurt those dumb yapping things. Fucking foxes. My dad grabbed me by the ear, shoved me in the car, locked me inside. He was furious I wouldn't partake in nature's hierarchy, the barbarity of what we all are. I sat in that broiling car all day, trapped. Crying. Pounding the windows. Then this . . . stillness took over. I spent hours staring into my lap, knowing at least I had made my own decision. But I swear to God, I'm spending the rest of my life trying to get out of that locked car."

I've never stopped wondering what was in Pinky's black envelope. What deep, dark secret he chose to write down. I walk back over to the bed and lie down next to Luke. Pinky puts his empty glass on the table. "I'll leave you two alone. His memory might be blurry when he wakes up. Probably for the best." He slips out and closes the door behind him.

It's hard to get Luke to walk. I have to prop him up. He looks dead drunk, so we slip underground, all of Luke's weight leaning against me, and head to Faber.

Luke immediately falls asleep again, on our mattress. After an hour, he stirs and sits up. His eyes are dull. His hair is drenched. He sticks his fist against his mouth. "I'm going to puke." I dash over, grab a trash can, and put it in front of him; Luke retches into it. He rips off his shirt, drops his head between his legs. I get a towel and gently mop his back. His vomit looks bloody. "What did they give you?"

"Couple spoonfuls of red liquid from a brown bottle. They called it the Big Cherry."

I do some furious googling. "Was there another name?"

"Noctec?"

"Uh . . . that's chloral hydrate. It's a sedative, it's *a date rape drug*. How many spoonfuls?"

"I can't remember."

"They could've killed you. And her."

"I don't think they gave Gretch any of it. They were trying to aerosolize chloroform, but they were worried about inhaling it themselves. I think they literally put a rag over her mouth." He holds his head. "I can't remember . . ."

"Where did they take her?"

"I don't know."

"Who's involved?"

"Small group. It started over a week ago. They planned exactly when they'd let the public know she was gone. I came in later. I had to help sedate, restrain her. She fights every time."

"Holy shit!"

"I'm not the one who actually took her. I don't know who did that."

"Why did you tag the grate?"

Luke frowns. "I didn't."

"Your memory is screwy."

Luke crosses his arms over his head and rocks back and forth, moaning. I sit behind him, enclosing him with my legs, his head against my chest. "It's okay, it'll be okay," I keep murmuring, not quite believing my own words. Oh God, I don't know what to do.

"I know what you're thinking, Lonely, but they're already a hundred steps ahead of you."

He's right. Contacting anyone would probably be pointless. Some favor would be called in, some *in* would be exploited, and I'd be screwed. "Now I see why they wanted us to get into Faber so bad." I feel empty and defeated. "It's our home . . ."

"It's not. They need it for her—during spring break." He looks at me with the blank terror of a child. "Do you hate me? Nothing would be worth losing you."

"No, I love you. That's the worst part. Or, at least, I love the Luke I thought I knew."

This really gets him. He leaps up, like he wants to get in the ring with me. "No one ever knows everything about a person! Stop chasing that, you'll never find it. You choose what to see, Lonely, you always have."

"Because I'm a romantic? I chase perfection and hate lies. The tragedy is all my own?"

"You turned your dead attacker into an imaginary friend. Think about that."

"Don't go there."

"I'm damaged goods, Lonely, and you always knew—"

"So it's my fault for getting in too deep? AND WHAT AM I?"

"You have to accept me as I am."

"Haven't I? Isn't that all I've ever done? I'm the one-eyed freak who talks to psychotic ghosts, you're the gorgeous jock with a rich family who spent Christmas in Milan. I don't think you get to play the damaged one." Although maybe that's not entirely fair.

Is being intimate with someone only knowing as many pieces of them as they allow you to know, the scraps of memory and dreams and trauma and aspirations that make up their core, that they're willing or able to share? Does anyone really know the whole truth of anyone?

"I'm sorry I got you involved in this, Lonely. I will have to live with that."

We both will.

CHAPTER THIRTY-TWO

DISAPPEAR INTO ME

I see Gretchen forty-eight hours later, the day before spring break. Luke and I arrive at Faber, and she's just *there*, like a FedEx delivery got dropped off.

She's in tatters. Semiconscious. Cuffed to a chair. (Luke was given the key.) She's been bound in a variety of ways and the different bindings have caused all sorts of bruising. She's skeletal. Her hair is all tangled. There's blood on her torn clothes. Framed against one of the tower windows, it's like she's in a poisonous retelling of "Rapunzel."

When she first sees me, there's confusion, a smudge of betrayal, then a thin, stretched sadness, like her smoked-out eyes are asking, *How could you?* I look away. The self-disgust is too much. I'm going to have to end this before anyone really gets hurt.

If I don't, I'll have completely lost myself.

Everything so far has been orchestrated with incredible meticulousness, everyone's role delegated from the start, every step planned far in advance, like we're dancers in a devilish ballet. Luke and I have been assigned to watch her for the duration of spring break, in Faber. Then she'll be moved out. We've been given a strict schedule to follow. We have to give her a NyQuil-sized cup of the Big Cherry twice a day, at specific times ("If she puts up a fight, tell her you're happy to inject her instead," Pinky said, handing us a kit with a hypodermic syringe).

Pinky loves that Gretchen and I have an established friendship. He thinks she'll trust me, be compliant. Meals will be dropped off twice a day as well. We're supposed to feed her when she's half-awake, so there's less chance of her lashing out, like she's a wild tiger. Given how thin she is, I'm not sure how well that's been working out. Hannah Locke will arrive three times a day to take her to the bathroom while we wait outside.

We've all been glued to the investigation. While the authorities *think* an outside assailant somehow broke into Gretchen's dorm room and abducted her, they've never stopped combing every inch of Essex, while conducting DNA analysis on some bloodstains they found. Pinky told us the authorities do not, in fact, have updated plans and blueprints of the campus and the tunnels, like we do. He hints Society has a reach into the FBI and the Secret Service, and while that seems frankly unbelievable, Society is scarily plugged in. They always know what location will be searched next. They make their move well before the authorities make theirs. Gretchen simply gets rotated to various secretive locations on campus.

The main trick besides keeping her hidden is to keep moving her around.

The media haven't backed off. Reporters throng the perimeter of campus day and night.

Her dad hasn't stepped down, despite increasing calls for him to do so, which might be why this whole thing is being prolonged. Section 2 of the Twenty-Fifth Amendment is being considered.

After I see Gretchen, in Faber, for the first time, I text Pinky the numbered code for "We need to meet." Fifteen minutes later, under a willow tree outside Strauss, he saunters over to me.

"She doesn't look good. She needs to be . . . like . . . groomed."

Pinky cackles. "You want me to book a mani-pedi and a deep-tissue massage?"

"You know what I mean. Cleaned up, for God's sake. You can't leave her like that. You need to rethink the bindings. They're cutting into her skin."

"Can't do."

"She needs . . . like . . . a tampon, I think."

A firm nod. "Can do. I'll send in Hannah to deal with the girly stuff." Pinky whips out his phone, sends a text. "Can you boys vacate at four?"

"Sure."

"If you try anything, they'll kill her, and that'll be on you." He looks up from his phone with a big grin; anyone walking by would think Pinky just told the best joke in his arsenal. "I want to make sure you fully understand."

I can't see his eyes, but I know he's not kidding. "I understand."

"Since you're a little green, there, my lad."

"I can handle this."

"Luke?"

"We can handle this."

"What else?"

"Can someone bathe her? Change of clothes?"

"I'll try." Pinky takes in the campus, chucking his phone from one hand to the other. "It's a shock for everyone, seeing her the first time. She's not at a D.C. country club like she's used to, and she's overplaying her distress; it's a natural survival mechanism. You'll get used to it."

"Oh, will I?"

"Be careful feeding her."

"That's another thing."

"She's been doing this hunger strike shit. She'll wise up. But those brief windows of time when the Big Cherry wears off, she can be a viper. Biting. Scratching. Watch yourselves. I assume I'll be receiving a candidacy statement from you?"

I close and open my eyes. "Yes." Our candidacy statements are due May 1. There's a nominating tribunal, where anyone can nominate anyone else for the BoD. This is considered an important meeting. It sets the tone, flavor, and makeup of Society for the remainder of our time at Essex. We have to write a platform with our ideas for Society, what we'd bring to the BoD as a whole. I need to attain as much power as I can in order to protect myself.

"I know you miss Nisha. She's a great girl." Nisha's been off visiting colleges with her parents and is taking an extended spring break. We haven't talked much lately. I'm afraid my distress will be too obvious. "When we're all back, I want you guys to work on the 1752 Room. I'd love for someone to finally crack it. Would be great if it was you two. It'll help you get favored for a place on the Board."

"Is that what this is still all about?"

"Society is about exploration." Pinky lowers his green-tinted sunglasses. His eyes are like corrugated ice. "It's always been that."

"Uh huh."

"Think of everything you'll gain. Your family freed of their burdens. You still get to hold Luke close at night. When you weaken, buckle under pressure, remind yourself of those things."

But what is weakness? Sticking with Society's plan or rebelling against it? My conscience is scrambled. My brain is muddled. My heart only wants Luke. My soul wants my family safe and intact. I know what we're doing is horrible.

I keep trying to reassure myself *they're just going to hold her for a short while, no one's going to harm her,* but I don't fully believe it. And I know Gretchen is suffering. Plus, that echoes what I told myself when I took those photos of her.

God, what have I become?

"Her dad doesn't love her," says Luke after Gretchen takes her dose with a steely acquiescence and conks out, her neck hanging down in a disturbing way, hair draped greasily over her shoulders. "Like, I feel that." He paces the library, syringe in hand, darting around with it like it's a rapier. Hannah did come by to clean up Gretchen—trim her hair, snip her nails. *Were they not doing that before?* Someone will return at nine to uncuff her (three of us have to be present whenever she's unrestrained, with a fourth doing external patrols) and move her onto a mattress so she can sleep properly.

"I'm not going to be able to do this for much longer," I state.

"Why doesn't your dad love you?" Luke moves in, tilting his head at her, in a taunt. This would seem diabolical if I didn't know Luke. He's not used to being conflicted. If someone or something makes him uncomfortable, he claps back. This is the boy who flips me off during sex. He's used to snapping towels at his fellow jocks. He doesn't hate Gretchen, but he probably hates her stupid dad for putting him in this position.

I hate her dad too right now. "Luke."

He hangs his head and throws the syringe across the room. "This is bullshit."

I walk over and pick up the syringe from the floor.

"What did you tell your parents? About being here for break," he asks.

"I said I was consumed with work and needed to hang around campus. There's no way they could afford another flight anyway." I'm stuck in this nightmare. I can't focus or sleep. I'm punchy with anxiety and can't ground myself.

Since Gretchen got here, the library, romantic in the beginning, feels like it's crumbling; the spines of all the old volumes look moldy, the windows unwashed, crusted with bird shit. The walls bubbled and distorted with accumulated water damage from old leaks.

At nine, they come, in their silver masks, to relieve us. The windows reflect the turgid strips of night, the oily sky braided by quivering stars. We will never have the night shift—a promise from Pinky. Luke's room at Garrott is open during break. In bed, I lay my head on Luke's chest.

"Sometimes I imagine us traveling places," he says.

"Like where?"

Luke digs around, heaving maps and travel books onto his bed. I remember from my care package he's into that kind of stuff. "Like wherever. Places."

Places. My fingers graze a local guide of Kyōbashi. "We should go everywhere." I listen to Luke's heartbeat, my head on his chest. It's one of the few things that center me.

He tells me about an anonymous British dubstep musician he's obsessed with. The music is fractured, haunted, full of insistent breakbeats and vinyl crackle. It sounds rainy and urban, the sonic equivalent to Luke's art. He plays me a few tracks, sharing a pair of headphones connecting us like an umbilical cord. He says, "Tell me about your dad's haunted house."

While listening to a track called "Night Death," I finally do, while rubbing his St. Jude pendant between my thumb and forefinger as I speak.

"Wow," says Luke when I've finished. "That's fucking fly. Wow . . ."

And then, after a long pause, he says, *Thread the darkness out of me.*

That night I have a dream I'm yanking a long, thin, wet black snake out of Luke's throat while his tinted eye flashes at me like a broken traffic light. That's when I start seeing snakes everywhere. Writhing, glistening amorphous shapes in the corners of my eyes.

I wake from a nap on our last afternoon guarding Gretchen at Faber, and Luke is sitting on the floor, one booted foot crossed over his other leg, emblazoned in a beam of sunlight. He's reading Shakespeare sonnets to Gretchen, the open book propped against his knee. Her eyes are dull, but not as vacant as usual. Luke is radiant in the sun, handsome as ever, the syringe glinting by his side. An angel with a venomous fang.

Luke and I started having sex more regularly than ever during break. That was the only thing that muted our guilt—disappearing into each other. He even said that out loud, surprising me by wanting to switch. *Disappear into me*, he said. It was tinged with terror.

Gretchen gets moved out. As the spring term begins, Faber is ours again. We decompress at night, playing house again, watching a DVD of *Breathless* we checked out from the library on our tiny TV. Luke coos the French title in my ear: À *bout de souffle* . . . And then we hold each other in a rigid grasp, watching Jean Seberg sell newspapers along the Champs-Élysées.

During the next few days, all my Society skills come into play, helping to install Gretchen into other places. Society moves in the dead of night, staying underground, stealthily avoiding cameras; Gretchen drugged, bound, and gagged on a wheelchair, covered with a dark quilted packing blanket.

It's astonishing what Society can get away with. The whole world is searching for Gretchen. But months ago, Pinky showed me what they're capable of. He waltzed into a famous museum late at night and told me he could snatch a priceless painting right off the walls.

I have to clone an RFID badge to help get Gretchen shuttered away in a storage space of Cook Gallery, which hasn't been used since 1986. I lock-pick into Tanner Hall and squeeze myself into a tight crawl space to de-wire an aging security system affecting the upper floors.

The campus becomes a chessboard, and we move through it invisibly, like diligent spirits.

Gretchen is placed in a creaky attic for a night, inhabited by nervous wasps, that used to be Tanner's lost and found. She's left among people's unclaimed musical instruments.

Meanwhile I think, *How long can this go on? How much can she take?*

I climb onto a sub-roof of Hillbrook House to disable exterior cams along the top floor, but there are none. There is a narrow frieze of three grapevines from the coat of arms of Connecticut on the exterior wall. I never noticed them before. I can't help myself. I take a photo.

Hillbrook House is never used. Instead, Gretchen is taken down into the tunnels.

I'm tasked with bringing her breakfast for the next few days. She's been placed in one of the newer utility rooms. She's wasting away. Covered in wasp stings and what I'm terrified might be rat bites. The first time we're alone together, she finally speaks.

Her voice is like a broken whisper, a distant wind. "Oh, Cal."

I kneel in front of her, behind the tray of food I placed on the floor. "I'm so sorry . . ." It feels like my guts have been pulled out through my eyes.

Gretchen clears her throat, a deep rattle, which shakes her whole body. "I know it was you . . . who got me the haircut and cleaned up. Thank you. They're holding something awful over you, aren't they? Is it your dad?"

I nod weakly.

"Family first, right?" She manages a strained laugh. "Don't lose yourself in this. You've gotten involved in something horrible. That's not you, I know you."

Does she? Look how far this has come. "They said they'd kill you if I tried anything."

"They're going to kill me anyway."

"No." Although I'm terrified she's right.

"They know how to do it, Cal. It'll be clean."

Clean. And then, suddenly, I have an idea.

She can be a viper. Biting. Scratching . . .

"Bite me," I blurt out. "Make sure to break the skin. They won't want traces of my blood anywhere. They'll have to untie you, clean out your mouth, clean the walls."

As soon as I say this, I wonder if they've been using Luke's blood, his phantom DNA, to further throw off the authorities. I remember his bandaged fingers. Oh God . . .

She stares at me for a long moment. And then finally, reluctantly, she nods.

I take the syringe from my back pocket and slide it into her open, bound hands. She closes her fingers around it. Consequences, whatever they are, have washed out of my brain.

This has gone on too long, and I need it to be over. "Please forgive me, Gretchen." Like when I was branded, I mentally calculate the amount of pain to come as I offer her my wrist.

Whatever she attempted failed.

I'm summoned to Old Shaw later. Pinky removes the sloppy dressings I threw on earlier to hide the wound. He disinfects my wrist and bandages me with a strange hint of tenderness. "She got you good, huh?" The injury is bad enough to offset suspicion, but probably not all suspicion. I don't know where the syringe is, and I won't be able to ask her. I know they'll be watching next time. "Stay strong," Pinky reminds me. "Remember what's at stake."

The next morning, my wrist throbbing, I notice blood all over my shirt.

Out, damned spot!

I only have the one shirt; I haven't had time for laundry. But I cannot arouse suspicion.

Did they stick a spy cam or a mic on the pizza bag? Probably not. *Who knows?*

But in case there are eyes and ears on me, I play along. When I get down there again, the defeat in Gretchen's eyes pulverizes me. *I'm sorry, I'm so sorry*, I think as I point my finger at her. "No biting this time."

But then I get another idea.

I take out my phone, make sure it's on silent, and take a photo of her.

* * *

"I got into Chicago!" Nisha squeals over the first coffee we've had in forever at the always bustling Café Bianco.

"Congrats!" I'm so happy for her. Her future is all mapped out, waiting for her. I can't fathom what that level of freedom must be like. I'm insanely jealous.

"Thank you! How are you? How are you and Luke doing?"

"We're doing good, thank you." I try and manage a smile.

"God, the two of you," Nisha muses, "what you guys felt about each other was so apparent from the get-go"—she clutches her heart—"even in your first explo together . . ."

The painter and the poet!

"How you reflect each other," she says, "the way you mirror each other's way of seeing."

I remember Luke's drawing, the way he rethought my eye. "He's the practical one; he draws what he sees. I'm the poet, right, I . . ." I do the opposite.

You choose what to see, Lonely . . .

"Are you . . . going to blow off the rest of the semester and party or what?" I ask.

"College cares about your grades till the bitter end. Anything given to you can be taken away." That hits me harder than maybe she intended. "Also, Society. It's been with me for four years of my life. I want to see it through to the end. I want to try and find the 1752 Room with you. That'll be my last explo."

I take materials out of my backpack. "I've been doing research . . ."

Nisha leans over everything. "God, did you map out the entire system of steam tunnels?"

In every waking moment that wasn't taken up by homework, classes, Luke, or Gretchen, yes I did. "I was thinking about Jeffrey and his explo during Rush. He made it into Barry, remember? He found a hidden passage from Quinlan's courtyard and squeezed through a partially bricked-over entrance. I kept thinking there must be a way around. Access from underneath? I tried once and failed." I point at the map. "But I think I found a workaround. Here's the quadrangle. Barry. Fielder. Quinlan. Franklin. There's supposedly an underground space that used to be a chapel at the base of Franklin. This junction of tunnels—*still unexplored!*—might—"

"Cal." Nisha lays her hands over mine, stilling me. "This is just Society."

JUST SOCIETY?

I didn't realize how fast I had been talking, how high-pitched and insistent my voice had become. That sweat was dripping down my face. That I look . . . completely unhinged.

Nisha tightens her grip on me. "You already made Veteres. This is just fun."

Fun. I wipe my brow with the back of my hand. "I've always had to try a little harder than everyone else." I try and laugh some of the tension away, but my hands are shaking. "I wish I was you right now, college on the horizon, this whole time behind me."

"Don't wish your life away."

"I'm not, I—" I get interrupted by a siren, a police car zooming by. A familiar sound now.

Nisha gazes out the window. "God, do you think they'll ever find her?"

"I hope so."

She smiles, filled with warmth and admiration. "Make good choices. That's what I've always loved the most about you. Your pure heart."

The way you mirror each other's way of seeing . . .

Luke only showed me that one drawing of me. And how it evolved over time as the way he saw me evolved. Every other drawing had multiple studies, gaining depth as he worked out his thoughts, his vision for each subject. Was I that fully formed in his creative mind from the beginning? Or are there studies of me somewhere I've never seen?

I stand, suddenly, unsteady on my feet, the chair scraping across the floor. "Excuse me."

In the flower-scented restroom, I stand in front of the mirror. I have new clusters of sores in my mouth. I feel feverish. I'm sick again. I take out my phone. "Brent," I say. "Talk to me . . . *please* . . . I don't know what to do . . . BRENT! I can't hear you anymore. TALK TO ME GODDAMMIT!"

Nothing.

Fuck it. It takes five seconds to look up Clayton Cartwright's venture capital firm—Wildcat Global Management. Clayton is the very definition of a mover and shaker, but he's also just another finance bro with a website and an email address.

I compose an email, attach the photo of Gretchen: thin, covered with bruises and bites. I put GRETCHEN CUMMINGS in the subject line. He'll see the email if it comes from Essex; he'll pay attention if it has Society's formatting. *She's suffering. Is it worth this?* I write. Because maybe Archi doesn't know, maybe they need to see it. I send the email.

CHAPTER THIRTY-THREE

GRETCHEN, DRESSED IN COBRAS

I burst into Faber twenty-five minutes later and turn the place upside down. I find Luke's Moleskines stacked in a far corner. It takes no time to find one with "Cal" ludicrously, plainly, written on the front. Inside, there are sketches of me—faintly drawn, the type of studies I saw for his other subjects. He dated each drawing. There are sketches of me crying behind Hertzman before we met. Sketches of me sitting in chem. He was either in love with me from afar, before I ever thought conceivable, or I was a kind of prey, and he was sniffing me out like . . .

Like a . . .

As I'm crouched over the notebook, I sense him behind me.

"I fell in love with you," he says in a flat, faraway voice. "That's what happened."

I don't move. "You told me I wasn't the lamb. I believed you."

"You're not."

"I had to believe you. I had no choice. I fell in love too."

"You're not the lamb *anymore*," Luke adds, "that's what I meant to say."

Are you small, delicate, fair, queer? Did you wonder why they picked you?

I swallow. "Because I was . . . the lamb?"

"Yes."

We haven't . . .

What? Consummated things? You will.

"Because you . . ." But my voice sputters out.

There should always be pain. So we'll know how things might end.

"Because I was the one who chose you."

I'm paralyzed, staring at the Moleskine. Luke will act petulant—get angry, defensive, because he's the one who fucked us. Sure enough, he throws a backpack out from behind the mattress and rips it open. It's filled with cash. "Bitch, I chose LIFE!" he screams. "I HAD NO CHOICE!"

I'm still crouched over the notebook. My tears slowly drip onto the sketch of me, warping it. "Society provided you with the Adderall?"

"They allowed Essex to look away so I could do my thing. I had my own contacts."

"This was about running away from your dad?"

Luke rips off his shirt. The scars seem to glow with an X-Men-ish intensity in the bleached afternoon light of our secret tower. The scars I've brushed tenderly with my fingertips when he's embraced me in bed at night. "DO YOU NOT GET IT?"

"I get it. You fell in love with me . . . but Pinky was in love with you. So you rebelled. That's what dinner at The League was, right? He met you halfway, but you continued to test him.

That's what happened with the security guards at Hoyt?"

Luke turns away. "That was all Pinky. He needed to see if the guards were bribable; they're assigned places where we might have needed to hide Gretchen."

"Who's the lamb now?"

"There is no lamb now. This is too big an operation."

"When did they change their minds about me?"

"After your story came out in *Bombast*."

I stand, teetering. "Right. I was candid about my family. They investigated further. Saw my parents were in trouble. Saw how serious you and I were getting. They knew I could be manipulated. I'd have to be a part of Gretchen's kidnapping or risk losing everything."

"The last thing I ever wanted was to hurt you, Lonely."

"When I lost my virginity to you, *Bombast* had already come out. Was I the lamb then?"

Luke whispers, *"What does it matter?"*

"It matters." Luke is in front of me, shimmering, like he's wading into a pool. But then I don't see him anymore. "Did it ever occur to you we were never meant to see the world in four dimensions? There are walls and locked doors for a reason. It's too much seeing!"

"Lonely—"

"You had to erase the tenderness of our first kiss in the closet, that's what you were doing. That whole time, erasing that first moment. That's why you had to blind me. Because I saw what you really were. How you enjoyed watching me choke on you once a week, and that time you laughed when you got your jizz on my shirt, laughed in that filthy, empty way of yours while you walked away, but you were also horrified, because I did that, and you were desperate to believe it had nothing to do with me."

We are their puppets. Stuffed with straw and sapphires.

"Holy shit," says Luke, snapping his fingers in front of my eyes. "I'm not him, Lonely!"

"I romanticize everything. I see what's convenient. Look at what I did with you!"

"Lonely!"

"The things we all have to give up, the things we have to trade in this world."

The snakes flick their tongues, and hiss, as they hang, coiled, off the walls.

"Uh oh," says Pinky, standing in the middle of the library, dressed to the nines, pulling black gloves on as we whirl around to face him, *"I hope I didn't interrupt a lovers' quarrel."*

"Well," says Pinky. "The time has come, gents." He smiles at me. "It's not just 1939, 1942, 1949, by the way. The three dates you fixated on. A suicide *here*"—he puts suicide in air quotes—"a brief disappearance *there*. Been happening for decades. It gets covered up. But *this time*, it's high profile. Can't be covered up as well. I told them it was a mistake. But the hungry lions of Archi need to be fed. We're going to say our farewells to our dear friend Gretchen now. Here's a tough life lesson, boys. Sometimes parents choose power over their children. You'd think—*that's depraved!*—is it possible? I'm here to tell you it is.

Sometimes it comes down to that. Money. Power. But grief is the great equalizer."

"Grief?" I rasp.

"The death of a loved one removes someone from power faster than a protracted disappearance. Especially—like VP Cummings—if they have other children. 'Cause maybe they didn't get our message? Personally, I think that's impossible. It's just dangerous amounts of ego. So here we are. Pulled by their strings. Stuffed with straw and sapphires." He winks at me.

"You can't kill her," I say.

"Relax, kid, the hard part's over."

"Pinky, you can't."

"Shit, you don't look good. It's about keeping the socially disadvantaged socially disadvantaged. The rich stay rich. The powerful stay powerful. Nothing can obstruct their unfettered extractive capitalism! But every so often, a new bloodline sneaks in. Congrats, Cal. You'll be rich and powerful too one day. And you'll pass that down to your children—"

"Pinky—"

"Should you choose to have any. Shall we?" he says, gesturing out the door.

As Pinky weaves us through the tunnels, he gets chatty.

"Those master keys, remember, from your initiation? Rumor has it they unlock the biggest secrets of Essex, but no one's ever been able to figure out what buildings they unlock. Personally, I think they don't exist anymore. But the secrets still do! So now the keys are just symbolic." Pinky stops short. He grabs a paint can out of his satchel, shakes it, and sprays an exact replica of Luke's tag on the wall. "He hates when I do this." He laughs at Luke, who watches him vacantly. "But I have to cover my tracks. Onward!"

When I hear that familiar whooshing sound, I know where Pinky's leading us.

"We're going to the aqueduct?"

"A grand end to a grand ol' time."

At night, the aqueduct is even more eerie. The grates above striate the inky tributary with shavings of moonlight. The water itself is like an undulating serpent.

Gretchen is lying motionless on the narrow stone walkway. A group of SMs, in masks, stand in a circle, shining flashlights down. At first, I think she's covered in slithering cobras, my sideways visions come to life. But they're garlands of black roses, laced around her throat. "Well, isn't this *baroque*," Pinky snorts as he approaches. "But this is how they wanted it."

They must have gotten my email. They reacted fast. And this is their response.

An SM rolls Gretchen's empty wheelchair into the water. It gets swept away.

Pinky waltzes over to me. Every muscle and joint in my body throbs like I'm being pulled apart, limb by limb, tissue by tissue. "You did good. I know this was hard. But we lifted you out of that hick town where you would've rotted into a husk like your dad. It's what you always wanted. Remember that."

He knows his words sting; he enjoys watching my face get red before he turns away.

"All right, everyone," says Pinky, "let's heave her in, as a group, on the count of three." I'm about to throw myself on top of Gretchen but Pinky crouches over her. "These are sloppy. For God's sake, guys, seriously?" Pinky starts arranging the flowers, making the presentation neater. Then he stops and regards Gretchen, Ophelia after the Mad Scene, almost like he's having second thoughts. But then he gives her one of his little salutes. "So long, Gorgeous."

"I tried to help her," I tell Pinky. "Maybe I wasn't willing to risk everything. Maybe I'm not who you think I am, after all."

Pinky runs a hand through his hair, ruminating. Briefly, everything stops. "It's harder when you see beauty in the world. Especially in the small things." He grins luridly.

I have the oddest, most Society-ish thought ever. They used red roses and painted them black. The red peeks through the black. They should have used white ones. I would've done a better job. I also notice Gretchen is in the same tattered dress. They never gave her a change of clothes, like I requested. And her dress has pockets . . .

Her eyes snap open.

They've probably been giving her the exact same dose this whole time. And she's built up a tolerance. In a flash she reaches into her pocket and stabs Pinky in the side of the neck with the syringe I gave her. Pinky screams, grabs his neck, and Gretchen knees him in the crotch.

Pinky, gasping, rolls away; he teeters on the edge of the walkway, trying to regain his balance. As he's about to fall in, a sickening fury overtakes him. He grabs Gretchen by the legs as she's kicking at him, and they both slide over the edge. There are two splashes.

For a second, I see their bodies, in and out of the slips of moonlight. In, then out, then in, then out, as if they're trying to avoid being swallowed by darkness. A yelp, a grunt, a cry, muffled by the rushing water. Then the current heaves them both away.

The SMs shout and scatter, their masks glinting in the distance as they disappear around corners. Like scared children. I make a move toward the water, but Luke yanks me back. "They're gone! It's too late. We have to get out of here!"

As we run through the tunnels, I realize I'm leading and Luke is following. Over time, I finally achieved my goal. I wanted to best Luke at steam tunnel cartography. I wanted to be better than him at *something*. We stop running when we reach a junction, panting, heaving, and Luke asks which way. I almost laugh out loud at the question. "You don't know where you're going. You only know part of the system, the southeastern quadrant mainly, where we originally were, back in the fall."

"I'm all turned around, Lonely."

"Why did you pick me?"

He pauses. "You were . . . the easiest pick. You weren't one of us."

I'm too numb at this point to be hurt by the most hurtful thing he's ever said.

Luke starts to cry, falling into me. I stroke his hair as he comes undone against my chest, with these terrible, racking sobs. "I'm so sorry! That's why I fell in love with you, that's why you became my Lonely Hearts. You weren't them, you weren't like anyone else, not in Society, Essex, not like anybody I ever met. That's all real, I fell so hard, I feel so much for you, I don't know what to do. I was gonna run, but all I could think about was taking you with me, being with you forever."

"Be with me then. Forever." I have to rid this desire inside me: to be loved so badly, to trust people unconditionally, to hand them my heart, refusing to see the truth of who they are. There are too many voices screaming inside my head, and I am so very hot and so very sick . . .

I grab at my face.

I take Luke's hand. He squeezes back, but then realizes what I've placed in his palm. He tries to keep his composure as I grab the back of his neck and force him to look at what was once there and now isn't. "Be with me forever. But see me as I really am. And everything they took from me." I draw him into a tight hug and I feel his ribs and how fragile he really is . . . but all I want to do is escape all of this. I shove Luke away and I run.

Luke yells bloody murder, chasing after me, trying to keep up as I race down the tunnels. But it's like I've exited my own body. I reach the section of the tunnels I marked on my map with a red X. I know to avoid the dangerous section, to make a sharp right . . .

I can tell Luke isn't behind me anymore. And then I hear him screaming.

It's a terrible, terrible screaming.

But I can't stop running. I'm like a spooked horse. I don't

stop when I'm underneath the quadrangle, even after I access the basement of Franklin Hall from a trapdoor and cross the nave of what used to be a chapel from the 1880s, the pews still intact (but the pulpit collapsed), broken stained glass littering the floor. I was right! *I was right! I can get in . . .*

I mapped out everything in my head. I needed to complete every goal I set for myself. I began judging my own worth by succeeding with every explo, solving every puzzle, every bit of research a piece in that puzzle. I needed to win! I became the best SM Society could ever hope for. Because, deep down, I always knew I was their stupid lamb. When I find the half-bricked-over entrance, on the opposite end from where I first attempted this, I know it'll lead me to the catacombs. I'm small enough to climb over the partial obstruction.

The temperature drops. There's a twining in the pit of my stomach, like angry electric eels stinging. It's not only Luke screaming that I can still hear, it's like the catacombs themselves are screaming. I rush through the narrow stone corridors; they aren't really catacombs, though—they are ossuaries, containing rows upon rows of human remains. It's all real . . .

The walls are stuffed with skulls and tibiae and clavicles; some are stacked in piles, arranged in sculptural formations, illuminated from above in crusty yellow light.

I run faster and faster, all the grinning skulls streaking by. There are so many bones, so many dead, and I run and run until there's a lit square at the end, and I reach a room that looks like a gallery in a museum. Blue walls with gold wainscoting at the bottom. Our school colors.

In the center of the space is a glass case, sitting on a stone pedestal. Inside is a skull.

"Hello," I say, panting, to the man standing there.

I was found by campus security in the dry moats surrounding Franklin Hall, in the quad, kneeling in the flower patches, cutting myself with a piece of broken stained glass. Campus security traced my movements. That's what led them to Luke. He managed to escape the tunnels and was found on the other end of campus.

Apparently, I told security I had been chatting with Alexander Essex about the Civil War, Reconstruction, the school's system of reparations for all the kids who drowned in the Great Flood of 1809. That's what school officials told me, anyway. I have no memory of that night.

Essex flew me home to be evaluated. The cuts were mostly superficial. I didn't remember hurting myself. I spoke to a psychologist and a psychopharmacologist.

Two days after I got home, I received this email:

~ no subject ~
Clayton Cartwright <CWCartwright@WildcatGlobal.com>
To: calixte.ware@essex.edu

OEUE

Mr. Cal Ware,

Your contributions to S-ciety have been noted and appreciated.
All will be taken care of.

WLM,
CnCtwt

CNSP

A day after I received this email, the charges against my dad were suddenly dropped. There was "insufficient evidence."

My mom was getting better. Her current course of treatment was working. The school encouraged me to take as much time as I needed for my mental health, but I wanted to get back to finish the school year. It was a condensed, but necessary, convalescence that would continue once I returned home for summer.

APRIL

Gretchen Cummings survived.

She was found wandering the woods on the edge of campus, thirty-six hours after the events in the aqueduct. Like me, she wasn't mentally sound by the time they found her. And once she was whisked back to D.C., "mental health issues" is what her family cited as the reason for her disappearance. Gretchen never mentioned the kidnapping.

Her dad eventually backed off on the wealth tax. It never passed.

Tath took over as interim CEO of Society. On the morning after my D-Comm testimony, I found out I wouldn't be expelled (which I already knew). But I was put on academic probation for the remainder of the year because we're not supposed to be in the tunnels, and someone had to get punished for something.

There was only a month of school left, so it hardly mattered and didn't affect my scholarship. I had a coffee date with Nisha; on my way over, I sent in my candidacy statement to the Board. Fixing my tie, slapping on a pair of new sunglasses, I looked around at the campus, blooming in the spring—a splash of Monet colors—and smiled for the first time in forever. I couldn't help it; the dark clouds were lifting. The snakes were gone. Everything was so damn pretty, and so much lay ahead.

Summer was yet to come, but I was already excited for junior year.

TEN YEARS LATER

Luke lost his right arm in the tunnels that night. They amputated it at the shoulder. He never returned to Essex, and I never, ever stopped thinking about him. I will have to live with what I did—or didn't do—for the rest of my life. The regret doesn't fade; like the HSV-1 virus, it hides away and emerges when I'm run-down and weak.

I checked up on him as soon as he left Essex. He never went to juvie.

Later, he dropped out of Cal Arts and became an instant star. The sexy one-armed genius! He learned to paint with his left hand, and between gallery shows across the U.S. and Europe, he painted a mural in the office of a tech startup in Silicon Valley, mostly as a favor. They paid him in stock, which he never expected to be worth anything. When the company blew up and went public, Luke's shares were worth around $100 million on the eve of its IPO. That probably embarrassed him more than anything, sullying his street cred.

When I graduated from Harvard Law and joined a law firm in Boston as an associate in commercial litigation, it was announced in *Essex Magazine*—our alumni mag—and elsewhere too. Soon after, I received a text from an unknown number. The text said: *Moon Tears*. It had to have been him. I never texted back. Months later, I finally worked up the courage to call the number. It had been disconnected.

A year ago, Luke was heading back from a party in Martha's Vineyard with a carful of drunk luminaries when their Mercedes SUV veered off a back road and crashed into the Vineyard Sound. By the time divers freed him from the wreckage, Luke was brain-dead. He was taken off his ventilator after two days. He was twenty-five years old.

I wonder at least ten times a day, if Luke still had his right arm—*would he have been able to escape the sinking car?* Probably not. But I'll never know for sure. Everything we do, even in our youth, has reverberations, echoing into the future cosmos.

And sometimes true tragedies come in waves, spread out over years. Luke was one of those people who naturally attract trouble. Some people are like that, I've found. That's partly what made him so tantalizing to me: gleefully skirting the line of danger, where rules are fluid. All that romantic torment! I was naïve and blind and young and infatuated.

Luke being Luke, of course he was an organ donor.

I only used my influence as Archi once in my life (so far)

outside the web of Essex. It was to contact the recipient of Luke's heart, a man who lives in Utah. I'm not sure what I was expecting to happen. But he was kind enough to respond. He sent me an MP3 file of Luke's heart beating in his own body. I will never tell a soul I do this, but I listen to that MP3 sometimes, at night, before bed. Luke's heart beating beside me.

It had to go inside someone else's body for me to hear it again.

Ah, the power of nostalgia.

Now I get it.

Pinky Lynch was never found. Conspiracy theories abound. People swear they've seen him partying in Tulum, traveling through Machu Picchu, exploring the Maldives, backpacking through Thailand. That he changed his name and owns a bar in St. Croix; hair long, bearded, bronzed by the Caribbean sun, finally escaping the clutches of his awful family, with their old money and conservative ideals. Yeah, nah. I think he drowned, his body swept into and devoured by the Connecticut River. He never did get out of that locked car, his family chasing their foxes.

Nisha dropped out of the University of Chicago after a year (it wasn't a good fit) and transferred to GW. She's now a public defender in Maryland, and she's engaged to a law professor at Georgetown (a cool guy). I fly there once a month to spend the weekend; we always do an escape room. I consider Nisha my best friend, so maybe it is true what they say—in some cases, you do keep your Essex friends for life.

*　*　*

Gretchen Cummings graduated from Princeton and joined a consulting firm in New York City. She also co-founded a charitable foundation called The Sisterhood Fund, dedicated to women's reproductive rights and ending gender-based violence. I made a sizable donation to the foundation (anonymously). Though she never returned to Essex, she's a big donor.

I visited Essex, for the first time since I graduated nearly a decade before, to attend a fund-raiser. I happened to see, in Dallow Memorial Hall, a framed photo of Luke and me. We're facing the camera, as if someone called our names while we were singing the Evensong. We're both grinning: his smile like gossamer, threading through time to find me again. I don't remember the photo being taken. It's so damn chummy. If you look hard enough, you can see two boys, happy but confused in their own separate spheres, slowly falling in love. The brilliant sunlight that streams in through those famous stained glass windows is already fading it away.

Even though I'd always felt old for my year, I was the youngest CEO that SoSE ever elected. They usually pick seniors. I was a junior, the only time I ever got to feel ahead of my time. CEOs lead the Board, and the Boards flavor Society. It's up to the CEO—and the BoD—to decide what the Neophyte curriculum should be like, and what skills will be emphasized.

I became CEO—and an engaged member of Archi—to make up for the horrific crime I helped commit during my sophomore year; to maintain control, and make sure Society continues to do what it's supposed to—*explore the school's history and learn its deepest secrets.*

I will do everything I can to make sure it never caves to Archi's dark side again. I helped lay the groundwork for new fund-raising initiatives so the school doesn't have to rely solely on Archi's tangled network for its endowment anymore.

I'm always waiting for a Neo or SM to find the 1752 Room (since to this day I'm not sure I ever did, and never attempted it again). Or penetrate the interior of the Tomb. Or figure out what those master keys unlock. So far, no one has.

After my sophomore year, after Luke, Society became much more of the brotherhood that was initially promised. I'm friends with many of my fellow SMs to this day, and I follow up on my fellow tap class members regularly. We all had a mini reunion at Isabella's wedding in Sonoma a year ago. A lot of wine was drunk.

I visit my parents often. My dad is designing haunted houses again—with waivers. My mom went back to work as a school administrator. As for everyone else I knew during my time at Essex, they're like the tails of a comet, sparking across the world. Emma Braeburn is a pastry chef, living in Paris. Jeffrey is getting his PhD in psychology in Oregon. The Pope is still Head of School.

Society, what it is and what it was to me, rushes back in odd moments, furiously strong.

I keep a bobby pin in my pocket as a sort of tribute, a habit I picked up soon after I graduated Essex. The irony isn't lost on me: the grand archways, glowing libraries, and mysterious tunnels that marked my time there, which seems more and more like a dream every day, something that couldn't have possibly existed, reduced to nothing more than a bent hairpin now, which I've only needed to use twice in my life. Until last week.

Recently, I moved into a new apartment complex. As I was coming home from work, there was a woman rocking a stroller with one hand in front of the apartment next door. Her baby was crying.

The woman smiled at me, her other arm at her side, her phone pressed against her hip. "I'm sorry about the crying. I'm an idiot and locked myself out." She gestured to her baby; that familiar exhaustion mixed with adoration that young moms have. "I left his bottle inside. The super isn't picking up."

And there he was again.

Standing in front of the limo, light spilling out. His ridiculously handsome face.

Kissing underneath the pterodactyl.

The scrolls, the skulls, the codes, the keys.

"No worries," I told the woman. "Are you my new neighbor?"

"I believe so," she said. "It's nice to meet you."

I'm just trying to survive my stupid life, Lonely Hearts.

Omnia ex umbris exibunt. Tibi oculi aperti erunt.

"It's nice to meet you too. You're in luck." The bobby pin was already out of my pocket, and I was already moving toward her door. "I think I can help."

ACKNOWLEDGMENTS

This book took nearly a decade to write, in various stages, in many different incarnations, across divergent periods of time, and I was lucky enough to have loving guidance, feedback, friendship, support, and mentorship along the way. So, without further ado, THANK YOU:

To my brilliant, sensitive editor, Mallory Kass, who saw all the trapped glowing light within these words and shined it all back on me. I'm forever grateful fate brought us together.

And thank you to:

David Levithan, Chris Stengel, Rachel Feld, Daisy Glasgow, Aleah Gornbein, Janell Harris, my copyediting, proofreading, and production team, and the whole Scholastic sales team.

Victoria Marini, Debbie Deuble Hill and the team at APA, Heather Shapiro and Baror International, everyone at IGLA, the Highline Collective, and Volume Five Lit.

Kara Thomas, Tiggy McLaughlin, Jonathan Talerico, Brendan Newman, Erin Hahn, Tom Ryan, Sara Faring, Lindsay Champion, Maxine Kaplan, Caleb Roehrig, Dana Mele, Adam Sass, Mason Deaver, Emily Wibberley, Austin Siegemund-Broka, April Henry, Skye N. Norwood, John Morgan, Camryn Garrett, Justine Jablonska, Karen M. McManus, Henry Kessler, Robin Lord Taylor, Maulik Pancholy, Beth Kingry Arnold, Colin Verdi, Joy

McCullough, Dahlia Adler, Elvis Ahn, Scott Hoffman, and Kathleen Glasgow.

And a very special thanks to John R. Christian.

With undying gratitude to my dear family: my amazing parents, Evelyn & Harvey; my hugely supportive brother Jordan; my luminous sister-in-law Lorin, always my first reader; Isla Bea (my niece, eight years old at the time she told me to "write better books because none of my summer camp counselors have ever heard of you"); and my adorable nephew, Henry Gray.

And, with all my heart, to my partner of twenty-four years (!!!) Brian Murray Williams.

ABOUT THE AUTHOR

Derek Milman has worked as a playwright, screenwriter, film-school teacher, DJ, and underground-humor-magazine-publisher. Derek received an MFA in acting from the Yale School of Drama, and subsequently performed on stages across the country, appeared in numerous TV shows, commercials, and films, and worked with two Academy Award–winning film directors. Derek's debut novel, *Scream All Night*, received a star from *Publishers Weekly*, and has since become a Halloween cult favorite. Derek's second novel, *Swipe Right for Murder*, received a star from *Booklist*, was named one of the best YA books of the year by *Seventeen* magazine, and was cited by *EW* and BuzzFeed as one of the best books of the season. *A Darker Mischief* is Derek's third novel. He resides in Brooklyn with his partner and their books, Criterion Blu-rays, and colored vinyl.

You can visit Derek online at DerekMilman.com or follow him on X/Twitter and Instagram: @DerekMilman.